KT-500-177

The Mouse Deer Kingdom

CHIEW-SIAH TEI

PICADOR

First published 2013 by Picador
an imprint of Pan Macmillan, a division of Macmillan Publishers Limited
Pan Macmillan, 20 New Wharf Road, London N1 9RR
Basingstoke and Oxford
Associated companies throughout the world
www.panmacmillan.com

ISBN 978-0-330-45443-8

Copyright © Chiew-Siah Tei 2013

The right of Chiew-Siah Tei to be identified as the
author of this work has been asserted by her in accordance
with the Copyright, Designs and Patents Act 1988.

The writer acknowledges support from Creative Scotland towards the writing of this title.

All rights reserved. No part of this publication may be reproduced,
stored in or introduced into a retrieval system, or transmitted, in any form,
or by any means (electronic, mechanical, photocopying, recording or otherwise)
without the prior written permission of the publisher. Any person who does
any unauthorized act in relation to this publication may be liable to
criminal prosecution and civil claims for damages.

This novel is a work of fiction. The names, characters, events and places
depicted here are the work of the author's imagination. Any resemblance to
actual persons, incidents or localities is purely coincidental.

1 3 5 7 9 8 6 4 2

A CIP catalogue record for this book is available from the British Library.

Printed and bound by CPI Group (UK) Ltd, Croydon, CR0 4YY

This book is sold subject to the condition that it shall not, by way
of trade or otherwise, be lent, re-sold, hired out, or otherwise circulated
without the publisher's prior consent in any form of binding or cover other than
that in which it is published and without a similar condition including
this condition being imposed on the subsequent purchaser.

Visit www.picador.com to read more about all our books
and to buy them. You will also find features, author interviews and
news of any author events, and you can sign up for e-newsletters
so that you're always first to hear about our new releases.

In memory of my parents

For the sons and daughters of Malaysia,
the land that has bred and nourished us,
to which we all belong.

MANCHESTER CITY LIBRARIES	
C0009835547	
Bertrams	04/10/2013
GEN	£8.99

Acknowledgements

Grateful thanks to Xinran and Toby Eady for keeping my dreams alive, and to Paul Baggaley at Picador. To my wonderful editors, Charlotte Greig, and Kris Doyle and his team. I am indebted to Willy Maley for his time and kind words, and to Alasdair Gray and Rob Maslen.

Many books assisted in my research; they include Leonard and Barbara Watson's *A History of Malaysia*, and by Colin Nicholas, *Towards Self-Determination: Indigenous People in Asia*, *Orang Asli Women and the Forest*, and *The Orang Asli and the Contest for Resources: Indigenous Politics, Development and Identity in Peninsular Malaysia*. Tan Teong Jin's *Travels in the Malaysian Rainforest* provided valuable information on the tropical jungle. I also referred to writings in Chinese, among them, *Penang Conference and the 1911 Chinese Revolution* (Zhang Shaokuan) and *Kang Youwei in Singapore and Malaya* (Zhang Kehong); and in Malay, *Stories of Animals from the Orang Asli* (Lim Boo Liat), among others. Khoo Salma Nasution's *Sun Yat Sen in Penang* contributed to the background of Part Two of the book.

A special thank-you to Colin Nicholas for the trips to the Orang Asli villages, and to the Centre for Orang Asli Concerns for allowing access to archive materials. And to Creative Scotland and Cove Park for their support.

The writing of this book would not have been possible

without the constant support from friends and family. To my family, especially my sister Chew Peng, Big Brother and sister-in-law, and my friends Siew Kook, Chew Fong and Seng Wee – I am grateful for the tropical warmth you exude, from thousands of miles away, that has kept me comforted while I write, alone, in my little flat; also to Lin Chau, Andrea McNicoll, Eunice Buchanan, Dorothy Alexander, Jackie Killeen and Richard Bull. To Jocelyn Gray, for the walks and talks. To Margaret and Michael Welsh, for your kindness, as always. To Irene Patton and all at the School of Philosophy, for being Good Company.

And to Ian Boyd, for always being there.

'. . . the earth does not belong to man;
man belongs to the earth.'

– CHIEF SEATTLE, 1851

Prelude: Engi

MAY 1938

My father once told me, if there was an outside man I could trust, that person would be Taukeh Chai. I was seven and naked, my first loincloth hidden still in the inner bark of the *terap* tree, yet to be peeled and made into the material to cover my boyhood shame.

That day, I squatted with Father under a tree and peered out between bird's-nest ferns at Taukeh Chai the Chinaman, standing in the clearing at the edge of the forest.

Why doesn't he just leave and go home? I stared up at Father; he pressed his forefinger to his lips, shaking his head, smiling, eyes squeezed into slits on his crumpled face. He was happy. He did this only when he was happy, when he returned from his hunting trips with a wild boar on his back. A really big one. Father was a good hunter, the best of the tribe. Only a giant boar would make him smile until he lost his eyes. But he didn't go hunting that day. He was seeing off the Chinaman whom he'd looked after for two weeks. He'd taken me with him.

When I looked ahead again the Chinaman was gazing in our direction, his eyes searching. I sniggered quietly, covering my mouth with a hand, and shrank further into the clump of foliage. Father rapped lightly at my head, another warning, though his muted laughter didn't escape me. We knew he didn't see us – how would he? We are chameleons in the wild, camouflaged among the trees and leaves; but I saw him waving into the air, his hand slow and heavy. On a ground void of shelter there was a lone figure, small, exposed, vulnerable.

Did light play its trick or did he really cry? Under the naked sun his eyes gleamed suddenly like the morning dew reflecting dawn rays; he wiped the back of his hand over them hastily, shaking his head. He continued standing for a while before threading the path out of the forest. Father had his big grin still hanging on his face when we walked back to our quarter. It was then Father told me the Chinaman was a friend – his first outside friend.

His name was Chai Mingzhi. Father called him *taukeh*, 'boss', even though he wasn't one yet. Not then.

*

I was born in the forest; so was my father. As was my father's father, and his father. How many forefathers were there before them when the first took his place on this land? That I'm not able to count, but Father told me:

'It began from the day the world started. When the sun and the moon began to take their turns in the sky, and birds emerged from the horizon, flapping their wings, singing. When the soil spread over the barren land, and green trees and red flowers, animals and snakes, beetles and butterflies rose from the earth and found their territories. Then the land opened up, became a river, and fish and prawns squeezed themselves out from the riverbed and swam freely in the water.

'We were as free as the animals and fish in our world.' Father paused, his bleary eyes gazing deep into mine: 'Listen carefully, Engi, my son: there wasn't an outside world during those early days; there was only Our World, the forest that was, and the forest was everything on this land.'

Father told me this when we sat under the rambutan tree after dinner, he chewing betel nuts wrapped in *sireh* or smoking self-grown tobacco rolled in leaves, while we children surrounded him hungry for stories the way he and his siblings once urged tales from their father, who got his from their grandfather.

I had always been a keen listener, always fought for the best seat, close enough for Father to reach my shoulder: a light touch, a squeeze, a look in the eyes at times when emphasis was needed. The hardest squeeze would come some time during Father's pipe-smoking break, when he lowered his head to face me, lowered his voice too, deep like a boar's grunt:

'I want you to remember all these, Engi. One day you'll tell them all to your children. Promise me, my son.' I would simply nod, my young head filled instead with questions about the outside men, eagerly pressing Father to move on.

When did the first of these people come? Father couldn't tell exactly but said they came by sea from the opposite shore, Sumatra that is now: they cut down trees, they made their homes here.

'Our ancestors kept quiet; they did nothing to stop them,' Father said. 'Because they thought there were enough fish and boars for extra people, our ancestors were contented with their little corner in the forest.

'Later, though, these outside men felled more trees, built more houses, and the edge of the forest receded by day, by month, by year. Before long, they broke into the forest, killed our people, burned our huts.

'There were more of them than us, and the daggers they brought with them would kill our people instantly with their wavy blades when they pierced into the bodies. They called it kris, their deadly weapon. Our blowpipes are made for killing animals from a distance; they are not designed to harm a human in close contact.

'They killed the babies, took away young women and men and made them slaves. They made the women sleep with them, and cook and clean for them; they made the men work in the fields. They said the lands were theirs, and they were the rightful "sons of the soil". Because the land was called *Malayadvipa* by the ancient Indian traders, they became the Malays.' A hand on my thin shoulder, Father spat a big lump of chewed betel on the ground – tuh! – bloody red against the dark earth.

After each harvest, Father told me, our ancestors burned the land and retreated deeper and deeper into the forest.

'Another group of people, the Chinese, then journeyed ashore across the ocean from the north. Where they came from, there were dragons hovering on the yellow land, whipping up yellow dust as they danced and hopped, sprinkling it on the people underneath. With that their skins took the colour of the earth.

'It was four hundred years ago.' Father counted his fingers. 'This first lot of Chinamen and women didn't give us trouble. Their dragon boat brought with it, in the entourage of hundreds of young men and women, a princess who was sent to be the wife of the Malay King.'

*

I would only learn of the Chinese princess years later, in 1905, five years after Father and I saw off the Chinaman at the edge of the forest. I was twelve, brimming with pride for my first hunt of the boar all by myself, and eager to rush out there for more, not knowing that it would also be my last.

That year, Father sent me to Taukeh Chai to be his apprentice.

*

She was Hang Li Po, the princess, married to Sultan Megat Iskandar Syah, the second ruler of the Malacca sultanate. I read of her in a book from Taukeh Chai's study, of her being the daughter of Emperor Yung-Lo of the Ming Dynasty, sacrificed for a diplomatic kinship.

During the two-hour daily reading session that Taukeh Chai scheduled for me, I squatted restlessly between neatly stacked-up shelving units, pretending I was in a corner of the forest. Leaning against the wall, my rough, sunburnt body fidgeted awkwardly in the stiff, over-starched linen; my skin, where it escaped my new shirt, starkly dark against the whitewash behind me.

Had she, Princess Hang Li Po, ever grudged her father for sending her away? What went through her mind as she was carried in the royal sedan to her new home? Did she miss her palace, her parents, her siblings, her summer gardens? Did she miss sitting by the window reciting her favourite poems which her husband was unable to comprehend? If she had learned the new language of her new world, would she forget the old?

Cowering there, I read the fate of a dislocated young woman, speculating on her pain, her suffering, asking questions that had no answers.

The forest of books was never the dense, shadowy woods of my natural world, and quite often, simmering in the unbearable heat of the populous town, I thought of the clear stream and yearned to have a dip in it.

*

In Taukeh Chai's study I also read about another outside man called Parameswara, who'd become the ruler of Malacca in 1401 before the first white men stepped on this land. An outside man he was, as his ancestors were from the Srivijaya empire of Hindu descent who'd settled in Palembang. Forced out by the Majapahit, they found refuge in Temasek which is today's Singapore. A new palace, a new life; generations passed. Yet the Majapahit would not leave them in peace, and during his time, Parameswara, the young Prince, began his own journey across the strait to the Malay Peninsula. He would find his way to Malacca, would build his kingdom there after an encounter with a mouse deer, would bring wealth and glory to the sultanate for generations to come.

How similar, I marvelled as I read on, the second part of Parameswara's journey was to Taukeh Chai's! From Singapore to Malacca, from rags to riches; both foreigners. The only difference is the former made this land his, declaring his empire on it, while the latter? Always finding himself and his compatriots holding on to a clump of loose soil, dangling on an escarpment, and there are approaching feet, stamping on the hands that have worked in the mines, the plantations, that have fertilized this part of earth with prosperity, and wishing them to fall. How could the human heart be so cruel? If we could take them all in, why couldn't they, the incumbents, take in the newcomers?

*

Even now as a forty-five-year-old living in the forest I'd once left behind, the questions would rise and ebb at times. In the deep of the night I would sit on the *mengkuang* mat in a pool of flickering candlelight, pen in hand, striving to chronicle the life of the man who changed my fate: Chai Mingzhi, my guardian of twenty years; the thorn in my heart. I would see them, Parameswara the ancient knight riding high on his war horse, trotting around, taunting Chai the pigtailed Chinaman whose face is obscured in whirls of dust, and I would drop my pen and sigh. How could I write about my subject if I couldn't even have a clear view of him?

Eventually, I pushed everything to one side, the project abandoned.

Until two days ago, when a forest collector found his way to my shelter.

The messenger, a young Chinese man I'd never met, refused the tea I offered, refused also to enter my hut; stood instead, a hand on the wild rambutan tree, towering over me. 'He wants to see you, that Taukeh Chai.' I looked up at him, my back leaning against the doorpost, my mind trying to work out what that meant. It's been thirteen years since I last saw my former guardian: thirteen years of silence between us.

The young man had certainly heard of me from the elderly of the community; his curious eyes searched me for traces of the boy in the stories that have been circulating in that seaside town of Malacca. Aware of my stare, he scratched his head, an awkward smile on his face, and said hastily: 'Not a good time, you know. Not a good time for your old boss, for us all, the Chinese.' And with equal haste, he blurted out the happenings at the Minang Villa, the proud residence of my former guardian.

'. . . Riot . . . Minang Villa . . . land . . .' His voice seemed to sound from a distance away. Unreal. '. . . Attempted arson . . . he was attacked and had a stroke—' I straightened my body abruptly. Been attacked? Had a stroke? When? How? Why? How is he? I heard nothing else from the messenger, knew nothing as to when he walked away.

I will return, I murmured.

Two days now since the visit of the Chinese messenger, memories of the past rise and surge, the force so strong I can no longer ignore it. Today, on the eve of my return to the Minang Villa – my first in thirteen years – I search through the notes taken over my time in the outside world and trace back to the beginning. I try to clear a path solely for Chai Mingzhi, only to find Parameswara, again, in his royal costume, sticking his head up, peeping. And suddenly I know. I know I can't abandon him, the same way historians of the Malay Peninsula can't abandon the like of my guardian and his compatriots in their chronicles.

I'll let him surface, Parameswara; I'll let him punctuate episodes of the Chinaman's life. On my exercise book, two lines are drawn – one of Chai Mingzhi's life, in the early twentieth century; the other, Parameswara's, from the late fourteenth century – with a five-hundred-year gap between them. Only by comparing the similarities between their journeys will the differences in the outcomes appear stark.

I am ready to begin my story.

PART ONE

Two Men, One Journey, Five Hundred Years Apart

1

The Journey Begins

SOUTH CHINA SEA, JUNE 1900

Dawn. The chill woke him. Snuggling up, he opened his eyes to a still-black sky, confused, not knowing where he was. Lying still, he listened – the waves, the low droning of the engine, the tiny movements of the many bodies around him – and gradually walked out of his dreams. He pulled his collar up against the sharp wind, glad for another day gone by.

He was Chai Mingzhi, a sixth-ranking mandarin of the Qing Court. He was on his way to Nanyang, the South Seas – like many others, most of them starving peasants turned contract workers, aboard this cargo ship – together with his sister Meilian and her daughter Jiaxi, and his friends Tiansheng and Martin, an English, who was also Meilian's fiancé.

The deck was quiet, suffused with the rhythmic breathing of sound sleep from the exhausted bodies crammed around him. Like them, he was driven out from the hold to the deck – from the inside heat, crowdedness and smells of sweat, urine and excrement, to the airy outside – despite the chill that would sometimes seep into the bones in the small hours, as long as Captain Cochrane permitted.

Tiansheng must be somewhere close by, he knew. His

friend would not leave him out of sight, always watchful, always ready to extend a helping hand when needed. A stumble on the deck, and support would come swift and strong from behind. And sometimes, even when not needed. An eye glued to his back, unable to be shrugged off. *It must have been wearing him out*, he sighed. And Tiansheng was one year younger than he was! Sleeping soundly now, Tiansheng was, perhaps, among the rest on the floor. Taking care not to stir, not to make a noise, Mingzhi tied a knot in the loose end of his cotton belt, something he'd done yesterday, and the day before, and before – each of the passing days since boarding the ship. He counted: six.

It is only the beginning. He let go of his belt, fidgeted lightly, trying to make himself comfortable. He thought of his sister, Meilian, and wondered how she and her daughter Jiaxi were coping on the other side of the deck. *Martin will take care of them; I'm sure he will,* he convinced himself, knowing he should trust his future brother-in-law.

Mingzhi heaved a sigh, relaxed.

Lying there, he tilted his head and stared out at the horizon, at the streaks of red, orange and purple criss-crossing the background of dark blue. He'd been waiting for it, the best moment of the day, before the cries for food, for water, for space began. Only at this moment he was free. Alone. Being cradled in the ever-changing sky above and the soothing sound of the water below.

Waiting for tomorrow.

And tomorrow.

*

It was noon when he saw Martin appro[ach]
ing through the crowd, most of them out
now, sitting, squatting or sauntering among
onboard.

'Come with me. Let me talk to Captain Coch[rane].
Let me tell him who you are.' Martin, who had found [a]
friend at the stern, sounded pressing, almost pleading. 'A
sixth-ranking mandarin has boarded his ship – what an
honour! He would happily let you share his cabin. Think
about the cosy room. The meat and the wine.'

Mingzhi shook his head, silent. It was a quiet afternoon. From where they stood, he could see speckles of
silver on the sea surface, glinting in the noon sun, fishes
whose names were still unknown to him.

At Martin's request the English captain had let this
fellow countryman of his, his fiancée Meilian and her
daughter, two of a handful of women on board, shelter
at the companionway leading to the captain's cabin,
away from the hold that was overcrowded with cargo
and people. The commander of the ship had, however,
turned a deaf ear to Martin's mention of Mingzhi and
Tiansheng.

'You give them an inch and they're ready to climb
over your head. They should think themselves lucky,
those two CHINESE women. I might change my mind
any time, you know?' The captain had thrown a side
glance at his fellow Englishman and walked away.

Despite much persuasion from Martin, Mingzhi had
forbidden his friend from revealing to Captain Cochrane
his mandarin status.

'Think about Meilian and Jiaxi, then. It will be at least
a month before we arrive in Singapore.' Martin came

... Mingzhi felt his friend's hot breath on his face. 'Look at them. Do you want them to suffer all the way to Nanyang?'

His back against the railing, Mingzhi peered across to where the mother and daughter were, at the top of the companionway, crouching, sheltering under the narrow sunshield. Her hand holding on to her mother's arm, Jiaxi stared up and caught her uncle's eyes. She nodded, did not look away, did not appear pitiable, a faint smile on her face. *A brave girl she is, only fourteen.* Mingzhi nodded in response, relieved.

'Let me go and talk to the captain, OK?' Martin raised his voice this time, impatient to proceed with his plan.

'No, don't.' Mingzhi turned to face his friend. 'No one would know my past. Not now, and never in future.'

'But—'

'Mandarin or not mandarin, it's all over now.'

Martin's shoulders dropped. He shook his head as he retreated, making his way back to his fiancée.

*

The eighth day, and there had been a tumult among the passengers since the morning, suppressed talk at first, gradually becoming louder. Mingzhi looked across the crowd at Tiansheng who, surprisingly, averted his gaze. *What is it? He doesn't want me to know?* He pushed his way to his friend.

'What's the matter?'

Tiansheng's head drooped; not a word.

'It's the Imperial City.' Martin, who had just joined them, appeared worried. News had been spreading among the sailors, he said, and now leaked to others on board. British troops, he explained, using the Boxers' attacks as a ruse, had allied with the Russian, American, French, Japanese, German, Austrian and Italian; they had marched into the Imperial City and broken into the Forbidden Palace.

Mingzhi felt a sharp pain at his heart. He glanced around and saw his fellow passengers' indignation: the suppressed whispers, angry veins, red faces and teary eyes. Holding his chest, he quietly stepped away, gesturing to his friends not to follow, and retreated to a quiet corner.

There were peals of laughter from a couple of English seamen near the stern.

'So they call it the Heavenly Palace? Heaven or hell, it's all ours now!'

'Look at them, a bunch of sick yellow men of Asia. A look at them makes me sick, too.'

Mingzhi shrank further, hands clasping tight at the railing.

He was glad that he had stood by his decision not to reveal his real identity to Captain Cochrane. A runaway official from the Qing Court, which had supported the anti-foreigner rebels, would have been conveniently singled out to be their clear target. Yet he felt it still, the mocking and the sneers.

Never ever board the Englishmen's ships, some of the evacuees had warned them as they were waiting at the river port in the southern town to chance the ocean. They had described the humiliating treatment by arrogant westerners, the struggle for space between overloaded cargo in a vessel not meant for accommodating passengers. But the decision to leave had come quick and unexpected. They were fortunate enough, with Martin's connections, to secure places on the ship alongside four hundred others, mostly workers contracted by English companies in the tropics. From the deck he had watched the rest of the evacuees – many of them sympathizers of the Boxers – clamber onto their boats. They had darted at passengers on the tall ship – among them Mingzhi and his party – occasional contemptuous stares and, at the English seamen, a grudging gaze. He had flinched, uneasy.

They were right, he sighed, pulling his gown tighter against the cold wind.

Standing there, alone, Mingzhi fixed his gaze on the distant horizon. There were only glitters of silver in the bright noon sun, wavering in light breeze, bubbling off. He strained his eyes for a glimpse of yellow earth, some seagull, so hard that his temples throbbed. No, the land he'd fled from was no longer in sight. A sudden constriction in his stomach had him doubled over; he clutched at the iron bar, a hand on his abdomen, retching. Tears squeezed out of his tightly sealed lids.

When it was over, sitting on the deck floor leaning against the railing, he tried to think what he could have done if he were there. Nothing. *Nothing I could've done,* he mumbled. Even before, he'd been struggling to meet the demands from his greedy superiors. With the government's coffers now empty, the corrupters would be more corrupt, would have pressurized him further with impossibly higher tax targets. *I was right to leave,* he convinced himself. Exodus like the one he was in, he envisaged, would happen more frequently, with greater numbers.

To foreign lands.

America, Europe, South East Asia.

Anywhere, just not staying in their homes.

And he would be in the tropics in a matter of days.

*

The tenth day, and the storm struck in the deep of the night, quick, without warning. From nowhere the wind swooped across, beating up mountains of dark water. Asleep and unprepared, he felt the strong impact, a sharp pain, and found himself thrown onto the many bodies crammed around him on the deck, into the heat, the sweat, the cries and screams. Together they were hurled around like the miniature rabbit and turtles in his childhood games. Helpless hands rose and bodies struggled to squeeze out from the piled-up human flesh.

Mingzhi was jostled, pushed against something hard and knocked his head. He groped at the slender fixture behind him. The spar! He grabbed at it and pulled himself free from the crowd, clinging tightly to it. Another surge came before he could catch a breath, more forceful this time. The ship keeled suddenly then plummeted. His hands and legs wrapped around the spar like a needy child, he felt the many bodies rolling past, sometimes crashing onto him. He heard their helpless cries and sounds of retching amid the crashing winds, but there was something else. He pricked his ears, and although quite faintly, he could make out the sounds of objects plunging into the water. Flop! Flop! Flop! He let his imagination stop there.

He could feel the wind lashing like a riding crop onto his lean body, weakened after ten days at sea, but nothing came to his open eyes. Only blackness. Amid it, the occasional blinding cracks of lightning, then the vague shuffling figures around him, the inky water that reeled – splashing on board at times. Cries of infants pierced the adults' moans of pain. He thought of the little ones pressed against their mothers' bosoms. *How are they going to survive this?* He closed his eyes. The howling waves, wind, thunder shouted loud into his ears.

The next attack came like an explosion. *No!* He lost hold of the spar, slipping down with the rest to the other side. He fumbled: hands reached out frantically. The shrouds! He clutched at one of them, felt the burning sensation on his palms and knew they were bleeding from the quick chafe. Crouching, he gritted his teeth, swore never to let go this time. Around him, there were sounds of banging, of bodies colliding with bodies. More tearing moans, more retching, more shrieking cries. More sounds of successive flopping. This time he couldn't help wondering, who could they be? Old Chong the elderly peasant who'd ignored kind advice to shelter in the hold, insisting on staying on the deck to 'get closer to the sky'? Or Young Li, the sixteen-year-old who'd had his arm chopped off by the equally poor farmers for stealing food from them? Or—

His heart stopped. He struggled to get up, pressing his hand down, and it landed on someone's back. He ignored the yelling and the curses that followed and called out—

'Meilian!'

'We're here! We're fine.' His sister sounded weak, a distance away, from the direction of the captain's cabin.

'They'll all be fine.' A pat on his shoulder. He looked up. It was Tiansheng; he'd found Mingzhi and moved closer to him from wherever he'd been, as always. 'Martin is taking care of them.'

Mingzhi crouched again, his back against Tiansheng, staring into the dark water ahead. He thought of the boats he'd seen during the day, the junks that were much smaller but packed with people, the starving peasants who wished for a better life, who would work in the mines and on someone else's farms. He thought of the paper boats his uncle had taught him to fold as a child, that would, each time, sink fast in the clear, tranquil water of the lily pond in their garden, ruffled only by occasional breeze.

But this was no breeze. The wind howled and whipped across; sharp blades sliced from all directions, slashing at his naked face and limbs, and his gown clung tight to him. With that, something came to his mind, a vague picture of a similar kind, of ferocious wind slapping against a trembling, lean body. His sister's.

It was Meilian's wedding, he remembered.

He was six then, had just started school, and had been enjoying his after-school hours with his sisters, sharing his newly acquired knowledge, practising calligraphy with them, who'd been deprived the chance of education. While his second sister, Meifong, quickly lost interest, impatient with ink-grinding and memorizing the poems, every day the eldest, Meilian, would wait patiently inside the specially curtained corner in Mingzhi's room, anticipating another poem, another story, another form of calligraphic stroke.

Read for me, she would say, pointing randomly at the neatly written blocks of verse on the threaded pages. And

Mingzhi, eager to impress his sister, had always been quick to obey, rattling them off, his effeminate childish voice filling the space behind the cotton shield, wrapping them in it. Only them. He would stare up at his sister, at her dreamy eyes, sometimes brimming with tears, sometimes sparkling with – delight? Astonishment? Anger? Somehow he knew, though, whatever it had been, he was supposed to keep it to himself, a secret they shared.

Before long, Meilian was able to browse the book for her favourites, even from those he hadn't yet learned, reading them softly, and eventually memorizing them by heart. He would hear her repeatedly murmur:

> *After drinking wine at twilight*
> *under the chrysanthemum hedge,*
> *My sleeves are perfumed*
> *by the faint fragrance of the plants.*
> *Oh, I cannot say it is not enchanting,*
> *Only, when the west wind stirs the curtain,*
> *I see that I am leaner*
> *than the yellow flowers.*

How could a person be leaner than a flower? He asked her and Meilian sighed and shook her head: 'You'll know it one day.' Her melancholy escaped the child's innocent ears. Now clinging to the shroud like a monkey, he pressed his face on the roughness of the hemp rope, feeling his cheek chafed with each convulsion. *We could all be leaner than this. Our lives.* That same year he would learn also what life meant when his second sister Meifong lay unconscious in bed, succumbing to the deadly plague that had swept the village, and later, when his mother's shrill cry came through as he and Meilian cuddled together and shivered in his room.

The next thing he knew was Meilian's wedding. To chase away all bad luck that had befallen the family and bring forth good fortune, his grandfather said. It was gusty on the big day, so strong the wind that the fat string of firecrackers, ignited upon the sedan's arrival, danced like a wild dragon on the doorpost, spurting fire, blurting out its anger. He winced, uncharacteristically, against his earlier anticipation of the spectacular displays he and other children of his age were usually fond of. It was then, when hiding behind his uncle in the crowd, he stuck out his head and saw her – Meilian, covered up from top to toe in red, being led out from the mansion. The wind surged across towards her as she stepped over the main-door threshold for the first time. She swayed and trembled in her heavy costume and for a second, stopped – only a second – and was quickly ushered forward. Her crimson gown and the equally striking long veil under her headpiece slapped against her body as she climbed into the red sedan.

She was fourteen then, the age of Jiaxi, her only daughter, now.

I've promised them a better future. I will see to it! Mingzhi thrust his fist on the floor. Lowering his torso, he let the wobbling waves rock him. 'A natural cradle' – he recalled Martin's words. *Martin the optimist*. He smiled quietly as he remembered how his friend had, during the calm start of their long journey, jokingly held Mingzhi's shoulders and rocked him to the near-rhythmic motion of the ship.

But now they were plunged up and down, and his stomach surged, aggravated by the fishy, sour smell of vomit that rose with each convulsion, each passing of the wind. He held his breath, suppressing the rumbling in his chest, and shut his eyes and ears, too. *Think, try to think of something. Anything.* Like the piece of gold, the only one they had, sewn into the inner pocket of his gown. He felt it with his hand, knew it was there. He felt also, as he concentrated, the bundle on his back, the hard edge that jarred at his spine.

It was the duplicated book of the family tree of the Chai clan.

On the night before leaving, he had carefully copied down the details from the original. He would keep it on the ancestral altar of his new place, perhaps, if he had one, or simply in a solid wooden box. *Don't they produce durable, beautiful teak there?* He would lock it away and start his *own* record of the family tree. The sea had separated them all: the place he came from and the people, their lives and their doings, right or wrong, moral or immoral. It didn't matter now, for all was to be forgotten, like the old clan book, click, locked away and never to be looked into again. *Why bother bringing it along, then?* His mind turned blank for a second, then quickly he shook his head.

Stay focused. He would begin the book with his very own name. *No.* He bit his lips. There would be new rules in the new place, and Meilian, as the eldest of his would-be household, despite being a woman and having a married name, would take precedence over him.

He imagined wielding a giant brush saturated with thick black ink and writing swiftly:

As he planned the list to be filled in his family record, his hand landed on the floor—

Some sticky liquid was pasted on his palm and fingers. The fishy, sour smell returned, even stronger now. Unable to contain it any longer, he threw up, and gone were the book, the writing, the listing. He was back to the chaos around him: the people, the noises, the reeling. He stared up. A flash of lightning tore across the sky and he saw, in the near distance, Tiansheng's watchful eyes. Mingzhi lowered his head.

He closed his eyes, held his breath and let his body rock, again and again, to the movement of the water underneath. He knew the rain that would follow would wash away the filth, just like the many other nights.

We have to survive this. Tiansheng lifted his face, staring hard into the darkness above him. *I will not let fate take over me; never again.*

At least twice he'd grappled with Death, and twice he'd made narrow escapes. To him, life couldn't have been any harder.

He had been an opera apprentice, stage name Little Sparrow. He was sold to the Northern Opera Troupe as a child by his starving parents. First came the hard training, day and night, interlaced with frequent punishments for a wrong step or an awkward twist of the wrist, or a slip of the lyrics. Long hours spent squelching, stretching his vocal cords to the highest notes, or half-squatting on a bench under the scorching sun: bent knees trembled, head spun. Then the strenuous, perilous journeys: trudging in the wild and the mountains, crossing the surging Yellow River and drifting along the Yangtze.

Over the years he watched new actors, new musicians, new runners bustle in, while the old, the incompetent were quietly discharged. He watched insecure, eager actors fighting against each other: seniors hiding their best tricks from juniors, juniors stabbing seniors' backs. He watched them curry favour with the troupe manager and flirt with the rich and powerful in the cities and towns and villages where they perched, and grew lonelier.

He found no confidant in his world.

He watched the gaudy blood-red NORTHERN OPERA banner fade into dull pink as he pulled it off the bamboo pole after every final show in the city or town or village they stopped at. Then moved to another town, stuck in the pole, hung the banner. The spindly stick swayed feebly even in the slightest breeze; extending itself up into the air, drooping, the laced satin announced not the troupe's fame but the teenager's solitude, his despair.

In a hilly village in Shanxi, he saw an old busker play a bamboo-leaf flute outside a shack by the gravel path as the carts of costumes and set pieces trundled by. He saw that the musician squatted firmly in the suddenly raised yellow dust, eyes closed, soft, trembling notes hovering in the evening air, unperturbed by the surrounding hustle. Walking past, the teenage opera singer thought he saw a glimpse of smile among the deep creases on the weather-worn face. A smile of contentment.

That night and a few more that followed, he sneaked out of the village temple where the troupe settled and staged their shows, went to the old man and learned the trick (he scrunched fifty leaves before perfecting the flute) and the music (simple, basic melody) from him. At first he was thrilled, immersed in the fine, wavering sounds: his world; a flicker of hope. Later, as he dipped deep into his music and began to create his own tunes, the tinge of sadness was so palpable he knew he would never be free, physically or mentally.

Nothing will get me out of this deep abyss, he realized. Training, punishment, performance, travel. Training, punishment, performance, travel. *This is my fate,* he told himself, and resigned himself to confiding in his flute. Sitting long hours in quiet corners; tremulous notes threading through silent nights. Until he arrived in the remote village, entered the mansion the troupe performed in, which was Mingzhi's home, and discovered an equally lonely soul in the young man.

Every night the two sneaked out of the mansion and met by the river, sitting and talking long into the small hours, happy and content. He did not know then that their friendship, disapproved of by Mingzhi's grandfather, would cost him his position in the troupe.

'Who do you think you are? A sing-song actor wants to link arms with the heir to a landlord?' the hooked-nose troupe manager, who'd bought him from his parents with two sacks of rice, taunted. 'We will manage without you, but we can't without those landlords. Birthdays, new births, festivals, harvests. How can we survive without any of those? You tell me. Only those rich men can afford them.'

The middle-aged man who had seen the young apprentice grow under his shelter turned his back on him, his voice echoing in the vast courtyard:

'Don't blame me. You sealed your own fate.'

Thump! The door closed behind the budding actor.

Flashes of lightning criss-crossed the sky. Tiansheng glanced at Mingzhi in the near distance, his shrunken figure. All of a sudden, and for the first time, the questions came to him: *If I'd known then, would I have befriended him? Was it a blessing or a curse, to be thrown out of the troupe?* He wondered if he hadn't met his friend, would he have become a lead opera singer? Would the name Little Sparrow shine through all corners as his predecessors' did?

Immediately he was stricken by his shameful thoughts. He straightened his back and fixed his eyes ahead to where the crouching shape was, and concentrated.

A rumbling sound moved across the water. He heard it coming; the rain now pattered heavily on the deck like a hail of bullets, shooting forcefully at his head, his shoulders, his back. *Just the right time.* In dire need of a good wash to clear his mind, he let his face take the blows in full. Around him, people cheered. Heads tilted up, chapped lips opened wide, they let the sweet juice of the sky moisten their dry throats, fill their empty stomachs; let the heavy beads hit hard against their exhausted bodies, skeletal limbs.

Tiansheng, with his eyes closed, wrapped in a noise cocoon with sheets of rain over him, fell abruptly into a scene hidden in a secluded corner of his mind. There was shouting, there was beating, there was kicking. He saw that he was the one being shouted at, beaten, kicked. He saw that, in the midst, he'd raised a knife and thrust it into the bare chest of one of his attackers; he saw that that was none other but Mingzhi's estranged half-brother; he heard a tearing scream; he saw his victim collapse before him, his eyes roll up – *No!* Tiansheng opened his eyes. The spasm and the blood that would have followed retreated to their hiding place, only awaiting the right time for a comeback. They would follow him like the invisible stamp of 'murderer' on his forehead.

He wiped his face again, as if to clear away the imagery. It was just another night. The rain would stop, so would the thunder and lightning. As would everything else. So he wished.

Meilian, huddling together with Jiaxi on the companion-way, rested her body against the side wall, a hand holding tight to the edge of the wooden panel under her, another around her daughter. A short while ago Meilian had heard it coming, the rain, thundering on the overhead shelter so narrow, and beads of water were soon beginning to splash onto her body. Shivering, she thought of it falling full on her brother.

It must be unpleasant. Meilian thought of her brother's court office-cum-residence in Pindong Town, the silky satin over the soft mattress in his bedroom. He was a mandarin, Mingzhi, dined on delicate bird's-nest soup and fine *o-long*, dressed in the official eaglet-emblem that declared his power and authority. She thought of the many sleepless nights he spent studying, the three rounds of tedious exams, the long, heart-gnawing anticipation for the posting. His pledge to help the people. *He gives them all up.* She was certain that he did it for her, as always. *Only he would care.*

The day when she stepped into the sedan to the man twice her age, Meilian thought her life was over. As second wife, her only function in the household was reproduction. A son, that was all they needed, to continue the family line. Those barren first years and after giving birth to Jiaxi (*A girl, useless!*), Meilian bowed her head – lower than the maids' – against her mother-in-law's cynicism.

Her husband – the son of Mandarin Liu, the commanding official of Pindong Town, fifteen miles away from her village – was nothing like his authoritarian, money-grubbing and power-crazed father. A skinny, timid man, he was never rude to her; never did he care for her either. Put simply, she was one of his many opium cases (silver, ivory, gold) in the glass display cabinet, only catching his eye once in a while; but more often, he would past it by unnoticed. He knew Meilian's function well and dutifully played his 'good son' role, squeezing the remainder of his energy (after his opium and brothel consumptions) onto his young wife, who'd never hissed a protest.

The dutiful son squeezed the last of his energy to produce a son before collapsing in his opium couch, a year after Junwei's birth.

At her husband's funeral, Meilian staged the best show of her life to the surprise and satisfaction of the critical, gossipy relatives and her mandarin father-in-law's favour-seeking visitors. She wailed and howled and beat her chest like most wives in mourning would at the wake, chanting: 'Why did you leave so early? How bitter my life has become!' In her heart she was laughing out loud, for the absurdity of such a performance expected from a widow and the unexpected talent she newly discovered. The effect was the unstoppable tears that rolled out of her otherwise dry eyes, drained from the many nights weeping in lonely darkness while her husband, after fulfilling his duty, drowned in his post-opium sleep.

A son, a daughter. Life would be different from now on with only them, she'd thought.

She was over-optimistic.

Junwei was only six when a murder took place in a brothel in Pindong, involving Mandarin Liu's nephew who, according to eyewitnesses, was the clear culprit. Having just lost his only son, the mandarin had transferred his hopes to his nephew. Using his position, Mandarin Liu conveniently found a scapegoat to seal the case. It didn't seal the mouths of his long-term enemies, though; the incident was a godsend opportunity for them to lodge a report at the heart of the Forbidden Palace.

But he was lucky still, Mandarin Liu, being tipped off by an informant a night before the siege. That night, he summoned his family members to the central hall. Standing in the spacious room, he gave his instructions on what to pack and what not to, and for carriages to be ready at the back door. 'Quick, careful, not a noise,' he commanded, his voice as firm as his face.

Then he turned to Meilian.

'Such an inauspicious woman! First my son, now the

family!' The old man spat at the daughter-in-law he would rather not have. 'You will not come with us, nor will your daughter. Never!'

Pale-faced, Meilian rushed back to her room, where Junwei was soundly asleep. Earlier on that frantic night, Meilian had combed her son's hair as she always did before bed. The wind during the day's courtyard play-time had messed it up and the claw stuck in it, a sudden pull. 'Ouch!' Junwei frowned a naughty boy's frown: mouth twisted to one side, eyes narrowed, blinking, blinking.

'Promise me, don't hurt me again, Mum.' His mouth jutted out, his cheek bulged with indignant air. Meilian squeezed his rounded face, her heart melting into waters. 'No, not tomorrow, not the day after; I promise.'

There was no tomorrow for them. Hours later, Junwei was snatched from his bed, his tiny hands rubbing his sleepy eyes. Away.

In her bound feet Meilian wobbled to the hall. It was empty. She hurried to the back door, only to see the last of the carriages bolt off in a swirl of dust. Gone.

'Junwei!' Her hysterical shriek tore across the darkness, and then silence, as though nothing had been, nothing had happened. Even she herself had never existed.

'Mother.' A soft, slender hand clung on to her own. Meilian turned and saw the daughter she had forgotten. 'I am here.' Jiaxi, standing by her mother's side, quietly led her away.

It was Mingzhi who took her and Jiaxi in, provided them with a shelter, taught her to read and write, to learn

English. Mingzhi who brought her to Martin, her second chance in life.

Meilian closed her eyes, the rumbling of the rain loud in her ears.

Jiaxi, her head on Meilian's bosom, felt the heaving in her mother's chest, felt also the soft, helpless hand loosely wrapped over hers, and saw the ruffles under the older woman's lids.

On the top of the steps, Martin, fixing his gaze on Meilian, wished he could hold his fiancée's hand, too, and take her in his arms, but knew she would be frightened away. *Their culture.* He sighed. It had been the same urge when he first saw her.

By then Meilian was widowed, abandoned by her father-in-law, and living under Mingzhi's care in Pindong Town, where Mingzhi took his office as the town's mandarin. To cheer Meilian and Jiaxi up, Mingzhi accepted his English friend's offer, travelling northwards to Peking for a much longed-for reunion, taking the mother and daughter with him. He did not know he would be caught up in the rebel Boxers' movement that would change his fate.

Nor did Martin.

Perhaps he'd been so absorbed into the local life, Martin had forgotten he belonged to the group labelled 'the foreigners', the 'enemy' to the ancient kingdom under threat. As he anticipated his friend's arrival, the Englishman was oblivious to the brewing tensions that would erupt in the Imperial City soon; more oblivious when he saw Meilian, stepping down from the carriage after Mingzhi and Jiaxi, pale from the long journey.

Hiding behind her brother, Meilian was a tender stalk of lily: pure, fragile, needing protection. *A hug, I would give her a hug.* Of course, he'd suppressed it, as he did now.

The rain bucketed down on him. Drenched, he fidgeted in his shirt and trousers that stuck to his body, another layer of dirt on top of the film of grime on his skin. He had never felt so filthy. He closed his eyes and drifted to his family home in another far-off land, to the spacious kitchen always cosy with smiles and hot bread and steaming soup. To the smell of freshly brewed tea. To the giant wooden tub, the warm water in it, the soothing sensations across open pores.

His eyelids squeezed tight.

Over the years, while he grew to become more adept at wielding the chopsticks, celebrating Chinese New Year and the Mid-Autumn Festival with local families, his expatriate colleagues found comfort in brothels carefully designed for their type. Red lanterns, soft *guzheng* music, seemingly vulnerable girls whom they could, metaphorically, spin on their fingertips, crush between their claws. A few times he was dragged along, before returning home, feeling ashamed, regretful. Empty.

Meilian was different. For the first time he felt warm, solid inside, simply by holding a door open for her, pouring a cup of tea, getting an extra serving of rice. For her.

He hadn't told his parents about Meilian. *What would their reactions be?* School teachers of a small English town having a Chinese (widowed, bound-footed, with a teenage daughter) for daughter-in-law? They had reluctantly agreed to their son's plan to learn trading in China. Five years, not more than five years, they had said. Martin knew his parents could tolerate him being away longer than he'd promised, could tolerate and even be happy at his leaving China for Malaya (*It's safer in a British colony!*). But this. The itchiness on his body became more unbearable.

He fidgeted again, shook his head and opened his eyes.

The two tiny figures in front of him huddled together like a pair of startled birds. Watching them, Martin's unsettled gaze turned soft, gently embracing his beloved. He smiled, like he usually did, his bare teeth a sudden flash of brightness in the chaotic gloom. He moved closer to Meilian, leaving a careful gap, just enough to avoid body contact, blocking the slanted rain from the mother and daughter.

'Get down inside!' Captain Cochrane shouted across from the wheel, his voice distorted and unintelligible in the deafening wind and rain, but Martin made out his gestures. He urged Meilian and Jiaxi to enter the cabin. Meilian, holding the beam tightly, did not budge. 'Get Mingzhi,' she said. 'Get them—' Bang! A convulsion cut short her words; they were knocked against the wall and then stumbled down the stairs. As she felt a sharp pain in her shoulder, Jiaxi, overwhelmed by a sudden fury, did something she'd never done and never thought she would do before – she twisted her hand off Meilian's, held it in hers and pulled her mother with her into the room. Martin followed suit.

Another shock came just as they slumped onto the carpeted floor. Bulbs flickered, then it was pitch black. Jiaxi answered after her mother in response to Martin's concern, before quietly dragging herself away from

Martin and Meilian to another corner. Leaning against the wall, she peeled off her cotton shoes and stretched out her legs.

She was angry. With everybody, everything.

Nobody cares about me. She arched forward and massaged her feet, mildly deformed from a (first delayed, later truncated) foot-binding effort. *Nobody cares what I think, what I want.* She plied open her slightly inward-curled toes, kneaded them lightly with her fingers. It wasn't about the storm, nor was it the discomfort on the ship. It was the decisions *they made*, one of those being putting her on this sea journey, subjecting her to this disaster. *No one has ever consulted me, not on anything!* It all started with the Peking trip. It was Uncle Mingzhi's idea: a chance for the mother and daughter to visit the city. She was overwhelmed then, eagerly packed her best silk-gowns-for-important-occasions (sky blue, pale green, clear lilac) a week before departure. Now thinking back, it dawned on her that she and her mother were secondary. *It was merely an excuse!* She rubbed the sole of her foot hard against her tender flesh. *It was all because of the men wanting to have a happy reunion!* Her angry thumbs moved faster, pressing even harder, as if the pain they inflicted on her sole would nudge away her fury.

It was fun at first, she must admit, the tour just a fortnight ago – Western ladies in their puffy dresses and delicate umbrellas, streets and alleys bustling with carts and people, the Forbidden Palace standing grand and solemn – until the Boxers marched into the streets, encircling the restaurant they dined in. 'Down with the foreign devils! Down with the foreign devils!' Men in black equipped with long swords had hemmed them in from all sides, shouting, rampaging, burning. They were trapped in the chaos.

Jiaxi, shuddering in the pitch-black cabin, had in her mind's eye the shock, the running and chasing, the encounter with the rebels flashing in fleeting sequences: clear, vivid, magnifying. There was them escaping the restaurant that was ablaze; there was them confronted by a group of Boxers in a dark alley; there was a sword pointing at Uncle Mingzhi's forehead; there was her, pulled down by Meilian onto the ground, kneeling, kow-towing for his life. *Only because we were with Martin!* She pulled back her legs abruptly and folded her knees in her arms.

She wasn't against Martin for who he was, that much she was certain, having spent time with Father Terry, the British priest of Pindong Town, learning from him, help-ing him manage the church-run orphanage. In fact she was delighted for Meilian to have a second chance. Her indignation came from the fact that they – or she, to be exact – had to flee the country because of him. Then again, she wasn't against the chance of opening up her horizons. Exotic tales of the West from Father Terry had long implanted in her fantasies of the wider world. The castles (with them stories of princes and princesses, queens and kings, knights and villains), the English coun-tryside with oaks and elms and pines, the frozen lakes in deep winter on which children skated and glided. She'd dreamed of dressing in one of the puffy frocks she saw in Peking, spiralling up an ivory castle, standing on top of it, peering ahead at the layers of green in the distance, the wind embracing her. But no, no castles, no frocks; they were heading to a hot and humid and mosquito-infested region! The thought of the blood-sucking insects aroused itchiness on her thigh. Flap! Her intuitive slap on her flesh gave herself a fright.

'Jiaxi?' Her mother's voice sounded empty in the blackness. 'Come over here.'

'I'm fine, Mother.' She sat stubbornly still, holding her breath.

It was Meilian who needed her, she concluded. *Not I her.* They would have been drenched and bruised all over being banged and knocked about in the narrow stairway, if it hadn't been for her decisive move. That pull was a divide. With that pull, she decided, everything had changed – she had now officially entered her adulthood. *It's time that I protect you, Mother.*

Since childhood she had drifted alongside her mother, striving to make themselves invisible under the roof of her greedy, calculating paternal grandfather and the scrutiny of his equally indifferent wife. Over her growing years she had noticed how her mother, the second wife to her opium-addict, brothel-frequenting father, was sneered, shouted, finger-pointed at. She'd watched how they – the same cruel adults – had converged on her younger brother Junwei, their coldness melted in sudden smiles, in bowls of bird's-nest soup, scallop gruel and ginseng tea held out for the little boy, and retreated to her rightful shadowy corner.

She had watched the boy from a distance the way she watched her father, a keen absentee from the family, then from her life permanently when she was nine. He died an opium-addict's death. Shrivelled, shrunken, skeletal. She had peered out from her corner when he was carried home from his favourite brothel. Coagulated foam encrusted his withered lips and part of his grey-black face and neck. That was, as she saw it, only a stranger lying cold and still on the stretcher, and felt nothing. Nothing at all. At his funeral she was more disgusted than embarrassed at Meilian's hysterical display of fake affection.

Later when the family abandoned the mother and daughter in their frantic flight, she was quietly relieved, despite Junwei being taken. She felt free, liberated, the pressing issue of survival nudged to the back of her young head.

Her mother was inconsolable, doused in tears, struggling to stay strong for her, she knew. The rejection of her maternal grandfather had added to Meilian's bitterness, though Uncle Mingzhi's unreserved kindness warmed them. Already a mandarin then, her uncle, utilizing the facilities that came with his status, had administered her learning with a tutor, arranged for the mother and daughter to study English with Father Terry.

It was the priest's teachings and his books that, she realized, had made her feel exceptional, standing above girls of her generation and those of the generations before. She was unable to comprehend yet marvelled when told of Florence Nightingale, Marie Curie, the Brontë sisters. Different professions, equally outstanding – all women. It dawned on her one didn't have to be an empress to be known, or to marry a rich and famous man to be successful. With that, she thought, she might well one day be someone special.

Anything was possible in English tales (a frog could become a prince, a maid a princess), anything could be realized in the English-speaking far-off lands, she conjectured, silently harbouring the fantasy. Was that the reason

Uncle Mingzhi insisted she should acquire the knowledge? So that she would have aspirations like his? Her mother's descriptions of a determined, diligent brother who worked his way up to shrug off their grandfather's grasp – the confined mansion he lived in, the opium farms their grandfather operated – had always fascinated her. The man who became a mandarin at twenty-one was a legend, her hero. She treasured the privilege her uncle bestowed upon her, respected and adored him. The rest, too, she noticed, looked up to him for decisions, his official past a stamp of authority.

She was slightly troubled and confused by Uncle Mingzhi's choice of friends, though. Not so much Martin – his politeness, the fact that he'd seen her uncle through his difficult time with practical business know-how had won her admiration – but Tiansheng. That former sing-song actor who'd later learned trades from Martin and become his assistant, she heard, was a murderer. Worse still, from the snatches of details she had gathered from all possible sources, except for her mother and uncle who'd been tight-lipped on this matter, she'd deduced that the man had killed none other than her second uncle, whom she barely knew.

Since their first meeting in Peking, she'd been keeping a careful distance from Tiansheng, avoiding eye contact, not talking to him. He wasn't interested in conversation anyway. He was, as she'd observed, a phantom in the background, awkwardly reticent and void of expression, his emotions unfathomable. *This makes the most dangerous sort.* She would protect her mother from this man, she quietly promised herself.

The rocking and undulations were dying down.

Noises of people – not rain or wind or waves – began to come through the door from outside the cabin. She put on her shoes. 'It's over.' Martin's words came with the scratch of a match. She blinked at the abrupt brightness. In the dim circle of the yellow glow, she saw that her mother's dreamy eyes were lost in a dark corner. *She is thinking of Junwei. Again.* She held her breath, holding back her annoyance, moved across and took Meilian's hands. *Look at me, Mother. Look at me.* She tightened her grip and put her arm around the older woman's lean shoulders.

Mingzhi loosened his grip of the shroud, shrugging away Tiansheng's helping hand, and uncoiled himself from it. He looked up at the sky, dimly lit now, and realized how long the whole thing had been. It appeared unusually clear, he noticed, so that the dawn hues, the red and orange and purple against bruised blue, seemed strangely bright, unreal. Could it be a display from the Heavenly Palace, a reward for their endurance? He thought of the stories he'd heard as a child, of the Jade Emperor, the heavenly ruler, rewarding honest and upright officials. He, a runaway mandarin, would never be on the emperor's honour list.

Will He give me a chance to make amends in the new land? He gazed ahead as the colours changed and shifted, and found no answer in them. Neither did he find the silence, the solitude he enjoyed on usual mornings. Noises began to flood in: cries from those who'd lost their loved ones, shouts from the seamen to help with clearing the mess on the deck, loud and rude and unfeeling. When he retracted his gaze and stared down, next to his leg was Young Li, lying still, eyes protruding, mouth slack, the only arm stretched out limply. The sharp end of a broken metal pole had pinned him through his chest.

*   *   *

Let's travel back five hundred years, to a time when the sharp end of a kris has pinned a Majapahit fighter through his chest.

It is the late fourteenth century. The date unknown. The place, a little island called Temasek, which will become Singapore four hundred years later. But for the time being—

The owner of the kris, Parameswara, thrusts his weapon further into the Majapahit fighter, the last of them in this attack. But he knows they will come again, so will the Javanese – they will seek every opportunity to banish him, to conquer his island. He knows also his men are weakening, his resources scarce. He stands stock still holding his weapon, the sharp end of it in the heart of the dead: two frozen figures linked by a thin piece of metal. The remainder of his followers watch, holding their breath.

He was a prince of Hindu descent, Parameswara. His ancestors, of the Srivijaya empire, had enjoyed the glorious years of the thirteenth century in Palembang on the island of Sumatra before everything ended. They had fled once, had abandoned their beloved home, had made this land under him theirs, before passing everything on to him. He had been prancing in the glamour and glory built up by his grandfather and father. Does he have to leave and find another land? If I do find one, do I call it home? How about this, and the one before? He is confused. The hand that holds the dagger feels numb; his legs begin to shake. He takes a quick glance at the men around him. Their eyes are fearful, their faces haggard, their limbs feeble.

He has to make a decision.

Parameswara yanks out his dagger; a red stream splashes onto his gown, his trousers. His face bloody, his expression grim, he stands firm, legs hard as rocks, raising his kris as far up to the sky as he can reach—

'Let's go!'

His voice bellows into the calm breeze of the tropics.

2

Nanyang, the Land of Opportunities

They sailed into the calm breeze of Singapore port two weeks later.

Mingzhi kept his eyes on Martin as he stepped onto the gangplank. More people were disembarking and he was jostled along towards the land, separated from Tiansheng who'd been close behind. When he looked up again, the tall figure at the front was no longer in sight.

He was in the middle of a busy traffic of people, passing him by from both ways like phantoms. There were quick exchanges of words, strangely familiar in this strange, unfamiliar place – the language from the land he had left behind, in dialects known and unknown. *Impossible*. His head bobbed under the fiery sun; everything before him flashed white, a blur. He rubbed his eyes, could see clearer now.

People were making trips between the piles of goods on shore and the ships at the pier, loading and unloading. Muscles pulled tight on bare shoulders, arms and calves underneath rolled-up sleeves and trousers, plaits circled on half-shaved heads. Their skins were a crude tan, sunburnt, but their faces, brown too, had unmissable residues of jaundiced yellow. Like him.

The Chinese.

'Hey, here, hurry up!' Martin called over from yards ahead, long hands waving. Meilian and Jiaxi too, all craning for him. Mingzhi raised his hand in reply and made his way forward—

'Where do you think you're going?' A loud voice rang close to his ears. 'Over there, move!'

He stood still, not knowing what to do. People with their burdens moved straight past; no one stared or stopped.

'I said move and join the queue over there!'

Mingzhi was pushed on his shoulder; the force made him swivel round. Inches from him, a man stood glaring, a finger pointing behind Mingzhi, who turned to look. In front of a makeshift shed, his fellow passengers from the ship formed a long queue. There were other men, shouting orders, checking names against their book.

'Go over there and register yourself!'

Another roar, another shove, and Mingzhi stumbled on the ground.

'Hey, stop it! He is with me!' Martin rushed forward. Tiansheng, stuck in the crowd, noticed the commotion and pushed his way through to help his friend up. Surprised at Martin's intervention, the man squeezed out an awkward smile at the white man, then turned to Tiansheng and Mingzhi: 'Go! Don't make trouble here!'

In the scorching noon sun, the five of them huddled together, encircled in the joint shadows under their feet, a forgotten outlying island in a bustling sea of people. *What now?* Jiaxi turned to Meilian for an answer, Meilian to Martin, Martin and Tiansheng to Mingzhi, who kept his head down.

Getting impatient, Martin, upon spotting an English officer patrolling the port, walked up to him, leaving a gap in the shadow-circle. Before long, hand-shaking and small talk turned to laughter and shoulder-slapping, loud in the afternoon air.

He was a trader, Martin Gray. The only son to his teacher parents in a small Gloucestershire town, home meant warmth and discipline; life meant school, homework, books. He hated it, spending instead his after-school hours ducking away from his overly loving parents: in the name of studying with friends, frolicking with his playmates by the railway.

Outspoken, quick-witted (in his ability to invent new, eye-opening games) and resilient (with bouts of careless laughter), he became the obvious leader of the town's average children, though his abrupt, unpredictable acts sometimes left them perturbed. A killjoy. He would, in the middle of a pebble-throwing game he initiated, in the middle of childish jokes and hilarious laughter – suddenly feeling agitated, feeling he didn't belong there – abandon it and usher his playmates to trail the rail tracks with him. He would walk for miles, his puzzled friends, tired and frustrated, shouting behind him. He would, at times, climb up the hills and peer. Two long, parallel black lines snaked in the serpentine valley of woods, heading to destinations that were only names on the maps in his geography books. He would watch smoke puff up, trailing from the front of the linked compartments, appearing and disappearing between the greens, and tell himself he would, one day, be in one of them.

Years later, he was.

Much to the embarrassment and bafflement of his model parents (intelligent, diligent), Martin finished high school with results so poor that a place at college was clearly unattainable. And so, despite their initial expectation of an academic career – a professorship eventually, an upgraded version of the profession they'd been duly practising most of their lives – for their only son, they had, after much persuasion from him, succumbed to his plan of taking up a trading apprenticeship in London with an acquaintance of his father's.

He embarked on his first rail trip north; the trainspotter was now a passenger, the outside voyeur now viewing from the inside. From his front-facing seat he saw the world – the trees, the houses, the town he'd grown up in – flash past like giant toys while he sped ahead. Everything seemed unreal. He saw also, through the half-raised glass panel, trains from the opposite direction coming his way, passing the open window, chugging away behind him. He was appalled – the future he was heading to was, in fact, someone else's past. And whether they'd failed or succeeded, attempting to come back or giving up totally, life rolled on like the train they boarded. It struck him with a pang. *There's only one chance in life,* he concluded. *Either you grab it or lose it.*

After three years – long enough to pay his dues – in the office of his father's friend, he found a job with Mackenzie Brothers & Company, who had business in the Far East, and two years later he volunteered to be posted to China. To him, the job was all he had dreamed of: sourcing merchandise for his company. Exotic oriental handicrafts, exquisite ceramics, fine textiles – anything that was a marvel to the West. The constant travels involved, the amount of time spent on the road, at first within the neighbourhood of Shanghai, then Peking, with occasional trips to cities and towns further afield, quenched his wanderlust.

When he sighted Mingzhi – who was on his stopping-by trip in Shanghai after his third round exams in Peking – in a secluded corner of a small bookshop, browsing the atlas, navigating his sea journey on the world map with his fingers with such concentration, such scrutiny, he knew instantly. He knew that this was another con-stricted soul waiting to be liberated. He recognized a similar wanderlust in the quiet, polite young man. That was, when he thought of it now, the bond of their friend-ship.

The story of Mingzhi learning English from a foreign priest against his grandfather's will confirmed Martin's conjecture about the reticent Chinese man's curiosity for the wider world. Over a pot of tea in a quiet teahouse, he related to his new friend travellers' tales that had entranced him on his long West–East journey across the oceans. Adventures in less explored territories in lands yet to be named; encounters with the natives in the depth of the forest, with language incomprehensible, ways of life too primitive to outsiders. He saw how Mingzhi listened, eyes gleaming, his tea forgotten.

'You don't have to go too far to find them, though,' Martin was quick to point out, saying there were people of that sort in South East Asia. 'You have only to sail southwards across the sea and then trudge deep inland towards the mountains.' The aborigines there, he said, had the jungles for their homes. To survive, they would hunt animals with blowpipes, the darts doused in poison.

And humans, too – intruders and rival tribes – their heads chopped, a declaration of bravery and glory hung high over the doors.

'You don't want to go there, do you?' he teased, and watched his new friend's face pale with shock.

That was then, when one was still new to the country, the other ignorant. When the fact of starving peasants braving the ocean in boatloads for the lands Martin described, draining their sweat and blood onto the foreign soil, was a distant reality hidden still from the young men, safely tucked in their respective worlds.

As for now, Martin waved a scrap of paper in his hand as he hurried back to the group, shouting already as he ran, his face red with excitement.

'All sorted: where to stay, where to eat, where to find work!' Breathlessly, he presented the paper to his friends, a list of names and addresses. 'Bob Greenhorn, that officer I spoke to, a good man he is. We'll be fine here with someone like him around.' He patted Mingzhi's shoulder, a reassurance.

Mingzhi did not answer, glanced around him – the continuous trips of loading and unloading, the many steamers and barges that lined the port, the stone-faced guards, the workers weighted down by their burdens.

'We're not staying, not in Singapore,' he said quietly; 'we'll travel further north, to Malacca.'

'Why?' Martin frowned. 'Look at this. Here's where all the business opportunities are. There's so much we can do. Set up a company. Shipping. Import–export. The world is moving faster and faster. This is just the right time.' He turned to Tiansheng. 'Don't you think so?'

The young man seemed not to have heard him, said instead he would go find a boat and hurried off.

'Hey, wait—' Martin shouted as Tiansheng disappeared into the crowd.

'We'll do the same there. A house, a business, all the same,' Mingzhi reassured his friend.

'But, here—'

'We'll find something, I'm sure.'

Martin turned to Meilian and Jiaxi, only to find them averting their eyes, determined not to get involved. He sighed, scratched his head and did not argue further. He looked up and saw that Bob Greenhorn was still strolling around. Martin went to him yet again; another set of contacts, different information about a different place, were needed.

Mingzhi took a final look at the men waiting in the long line, his fellow passengers from the ship. Ignorant, poverty-stricken peasants lured into signing contracts to feed the many starving souls at home. Only hours ago he heard their whispers, of a guaranteed job, of sending money home, of a better life. But now his careful eyes observed: their paces hesitant, their bodies shrunken, by fear, by uncertainty.

He looked away in the direction of their new destination—

'Let's go!'

His voice dissolved in the tropical heat.

* * *

Parameswara travels northwards away from Temasek, the island that would become Singapore, where four hundred years later, cargo ships would sail in and berth at the dock like flocks of sparrows perching on the cables across the skyline. West to east, east to west. Loading and unloading; exchanging tea and spices and silk, and what comes alongside these commodities: culture, language, ways of life.

And an empire would flourish for another hundred years, with the tea and spices and silk from the lands that are not theirs.

The Prince-in-exile does not know all this, of course. For now, he sits on the stump by the Muar River. He has decided to settle here: build his palace, nurture his family, establish his kingdom. But the water is too muddy, the land too soggy, the place too secluded. So he has to continue his journey. He contemplates the babbling water: If I do find somewhere to settle, do I call it home? How about this, and the one before? Can I call them all – the one I was born and raised in, the one I seized, the one I may find in future – home? But then, where exactly do I belong?

The river remains silent.

3

The Mouse Deer Kingdom

It was dry and sunny when they arrived in Malacca. Perhaps it was the coconut trees, swaying and lining the beach, perhaps it was simply the cool breeze, Mingzhi did not say no when Martin set off to track down the contacts from Bob Greenhorn. On his return, with detailed instructions in his hand, they boarded a bullock cart and were driven along the river to an abandoned house-on-stilts.

It had been left empty for a year, they were told. 'The old fisherman and his only son,' Martin said, 'went to the sea not long after his wife's sudden death and never returned.' Nobody had since claimed the place, he reassured them, and nobody would. Why? 'They say *pantang*, inauspicious, one death after another.' A finger on his lips, he whispered, 'They believe there's *something* lurking in there.' Meilian and Jiaxi stepped back, pale-faced, only to find the Englishman laughing at his trick.

Mingzhi noted four things when he entered the shelter. First: it was empty, robbed of whatever had been there; second: there were no rooms, no partitions, only naked walls and floor; third: cobwebs had infested all corners; fourth: the broken roof – where wands of light sneaked in through the torn attap, sprinkling iridescence on the patterned cobwebs. He picked his way through them, ducking and whisking off the colourful threads above his head and the mosquitoes that were droning close to his ears. He saw, as he glanced down, clear imprints of his feet on the dust-coated floor, the evidence left by a trespasser.

There was a sound of chirping. He stared up, squinting against the light. A tiny sparrow stuck its neck out from its nest on the beam, inches above his head. It gazed at its surprised visitor, inquisitive, head turning this way and that, as if studying him, deciding foe or friend. It didn't take long to make the decision. A swift move, and it dashed through in between the torn pieces of woven nipa. Away.

It was blue, the sky, Mingzhi saw through the gap where the bird had disappeared. He reached out his hand, parted the attap and peered out. The cloud was a brilliant white against the blue, static and solid, like a boulder being lifted onto the sky and stuck there permanently, so much so that it seemed as if the sparrow could just make a nest in it, would go wherever the cloud took it.

A mobile home.

Rootless and rooted.

And everywhere and anywhere was its nesting place.

But he couldn't see it, the sparrow; wondered if it would come back, if it would return to the nest.

He wished it would.

'It's only for a night or two,' Tiansheng's voice rose behind him. 'We'll find a proper place soon.'

Outside, the rest were waiting.

'There's nothing to be worried about.' Martin pointed out the convenient location of the house: quietly tucked away at the far end of the Malay settlements and situated just next to a vegetable farm owned by a Chinese family. 'It can be passed off as part of the farm.'

Mingzhi peered in the pointed direction. Occasional brown patches of attap roof were vaguely visible among the tall, luxuriant trees a short distance away. There seemed to be no sign of activity, only tranquillity, broken by rustling wind and sporadic cries of birds and unknown beasts. Turning back, there were Meilian and Jiaxi's tired faces. His eyes turned soft.

He nodded.

*

A kampong house had never been the plan.

Mingzhi wielded the coconut-fronds-for-a-broom across the front clearing, back and forth. He'd seized the job from Jiaxi (*Too laborious for a skinny girl with deformed feet!*), told her instead to assist her mother with dinner preparation. For half an hour he had been working on it, smoothing out the gravel, so that Meilian with her tiny feet would not trip over stones or undulations or puddles. Back and forth, back and forth. Sweat gathered into beads and then rolled down his reddened face.

For three days now, Tiansheng's efforts to acquire a *proper* house had been fruitless. The associations of their respective clans, purposefully formed to assist new arrivals from the same region who shared the same dialect, when approached, were evasive with their answers. Later, when he spotted a TO LET sign and made a direct enquiry for a double-storey shop house on the seafront's main street, everything became apparent – the potential landlord, a man of Hakka origin like Tiansheng, slammed the door before him on the mention of Martin, a foreign devil.

Martin seemed unperturbed, though. Perhaps the Englishman was again possessed by the exoticism he fantasized about in a foreign soil, as he'd been in China. Mingzhi stopped sweeping. He remembered Martin's old-temple-converted residence in Peking, the scrolls of mountains and waters overcrowding the walls that had made Mingzhi scratch his head, speechless. On their first night in the hut Martin said that it was fascinating, as he felt and sniffed the nipa-woven mat beneath him, fresh from the marketplace, before sinking deep into sleep. Minutes later they sprang up, scratching and slapping. Mosquitoes! The paraffin lamp was lit, and they wrapped themselves from head to toe in sheets and blankets, but unravelled in seconds, sweating and panting, then covered up again, then uncovered. Mingzhi sat up all night and kept watch over the two figures in the makeshift curtained corner, his sister and niece, as the sounds of darkness closed in: insects, something slick and quick between the stilts, beasts and birds in the woods and the river.

He put aside the broom. Earlier, with a new machete he'd cleared overgrown grass and thickets, a paradise for the mosquitoes. He'd combed the immediate surrounding area, filling up puddles with earth, emptying rainwater-filled coconut shells, discarded pots and pans and broken urns that had come into view. The bloodsuckers' attacks came even in broad daylight, and every morning the sight of the swollen red marks on Meilian's and Jiaxi's faces troubled him.

The day's heat was fading; he felt it as the slanted sunlight splashed a bright orange across his white shirt. From the back of the shelter, smoke, thick with the aroma of dried shrimp and yam, whirled up. What would the other dish be? Meilian always managed two dishes on the table – oops, on the mat: there wasn't a table yet. A simple boiled vegetable with pak choi bought from Farmer Chong, their neighbour, or stir-fried *kangkong*, the swamp cabbage, with the leaves Jiaxi collected by the stagnant shallow. The teenager, after spotting a Malay woman pulling a string of the plant off the riverbank, had experimented with a stir fry and found it a delicacy. *A smart girl she is.* He nodded, a rare smile on his face.

Martin would return soon with sulphur to spread around the house, to stop their fear of snakes wandering about, sneaking up on the house. And Tiansheng, too, with news he anticipated hopefully. *What if it's another disappointment?* There were no signs of approaching figures on the path leading to town. No signs of other human beings. The quietness was so intense that the faint gurgling of the river reached him through the brushing breeze, rich with a mingling of fresh damp soil and green grass. Familiar. He thought of another river, another place, the long, lonely yet soothing hours sitting by the water during his adolescent years.

He would take a walk along the river, he decided.

*

Venturing into the port-town, Mingzhi was surprised at the great number of Chinese, all huddling together to recreate a sense of home. The clan houses, for the Hokkien, the Cantonese, the Teochew, the Hakka, the Hainanese, said it all: a roof for persons from the same region. Inside the whitewashed halls, portraits of prominent figures, the clan heroes, hung high. Men in whiskery white beards were transported in rolled-up scrolls across the oceans; maybe it was the homesickness, maybe it was the too-humble room, they glared down in protest at their descendants, their faces solemn, their snowy moustaches upturned.

In the main streets he found grocers, tailors, blacksmiths, jewellers, textile and hardware stores, and teahouses – any kind of shop he might have seen in cities like Peking. Even coffin- and tomb-makers. Culture was packed and shipped and sailed over the sea: square characters nudged away the crab-walking scripts, chopsticks were held firmly between fingers, temples stood tall among the mosques and churches. But the differences, he knew, were irrevocable, emanating from the place, the water, the air. The sense of belonging.

*

The way things progressed seemed natural, inevitable. First, because Meilian needed to be able to whip up a proper meal, a kitchen corner was added to the rear of the shelter, equipped with a coal stove and a shelving unit. Then, considering the price of meat at the marketplace, Tiansheng brought back young chicks and ducks, encircled them in his handmade bamboo pens. Little yellow balls of fluff running wild, chasing each other. Chick, chick, chick. Quack, quack, quack. Soon there were also a bed of sweet potato creepers, a bed of choi sum, a bed of cabbage; a continuous supply of fresh vegetables within easy reach.

Tiansheng, too, for the convenience of the mother

and daughter, partitioned the living space with screens he tactfully designed by neatly tying together strips of split bamboo. Only two secretive days of working by the bamboo growth, and there was a room for the women, there was a corner for the men, there was a common sitting and dining area, which had sprung up unannounced, much to Meilian's surprise and appreciation, though Jiaxi had been quiet.

Martin, unable to resist his new friend at the Club, traded two of his precious Suzhou silk kerchiefs for a framed *Spring in English Countryside* in watercolour. Clusters of temperate cherry blossoms bloomed on the dull, naked wall of the tropics, pink against the dark-brown nipa. Later, he put up black-and-white prints of England, pasted the likeness of his homeland on the wall in the women's corner for his fiancée. 'Factories, coal mines, Tower Bridge.' He pointed at them for Meilian. 'Birmingham, Sheffield, London. My country, and it will be yours.' He peered at her suddenly flushed cheeks and suppressed the urge to kiss her.

Because of Mingzhi's itch for calligraphic writing, a tabletop was salvaged from the occasional flotsam by the river, a large piece of sun-dried banana leaf laid on top of it, and he began practising – fingers for brushes, water for ink. Dark wet strokes and lines cleared in minutes; poetry and prose drafted carefully, evaporating before he finished. Jiaxi joined him sometimes, uncle and niece sitting together, the elder giving guidance to the young: demonstrating, correcting mistakes, pouring on generous words of encouragement.

*

Days gradually turned to weeks. Mingzhi was sleeping better now, inside a mosquito net set up over his mat, no blanket, shirt off – the heat was becoming bearable. Night noises no longer woke him.

*

Returning from yet another disappointing house-hunting trip in town, Mingzhi walked through the newly added bamboo fence, past the blossoming clumps of red hibiscus by the gateposts, into the noisy greetings of the chickens and ducks, into the smells and smoke from the kitchen lingering still, and entered the hut, moving towards Meilian and Jiaxi who, with warm smiles on their faces, were sitting on the mat before their keenly prepared lunch, waiting for him, Tiansheng and Martin.

Standing there, he felt a sudden grip at his chest: the place had now a shape and a face.

And a heart.

*

Evening again, and Mingzhi was on his daily pre-dinner walk. He would usually thread the better path southwards, stop short before the kampong dwellings, then turn back to the hot dinner readily laid out by Meilian and Jiaxi, but today, he decided to venture further, northwards this time through the overgrown reed.

He regretted it. The wild plants had disguised the marshy land that was further sodden by an overnight downpour, and his feet kept sticking into the mud. Gingerly, he retracted his footsteps.

'Ouch!' He slipped and stumbled into a shallow pool. He pulled whatever he could reach, but fell again when the branch he held snapped. There was something at the bottom of the murky water that jarred under him – a wooden board, blackened with mud, bulging with dampness. He picked it up and scrubbed the surface of filth and moss with a handful of grass.

Some ancient writing appeared – deep carvings of strokes rose, after age and weather, like an old sage, travelling back in time from hundreds of years before, with such courage and perseverance, still strong, still wise, with abundance of knowledge to share. It was the incipient name of the ancient river, Sungai Bertam, which had been renamed Malacca River, Mingzhi deduced. He wedged the signboard between the forks of a *banyan* tree by the babbling water, the way he thought it would have been.

Cleaned.

Sanded.

Gloss-painted.

Same place, same wording, different time.

The old sage in his new gown and hat rose tall; his wise eyes glanced through the past and stopped at the present. He should look further, he knew, into the future. But was there a need for it, if the future was only a repetition of the past?

The river remained silent.

Later, Mingzhi took down the board, turned it over and carved on it:

蔡宅

CHAI FAMILY

Square Chinese characters in forceful calligraphic strokes on one surface and the initial soft, curvy lines of Arabic on the other, sharing their existence in harmony. Equally ancient, equally artistic, leaning back-to-back against each other.

With Tiansheng's help, Mingzhi nailed his claim to the Fisherman's Hut above the door of his new residence on his new land.

*   *   *

He is tired, Parameswara, after the long trudge north-wards, now arriving in a fishing village: quiet, calm, a river leading to the sea. By the gurgling water, a signboard stands quietly behind the tree he is leaning against:

SUNGAI BERTAM

Bertam River.

It's leafy, the tree he sheltered underneath, and the wind light, desultory and cool, arousing the mountainous exhaustion that has been lurking inside him, pouring out in torrents now, seeping into his every pore, every vein. He dozes off.

He is in a palace: grand, splendid, commodious. Leaning back in the gold-encrusted throne, devouring food that comes plentiful on silver plates and bowls, admiring court women swirling on the glittering marble floor. They twist their waists and turn their bodies, the dancers, big, rounded eyes winking forth charms and beauty. And they are mine! *He raises his hand, beckons, and the girl in the lead, the prettiest among them, treads towards him. Smiling.*

He opens his arms.

'Your Majesty! We've fought them all! Siam is ours now!' His chief knight bursts in, brimming with excitement.

Parameswara's elated laughter bounces against the hard walls and floor, echoing in the spaciousness. Long, loud, deafening. But there is something else in it, an alien noise—

The sounds of barking wake him, and Parameswara opens his eyes to a small, vulnerable mouse deer, confronted by his hounds.

The tiny animal – face like a mouse, body of a miniature deer the size of a hare – retreats, but the river cuts its route. Seeking their chance, the attackers encircle their prey, their barking intensifying and they advance towards it.

It has no way to escape.

Then, like a flash of lightning, the mouse deer lurches towards the leader of the beasts and kicks it on the head and face with all its might. A shrieking howl, and the dog falls into the river. Surprised, the rest of the hounds step back, their tails hidden between their legs; they will not launch another attack.

Parameswara watches as the victor trots away, its head up-tilted, and it leaps as if it were flying. He looks around: the land, the people, the river. If even a little mouse deer could be so brave, so fearless, he thought, there must be something magical about this place: the people, the water, the land and everything on it. This is a sign. I shall build my kingdom here.

He points at the tree he is leaning against.

'What is it called?' he asks.

'Malacca.'

'Malacca: that's my home for now,' Parameswara declares. 'My kingdom!'

4

Far Far Away, Up on the Floating Cloud, There Was a House

The day she told her uncle of the visits from the kampong children, Jiaxi woke in the middle of the night to his sleepy muttering: 'No, no!' Through the bamboo screen his tossing and turning were unsettling, his breathing heavy in the quietness.

She'd noticed the stealthy visitors since they took refuge in the Fisherman's Hut. First were the children. Naked (the really young ones) or in tatty shorts, they appeared between trees and bushes. A quick show of the face – sometimes a grimace, other times a giggle – and they were gone, their chuckle bouncing in the air like the clinking of marble balls. Then came the men, the deliberate passers-by: bare-footed, sarongs wrapped around their waists, a hoe or a net or a basket on their backs, a ninety-degree tilt of their heads towards the house, eyes searching; they turned back in a fluster when their gazes were caught by their targets', and continued walking. The women she encountered when washing or fetching water from the river were more careful, watching from a distance in a group of two or three at first, whispering among themselves, nodding and smiling at her. Once, though, one of them pulled a few strings of *kangkong* and handed them to Jiaxi, mimed eating. She stir-fried them and the dish won her praises from her *family*. Later, coconut cakes wrapped in banana leaves were found on their doorstep. *The women*. She smiled and planned to reciprocate with sweet dumplings.

She had not then told her uncle of these friendly encounters, the search for a house and livelihood enough for his worries. These kampong people seemed to have a means to determine the right time to call upon the new settlers – when the men were absent. Later, it dawned on her that the route to town passed inevitably by the village dwellings. They must have been watching. She laughed quietly, as she imagined the peeping eyes glued on the two men in pigtails and a suited white man as they walked past. What a scene. That was, she concluded, innocent curiosity about a foreign family, a joke she shared with her mother.

Just lately, the children had become bolder. A few pairs of chopsticks to begin with, missing from the bamboo holder in the open kitchen shed at the rear of the house, then the bamboo steamer. *Curiosity, pure curiosity,* she thought: those ethnic wares must have made them wonder about their usage. They never took the food, though, the waxed sausages, the salted cabbage left untouched on the hook hanging down from the wooden beam. When one morning on her first round of feeding she counted one chicken less, despite her mother's objection (*It could be the fox*) it was made known to her uncle, and stories of the past encounters unravelled.

'We'll have to make it official.' The next morning she overheard Uncle Mingzhi, having risen early from his bad-dream-infested night, talking to Martin. 'We have to make this house ours.'

As he was acquainted with the British traders, Martin had been given the task of exploring business opportunities: long hours spent in town, of which most were invested in the Club. Tiansheng, now silent on the matter of house-hunting, had begun to make enquiries at the shops, too, with Uncle Mingzhi for company sometimes. Conducting a field survey, they said, a term his uncle had learned from Father Terry in Pindong Town. She'd never been to town, nor had Meilian. *This is unfair!* Her hand that was stirring the gruel – their breakfast, to eat with pickled cabbage and fermented tofu – moved faster. She'd been up with Meilian at dawn, as usual, to prepare them. *To fill the men's stomachs!* She hit the watery rice with her ladle.

'There's no need for it.' Martin sounded impatient.

'If we were to stay here—' Her uncle was cut short.

'It's perfectly fine, I was told. Yes, it seems a younger man from the kampong is coveting the title of *Penghulu* – the head of the village – and he tries to stir things up among their people, Jamerson the colonial secretary's assistant said. This may force the older man, the current leader, to take action. But they won't get anywhere as long as Jamerson and his boss are in charge.'

'But the village people—'

'We'll make this place appear to be part of Farmer Chong's territory. He's just next to us; it can easily be disguised. I bet those people will quickly leave us alone.'

'A legal document or something like that would be good. We'll pay for it. We'll sell the gold,' her uncle insisted.

'Save the gold for the business, my friend. A shop lot or some sort. We'll need one. We've discussed this, haven't we? I'm in talks with a couple of people. In fact, I'm meeting one of them today. Real good opportunity, he said. I've been itching to know more!'

After a moment of silence, her uncle pleaded, 'Just make it legal. Ask your friends at the Straits Settlement Office, will you?'

The pause was lengthier this time. Jiaxi lifted the ladle from the pot, stayed motionless, waiting. When the answer finally came through the open door between the kitchen and the living room, it was low and firm: 'OK. I'll see to it.'

Meilian, scooping out pickled cabbage from a clay urn, heard the exchange, too. Yesterday her fiancé had said he would get her and Jiaxi textiles for a new pair of samfu each. She stared down at her cloth – one of the only two pairs she had – worn and smudged in places, and knew Martin had noticed, too. She blushed with a scowl, embarrassed, pleased and worried at the same time, the important question of the source of money for it dropped before Martin's smiling face. The last of his silk kerchiefs had been traded for needles and threads and materials for shoes, she knew.

He was a good man, still insisting on serving her at meals, much to her embarrassment. Chopsticks full of pak choi, ladles of thin cabbage soup, second helpings of boiled rice. Attentive gaze and grateful nods passing between them, her heart filled with contentment; the hard floor and rough mat, and the crude diet forgotten.

Yes, his gaze. A surge of warmth spread inside her. The

day she stepped out of the carriage in Peking, exhausted from the long journey northwards, she raised her head, met his eyes and immediately drowned in a pond of blue. Calm, tender, inquisitive. Wanting to know. As if she were an ancient vase of the Tang Dynasty, waiting for him to unearth the mystery surrounding the delicate carved lines: the ruffles between her brows. The seemingly permanent scowl.

An ancient vase she was, being polished with gentle words, sunlit smiles. Someone born to serve was now being served. And she shone, the past nudged away. She was more than happy to live, to begin a new life elsewhere, anywhere, with him, with Jiaxi and Mingzhi. Her family.

Yet still, something was missing.

As she stirred the pickled cabbage, a face appeared in the urn, smiling, winking; a naughty boy's frown.

Her stomach constricted.

Jiaxi saw her mother stand motionless, her eyes lost, and the girl's heart sank. *I'm here, Mother*. She hit her ladle hard against the sides of the pot, shaking stubborn gruel off it. Thud, thud, thud. *Please, Mother, look at me, please*. She saw herself slip into the dark corners of her past, watching, observing, an outsider again; anger rose and surged to her ladle-hand. Thud! Thud! Thud! 'Eh?' Meilian, awoken, turned to her daughter, her face a blank.

Still angry, Jiaxi looked away and stirred the pot of food more vigorously.

'For you.' A voice rose from behind them.

The women jumped. Tiansheng had soundlessly sidled

into the kitchen as he usually did. Jiaxi watched as he handed Meilian yet another piece of his work, a tray made from bamboo strips this time. She saw his eyes fixed on her mother as he spoke, and became anxious. She restrained the urge to pull Meilian away, ask her to stop smiling. Not at him. The kitchen, the partitions, the fowls, could they be his tricks to impress her mother, she wondered? *Be careful, Mother.* That man, always the first to rise, should've been making use of his time, going out there getting them a house in town. Didn't Uncle Mingzhi say it clear and definite? She hadn't been in town, had been eagerly expecting the move. Tiansheng's creeping about in and around the hut set her on edge. The need to keep watching the man, to protect her mother, and even Uncle Mingzhi, had grown stronger.

Just lately, after much persuasion her mother had reluctantly confirmed to her the rumours of Tiansheng's murder of her second uncle.

'It was complicated.' Her mother had insisted on the man's innocence. 'He was merely trying to defend himself.' Tiansheng was an honest market trader then, striving to make ends meet, her mother had added, saying that the gang attacked him for protection money and her Uncle Mingyuan was stabbed in the midst of their grappling.

Meilian's descriptions of a gambling, brothel-going, gangmaster brother, who was accidentally killed when he and his hatchet men were bullying a vulnerable hawker – who happened to be Tiansheng – didn't stick in Jiaxi's ears. *He is a murderer all the same!* Jiaxi toyed in her head with the idea of a warning, a hint, to Uncle Mingzhi. The only piece of gold her uncle had brought with him from his family hoard in China was the source of their future, their livelihood. It was too precious to fall into a criminal's hands. Jiaxi made a decision: a plan had to be worked out soon enough for her uncle to uncover the true face of an unworthy friend.

Alone in his partitioned corner, Mingzhi took out his pouch from the inner layer of his vest and weighed the contents on his palm, speculating on their worth. Peking's fall to the Eight-Nation Allied Powers had devalued everything from the Land of the Dragon. Everything. Pride, dignity, wealth. 'We Chinese are brothers; I'm doing you a favour, you know?' Taukeh Tan, the grocer and money-changer, had said, a few pitiable coins held out in exchange for the young man's silver, before adding: 'Nobody wants Qing money nowadays,' with a sly grin.

He put aside the pieces of silver and stared intensely at the gold still in his hand, its shininess the flames in last night's dream. He saw vividly the fierce fire on long torches, and the floor, the walls, the roof that shook in the convulsions; heard the shouting in sharp, quick, unrecognizable syllables. Outside the window was a sea of shuffling black figures, taut faces and green veins of anger illuminated in bright fire. In a corner Meilian and Jiaxi huddled, but Martin and Tiansheng were nowhere to be seen. '*Pergi! Pergi!*' The shouting grew louder as the crowd charged forward and burst the latched, barricaded door. *Go! Go!* Strong, forceful hands reached out for them, pulling, dragging, pushing. There came Meilian's and Jiaxi's screams of fear.

No!

He cringed, holding the gold piece tightly in his hand. A change of plan was inevitable, he concluded.

Later, he sought out Tiansheng who was smoking under the shelter by a stilt, and discussed with him a means of almost zero-capital, low-risk income in place of their initial idea of a high-investment business.

'Our priority now is to secure the house.' Mingzhi landed his hand on Tiansheng's shoulder: he was in charge again.

With Martin's promise to settle the matter, he added, he and Tiansheng would now focus on anything that would bring them not only rice and meat, but also extras to hoard up their coffer, for a proper house as soon as possible.

'I've been getting advice from Farmer Chong and shop owners in town.' Tiansheng, glad finally to have the chance to broach his plan, said gathering forest produce was the answer.

'Let's begin with items easier to collect – durian, *petai*, *langsat* – whatever fruits we can get, and then sell them in the market. Not only the Malays love them, the Chinese and the white men are beginning to enjoy those exotic fruits nowadays.

'With the profits, we'll get a cart, go and find aromatic woods and rattan. The market is good, especially for rattan.' Tiansheng raised his voice, excited. While domestic households ran their chores around woven mats and baskets, westerners were allured by its durability, lightness, high flexibility. It was easy to bend and twist and turn, made more fashionable furniture. Tables, chairs, chests. Packed and boarded on ox carts or dinghies southwards along the Straits of Malacca to Singapore, where another journey began, in secure packaging, on bigger ships, going west west west.

They would bypass the Malay middlemen waiting upstream of the river, go instead to the wholesaler in town, Tiansheng added. 'I believe Baba Lim the wholesaler will give us a better deal.'

He's worked it all out. Pleased, Mingzhi nodded: 'Let's do it.'

*

How am I going to tell him? Martin kicked the pebbles that were in his way and regretted too late when a sharp pain shot up from his toes. *Damn!* He paused, lifted his foot, let the pain subside. His shoes, he noted, were so thin, so worn that coconut oil could no longer shine their dull, scratched surfaces. A new pair – that was all he needed. He shook his head, and with a bitter smile on his face resumed walking.

It was impossible to purchase the land they occupied, he had been told. It was possible, though, his friend at the Straits Settlement Office had pointed out with a sly wink, that over the years they would be forgotten, as the hut was next to the Chinese farm and could be disguised as part of it.

'Stay put,' Jamerson, the secretary's assistant, had reassured him, promising assistance within his capability. But Mingzhi with his Confucian teachings would never agree to that, he knew. *That's cheating*: the upright former mandarin's possible response flashed before him. He kicked again, and again screamed in pain.

He shook his head, decided to delay the matter as long as he could, continued instead with business-hunting. It was too much of a distraction, Mingzhi's sudden insistence that he make legal occupation of the house his priority. He needed to have something dusted, quick and precise. He had always been the pride of his former bosses, his records a splendour. Nearly two months without achieving something definite was a defeat. A shame.

Martin sped up along the river. He had an appointment and did not want to be late. Veteran planter Montgomery had mentioned a pioneer project, something called rubber, some milk-oozing tree transplanted from somewhere in South America, a guaranteed profit generator. He was intrigued.

This land, the Malay Peninsula, is a boon, he thought as he negotiated the puddles that filled the path after the overnight downpour. The forest, the fertile soil, the mines. The generous supplies of cheap labour inland and abroad. In Montgomery's words: 'You only have to strike it once and strike it right.'

While most other planters and traders drowned their time in the Club, Montgomery was one of the few who still talked passionately about business. Adventurous, with acute business sense, the forty-something Scot was serious about the new plants, eager to be the first to lay hands on them in this land.

And he was waiting for Martin in the Club.

The Club stood prominently on the main road facing the sea. From the peak of Bukit China – the hill that was the synonym of its Chinese cemetery – two miles inland, one could easily spot a white Victorian structure that projected itself up oddly from the uneven varicoloured rooftops (dark brown for attap, tawny or red – if painted

– for tin, brownish red or green for tiles) of the blocks of single and double terraced houses in town, wooden or cemented.

It was owned by the colonial government, a little recreational gathering place for the expatriates: officials, planters, traders and, on very rare occasions, wealthy Straits Chinese, the Baba Peranakan, who were guests of the white officials and planters and traders. Unperturbed by its awkward existence, the foreign building made itself at home in the foreign soil the way its owner and guests made the land theirs. Every day incumbents and newcomers would cruise in with pride and loneliness, drinking away the heat and the fear of malaria with mugs of British beer served by over-courteous Chinese or Malay waiters with their over-bowed heads. They wouldn't touch the *samsu* or the toddy brewed with palm flowers in the depths of the coconut or oil palm plantations. They wouldn't visit the roadside huts that sold *samsu* or toddy. That crude alcohol, those shabby stalls, were for the coolies.

They felt safe in the Club, the colonists, a fertile oasis of the West in the hot desert of the tropics. Ceiling fans, iced beer, cool marble floors. Heart-melting melody flowed from the enormous ear of the glistening gramophone, wafting under the high, chandeliered ceilings, between the wide columns of pillars.

After an evening of drinks and steaks and apple crumble, the officials, the planters and the traders returned to their villas, sat in their ample rooms and felt lonelier, missing their homes more than ever. And they anticipated the next day.

To the Club.

And the next day.

They gravitated to it like bees to pollen. Without realizing it.

Martin had tried but to no avail to avoid having meetings in the Club. He had preferred the teahouses run by the Chinese, the Lek Kee in Market Street being his favourite: round marble tables, a spittoon under each, cups of freshly brewed tea in the company of noisy market-goers and hard-working hawkers reminded him of Peking's teahouses and the roadside eateries in the alleyways. They had been polite, the waiters and their middle-aged boss, but before long, he had become aware of their stare: more suspicious than curious. The joy, the fun deflated.

His British friends, like his companions in Shanghai and Peking, would not set foot in the local teahouses and coffee shops, would only meet him in the Club. 'The bunch of coolies,' they snorted as they sipped their gin and tonics. Martin, in dire need of information about trades and businesses, over the weeks had somehow progressed from a reluctant patron to a willing visitor, as the gaze of locals at the Lek Kee had grown spikier, the tropical heat more unbearable in the small, crowded room.

He had gravitated to the Club without realizing. The music, the talks, the comfort. The familiarity. The Club's enclosed atmosphere was nothing like the grand, splendid nightclubs in Shanghai with their luxury dining halls and spacious dance floors. There, people came and left. A nod, a smile, blurts of 'How do you do?' and the evening was over. Here there was a close circle; everybody knew everybody else.

Yesterday, after a light lunch of cucumber and tuna sandwiches he'd long missed, he slumped in a recliner under the drooping green fronds of a potted palm. Music swimming in his ears, the remnants of cool cucumber and brined tuna lingering on his tongue. Sitting there, looking at the familiar figures and features, listening to the familiar language and accents, suddenly, for the first time, he realized he'd been away from home for too long.

'Dance with me!' Jean, a young, lonely mistress of a planter yanked him up. Martin let her, and they danced in the not-too-big space between the dining tables and the bar, turning narrow rounds. As he held her tiny waist, Meilian's shy, smiling face lurked before him. He wished he was holding her, dancing with her, like couples did.

Jean's frivolous laughter rang in his ears like the cackle of the pair of hens Tiansheng had newly added to his den. Amid it, a gentle 'shoo-shoo, shoo-shoo' stood out crisp and clear: Meilian, standing between the forever hungry chicks and hens, casting corn crush from a coconut shell. Her eyes on the furry fowls, her face soft and tender, an invitation for a kiss, an embrace.

But he'd never kissed her, never touched her face, never held her waist like he did with Jean. *Why is it for me to respect her culture and not she mine?* Immediately he was ashamed of his thought. It was her diffidence, her modesty, her quiet toughness – all the unique qualities he could look for in an oriental woman – that had initially attracted him. *What's wrong with me?* An uneasy feeling assaulted him. He feared. He feared he was incapable of holding it down. He feared he could tolerate it no longer. He realized, shamefully, that he couldn't trust himself.

We have to get married soon! Martin stopped abruptly before the music did; his dance partner's fervent eyes turned dull with dissatisfaction. *But what with?* He had to have something to show Meilian, to prove to her his worth. Tiansheng's over-diligent over-pleasing of his fiancée, which he'd noticed lately, had unsettled him. A rare scowl appeared on his youthful face. At the bar, Montgomery had been watching. He bought the troubled young man a beer.

Martin quickened his pace. Opportunity was waiting and he wanted to make the right strike.

*

Martin was later than usual that evening; too late.

'The forest south of the town: we should begin before the rain falls, machetes and a tough pair of legs are all we need.' Tiansheng detailed his plan at dinner.

As his friend droned on, Martin flicked in his bowl with chopsticks the soft stalks of *kangkong*, knotted like his heart, turning cold. He tried: 'Trust me; the only thing that can make money here now is rubber.'

'We'll make our first trip to the jungle in a couple of days,' Mingzhi said. Tiansheng rolled a cigarette, silent.

'Montgomery says we've to do it before anyone else does. Get a few acres, and we'll work together,' Martin persisted.

'It's too risky, six long years before harvest, all that uncertainty.'

'It's worth waiting. Remember the pottery business?

I helped you to set it up. I helped you to meet your tax targets. I was right then, and I won't be wrong this time. Trust me. You have the money for capital, and I will work out everything for you, just like the last time.'

'Get us this piece of land under our feet, that's what we need, that's all you have to do.' With a quick sweep of his chopsticks, Mingzhi stuffed his mouth with rice and slices of fresh bamboo shoots and wouldn't speak further.

That's unnecessary! Martin screamed inside him, but on his face was an awkward tilt meant to be a smile. After politely sitting through a tasteless, unfinished bowl of rice and vegetables and thin *o-long*, he made his first after-dark outing, sneaking away to the bright, spacious, music-filled Club, where his beloved brandy was waiting.

Standing on the land called Malacca, Parameswara peers at the distant hills and then stares down at the water below his feet. There will be a fort up the peak and the river and the sea are natural barriers. Of course, he doesn't know that bigger disasters will come from the faraway ocean, that one hundred and fifty years later a Dutchman called Afonso de Albuquerque will fire a cannon, bomb his wooden fort and replace it with a more solid, more secured stone farmosa. For the time being, Parameswara, still standing, still looking, feels safe. He thinks he has cut himself off from his enemies, his past. No, he will not look back to the past, the decision firm and absolute.

Parameswara pulls out his kris and raises it high to the sky: 'To new life!' The past hurled into the gurgling water and flushed into the sea.

In his new residence – far from the grandeur of his dream palace, but small, humble, a comfortable shelter for the time being – he lapses into his first soothing sleep in months, a break he is direly in need of in view of the future he envisages.

Indeed he sees far, peering beyond the quiet, tranquil fishing village; beyond the daily catch and the sampans plying the river; beyond the coconut trees and their fruits, the few hectares of paddy fields and the herds of cows and chickens and ducks.

He knows he has to plan carefully.

There have been noises, rising from among his men, urging him to claim more lands, to expand his territory.

How can I move further when my legs are not yet firm on this tiny piece of land? When the people haven't recognized my existence, haven't bowed under my rule?

Parameswara makes his decision: he will first make good use of the fertile land, making sure the people know he is doing the best for them.

It doesn't take long for them to witness the effort.

When banana, sugar cane, yam, sweet potatoes and many more begin to grow in abundance, MALACCA spreads its arms and legs like the stalks and branches of the trees that bear the fruits. All the way to the far-off lands. The name of a small town that is progressing with extreme speed flows to all corners, together with the name of its new ruler, wise and far-sighted, so the people hear, and more flock in to share the future prosperity that is visible through all signs.

And underneath the trees, the roots burrow deep into the earth, staying firm in the lands to which they now belong.

Parameswara makes a tour of the town (yes, it's a town now), sees the smiling faces of his people, the streets and paths that are becoming busier with each passing day. He nods and nods: it's time to plan the next step.

5

The Wild Boar Has Tears

Mingzhi landed his next step on a loose pile of twigs on the forest floor and nearly fell over. Regaining his balance, he adjusted the thin rattan straps around his shoulders, the wicker basket on his back a dead weight pressing down on him.

Ahead of him, Tiansheng's naked upper half appeared and disappeared between the long grass and saplings, thickets and drooping roots. Mingzhi kept his eyes on his friend's sunburnt back and blundered forward.

They were on their third expedition to the forest. On the first trip, their limbs were trembling from climbing the *petai* trees, as tall as ninety feet, their palms cracked with cuts from the bark. Mingzhi, clinging on the branch like a needy child, had glanced down, gasped and would not take another look. Still dazed, he tried to keep his eyes on his targets, the clusters of pods, long, twisting like green snakes, a distance away. He gritted his teeth, a hand holding tight to the branch, the other wielding the long bamboo pole to the end of which a knife was tied, stretching out, striving to cut the *petai* pods. Their guide, Farmer Chong's casual worker, waited for them impatiently under the tree, his head shaking as he watched Mingzhi's hands shake.

The two barely filled the bottom of their baskets.

They were lucky, though, as they spotted a trunk of aloe wood infested by fungus, hardened, black and aromatic, ready to be harvested. It was shared between the three of them, and Mingzhi and Tiansheng had their blocks sold at Baba Lim's shop and returned home with their first cut of meat in two weeks, much to Meilian and Jiaxi's delight.

The second outing, without the guide, they spent longer hours and proudly carried home half a basket each of the stinking beans, only to receive the news that the *Penghulu* had paid a visit. The elderly man seemed kind – Meilian related their conversation that was translated by Jiaxi – politely asking them to leave the house at their earliest convenience.

That night, Mingzhi's nightmare recurred: more attackers, increasingly violent. In his dream, they were all thrown out of the house and Mingzhi, lying on the ground, limp and aching all over, watched helplessly as a torch was hurled over him onto the attap roof. A brilliant red burst out in the silent darkness; everything seemed to have frozen, only the stunningly bright hue was expanding, filling up the night sky.

Afterwards, awake in sweat-sodden bedclothes, he heard the drone of rhythmic snoring coming through the thin bamboo shield from Martin's corner. *How can he be so relaxed?* He tossed and turned, covering his ears with his hands, his sheet, his pillow. Martin had made no mention of the legalization of the hut. The subject, when touched, had always been skilfully avoided. Before he had been able to confront Martin, there was the trip already planned by Tiansheng.

I'll definitely talk to him on my return, he promised himself.

Today, they would also scout for rattan, in preparation for their next trip.

They reached where they had stopped the last time and were now on a slope, ascending. *Let's move to the river on the other side of the hill.* Tiansheng gestured, standing on the high rise, his face obscure in the screen of sweat over Mingzhi's eyelashes. His friend had done a reconnaissance on their last outing, allowing Mingzhi a long tea break to recover from half a day of exhausting trudge before heading home. '*Can't expect much from a mandarin cum scholar turned forest gatherer*' – *that must have been his thought of me.* Mingzhi shook his head. But he was gathering stamina, feeling stronger this time. He was making good progress, he knew. It was only noon and they'd ventured deeper this time.

He only needed time.

Mingzhi held the trunks and saplings and branches for support as he pushed himself up, carefully securing footings on the damp soil, loosened by last night's downpour. Careful, too, to avoid jarring rocks and roots. On all fours at times, hands and knees and shoes caked with mud.

Tiansheng gestured again, quick successive hand movements. Too quick. *What?* Mingzhi rubbed his eyes. His friend's anxious calls came through, shrieking panic in short vowels. *What?!* Mingzhi, panicked too, saw Tiansheng drop his basket and clamber up a tree and eventually made out his friend's words: 'Step away! No, climb the tree! Quick!'

There were noises – thunderstorm – no, the thunder of hooves.

'Do it, now!' Tiansheng's voice was almost hysterical.

Mingzhi unleashed his basket. The noises grew louder. He could see something now, some dark specks, appearing on the peak of the hill, moving fast in his direction. Very fast. He clung on to the tree next to him and pushed himself up the branches. The trotting came closer. The earth shook. The trunk in his clutch vibrated.

Wild boars! A sounder of them, rushing down the hill, squealing and snorting, banging against the trees, trampling the saplings and young roots and decaying trunks, knocking off the rocks and stones along the way. The sudden rise of the river after yesterday's downpour had forced them out of their gathering place on the other side of the hill.

Mingzhi stared down as the pigs brushed past the tree he perched on. A heavy blow, a loud thump; another. More. And more. Thump! Thump! Thump! Hitting against his heart. Dark, ugly beasts, some with long tusks squeezed through between the trees. Too many of them, too fast, a wave of black thunder rumbling past. He locked his limbs around the stout branch like a child clinging on its mother, shaking.

He hung there for what felt like ages, did not notice when the noises and convulsions subsided, when Tiansheng called over from the rise. Hanging there, still in a trance, he finally heard his name, vague, distant. He looked ahead; his friend stood craning his neck.

'Are you all right?' Tiansheng, basket on his back, was ready to move on.

Mingzhi got down from the tree, still shaking, staggering down the slope for his basket, picking up the stalks of *petai* pods strewn on the track, going back up. He noticed the missing bark on the trunks, scratched off by the fleeing boars, the mess of trampled grass and saplings and rotten wood on the already loose earth. *If I didn't get a warning; if I hadn't been in time* ... A twig crunched under his feet and he shuddered, imagining himself under dozens of forceful hooves.

How would Martin react if he were here? Mingzhi tried to envisage his friend climbing a tree, but the picture was obscure, the images separate – Martin and a tree, a tree and Martin – drifting apart, couldn't be connected.

*

The night of their first disagreement, Martin came home drunk in the small hours.

'Rubber! I said definitely rubber!'

The stench entered the house as Martin blundered in. His eyes red and bleary, he staggered towards Tiansheng, pointing his finger at him: 'Going to the jungle? You put your mandarin friend here to shame. You put us all to shame!'

'Stop it!' Mingzhi pulled him away, while Tiansheng got up and walked out of the room at once. Meilian gestured for Jiaxi to return to their corner. She watched as Mingzhi dragged her fiancé to one side. Giant shadows shuffled like monsters on the walls in the yellow light of the paraffin lamp. Meilian stared at Martin, now slumped on his mat, leaning against the wall, at his red-veined eyes, his strained neck and occasional drunken burps. Like a stranger.

'We're going to be very rich, Meilian.'

He struggled to get up and hobbled towards Meilian. 'We'll make money with rubber. Yes, money!' His figure was a bear-like shadow on the wall, expanding as it approached, smothering her. Sitting on the floor, Meilian dragged herself backwards to another corner.

Mingzhi rushed to Martin: 'Stop it!'

Martin, in his drunken trance, brushed him off. 'We're going to make big money!'

His long hands fluttered in the air, cupping the invisible cash. Clank! His *Spring in English Countryside* fell on the floor; the glass frame smashed into pieces. A broken spring lay feebly in the steaming heat of the tropics, as if regretting its presence in a place it didn't belong.

Tiansheng, who'd been smoking underneath the house, dashed in. Martin pointed at him: 'You, you don't have to work like a cow. Not any more. We're going to be rich! We'll have a rubber estate!'

'Drop it now and go and enjoy with your white friends!' Tiansheng grabbed Martin by his shirt collar. 'We don't need money, we don't need you here!'

'Really? You couldn't even get a place to live without me!'

'If it wasn't for you, we'd have easily rented a room in town, *gweilo*!'

Mingzhi tried to hold Tiansheng back.

'Blame me now, eh?' Martin now pointed at Mingzhi: 'And you! Coward! All of you!'

Tiansheng shrugged off Mingzhi's grip, lurched at Martin, punched him in the face and was immediately hit back. A second punch from Tiansheng sent Martin back to the mat. Mingzhi pulled Tiansheng away. Meilian shrank further, her tears welling up. Martin's outstretched fist-for-vengeance hung feebly in the air before flopping down, and he spoke no more. His head askew, he was fast asleep, snoring away in seconds.

*

Not a word had been said about the incident, the awkwardness apparent, especially between Martin and Tiansheng. Mingzhi shook his head, lifted the straps, transferring parts of the weight onto his hands as he trod the final steps up to the rise. Tiansheng, relaxing by a stump, beckoned his friend, a packet of dumplings already open, a bamboo container of cold tea, too. Unloading his basket, Mingzhi stretched his arms and legs, felt through his shirt the indentations of the shoulder straps on his flesh, the bright red against now dark-brown skin. *Glad I still have Tiansheng,* he thought, and was immediately ashamed of himself. *He is my friend too, Martin. He helped me through my difficult time back then in China,* he repeated loud in his head, empty sounds leaving the lightest vibration in a wobbly heart.

'Down the hill, over the clearing, that's where we're going.' Tiansheng pointed, Meilian's sweet dumplings finished in two big gulps, washed down with cheap, unbranded tea so thin it was almost colourless. Mingzhi peered in the far distance, saw only a canopy of lush green, a mild patch of yellow somewhere in the middle, heard just occasional hoots amid the silence of an uncommunicative forest. Turning back, there were identical blocks of dense woods and thick bushes, so that the pig trail, the route he came out from, seemed to have been erased from his eye-map. Three trips now and still he was handicapped when it came to directions, kept on track only with Tiansheng's patience and acute sense, good eyes.

At moments like this, the books he'd read sprang to his mind – tropical forests, the vast species of plants and animals and birds and insects, all the names he knew by heart but mostly hadn't seen even in pictures. His learned knowledge of making out east or west by just looking at the sun crumbled in a jungle so luxuriant, so shady that it was empty of full-faced sunlight, and Mingzhi had no clear sense of his whereabouts when he was enclosed in it.

Useless.

He stole a glance at Tiansheng, leaning against a giant tree, sitting comfortably between its folds. *So at home.* Thinking of how keen he had been, when they first met, on teaching his friend to read and write (*Skills for life,* he'd said), a bitter smile rose on his face. Here and now, it was Tiansheng's life skills, earned from his days in the streets, sleeping rough and scavenging and trying whatever he could to keep breathing, that prevailed. He looked away.

As he took a bite of the sweet dumpling, his hunger, suppressed by the work and walk and fear, grew in a sudden rush. At home, he would stuff into torn-open dumplings lean slices of pork braised in rich dark soy sauce and five spices – on good days, or simply the sauce on bad ones – cooked specially to accompany the floury food. One bite and the gravy would burst from the edges of the folds, smearing the corners of the mouth where the sticky taste and smell would persist for half a day; but now, in the wild, he ate it plain, just as tasty.

Meilian had risen before dawn to prepare the dumplings, fumbling in the dimness of the paraffin lamp in the shed-for-kitchen behind the house, mixing and kneading flour and water and spoonfuls of sugar, steaming the balls of dough in layered bamboo trays over a carefully tended wood fire. Meilian the keeper of the house, his sister turned mother, held the five of them together. Cooking, washing, cleaning. Becoming the mediator between the three men since the air had turned tense and awkward after the fight, passing messages and things, skilfully adding in her words and thoughts with the hope of mending the damage.

He stared at the white texture in his hand, at the imprints of his fingers that broke the tender outer membrane and carved deep into the soft lump of flour, and a decision was made: he would make Meilian and Martin's wedding the uppermost priority, at the first instance when they'd secured the land title of the hut. The last mouthful he let linger a little longer on his tongue, let it melt in saliva; the sweetness intensified.

Jiaxi loved dumplings, had learned to make them from her mother, favouring those with red bean paste stuffing, which she was adept at cooking. *She should be in school, Jiaxi, should have a career*. Mingzhi thought of the only Chinese school in town, operating on donations from wealthy Chinese businessmen, whose children made up the majority of the students. His application for a teaching position had been placed at the bottom of a long list of migrant scholars eager to put themselves up for the right use but without an adequate reference. A list so long that he was certain he would never be approached. Tell them you were a mandarin, a *jinshi*, Martin and Meilian had persuaded, badgering him for days; he shook his head, his lips pursed tight.

It was Jiaxi he should make plans for. With an elementary learner of Malay brought home by Martin, she'd picked up the language almost effortlessly, negotiating with call-in hawkers with baskets of eels and *binjals* and matches on their heads while Meilian watched, helplessly, at her daughter's side. The fourteen-year-old was quick to recognize the nature of the various vendors – Ismail was generous, Minah calculating, Mr Yang cunning – and dealt with them accordingly, haggling patiently with Minah, pointing out Mr Yang's imbalanced scale, giving a couple of eggs to Ismail in exchange for extra stalks of beans. Now that her initial shyness had been overtaken by a newly acquired confidence, undeterred by her slightly deformed feet, Jiaxi revealed herself as bright, strong-willed, passionate about learning, setting foot firmly on her new land.

Just lately, Mingzhi found his niece reading from wrappers of groceries, the tawny outdated newspapers she'd collected, having carefully smoothed out the creases, spending hours gnawing at the words and sentences, trying to make sense out of them. One evening two days ago, she glanced up at Mingzhi from the paper she'd been reading since after dinner: 'They are opening a college, a women-only teachers' college.' Her young eyes sparkled in the faint light of a paraffin lamp. Reading on, the ember soon died down: 'For the Malays only.'

She wants to be a teacher! Mingzhi was suddenly excited, remembering the rural schools he set up during his mandarin days, the calls for support, the overwhelming response he received, the construction of the buildings on crude, barren grounds. *We can have a Chinese teachers' college, for men and women and no divide – rules have to change in this land – and I will train them.* The town was prospering, he'd noticed, and he was certain that previously less capable families would begin sending their children to school, that they would need more teachers, more classes in number and size. He had only to convince the rich men in town to support his plan, which he would draft scrupulously in detail, with experience he accumulated from projects on a larger scale. Prior to that, he would have to make himself more presentable to be in talks with the big *taukehs*, the bosses in Qing gowns and Western gold chain-watches in their pockets.

He would definitely go for rattan on their following trips.

For the time being, he imagined Jiaxi standing at the front of the classroom, writing on the blackboard, talking to the students, her young face shining with pride. He smiled and looked up. Across from him, half-hidden in the folds of the old tree with a cigarette between his fingers, Tiansheng peered over, puzzled at the sudden, unfathomable brightness on his friend's face, and squeezed out an awkward smile in return.

Mingzhi decided to keep his thoughts from Tiansheng. *Not yet; certainly not now.*

After lunch he worked strenuously with new energy, stimulated by his idea, reaching out for higher branches, cutting the clusters of *petai* with his pole-knife. Back on the ground, he gathered his harvest and his basket was now nearly full. *Worth a week's rice and vegetables at least.* He bounced the load on his back, remembered the block of aloe wood he collected earlier, and made a quick estimation. *And meat!* He licked his lips; a clay pot full of Meilian's signature five-spice mushroom braised pork swayed in his mind's eye. Black mushrooms and slices of golden, juicy meat in simmering honey-brown sauce. He would ask for a generous cut of the loins from Butcher Lee. Mingzhi swallowed a mouthful of saliva.

They would keep in the House Fund the money from Tiansheng's load—

Tiansheng!

He stared ahead. There were large patches of green (the grass, the leaves, the thickets and brambles) and brown (the trees, the branches, the roots), but the shuffling figure between them was nowhere to be seen!

He made a quick swivel east-south-west-northwards, saw only boles and bushes and creepers, big or small, lighter or darker, identical at every turning, every angle. Looking up, the trees shot high into the sky where his eyes couldn't reach, their accumulated leaves a giant cloak over the tropical woods.

'Tiansheng!'

His voice spread in the wild emptiness, bouncing back in long tails of hollowness: distorted, unrecognizable, a touch of eeriness. He shuddered, strained his eyes hard between the trunks again and saw nothing, still. Another call, another succession of echoes. No answer.

He was lost.

He waved his machete and slashed the saplings and

undergrowth that were in his way. Slash! Slash! Slash! *There must be some sign, some indication somewhere.* Panic surged through to his arms and his machete worked faster. Slash! Slash! Slash! Young and fragile plants fell, and he saw it now: a few patches of cracked twigs on trampled earth.

He squeezed through the bushes, keeping his body low, keeping his eyes on the vague clues on the ground, kept going; hands sore from the effort of pushing the plants apart, legs dragging on, caked with mud. The pointy leaves of the long grass sprang back at once and slapped against his body, already sweat-sodden; their blade-edges assaulted him with a vengeance, slicing his skin. Red scratches crawled on his bare arms and legs, unbearably itchy.

He began to feel the gradual heaviness of his limbs, the slowness of his movement, the diminishing daylight.

No! He shouted for Tiansheng again, brandishing his machete more vigorously.

There was a trail – a narrow, serpentine path of more crushed twigs and leaves on soil hardened from trampling. He was suddenly rejuvenated, pressing harder ahead in a mingling of fresh earth, decomposed leaves and wood that clogged the air. Above the mixture of rich odours he had grown accustomed to rose a stench, strong and raw, drifting over the forest floor. He sneezed.

Beast. That much he was certain, though he was unsure of what, despite the faint sense of familiarity.

He turned back. The trail seemed to have been cut off, obscure in the dense green, now darkening. He was trapped, could only move forward. Before long he saw it: a black lump of dung, two, and more, strewn along the track. Only then did he glance up at the trunks on both sides, the naked patches scraped off by some bristly hide.

A pig-run, he was on a pig-run!

There was a sound, the snarling of a beast. He shuddered in a spell of cold sweat. *Where are you, Tiansheng?* He clutched his machete, held it out in front of him in his outstretched hand, his eyes kept on the tiny shuffling in the bushes as he stepped back. They usually came in a group, he knew. He took a glimpse of his machete and knew it was useless, that he wouldn't have a chance if they came rushing over him.

The snarling grew louder, intensified. The dark patches of branches moved noisily.

'Tiansheng!'

His hysterical shout triggered an immediate reaction. A loud groan and it darted out, an enormous black shape lurching at him. He leaped to one side and brought down his weapon with all his might. A shriek, and blood spurted from the back of its bristly neck; a quick struggle and it was still firm on its hooves, puffing, glassy eyes losing focus. *No, I can't let it lunge at me again!* Panicked, Mingzhi raised his machete—

A thrust, another, and another; quick, repeated blows on its head. Sharp, helpless squeals deafened his ears; sprinkles of red showered his hands, his face, his body. Still, the big knife kept slashing down, before everything stopped. No more shrieking, no more squealing; only silence. Long, dead silence. He stood there, felt as if it were a dream.

He stared down at the dark figure in a pool of blood on the ground, the head that was now a mess of flesh and fractured skull. *No, it isn't a dream.* He shivered, fully awake now. Part of the boar's face, surprisingly, was intact, and there were no tusks. Lying there, its body – its belly – appeared huge and heavy. It was a sow, a lone, pregnant sow. The load she was carrying must have slowed her down, separated her from the herd. The machete slipped from his hand.

There was a sound, vague, coming from the bush where the sow had emerged. Mingzhi scooped up his machete, eyes on the source, muscles tensed.

It ducked out, a tiny dark shape, trotting and grunting, hesitantly, towards the now motionless figure on the ground. Mingzhi could see clearer now: an infant boar, squelching by the side of the dead beast, thrusting its head against the front limbs of the dead sow, as if trying to get her on her feet.

He dropped his machete again, ashamed. *She was trying to protect her child.*

In the last of the forest light, he saw that while one of the eyes of the animal he'd just killed hung loosely outside its socket, the other was surprisingly intact, wide open, staring up at him.

There were tears in it.

A sudden tiredness assailed him and Mingzhi felt dizzy. He heard noises, a quick pattering of hooves, the squealing of the young boar, all around him. *The herd; they are back for her.* The earth shook, the vibration channelled into him. He looked up; the forest swirled around him – the trees, the boles that extended like evil arms, the fluttering leaves, the shadows on the ground – dancing, drifting. He saw them reach out for him, huge, black patches, and there was no escape.

Blank.

Everything turned to darkness.

6

The Indelible Presence of an Absentee

There had been noises, quick, monotonous, drifting in and out of his senses as he drifted in and out of consciousness. At times some liquid filled his mouth and flowed along his throat. The warmth, the bitterness, the acrid smell surfaced only on good days. On bad ones, he could taste nothing, just water, the overflow and following that, the wetness around his mouth, his cheeks, his neck, and a hand that wiped it away in a swift movement. Even in the vagueness of his senses he felt it, the roughness of the callus-infested fingers and palms. One of the hands would hold up his head, the other feed him: crude skin brushed over his face, rubbing away the excess remedy. The touch was his only contact to a living substance, the indication of his existence. And nothing else.

*

It was you! Jiaxi screamed inside her when Tiansheng discussed with Farmer Chong and his workers a search party. *You left him there!* There was no lack of fruits in there, Tiansheng said, confident that his friend was unharmed but had simply lost his way: the forest too deep, too wide. Martin wasn't at the meeting. On hearing the news from Meilian, he'd gone instead to approach the colonial officials, who, after much persuasion, had agreed to call for a hunt. He did not talk to Tiansheng, just glowered at the young man behind his back.

I should have acted earlier. Jiaxi put down on the mat with a loud thud the tray of tea and snacks for the men deep in discussion, a glaring stare darted at Tiansheng who was immersed in sketching out maps and directions. Was she to share with her mother her thoughts about the untrustworthy man? Was she to unravel his plan, his intention of exposing Uncle Mingzhi's weakness in an attempt to gain control of him, of his gold? But her mother had been busying herself in the kitchen since Tiansheng's return with the news, baking, steaming, boiling soup and pastes, preparing food that didn't need to be prepared, wiping from her face tears she disguised as vapour and sweat. *Mother.* She sighed, and in that very moment she made two decisions: first, she would go and bring Meilian another handkerchief; second, she would, after all, press ahead with her plan. On his return from the forest, which she believed to be soon, her uncle would at last realize his mistake in his choice of friend. Pleased with her thoughtfulness, the young girl did not know then it was a decision she would regret for the rest of her life.

*

He woke three days later, tired eyes opening to a ceiling of loose nipa jutting out from the uneven attap: lying still, not knowing who he was, thinking hard. Gradually coming to him were slow, dreamlike images of the jungle, his basket, the boar rush, Tiansheng—

Tiansheng! He – they – must be worried sick!

He struggled to sit up, his body aching all over. A clamour stirred outside the shelter, people shouting in words he was unable to comprehend, the same noises he'd been hearing in his dreamy state, only this time they were – it seemed – pressing calls for someone in the distance. He glanced up to the source of the blinding afternoon sun that was slanting in, to the silhouettes of the people converged at the door. He squinted, yet could make out nothing.

There was a momentary darkness as a figure shuffled in through the light tunnel. He wanted to say something but his head spun, and he was immediately helped into lying back down by the same pair of hands that had fed and washed him over the past few days.

'Anan,' a voice said, a loud pat on a stout chest.

He could see clearer now: on a small weathered face there was a pair of dark, round eyes. He stared up at the tobacco-stained teeth in a blackened mouth. *The indigenous!* The tales of headhunting, of poisonous blowpipes trundled in his head. *No!* He pushed himself up and was again pushed back down. 'Let me go!' He heard the last of his voice, before dizziness swooped down on him alongside the shadow of the man before him, like a giant canopy, wrapping over him.

Blackness again.

*

When he woke again it was night. Immense stillness pressed in from all sides, the sounds of the forest close to his ears: the low droning of insects, the occasional cries of some beast, shrieking or howling or hooting, seemed to be right outside the shelter. Pale and feeble, he curled up on the mat, his mind on the house-on-stilts by the river. *What are they doing in this moment? Thinking of me on an equally sleepless night?* He thought also of himself tied to a pole above a fierce fire, a congregation of savage hunters around it: chanting, dancing in triumph, saliva dripping. Would he survive this? Would he be able to go home to them? He was surprised at how easily the word 'home' had slipped out. The worried faces in his mind's eye flashed in the yellow glow of a paraffin lamp.

A far cry of a monkey penetrated his mind-image and there were other noises, of people chanting or singing, and flashes of bright flames also, sneaking in through the gapped bamboo strips. *Is it time for the big ceremony? Time to put me on the fire?* He sat up in a fluster.

Meilian heard a far cry of a monkey, then the flutter of clothes next to her as Jiaxi sat up in a fluster. She knew Jiaxi had been awake, as she'd been the nights before, since the day Tiansheng returned without Mingzhi.

Another shriek rose from the distant darkness, sharp and piercing; her hair stood on end. She stared out through the open window, through the wired-squares Tiansheng had added for protection while they enjoyed airy nights inside, and peered deep into the black horizon. *He could be there, somewhere over there among the beasts and all that* . . . She held her blanket tightly.

The search team Tiansheng formed had been dismissed – unofficially – yesterday, when Farmer Chong and his helpers decided they'd better return to the farm, with an unspoken statement: *No chance for survival out there.* Martin's colonial police squads weren't so kind, though, frankly shook their heads and declared it a hope-less case.

Even Martin grew quieter, seemed to agree with his new friends. But Tiansheng refused to give in, continuing with the search on his own, leaving without Martin, whom he was still not talking with. Meilian lay back down, felt under her pillow the piece of gold her brother had entrusted, the money for a house that would mean nothing without Mingzhi. She stared into the darkness, and soon dawn was breaking.

There will be news. She could only hope.

*

'It's his fault.' Martin's words to Meilian rang through the thin bamboo planks into Tiansheng's ears. 'He has to sort it out. It's his responsibility.'

He did not hear Meilian's response, too soft. *Did she defend me? Say something nice?* He'd be thrilled if she did. Immediately he was ashamed of his thought. What right had he to be excited by the possibility of someone else's fiancée defending him? Even if there was, any excuse, however reasonable, would only deepen his guilt. Squatting in the shadow between the stilts under the Fisherman's Hut, he rolled a cigarette, lit it, took a puff and then brought it close to the wounds on his arm, the scalding heat lessening the pain. He had just returned from his second trip to the jungle and had stayed where he was, ashamed to enter the house, ashamed to face Meilian, to look her in the eyes. What would she think of him? All his efforts at trying to make himself useful over the white man now evaporated. *She will never lay her eyes on me again,* he was certain, but immediately the shameful feeling rose again. He should be focusing on finding Mingzhi. He shook his head; his friend came to his mind, a lean figure wandering in the vast forest. *It was my fault. I should've waited for him, should've checked on him now and then.* He landed his fist on the pillar; it didn't make much noise on the solid teak, only a low, dull drone. And numbness.

His friend was out there, he reassured himself. He would go again tomorrow, again on his own, his initial thought of asking Martin to join him in the search now abandoned.

*

It was easier than she had thought, the execution of her plan. While Meilian tried to divert her anxieties and her worries for Uncle Mingzhi with cooking, Jiaxi sneaked back into their shared corner and combed every inch of it for the piece of gold. *There it is!* – in a silk pouch under a pile of cloth. She tucked it in her inner pocket. Her heart kicking with excitement, she felt the hard edges of the gold with her hand as she went swiftly to join her mother in the kitchen. She had only to find the chance to hide it in Tiansheng's corner when he was away.

The chance she needed, however, would not be there.

*

The young Malay man's legs clasped tight on the spindly trunk of the coconut tree and he started climbing: hands first, then the feet followed, toes pressed hard against the trunk, pushing his body up. One-two, one-two, one-two – quick, without a break – and he was up there between the fronds. Martin watched him reach for the machete tied to the side of his waist, and in seconds bundles of green coconuts fell to the ground.

Was that what they did when they cut the petai? *Climbing up the trees and all that?* He continued his journey on the quiet kampong path to town for yet another meeting with Montgomery, and would later try again to persuade his official friend to begin another search for Mingzhi. How untimely, he had been thinking, and it was all Tiansheng's fault; the incident had disrupted his secret business plan, meant to be a marvel to all of them. He thought he would press ahead, letting Tiansheng the culprit sort it out; but today, he was agitated. The pulled muscles on the sunburnt, calloused limbs, the cuts and bruises on the young Malay man's body, lingered in his head. Mingzhi, his friend, had been a mandarin, a scholar, someone who had, referring to a painting, explained to him how impermanent was the tie between a lotus and the water it lived in, like the relationships between human beings, vulnerable, unpredictable. *How sentimental he was.* He thought of his two friends climbing the trees. He thought of the delicious dumplings made of meat bought with the *petai*-and-durian money. He stopped.

He would tell Tiansheng that he would join him on his next search trip to the forest. He would talk to him tonight.

*

The talk, the trip never materialized.

Tiansheng was lying in bed, his body a hot cauldron. *As though his blood is boiling inside him, as though you could cook anything on it,* Meilian thought as she wiped sweat off his forehead. *Anything. Fry an egg, boil a pot of water, steam a fish (if there were any).* She repeatedly soaked a piece of cloth in cold water and dabbed his face and hands.

In a moment, he would start shivering, and then in the next, the temperature would rise again. Intervals of hot and cold persisted since he had returned, face ashen like a zombie, and collapsed on the floor without a word. It was a miracle he'd made it through the village path before blundering up the stairs. *A tough guy, he is.* Meilian remembered vaguely snatches of stories about the former opera apprentice, his journeys across the mainland. *But here's someone else's land, the tropics.* She stared at the patient under her charge with a newfound respect.

'Malaria.'

The name came quick and confident from the white-bearded Chinese herbalist who, after five years in the tropics, had had his book of medicine expanded to include diseases brewed in this humid land between the overgrowths, in the clogged ditches and still ponds, from the muddy pigsties and stinking fowl pens. Viruses grew and mutated in their paradise, their ghastly eyes peeped and peered, looking for chances to launch their attacks by free rides that came in abundance from the buzzing mosquitoes, flies and many more insects still unknown to the sensei. He knew, nevertheless, the only prescription for this particular virus carried by a particular type of mosquito. *Quinine,* the sensei, sent for by Farmer Chong, wrote on his paper. The sound of it yellow and bitter, as was Meilian's face as she shelled out the money for the medicine.

The cold spell began to take its toll, and in his corner, Tiansheng groaned. He curled up, shivering, teeth clattering. Meilian pulled another blanket over him. *Who will go and look for Mingzhi now?* She would tend him until he was well again for the task, which Martin, her fiancé, she knew, was unfit for – would potentially get himself lost in the wild.

Ma-la-ri-ya. Jiaxi repeated in silence the newly learned vocabulary. She'd emptied the vats used to store rainwater outside the house, cleared the clogged drainage, as instructed by Meilian on the sensei's advice. 'I never knew water could be a threat to our lives in that way,' her mother had said as she poured the last open pot of water in the house through the window as if it were the virus itself. Jiaxi had nodded. With her mother at Tiansheng's bedside all day, chores were now hers to take care of for days to come – cooking, washing, cleaning – the piece of gold sewn to her vest forgotten.

*

'Let's have another drink.' Jamerson, the assistant to the colonial secretary, put his arm around Martin's shoulder and ushered him to the bar.

'Get your men. Try again.'

'Scotch?'

'Let's go deeper this time. He's out there, I know.'

'I love this place. You know why?'

Martin stared at him, his glass of whisky untouched. Jamerson sighed.

'You've been away too long, my dear fellow.' He took a sip of his drink. 'Think about it.'

Martin followed his gaze to the young Chinese waiter

with his forever bowing posture and a flattering smile that was permanently on his face, fanning an English couple having late lunch in the dining room.

Jamerson took a puff of his cigar and beckoned. Another waiter in the same white Qing shirt, same pigtail, similar bowing posture and flattering smile came with an ashtray in his hand. Without looking at him, Jamerson flicked the ash off his cigar, then waved the teenager off.

'Tennis tomorrow?'

Martin's heart sank.

*   *   *

Parameswara's tomorrow is bright and clear. They welcome him, the people, much to the surprise of the new ruler: taking him in as if he is their own, as if he has always been part of them.

Parameswara stands on the top of the hill that will become Bukit China, the Chinese Hill, where five hundred and more years later, after shedding their sweat and blood for an economy that will later become Malaysia, immigrants from the Land of the Dragon will find their resting place. They will find neither recognition for their contribution to this land, nor a peaceful rest on the soil fertilized with their sweat and blood, but the fear of being pulled up from their graves, the land taken.

The new ruler of Malacca does not have this fear. Standing firm on the hilltop, Parameswara peers at the sea, at the ships flocking from the east and the west, thinks of the spices and camphor and silk, and smiles. His fear, though, comes from across the waters and the borders. His land shall not stay alone, shall not be left exposed, vulnerable to the vultures' greedy eyes. He has to find a way.

Parameswara finds his way to the north: out of the Strait of Malacca, across the South China Sea. Standing on the bow he peeps through his telescope. In front of him is the land he has never seen: China, the symbol of wealth and power, of the protection he needs.

On that Land of the Dragon Emperor Yongle sits high and elegant in his dragon throne, admiring the offering from the faraway land – bunga emas, *the miniature money tree – with its golden leaves and petals sprouting from equally golden sprigs: glaring, exquisite. Expensive.*

In the splendid, yellow glow of the bunga emas, *the young man who kowtows before the Emperor seems honest and earnest, his eyes hard, his face taut: the unshaken determination of a great warrior.*

This is the man. *Yongle nods, and announces:*

'He shall be the King of Malacca!'

Recognition is carved into the tiny square of the Imperial Seal, safety bound under the yellow shade of the royal umbrella – granted by the Land of the Dragon, granting a kingdom that is free from assaults and whatever calamities might befall it. For the time being.

As for the future, a princess, Hang Li Po, will be married off to the distant country. For a closer friendship, but more for gold and silver. For the spices that come in abundance. For the guarantee of the continuous supply of them.

A retinue of five hundred attendants of the bride will be escorted by five hundred servants of the groom. Yellow skin matches honey brown; single slit eyes meet double-creased, rounded ones. Five hundred more marriages will then ensue in the new kingdom. Five hundred new families with five hundred lines of a new breed, with a new culture, new language, not Chinese or Malay, but Chinese and Malay at the same time: the Peranakan called Baba and Nyonya.

That would be my new kingdom, and I'd embrace all who'd contribute to fostering its prosperity. Parameswara nods with contentment.

7

The Fire

Mingzhi stood at the edge of the jungle and peered in the direction he had come from. Between the trees, the stout back of Anan's naked upper body, the frizzy head of his son were shifting away, two blobs of dark brown threading through the sunlit greens. A couple of times the seven-year-old Engi turned back, mouth cracked open for a wide, toothless smile, and waved at him. Soon they disappeared altogether.

How easily they move in it, Mingzhi marvelled, trying to remember the trail just travelled, the signs and marks Anan had pointed out to him as he led Mingzhi out of the nature-maze, now a blur of green. Come and visit some time, Anan had said, and mimed blowing his hunting pipe: *We'll go hunting together.* A big smile on his face, eyes squeezed into narrow slits, tight brow crumpled with lines.

Mingzhi nodded at the now empty woods: *I will.*

Ten days he'd spent under the Orang Asli's charge: herbal remedies day and night, roasted yam for meals, pounded herbs for cuts and bruises and the half-an-inch-deep boar-bites on his thigh. He picked his way through the puddles. Last night, heavy rain drummed on the attap roof and strung up more vividly the anxious faces of Meilian, Jiaxi and his friends. Once, with his limited Malay and hand gestures he tried to describe to Anan how his friend might have been trudging the jungle, panicked and frustrated, blaming himself for his disappearance. He mimed a woman with tears rolling down her cheeks, and suddenly his own eyes were filled with wetness. Anan, thinking his patient was missing his lover, had laughed a hoarse, childlike laughter. He'd held down Mingzhi's shoulders, *Lie still, you need more rest*, his palms pressed together against his sunburnt cheek, his head askew, miming sleep.

Anan my saviour, my friend.

He would return, not for hunting but something else. Anan and his tribal men were experts in collecting rattan: quick, efficient, knew where to get the best. He would work out a plan with Tiansheng and Martin, starting up a wholesale trade, perhaps, buying from the Orang Asli instead of cutting the palms themselves. Martin, with his business mind, would see to it, he was certain.

He stepped out onto the narrow track flanked by long grass. The basket Anan had carried along the journey earlier was now a significant weight on his back, filled with slabs of roasted boar legs and loins wrapped in yam leaves, the result of the hunting trip specially planned for his departure, and tusks and herbs that were gifts from his new friend. *Eighteen miles, another eighteen miles northwestwards and I will be back at the Fisherman's Hut!* He adjusted the load on his back and sped up, his mind busy rehearsing his reunion with his friends and family.

The scorching sun was getting on Meilian's nerves. Late afternoon now, and she was at the makeshift kitchen outside the house, peeling a tube of yam. The slanted glare shot right between the two rambutan trees, right through the wall-less shelter, right onto her. Through the thin cotton of her samfu, she could feel the burning heat on her back and the left side of her body. *I should have added a shield, at least something to hang over it.* She attacked the dark purple tuber with an unusual vigour. Thud! It fell to the floor.

'Mum?' Jiaxi, who was in a shaded corner rinsing the *kangkong* she collected by the river that morning, called over. 'You're tired. Let me do it.' She picked up the yam. Her mother had been restless since the morning, she'd noticed. First this new country, then her uncle's disappearance, Tiansheng's sudden illness; all too much for a woman who once was waited on by maids at home. She knew Meilian had been trying to be strong, trying to hide her tears from her.

It must be hard. Jiaxi, holding the tuber, quietly knocked the handle of the knife against the wooden worktop. Once, twice and it came off. She turned to Meilian: 'Take a rest, Mum. Let me take care of this.'

Wordless, Meilian retreated to the house.

It must be here somewhere. She began her search again, careful not to wake Tiansheng who was asleep in a corner, though she wished she could tell him, could share it with him; wished for him to help her look for it.

The gold.

It was gone.

It was only at noon today she had become aware of its disappearance. She had looked under the mattress she shared with Jiaxi, their pillows and spare clothing. Mingzhi and Martin's territories. She had even tactfully pretended to be cleaning Tiansheng's corner while he lay there, frail and pallid.

Nothing. Absolutely nothing.

An immense fear swooped down on her. *It's for the house!* Her hands shook.

It might've long gone, when she was worrying about Mingzhi, tending Tiansheng. So disrupted was she that she'd neglected her daily check of the piece of gold. *But when and how could it have happened?* There had always been someone in the house, and she had always carried it with her in her secret pouch when running chores outside the house. *Could it have dropped?*

She combed the vacant space between the stilts under the house, pulled away the branches in the hedge, poked the chicken and duck pens with a bamboo stick, hoping for a glimpse of the glittering gold.

Not a trace.

He was on a clear gravel path now, Mingzhi. *Another six miles.* He tried to move faster but the load on his back was weighing him down, getting heavier with each step. His toes and the soles of his feet were in agony, infested with blisters; they chafed in his cotton shoes, clammy with sweat and heat, getting tighter as his feet expanded in the searing tropics.

He sighed, put down his basket and sat in a bower by the roadside. He had been hoping to be home by dinner, a surprise to his friends and family, but would wake them up instead now with the delay. He took out the last of the roasted yam Anan's wife had prepared for him. *What are they having tonight? Sweet potato leaves? Dumplings with braised streaky pork?* He swallowed a mouthful of saliva, the yam cold and tasteless.

He looked up. The sun was setting, a criss-cross of brilliant yellow and orange on the sky, partially blue and white still.

'To success!'

In the Club, Montgomery's voice echoed in the marbled hall, the start of a night-long celebration pronounced. A hundred acres and a contract of coolies from India – an excellent deal according to Montgomery, who had promised to share with Martin practical administrative and operational matters.

Martin took his first bite of beef steak in weeks, his mouth filling with the medium-cooked red meat doused with brownish gravy. Sweet, juicy, warm. He closed his eyes and munched, savouring the texture, the taste, the smell. That would be the energy supplement he needed tomorrow, the trip to the forest that could be undertaken now that the deal had eventually been finalized. He would go on his own. He would find Mingzhi: he would deliver to him news of his business venture, would tell his friend to join him. Let's do it together, he would say. Before that, though, he would write a thank-you letter to his parents for trusting him enough to mortgage the family home, their only property, for a loan.

Montgomery raised his glass again and he responded with a big, soothing gulp of wine. Martin took another bite of the meat and gazed out through the open window at the sea. The evening sun was partially immersed in the horizon, now a bloody red. *Red, a lucky sign*. He was surprised at how easily he had switched to adopting cultural symbols of the Orient over those of the West, and would not, for a second, assume the colour was a warning.

Could it be the kampong children who darted out from the bushes now and then with curious faces? Or the men with their sharp gazes whenever passing us by? Meilian looked into the urns and pots now emptied of water, the cupboards and trunks. Nothing. Fear grew and expanded to every sinew; apart from that, the gradual emptying of hope.

It's gone.

She wasn't aware when Jiaxi took out the dinner she prepared, when she had a few bites of the rice and yam and swamp cabbage, when Tiansheng, recovering, got up for the first time to have his meal, when Martin did not come home for dinner.

It's gone.

When the sun finally went down, paraffin lamp lit, then put out.

It's gone.

When she went to bed.

It's gone.

She lay there, eyes open, but saw nothing and heard nothing. Not the geckoes cruising the walls and ceiling looking for partners, not the rats chewing the pillars or scurrying from one corner to another, not the monotonous humming of crickets in the bushes.

She did not notice the slight, surreptitious shadows outside the house; did not hear the muffled whispers, the occasionally light crunches of leaves and branches under tiptoeing feet; did not see the hands that pulled the CHAI

115

board off, the torches that would soon be hurled onto the attap roof.

Perhaps it was the full bowl of rice he finished today, perhaps it was the relief at realizing the disease had finally left him: Tiansheng lapsed into a deep abyss of sleep. He was swimming in his sea of dreams: free, relaxed, turning somersaults.

Haven't been feeling so good for a long time! He swirled and dived and darted up, at times slow, at times as fast as a fish.

Yes, I am a fish!

His hands waved with the rekindled skill of an opera singer from his early apprentice years. Soft, graceful, boneless. Currents tailed his fingers like flowing sleeves. He was on an underwater stage, resurrecting his role as Green Snake in a solo performance of *The Legend of the Lady White Snake*. He could hear the applause, wave after wave, and was drowned in it.

But it suddenly turned scalding, the water, so hot that Tiansheng woke and choked instantly. The smoke! It was thickly clouding the room. And flames already licked up parts of the walls. He sprang up.

'Meilian! Jiaxi!'

There was a weak sound of coughing coming from the flared-up corner. Tiansheng rushed over, covering his face with his sleeve. A loud rumbling followed him and something hit him on his back. He felt a sharp pain, but there was no time to stop, to check, to think. *Get out of here!* That was the only thing that mattered. The wall behind him had collapsed; the attap roof, torched up, was sliding down and would smash on him any minute.

Everywhere was fire. 'Jiaxi! Meilian! Get out, quick!' He choked and coughed. 'No, I've to find the gold, I've to get it!' Meilian's hysterical voice seemed to come from a distance away. In the flashing red flames Tiansheng saw a pair of helpless hands, stretching out through the darkness; he yanked them out, pulled the figure with him and leapt out of the burning wall onto the front clearing.

The house, ablaze, toppled to the ground like a deflated fireball.

Half a mile away, without a lamp, Mingzhi, feeling his way through the pitch blackness, saw the sudden, strange brightness, red against the dark sky. *Must be some kind of celebration; their festival.* He thought of the bonfire that Anan had started for him last night, a farewell. The dancing and singing and music. *It would be interesting to see the kampong carnival, too!* He dragged his exhausted body forward, the blazing light his convenient target.

Martin's face was as red as the torch he carried. He was drunk, whistling and humming his favourite tunes intermittently, the music from the gramophone still in his ears. He was careful, though, reminding himself not to stumble, not to mud-smudge his white suit, his only piece of presentable attire. His hand that held the fire stretched out, rather than up, in front of his body, illuminating the track before him – the puddles and mounds, rocks and branches – so that he did not notice the reddening sky in the distance.

They entered the kampong almost at the same time. Martin, with his torch, was steps behind Mingzhi, who hunched under his basket.

It wasn't a fair, Mingzhi realized immediately. There were many people, true, but they were shouting, running here and there. Anxious, panicked, crying: '*Api! Api!*' – *Fire! Fire!* He realized, too, the glare and clamour came from the far end, the boundary between the kampong and the Chinese farm. His heart sank. He dropped the basket and ran.

Behind him, Martin, his eyes now wide open, dropped his torch and ran.

'Mother! Mother!'

Jiaxi, screaming at the roaring fire, elbowed and kicked at Tiansheng, trying to break free from his grip. 'She's in there; get her out of there, please, I beg you!' She screamed and cried and pulled at his hair, before passing out.

Meilian . . . 'No, no!' Mingzhi, just arrived, lurched forward and was immediately stopped by Tiansheng. 'It's too late now. Too late!' He gave a shove and Mingzhi was down on the ground, holding his head, his mind a blank.

'What have you done!' Martin, at the scene now, shouted at Tiansheng. 'Bastard!' He launched a punch on Tiansheng's face and was hit back.

'You're supposed to take care of her! Look at the state of you! Where've you been? Having a jolly time?'

'That's none of your business!'

'She might still be here if you were around!'

Fists were raised again and they entangled, anger, grief and resentment thrown in quick exchanges of fierce punches and kicks.

'Stop it!' Mingzhi rose to his feet. The two men

froze. For a few moments he remained silent, staring ahead at the spot that had been the Fisherman's Hut. They were still burning, the remainder of the pillars; there were still sounds of crackling from the now subsiding fire, like a satisfied eater's belches after a sumptuous dinner. It was a big meal, indeed. A house, a life; and the relationships between those who were alive would change from now on.

Quietly he asked Martin and Tiansheng to take Jiaxi to the Rest House, which would become their temporary shelter for days to come, thanks to Martin's connection with Jamerson. He ignored the fact that his two friends were not talking, not looking each other in the eye.

The villagers who had been crowding the front clearing had retreated. There was nothing to watch now.

Nothing was left.

No Meilian, no clan book. No gold piece.

His tears streamed, and he looked away.

There was something in the bushes, he noticed, something dark and square. He wiped his eyes with his sleeves, walked towards it and pulled it out.

CHAI FAMILY

The board, cracked at a corner, squinted up at him, the FAMILY blackened, smudged with soot.

Something flashed in his head. The board had been right above the door under the attap roof; it was unthinkable that it had survived the blaze, that it was outside the house. *Unless someone tossed it away before the flames started!* He remembered his dreams. He remembered the letter from the village head, his visit. He remembered the many other unfriendly visits.

Thump! He dropped his family name, his only possession now, his heart emptying. He saw himself drifting on the sea, floating between the swaying coconut trees, sprinkling crushed corn into his pens of chicken and ducks, having dinner cross-legged on the mat with his friends and family: chatting, laughing. *My tropical life.* He blinked, and everything was gone.

No! He gritted his teeth and picked up the board from the ground, grasping it tightly in his hands, until his fingers hurt, his angry veins green against his neck.

I am staying put! I AM STAYING PUT!

He bellowed inside, his eyes hard and dry. There were no more tears in them.

PART TWO

One Night, Two Places, Four Unsettled Souls

Engi

MAY 1938

Candlelight flickers; the glow has turned low, dim over a pool of wax. I light another and stare hard at it. I see nothing but the new flame, bright and red, filling up my vision. I see a house, wrapped in the blaze, topple to the ground.

I blink; gone is everything save the red grains at the back of my eyes. I sit motionless, shaken, as I feel his pain and sorrow. He, Chai Mingzhi, or Taukeh Chai, my guardian of twenty years.

'*Whoo*—' The whooping of a gibbon tears across the darkness, loud in the dead silence. Thirteen years now since my return, the serenity of the jungle still baffles me at times. I would confuse the repeating howls for eager shouts from mobile hawkers with their renowned long drawls, '*Bao*—oh, *bao*—oh, *bao*—oh,' calling out freshly made hot dumplings for breakfast. Even in my half-awake state those little soft, snowy white balls would roll into my mind, the sweetness of the braised pork filling rising from memory, tickling my taste buds, and I would lie there wondering about my existence, which is reality, which is dream. Because of the quietness, every sound amplifies. I would confuse some wild bird's gentle movements on the tree outside the hut for Taukeh Tiansheng's rapid rapping at my door, '*Quick, you lazy* sakai!', angry knocks calling for my swift response. I would confuse the flock of hens' clattering for street children's chattering as they gather and march noisily to school.

How frustrating. A combined total of twenty-five years in the jungle – twelve childhood years plus another thirteen after my return – leaves an impact lesser than a twenty-year gap in between spent in the outside world. Reality presides over logic. The law of mathematics I've learned from Taukeh Chai fails to explain the equation, to find logic for the inverted 'greater' sign. Did Father conjecture this? Did he foresee my quandary when he planned my departure and return? Questions pour on me in the early hours when the mind is most troubled. Was it fate, my venturing into the outside world? Why was Father so sure? Was it the conclusion from the shaman he'd been frequenting? Did the wise man, after calling forth the spirits of our ancestors, breathe on the stone of *cenoi* and see me drifting on it among the outside men, eating alien food in shirts made of fine cotton? On that magic stone of fate, did he see Taukeh Chai, holding my hand, taking me out of the jungle? Did the shaman see me snuggling up in a small back room, alone and afraid? Did he see my life and convince Father that was the path for me?

Twenty years after I walked out of the forest, twenty years of infrequent trips home – which had become rarer in the later years – at Taukeh Chai's approval, a messenger was sent for me to return. I had stared down at the scrawny body once strong and stout, a man I called Father, and wondered what he'd seen in me – a stranger to his world? Was it what he had intended? On his death

124

bed, Father was too frail to answer my queries. He glanced up at me, his bark-like hand weakly touched mine, and he smiled, his withered face all crumpled, his eyes turned into slits. I felt a loud pang in my head—

He was happy.

*

It was fated, my being uprooted to a foreign realm.

To stop my badgering to join him on his hunting trip that morning thirty-three years ago, Father promised to bring home the biggest animal he'd ever caught. *What will he capture this time? An elephant?* The thought of it excited me. No one had ever brought back that giant beast – its skin too thick, its body too huge, containing too much fluid for the blowpipe poison to take effect. But in my childish mind Father was capable of hunting down whatever he targeted. A tiger, a bear and surely an elephant, too. He was, after all, one of the best hunters of our tribe. All day I hovered restlessly around the hut, climbing up the wild rambutan tree occasionally, peering in the direction in which Father had disappeared. Come afternoon, a dip in the running stream disappointingly lost its usual effect; its coolness couldn't extinguish my anxiety, accumulating by every passing minute.

It was a strange day, I remember. A hornbill had been calling incessantly in the morning after Father left. 'Rang! Rang! Rang!' Loud shrieks tearing my eardrums; seemingly coming from a near distance. *Rang*, short for *orang*, 'man'. As children we had been told of the bird's kind warning upon sighting intruders. On hearing the first calls, I looked around, trying to locate the bird, trying to check also for invaders. I saw nothing. I cursed the 'mad' bird and ignored the cries, which died down later.

At dusk, in the fading daylight a familiar figure emerged, hunched under the load on his back. I jumped down the tree and rushed forward – but wait – there was a hand hanging down from Father's back, unmistakably yellow against Father's dark-brown skin in the still visible evening hue. I'd never seen a Chinese then, but instantly I knew, having heard about them all so often, the descriptions of them ingrained in my young mind. 'Rang! Rang! Rang!' The calls of a hornbill again tore the evening sky. I turned and ran to Mother in a panic, my eyes wide with fear and disbelief. 'Quick!' I shouted. 'The Chinamen!' My hands gesturing like a maniac, I urged her to go into hiding.

You see, the Chinese were the woman-snatchers, I'd been told repeatedly ever since before I could even talk, and I was taught to give warning at the glimpse of them. These second lot of the Chinamen, Father said, were an influx of coolies brought in by the British to work in the mines and plantations, their wives left at home, too far to be their comfort. Long hours of laborious work under finger-pointing, wooden-faced white bosses during the day would, in the deep of their lonely, homesick nights, whip up the animal desire that gnawed the human part of them. The Malays with their numbers and weapons they feared, but us – they knew we were vulnerable outside the jungle, they knew we had no way to find them, they knew they had the big, hairy white men with their deadly booms for their protection. And so our women – beautiful, defenceless – became their obvious target. They kidnapped them – when they were alone bathing in the river or doing chores on their own – and made them their wives. Just two weeks before, out collecting bamboo shoots, Mak Minah's fourteen-year-old daughter vanished, a tray of young shoots strewn on the ground. Still in shock we were. *What has got to Father? Has he been possessed? Has the Chinaman cast spells on him?* Shaking, I pulled the hem of Mother's sarong for her to go with me, to cower behind our shelter, ignoring Father's pressing calls for us, for Mother to fetch water. She wouldn't move. 'Rang! Rang! Rang!' My ears hurt; I clasped them with both hands and ran to hide in a corner of the hut.

Did I hear the shouts of the giant bird's concern that evening when Father came home with Taukeh Chai on his back? 'It was you. You made that strange noise.' Each time when we recalled the episode, Mother stressed with such assurance that the cries had come from me. She said she was stunned to see me jump down from the tree, my throat cracked with the frightening squeals, 'just like the bird'. She'd remembered with such clarity the cooking (three strings of wild *petai* with chilli, two *kuning* fish) she put aside that evening before rushing out of the shelter, that an argument was clearly uncalled for. To think back, perhaps it was an instinct, perhaps the ancestors, foreseeing the danger of losing their descendant to an outside man, had their spirits enter me, voicing their warning directly through me of the arrival of a stranger that would change my life forever.

Father wasn't alerted. Instead, he'd since conveniently transformed the incident into the signature tune of his evening show time. His curtain-opener. Rolled tobacco still clasped tightly between his lips, he'd leap off from the stump he'd been crouching on, holding his vocal cord and giving out a sharp, throaty 'Rang! Rang! Rang!' to an audience of giggling children and his son, me, who buried my blushing face between my knees. Stories, long or short, of spirits big or small, their comings and goings, of animals tame or savage, witty or fiendish, of trees and beasts turning into humans and vice-versa, poured into our young minds like the gurgling stream shaded under the *neram* trees. Clear, soothing, pleasant.

It was the river of tradition that we bathed in, imbued with generations of life and death, with soft whispers of tenderness from the spirits of watchful ancestors, with the souls of the forest that protect our existence.

Five years later, I swam out of it, into the outside world. Taukeh Chai's world. Those early days after my arrival in town, in the small back room I lay wide-eyed on the soft mattress in the sweltering evenings, thinking of Father, his stories, those that I would miss. I feared. Even as a child I feared. What would be left for me to tell my children, if I would have any? Staring at the ceiling, I tried to recall Father's animated voice, playing the tales again and again in my head in desperation. But the tones somehow didn't seem right, and I confused turtle for tortoise, weasel for mouse deer. Night after night, on the wooden ceiling I saw them fading away, one after another, while other sounds, other stories noisily rumbled in, eventually taking over.

Stories told by Taukeh Chai by my bedside in my new residence.

*

A body born and bred in the wild seems to have nur-
tured a natural resistance to the comfort of a civilized
world. Days after my arrival in town, one morning I was
attacked by a fever so severe that I lay on the edge of
consciousness, body heavy as a dead boar. The daily
routine established had me going to the shop with
Taukeh Tiansheng in the first half of the day and back to
the Baba Lodge, to Taukeh Chai's study in the second
half. I would usually wake up at dawn, wolf down a
cold dumpling soaked in sweet tea and then tag behind
Taukeh Tiansheng when he left the house, not a glance
at me, not a word exchanged between us. That morning, even in my half-conscious state I heard the door to
my room being flung open; I heard the rapping at the
headboard. I heard angry shouts: 'Get up!' 'Time to
work!' I heard argument. I felt a hand on my forehead,
and there came Taukeh Chai's firm, authoritative voice,
'Let him sleep,' deep in my ears.

Two days later I woke up to realize it was the first
open disagreement between them, the beginning of a
long and painful confrontation between the two persons
who were once bound tight like inseparable flesh and
blood. And—

I am the only witness to the mystery surrounding the
break-up of Chai & Tian Company!

I sit straight up at the thought, overwhelmed by the
sudden flood of the long-ago episodes, the ups and
downs, climaxes and anticlimaxes that have dominated
my guardian's life. They fill up my inside, nudging away
the stories of the ancient man called Parameswara. I take
a big gulp of tea, stretch and shake my head of tiredness,
ready to continue. Dawn will be calling in a couple of

hours; the night is too short to dwell on a life so eventful, so tragic.

Everything began in 1905, after Taukeh Chai's visit to Penang.

1

Mingzhi

He waited. On the long bench at the front of the steaming stall five Chinese coolies perched, slurping bowls of
rice porridge with fermented tofu, pickled cabbage,
salted fish and fried groundnuts for accompaniment. He
watched them locked with such concentration in their
noisy ritual of shoving the gruel into their mouths that
each seemed to be a muted, unconcerned individual.
Five eating entities that resembled one another: sun-
scorched, discoloured plaits hanging thin and unkempt
on their backs, shoulders stooped, heads buried deep in
their food, their arched bodies forming a symmetry to
the tiny sparrows resting in a row on the newly laid cables
overhead. Black specks dotting the gathering grey-blue
of evening, appearing smaller, lonelier than they actually
were.

Mingzhi shook his head, thinking of himself sitting in
a corner, alone. *What would they make of me? A stranger?
But aren't we all strangers on this land?* He laid his elbow
on the table but retracted immediately, and rubbed it
against his shirtsleeve to get rid of the stickiness. In the
dimming daylight, he noticed the significant film of stubborn grease on the wooden tabletop, and regretted his
suggestion of this meeting place, which he had heard of

from a travelling trader on a trip to Malacca. Of course, it was the kind of stall frequented by thrifty travelling salesmen – economic, fast, homely.

But what would Jiaxi think of it?

It was his first trip to Penang. Two weeks ago, when Uncle Lau told him of the visit of Dr Sun Yat Sen, a medical practitioner turned revolutionist, to Penang, inviting Mingzhi to come along, he did not hesitate. He would take the opportunity to meet Jiaxi, he told himself quietly. He hadn't seen her for five years. *This is absurd* – he shook his head again – *that an excuse has to be worked out for a long overdue visit*. A day before the trip, Uncle Lau had become bed-bound with a worsened rheumatic knee joint. Mingzhi was guiltily relieved, glad to save the explanation of the meeting arrangement with Jiaxi, which he'd kept from the older man.

He pulled out his watch. Thirty-five past six. The meeting was to start at half past seven, the venue yet to be located in this unfamiliar town. He had another glance at the watch before dropping it in his pocket under his gown. When he looked up again, there she was, arriving in a rickshaw that stopped across the street.

He watched her – a suddenly elongated figure – as she alighted from the vehicle, her body, as if just grown out of adolescence in that split moment, wrapped in a white dress. *Nineteen years old,* he realized, uneasy at the sight of the foreign attire. He wondered if she still wore samfus. He watched as her young face searched for him, her girlish chubbiness gone. He watched her scowl, a line cut deep between her eyebrows. Familiar. *Meilian*. He felt the heavy thud in his heart.

———

Was it a mistake to have let Jiaxi go? He shook his head: *What else could I have done?* It had seemed right then, when they met Tim Marshall and his wife Lina at the Rest House, where they had stayed for a fortnight after the fire. Amazed by Jiaxi's fluency in English, Mrs Marshall had taken a liking to her. Mingzhi, unable to reach out to his niece who had grown increasingly reticent, was glad for the companionship Jiaxi had to obliterate her grief. He had encouraged the friendship. *It's easier to talk woman to woman, especially an older one to a younger.* And Lina Marshall possessed the same kindness and trustworthiness as Father Terry, a figure the young girl revered.

'Come with us to Penang,' Mrs Marshall had suggested, when the family's tragedy was finally revealed to the sympathetic pair after a few sittings of afternoon tea. The couple were on their way to the island to take up teaching posts at the church-run Methodist school. Jiaxi had said yes without hesitation, without even seeking her uncle's permission. Mingzhi, despite his worry for the future distance between them, did not object. *A young girl needs a woman to take care of her, a good one.* Like Lina. And he believed in the Marshalls.

Also in their company had been a forever-smiling Miss Jean Lambie – a new teacher determined to explore the new land – whom the younger girl had been encouraged to befriend. Young and cheerful, the lady in her early twenties would spread her sunshine smile in her presence, the air lightened, the mood relaxed. *The right companion for Jiaxi in this time of sorrow.* Quietly relieved, he saw them off at the port three days later. No words still from Jiaxi who, standing on the deck, had her back to the send-off party consisting of Mingzhi, Tiansheng and Martin, her hands clutched tightly at her bundle (in which, without anyone else's knowledge, hid the *missing* gold), her eyes fixed on the unforeseeable far north. Impatient to be going.

She blames me. It had suddenly dawned on him as the boat was bobbing away, and in the bubbling froth loomed Jiaxi's face – no sadness, no hatred, just impassive. Two blank, staring eyes rippling off at a quick paddle.

She never wrote.

'We moved twice.' He sipped his coffee, repeating the lines he'd carefully written in immaculate calligraphy over the years – placed in sealed envelopes and entrusted to messengers, usually travelling salesmen – without getting any replies. 'The first was a back room at Tan's grocery shop, not long after you left.' He stared at his cup, the ring of stubborn brown around the white ceramic. 'Only Tiansheng and I.' Martin had found refuge at Montgomery's. It was a relief to them all. Even putting aside the awkwardness between his friends, they wouldn't have been able to get accommodation together after all, a white man for a roommate an obstacle too big. 'We called it the Rats' Nest.'

Suggested by his niece, the coffee shop across the road from the stall was quiet; the owners, a middle-aged husband and wife pair, were clearing tables left from the afternoon-tea rush, the throng now having moved to the eateries or returned home for the evening. He stirred the sweet coffee that didn't need to be stirred, a drink he was still to get used to.

'We slept on the floor. A table, two chairs, discarded

fruit boxes for chests. There were rats everywhere. Behind the walls, under the floorboards, on the ceiling. Waking us up at night, all those sounds of chewing and scuttling. They'd gnaw at everything: our shoes, the mats we lay on, the plants and roots and fruits we collected – we had to hang them in a basket on a hook from the beam. Once I was bitten on my toe. I thought there were tastier, more fulfilling foods in the shop for their stomachs.' He breathed deep and heavy, disgusted by his presumed humorous comment, which amused neither the storyteller nor his listener, disgusted also by his sudden, uncharacteristic garrulousness, by the trivia spewing out from his mouth like overflow-sewage from the gutters after a downpour.

Only thirty-one he was. Not young, not old either, though ageing seemed to have come abruptly in front of his staring niece, eyes clear and calm like a pool of spring water, fixing on him. *Is she counting my grey hairs? My wrinkles? The cuts and scars on the backs of my hands that escape my shirtsleeves?* Intuitively, he pulled down the hems of his sleeves.

Words, nonetheless, continued to flood.

'We went back to the forest – it was the only way; we had nothing left. Nothing but the board that bears the family name. But no, we no longer climbed the trees. Remember Anan? The man who saved my life when I was lost in the jungle? I made a deal with him. He and his son, Engi, and others from his tribe got us what we needed, not only fruits and aromatic woods. Rattan, camphor, bezoar stones, honey. Anything saleable. The smaller items Tiansheng sold in the market.' After months of getting meagre payouts from Baba Lim, the wholesaler, for their rattan, they found out about the business of shipping and about potential buyers in Singapore through a clansman of Mingzhi.

'Remember Uncle Lau, a distant relative from home? He came to our rescue. "Set up a company," Uncle Lau said, "and start selling in bulk." He is a trader himself, importing rice and flour from China and then sending them away through Singapore.' From Uncle Lau, he got contacts, learned to negotiate: the prices of rattan and camphor, of shipping, of labour – when bigger consignments were involved.

There were other skills he acquired from the veteran of the tropical peninsula: comfort money for customs officers, under-the-counter transactions of gold that came at rare opportunities; these he left out, ashamed of himself.

*

He was driven into the conspiracy of illicit acts he most despised, initiated by Tiansheng.

'Everybody does it,' his friend had shrugged, matter-of-factly, his tone surprisingly familiar, so that Mingzhi had confused it for the voice of the governor, his flower superior, who once said: 'Everybody knows how to meet their tax targets,' persuading him to dive into the murky waters of corruption. He was proud then to have had stayed out of the mud. But now? 'This is how things work in real life,' Tiansheng had added, and his undertone was apparent: *Without power, without resources, what else can you do? Your books, your morals can't buy you rice and meat.*

His partner complied with Uncle Lau's arrangements

without further consulting Mingzhi. Secretive deals in dark alleys, in the back room of a smoke-shrouded mah-jong or opium den and, sometimes, in tumultuous coffee shops in broad daylight. All so surreal. He'd heard stories from Grocer Tan, told during Mingzhi's early days as a newcomer wandering in town for possible accommodation and business opportunities; days which always ended with long games of chess on the bench outside the shop. Activities of the underworld were described in hushed voices between thoughtful moves. Protection money was an unlisted business expense for all traders. A victim himself, the shop owner sighed and shook his head.

Once, at the height of their game, Grocer Tan hastily leaped off the bench upon sighting two approaching figures. The burly men then, in a hurried pace, walked straight past Mingzhi and tailed the shop owner to the back of the store before leaving in minutes, as wordless and impassive as they'd come. He'd noticed on one of them his slightly bulging waist, and speculated about the amount they'd collected. He was careful to take longer than necessary as he picked up the pieces knocked over in the haste, allowing time for colour to return to his suddenly clammed-up chess mate, allowing his unusual silence. That night, he imagined Tiansheng sitting in the din and smoke of the opium den, across the table from the two burly men, head bowed, a red envelope the size of an open book held out with both hands. Not a word. He saw his friend's face, his flattering smile at the two men, becoming obscure in the hot vapour of bubbling black gum: distorted, unrecognizable.

In reality, though, he pretended nothing happened,

keeping his head down whenever Tiansheng sneaked out, red packets of money-for-favour safe in his chest pocket, their final destinations, the intended beneficiaries and the entire matter not to be discussed. As though by not seeing, not actually doing it, not talking about it, he was out of it. *How hypocritical.* A conspirer he was all the same, his silence already a nodding head.

In the deep of the night, though, his self-deception would crack into pieces as Tiansheng tiptoed away, the lightness of his careful footsteps striking out surprisingly huge vibrations in his ears, on his body, lying as stiff as a log on the mat facing the wall. Thud, thud, thud . . . Each accompanied by a series of echoing tremors, *sinner, sinner, sinner,* swooping into every inch of his skin, his flesh, his insides, until he wrapped his hands over his knees, over his head, shaking. On occasions when he'd lapse into sleep, the noises slipped into his dreams like the thumping of a ferocious giant, beating on his heart, and he would wake in the pitch blackness, gasping for air.

*

No, she should never find out. Not from me.

'Anan and his men knew where to get the best of everything: camphor, honey, sandalwood. Anything they can find. And rattan, too, cut, tied, and sent through the river; we collect them downstream, passing them on to the buyers. Orders began to flood in. At first we hired a corner at Uncle Lau's warehouse. Three years later we bought the vacant shop lot on the main street.' He could only keep on talking.

'"Chai & Tian Company", our signboard says. I insisted on having Tiansheng's name on it. He's done so much, after all.'

They came to them, the small, individual collectors, as they once were – the suppliers who'd been exploited by Baba Lim – offering in small quantities rattan and other produce. Because of the pair's experience with Baba Lim, because of their empathy for them, fairer, better payments were handed out, their budgets stretched to the limit. 'We will beat him.' Tiansheng, his indignation towards Baba Lim rooted deep, had vowed to overtake the bloodsucker he so abhorred, the leading man of their trade in town.

They'd slept in the back chamber of the shop, other rooms allocated for an office – with fruit crates for a desk and document storage – and the stock of forest produce that was constantly in transit.

'The second floor of the shop we used entirely for storage. Only a half-laid floor, the other half open up to the ground floor. A self-made pulley attached to the beam would roll the loads up and down. Tiansheng had designed it, a model he remembered from his days working at the docks.'

Still, the nightmare resumed with Tiansheng's after-dark ventures that had become more frequent as business progressed. During the day, in the windowless box-room-for-office, he sat in a gloomy corner and struck hard on the abacus for a balance that would be perfect for the tax office. Click, click, click, the wooden beads crisp and clear in the barren space, so that despite the dreamlike atmosphere he'd so carefully constructed, he was constantly reminded of the reality of his deed. Of the fact that he was keeping two books: one official, the other bearing the actual income, to be kept in the secret compartment under the floorboard, alongside a box of undeclared gold pieces and cash, fast accumulating with each passing day.

In the same room he wrote her letters, on evenings when the accounts – official and unofficial – were cleared away. Long, detailed descriptions of their business (legal), of the few games of chess and the rare copies of books (secured through the resourceful Grocer Tan) he managed amid his busyness, of his visits to the forest, to Anan and his son Engi, whom he'd increasingly grown fond of. As if by babbling about the bright side of his life, the dark side of it, unmentioned, would be obliterated by itself. He scribbled to the last of the daylight sneaking in through the open door, finishing with 'please write' before his signature. After a year or two without a line from her, he saved the two words, prying instead for a glimpse of the girl in occasional letters from the Marshalls, from the messengers to whom he entrusted his letters. 'Only to her hands,' he'd repeatedly instructed.

It had been futile, his attempt to conjure up from the snatches of news an image of a girl who was 'well', who was 'doing excellently at school', who was 'becoming taller and prettier'. He was, after all, handicapped when trying to sketch out a real picture of her, the girl who was now sitting in front of him.

Three months ago, he received a final letter from Lina Marshall, sent before the couple left for their new positions in another church-run school in Shanghai. 'She refused to come with us.' He read disappointment out of

her neat writing. 'A teacher herself now, she's more inde-
pendent than any of us would've thought.'

There was a sudden brightness; the hurricane lamp, just
lighted, was hanging at the entrance behind Jiaxi. Yellow
hue flooded, and the world before him was surreal, like
a forgotten painting on rice paper resurrected from an
ancient trunk, old, stained, faded. Her hair was gold-
gilded, absorbing the light, and underneath, her face
obscure in the gloom. Only then did he brave his first
direct view of her of the evening, his own face shadowed
in hers, saved from her scrutiny. *They were right; she is
pretty.* Like her mother. He felt again the ache in his
heart. But there was something else about her, the calmness, the maturity that were not her age to bear. And the
tinge of – sadness? – between her brows.

From the corner of his eye he caught a glimpse of
glitter, the metallic reflection in the glow, and traced the
source to the hairpins on both sides above her ears.
Silver, delicately carved with designs he wasn't able to
name. Foreign. *From Lina Marshall?* The question was
not brought out.

He felt his watch but did not take it out. *Past seven?*
He considered the darkening sky; the eaters at the stall
across the street were now black figures in the faint light
of paraffin lamps laid on the worktop and the tables. He
knew he would be late for the meeting.

There were more questions he needed answers for.
She'd returned to him through the messengers the money
he'd enclosed in his letters. On all occasions. He was
deeply hurt. Perhaps she was being thoughtful, saving
her 'penniless' uncle (as he was gold-less when she left)

the burden; but his writings had later described a gradual progress to prosperity, yet the notes were bounced back nonetheless. Her act, the way he saw it, was a rejection of his duty as her uncle. *How does she survive? Do the Marshalls, or the church, provide everything she needs?* He noted the silky reflection of her dress, the exquisite designs of the soft lace, the light touches of white and yellow adorning the collar and the hems of the sleeves.

I can afford that too. He regretted not getting a couple of textile materials for her. If there were a woman, if Meilian were around, she would have reminded him. *Meilian.* He sighed. None of this would have happened if Meilian were around.

'We were lucky.' He intentionally dwelled on a business that was expanding beyond his expectation. Sometimes, in fact, he thought he no longer knew what to expect. Things happened – or perhaps, were arranged, for instance, the move to Baba Lodge. 'We can afford it now,' Tiansheng had said; the ownership of a property that had once been their rival's was a triumph for his partner. So successful was their trade, they'd taken over not only Baba Lim's shop but also his house.

It was Tiansheng who had the signboard relocated to the new shop, with a big grin that was extremely rare on his face.

In the Baba Lodge two streets away from the shop, into which they had moved just recently, he and Tiansheng each had a room spacious enough for a double bed on an iron-posted frame. Thick mattress, soft pillow, fine blanket. Perhaps it was the whitewashed cement walls and tiled floor that would absorb all footsteps leading to another sin, perhaps it was the dinner that was by each passing day getting more sumptuous – the braised duck, sea cucumber and roast pork – prepared by an amah who also cleaned for them, he slept well. Noises ceased, nightmares were rare.

Across the road on the pavement outside the shops, a group of four or five children had ventured out for their after-dinner playtime, their young voices crisp in the increasingly quietened street. Some of them were bare-foot, he noticed, stepping into the shallow drains along the pavement, picking out something – fishes? Frogs? – from it at times, arousing bouts of laughter, bouts of hoo-ha. He thought of the food stall, the leftovers shoved into the open drainage. He thought of the grease and the slop sticking on their bare legs and hands.

He looked away. *How has she been living her life here? Does she have a close friend?*

From a distance, homecoming-calls of some woman were heard, shrill and loud above the children's tumult, shouting out the prospect of a punishment. The children dispersed, grumpily, water still dripping from their hands and legs. Before long, all noises died down.

'Tiansheng works extremely hard; we both do.' He tried to make out the designs of her hairpins – flowers? Beetles? 'We had to survive. We had only each other.'

There was a tinge of confusion in the suddenly attentive gaze, and above it, Jiaxi's knotted brows, a silent question. The floodgate of words slammed shut.

He sighed, a long pause.

'He didn't join us. He had his rubber estate. With Montgomery.' From where did Martin get the money for the plantation? Over the years Tiansheng had been repeating his doubts, speculating of a theft – when Mingzhi was still deep in the forest and himself down with malaria. A theory had even been worked out – that Martin, after stealing the gold, set fire to the house. His friend's hatred for Martin, to that extent, was unexpected to Mingzhi.

'Do you think Martin would do such a thing? I thought it was melted in the blaze, the gold.' He glanced at Jiaxi, only to find his niece pale and tremulous, her eyes brimming with tears and pain.

The fire. He looked away, pretending not to notice. *I shouldn't have mentioned it.*

2
Jiaxi

She got off the rickshaw outside the alley, relieved to see the lit window in the secluded lane, a knowing eye in the darkness.

Edward had been waiting for her.

She felt his body on hers, solid, masculine. *Hold me, yes, hold me tight.* She felt his touch, his kisses, the gradual hardening of his manhood; his weight a reassurance of her presence, rather than his. She clasped her arms around his back, pressing him onto her, and felt the squeezing of flesh against flesh, the rubbing of ribs against ribs, pelvis against pelvis, their sweat that had mingled together, inseparable. Their body heat. The emptiness inside was so immense, she held him tightly until her arms, her fingers, her chest hurt, until they were both out of breath.

'What is it? Want to talk?' He gasped for air as she loosened her grip. He knew her well enough to ask, not well enough not to.

She clung on to him again, did not answer, laid her palm instead on the nape of his neck, tracing from there the contour of his muscles, the slight curve along his spine, and below it, the tight bottom of a forty-year-old who wouldn't miss a daily ten-lap swim to preserve his youthfulness. Avoiding his stare, she hid her face above his shoulder, her cheek rubbing against his neck, feeling his softness, his warmth. His existence. Knowing she wasn't alone.

The room was dark, the candlelight blown out upon her arrival; the only source of brightness was the faint moonshine escaping the thin gauzy curtain. Even so, she felt exposed, her nude body conspicuous in a room poorly furnished, the bed the only prominent fixture. *What would he think of me?* She closed her eyes and saw her uncle, the lines on his face, his tired eyes, the lips that seemed to be not moving while he talked, as though he would rather be not talking, his greying head – at thirty-one years of age. She saw his gaze on her as she walked away, climbing into a rickshaw. She felt it there still, his gaze, cold on her nakedness.

With both hands she held her lover's head and pulled it closer towards her, showered him with a rain of kisses, like an unexpected torrential downpour of the tropics, or a monsoon deluge – he had learned these over his years in the peninsula. It was new, her passion. He savoured them, her biting kisses, the skimming of her teeth on his earlobes, his jaw, his neck, his chest.

'Are you trying to eat me?' His breathing grew heavier; the real game was to begin. He made the move but she pushed and turned him over, and the next second she was on top of him, her skin hot as burning coal. Inside her he was now twisting her lean body. The room swirled. Her strong legs and waist, her suppressed moans, their sweat and secretions. The air suffused with their odours.

In the midst she tilted her head and caught a glimpse

of the hook hanging down from a beam, left by the previous occupier; she remembered the pulley her uncle told her about, the rattan and the shop. She saw him, a sixth-ranking mandarin of the Qing Court, sleeping on the floor. She thought of the rats, the dirt and dust, mites and lice. She looked away and quickened the rhythm of her ride, grinding hard on her partner, heaving, as if making love for the last time.

When it was over, he felt the wetness on his chest, the spilling of her tears like rainfall, of her loosened hair, soft as silk as it brushed against his skin, her head in his embrace. The slight quivering of her body as she sobbed.

*

Edward's footsteps descending the wooden stairs, each echoing with a grinding creak; the smell of tobacco in the air.

She sat leaning against the bedpost in the still unlit room. She closed her eyes. A flood of images surged in her head. Miss Lambie fingering a colourful piece of sari, draping it over her head like a veil. Her laughter, her body – trembling with excitement – under the red and yellow and blue silk.

She covered her face with her hands, anticipating the bright flames that would envelop everything.

How absurd it was, that scenes of her early years in Penang would register themselves in her memory, without her realizing it. She'd wished then that they would prevail, would nudge away those from the fated night – her mother's worried face, the fire, the crumbling of the Fisherman's Hut, her uncle's sadness – but no, they quietly slunk away, leaving the images she most dreaded to claim their precedence. Day and night, day and night. Persistent, tormenting.

And years later, as if suddenly regaining their strength, these forgotten images of her early days in Penang gradually crept up from a hidden corner and reclaimed their place in her memory. They would resurface at a squeak of a door, a waft of perfume, a glimpse of the setting sun. Like now. Snapshots of a whole salted fish, red curry, yellow cumin, smoky cauldrons, a sea of giggling girls in blue uniforms and rustling green leaves would flash in her head, one or two at a time, then flare up in fierce blaze, leaving only blinding red at the back of her eyes, her temples throbbing. Any place, any time, any picture. Once, in the middle of lovemaking, she glanced up from under Edward and saw on the grey ceiling the gawking eyes of the construction workers, the eyes that had once been glued to Miss Lambie, fixing on her – naked, panting with lustful joy. She faltered as the red flames smothered over her, and in the midst, her mother's last words before bed that night, almost pleading:

'I lost it; I lost the gold. Have you seen it, Jiaxi? Have you seen it? Please tell me you have, please!'

*

Yes, I have, Mum. Here it is. The answer she wished she'd given repeated day and night, in silence.

If only time could be reversed.

*

Her first month in Penang she spent drifting. From corner to corner, room to room. A stringed puppet moved in response to Lina Marshall's worried calls for breakfast, lunch and dinner (the kitchen and, on festive occasions or in the presence of guests, the dining room), shower (the bathroom), reading and listening to music and socializing, or pretending so (the drawing room), bedtime (her room – the place she most preferred, to hibernate in all by herself). Like an apparition, she sauntered in the bungalow, her home for five years to come. The Marshalls let her, allowing her her reticence, gracious time given for recovering from what they thought was solely grief, the real pain hidden in the deep abyss inside her.

They lived in the convenient neighbourhood of the school, quiet, secure, with mostly middle-class expatriates for neighbours. On the suggestion of her husband, Lina Marshall invited Miss Lambie to lodge with them. Tom's reason of 'keeping Jiaxi company, since they've acquainted over the sea journey' stood tall and undisputable. The couple even made special arrangements for the two younger girls to occupy the only two back-facing rooms next to each other, while the Marshalls took the master room with a front balcony.

Miss Lambie, indeed, did not disappoint them. To cheer her up, she invited Jiaxi to join her exploring their new environment. A girls' day out, she'd say. Long days spent wandering in the streets of George Town in a rickshaw, stopping occasionally to venture in and out of the shops to quench the older lady's curiosity at the sacks of plain white rice, black mushrooms, dried anchovies and salted fish – which she wouldn't touch – in the Chinese groceries; in the Indian stalls, though, she'd let her inquisitive fingers run in the mounds of curry powder, her paleness against the toned, bright yellow and red, and then playfully land her colourful palms on Jiaxi, who, to Miss Lambie's disappointment, was unresponsive. A killjoy.

In fact it was the older girl who needed company.

A first-timer in the colony, Miss Lambie would not hide her marvel at scenes she called 'exotic', unreservedly exclaiming at the sight of the bloody red pulp of betel nuts being spat on the ground, clasping her nostrils against the strong, acrid smell of shrimp paste with a hand, and with the other whisking off the choking smoke as they walked past roadside eateries. Once safe from the smell and the smoke, she'd laugh holding her chest. 'Oh my God!' Her chortle rang to the raised eyebrows of the Chinese shopkeepers, the Indian money-changers, and the sweaty, half-naked coolies at the construction sites from where buildings would mushroom on the fast-developed island. Even Jiaxi, buried deep in her sorrow, was mildly aware of her companion's waywardness, though unperturbed by it, mindlessly dragging herself along with Miss Lambie's games of colonial adventure.

*

Miss Lambie's unladylike manners had somehow alerted Mrs Marshall, even though she was the least alert sort.

'Shall we remind her?' At lunch one day during Miss Lambie's absence, Lina Marshall had suggested to her husband that their lodger should watch her behaviour: 'She is a teacher after all. She is to set a good example to the students.' The undertone of 'setting a good example to Jiaxi' was left unspoken.

'Young and lively, that's the way I see it.' The man of few words had assured his wife that it was merely the excitement of newness, of foreignness, and that it would subside as soon as the school started, when busyness took precedence, when a routine was to be observed.

Lina, trusting her husband's judgement as always, had dropped the matter.

*

Because she'd never had a formal education, it was arranged for Jiaxi to attend the class three grades below her age group. 'Allowing time for her to catch up' was her guardians' kind reason. She'd never fitted in, not so much because of the three-year gap, but because of her heart, tired like an old woman's. Every day she sat in a classroom full of young daughters of expatriates and wealthy Straits Chinese, Indian Chettiars and Malay blue bloods: a fourteen-year-old with incipient breasts among a group of chubby-faced eleven-year-olds; their strikingly white, immaculately tailored uniforms, their pure, innocent eyes, their careless, girlish giggles were constant reminders of everything she wasn't. She felt aged, filthy.

I have to get out of here! Inside she screamed, loud and furious; on the surface, she was composed, a young lady with demeanour so graceful that praises – from her teachers and acquaintances of her guardians – were made known to the Marshalls, who would nod at each other with a knowing smile, relieved for the decision that they had once worried was too hasty.

They didn't see the beast inside her, the frustration built on guilt, shame and self-denunciation. The beast that was twisting and turning at the bottom of the dark abyss, awaiting its chance to burst out. That would come alive in the deep of the night, gnawing at her, ripping her from her sleep. At first she would pace the room, hours spent going round in circles, barefoot on cool parquet, until her legs were sore and tiredness drowned her. When the Marshalls began to worry at the breakfast table of night noises that were, to them, signs of rat infestation, she took to sitting by the open window of her back-facing second-floor room – the wind in her loosened hair, the humming of insects in her ears – staring aimlessly out into the darkness. The night sky above, a black alley below, and right outside her window an old mango tree standing alone. Silhouette of rustling leaves, of branches stretched like lunatics in the occasional gusts from the open field beyond the barbed wire, where unknown night activities were taking place.

She wasn't afraid. Fear had been trapped outside a heart numbed by a more dreadful experience, by guilt and shame.

So she sat, alone, the night noises surprisingly soothing.

Sometimes she dozed off, only for the dawn chill to wake her, only to find the edge of the window frame indented on her cheek and her arms; but more often, only the first light on the horizon, the first cock-a-doodle-doo could end her waiting. But what was left to wait for? She'd stare blankly at the mirror as though looking for an indication, as she pressed a hot towel on her eyes in the morning prior to the start of the day, before disguising the remainder of the dark rings around them with the foundation powder Miss Lambie generously presented to her. And no, no answer would come in return from the equally empty face that appeared in the reflection.

In such a state of mind, she had, somehow, learned to carefully pad under her uniform and her samfu layers of undergarments, as her body grew skinnier, her collarbones protruding more with each passing day.

And a month passed.

An accidental discovery changed everything.

*

The back alley below Jiaxi's window was sandwiched between the row of bungalow houses and a long stretch of barbed wire fenced against the abandoned fields. During the day, mobile vendors in pull carts or simply with baskets in their hands, on their heads or backs, strolled along the narrow lane, calling out their wares to the women busy in their kitchens. Chillies, bananas, sweet cakes, morning glory, pak choi, long beans, chickens and ducks, eels and *kuning* fish, threads and buttons and needles, knives and scissors, or offering to sharpen knives and scissors. Shrill voices pierced the otherwise tranquil morning. There came the haggling: waves of noises undulating along the row of back doors. By then, the Marshalls had a maid to cook and clean and go to the market for them, and this faithful middle-aged Chinese amah would dutifully demonstrate her negotiation skills, shouting as loud as the sellers for one cent or two, less or more.

In the evening, when the last calls for bread and buns faded away, when the back doors were locked against stray cats and dogs – which were too many to be spoilt by the colonists who loved cats and dogs over their own species – the lane regained its peacefulness.

And alone in her back-facing room on the second floor, she would have it all to herself.

But not that very night.

It began with the turn of a key. A click. Light, careful.

The back door.

At first she thought it was Lina Marshall taking out the garbage, as the fish guts and chicken bones would decompose fast over a hot and humid tropical night, the stench unbearable. She'd seen it earlier after dinner, the bucket of waste, sitting next to the sink where Amah was busy washing dishes. The middle-aged woman must have forgotten, too eager to rush home to her family. *I should've done it for Mrs Marshall.* She bit her lip, ashamed, and sank in her chair by the window.

The loud thud of a metal bin against gravel that she anticipated never came. Intrigued, she straightened her back and stuck her head out from the inside dimness to the blackness of a moonless night. There were movements, under the mango tree, she was certain, but of what, it was too dark to figure out. *Thieves?* Vague snatches of tales overheard at mealtimes, of break-in robberies, possibly by poor immigrants, for food and cash, flashed through her mind. *Shall I alert the Marshalls?* She hesitated, afraid of making a mistake, making a fool of herself.

There was a light 'shh', followed by heavy breathing, the rustling of clothes. Some object leaning onto the tree.

Hands gripped tight at the window frame, Jiaxi pricked up her ears, could barely make out the hissing now, leaking through the quietness.

'Don't make a mess; it's my new dress.' A woman's muffled voice, truncated in parts, breathless.

A man's low, throaty 'Em, hm,' came in reply.

Jiaxi shrank back in: heart pounding, face burning.

It was Miss Lambie and Tom Marshall.

Everything became apparent. Her guilt-laden mind suddenly cracked open; episodes of the Marshalls' mealtime talks flooded in: the man's insistence that the woman lodge with them, his defending her inadequate behaviour, his blaming the night noises his wife pointed out to rat infestation. His thoughtfulness, his foresight, his judgement were, after all, a man's slyness wrapped in an affirming voice and a solemn outlook.

The next morning, Miss Lambie did not join them for breakfast as usual, content instead with an early coffee in her room delivered by Amah, another unusual habit, which Lina Marshall once indicated to her husband as impolite but was again dismissed. At the kitchen table, Jiaxi, for the first time, looked up from her plate. She peered over the *Prince of Wales Island Gazette* in Tom Marshall's hands to a man deeply immersed in his reading, focused, solemn, sharing a news item or two occasionally with Lina, who sat graciously by his side, ready to smile if he would. *What a man of respect! And what a happy couple!* She could almost hear the hilarious laughter inside her, and was suddenly relieved.

She remembered the story from the *Book of Ghosts* about a creature who wore a painted human shell, and transformed itself into a beautiful woman so as to live in the human world. Men blinded by its charming appearance were lured into its bed, their essence extracted to enhance its beauty. The more victims hunted, the more human it seemed to become; yet still, the inhuman self underneath grew uglier, the urge to kill stronger. She shuddered. The tale she once convinced herself to be merely a tale seemed to have enacted itself in another form in real life. She thought also of the Western folklore, the Red Riding Hood, of the wolf masquerading as a human, and wondered if it was a permanent fixture, either the painted shell or the grandmother-shaped wolf, that was draped over every man, every woman. *What is true self*? She no longer knew. She glanced at Lina Marshall, the calmness, the contentment on her face – was it the real her? What was Lina's story then, her shame, her wrongdoings, hidden from her, from Tom, from everyone else? She was convinced there must be at least one, if not two, or more.

Nothing mattered any longer. Nothing.

She could still live a life – like Tom Marshall, like Miss Lambie – that's what mattered.

The change was instant, dramatic, with careful measures to avoid attention.

She worked out a plan. After a month of daydreaming in the classroom, she began to absorb every word, every piece of information delivered. Like a piece of blotting paper, soaking up fast. Soon another sheet was brought forth, and another; never were they enough to quench her thirst for knowledge. She read ahead on the lessons before they were taught, memorizing the content. She avoided being too conspicuous though, never asked questions, never volunteered to answer. And so, to the teachers, including the Marshalls, it was a surprise too big to contain when, at the end of year, Jiaxi scored the highest marks in all subjects.

'Remarkable,' her class teacher commented, recommending her strongly for an upgrade after an unprecedented interview, in which she not only answered eloquently all questions asked, but also brought out her queries on matters never discussed in the class, much to the marvel of her interviewers.

It was a unanimous decision that she be immediately promoted to the first year of secondary school.

*

School, home, church. Her days rolled on to meticulously planned schedules. The additional painting lessons from Lina Marshall she obliged, the one-hour break from study a luxury she'd rather not have. *A waste of my already too-little time.* For the daily after-lunch session she dragged herself into the spacious drawing room; in a corner in front of the easel was the enthusiastic tutor immersed in her own excitement for art, next to her, the reluctant student, letting her brush muddle with colours, her mind with thoughts.

With idleness now laid out like a sieve, the noises from the dark she'd put behind sifted through the tiny fissures and claimed their place. As she mixed together oily pastes for sunset hues, as she watched the streaks of bloody red and bright orange interlace, she heard the suppressed sighs, Miss Lambie's, mingled with her partner's throaty grunts; standing there, her breath grew short, her face red, her heart beating faster, the movement of the brush in her hand even quicker, pressing hard and rapid on the canvas – all so conveniently mistaken by her proud teacher for artistic passion.

Images followed. They leaped on her canvas, the naked bodies she had secretly imagined, locking together, twisting and turning, their skins fair against the green of the meadow, the blue of the ocean, the blackness of night.

Any colour, any scene. The beastly groans and acts would spring up; the lustful faces appeared large and clear.

Soon they began to invade her at night, the images. The occasional tiny movement, the noises below the window she'd grown accustomed to were the triggers. As she conjectured the couple's every move, every joyous feeling they shared, the beast in hibernation raised its head in response, wriggling inside her, striving to fill up the emptiness that would not be filled up, leaving her restless, tossing and turning in bed, the tropical nights unbearably hot and long.

Lina Marshall did not once suspect her student's sudden interest in mushrooms, that she would tirelessly sketch them again and again, in different colours, at different scales, but stalks of stout fungal growth nonetheless. Always a single stem, strangely long, its head awkward. The phallic resemblance somehow escaped the tutor's innocent eyes.

*

'Too quiet, that's all she said.' Lina Marshall related words from her colleague, Jiaxi's class teacher, describing a lonely teenager without friends. The Marshalls had been discussing their charge's abnormality over their evening glasses of sherry.

'Not anything we haven't already known, isn't it?' Her husband considered it to be the girl's natural attribute.

'She should at least confide in me, shouldn't she? Never ever has she spoken of her mother. No, not her uncle, either.' Certainly not to Lina, a blow to her readily laid-out motherly love. She could understand if the girl was still in pain, her loss couldn't be replaced by any means; but her silence about it, the polite distance she kept from the person supposed to be the closest to her, pained her kind-hearted guardian.

'Could she be homesick?' Tom Marshall speculated.

Jiaxi, passing by the drawing room with its open door, overheard. *How absurd. Where is home, exactly?* She never knew. Her father's house in Pindong Town? Her uncle's mandarin residence in Lixing? The little courtyard her uncle rented for her and her mother in Pindong Town? None of these was hers. She'd been nothing but a parasite in those dwellings.

She laughed behind his back when later Tom suggested a trip *back* to Malacca. A reunion with her uncle, he thought, would do the young girl good.

The trip never materialized. Homework, exams; the reasons stood tall and undisputable. Once, just before the travel arrangements planned for the long year-end break were finalized, Jiaxi fell seriously ill: food poisoning. The sour milk she kept had worked to her purpose, to nobody's suspicion, certainly not the white-bearded Dr Fountain.

*

Alerted now, she began first to join in the circles of her fellow students, pretending to listen with patience to their small talk about sibling rivals, unreasonable mothers, the boys in the school next door, or their jealousy for their co-students. How petty, how childish. She'd then relate the stories over the dinner table, her listeners smiling and nodding, the label of NORMAL stamped down with a loud thump. Approved.

*

She wasn't pretending when she agreed to join the Sunday after-church class, looking up to Father Harold as she once looked up to Father Terry, her elementary English teacher. Sitting in the small, airy room, listening to the similarly gentle voice, a familiar feeling rose inside her. Time and space crossed over and in a blink, she was back in the white orphanage-and-church building on a hill in Pindong Town, the children crowding around her, Father Terry's kind advice ringing in her ears. When the moments passed, she opened her eyes to the caring gaze of another caring priest, and felt warm.

Having heard of Jiaxi's past misfortune from Mrs Marshall, Father Harold had been paying more attention to his new student. A brave girl she was, he noted, always composed, despite the tragedy she'd been through.

To the priest, the young Chinese girl's thirst for the knowledge of the West was a surprise, too: always asking questions, always wanting to know more. An ocean – borderless and bottomless – waiting to be filled up. New developments in education and stories of women's achievements, especially, excited her. He noticed the gleam in her eyes at his mention of Elizabeth Blackwell, the first British woman doctor, and the Bedford College for Women in London established by Elizabeth Jesser Reid, a keen promoter of women's education.

She's going to be someone special herself, this girl, he remarked quietly.

*

She wasn't pretending either, when she grew closer to Miss Lambie. Jean's carelessness, her bluntness, her daring secret night activities were attractions to a girl with a secret of her own. A dividing line drawn across, she leaped from the bright, clear upper half, down onto the other side: dark, bottomless. Free. Behind the closed door of the older girl's room Jiaxi smoked her first tobacco, learned to put on make-up, to practise kissing on an orange. She knew now, after her initial resistance, to consume substantial amounts of milk, freshly delivered from the farm every morning. Miss Lambie had proudly advised: 'If you wish to be like me,' her fully developed chest pushed out, a result not to be disputed.

Outside the room, the smell of tobacco extinguished, the talks about men and what they did with women hushed down. She was, again, an innocent middle-school student.

She'd never revealed to Miss Lambie, nor did she to Mrs Marshall, her discovery of the adulterous affair. That wasn't in her plan, the family a shelter too secure to be letting go.

*

Edward wasn't part of her plan.

She was sixteen, dutifully going to the church every

Sunday with the Marshalls though she'd rather not, her studies being her only concern. But she didn't mind it that morning, doused in blissfulness. The day before, she received her end-of-year result, the first of the top positions she'd maintain throughout secondary school. A big first step towards her plan. She was quietly elated. A delicate white laced dress, a present from Lina Marshall, was her means of celebration, her usual pair of dull samfu put away. At the mass she sat next to the Marshalls in the middle row, the blunt morning sun of the tropics falling through the tinted glass of the high windows onto her, a brilliant glow. She closed her eyes; her youthful face, slightly tilted up, taking the light in full, was radiant with long-lost excitement.

She was being looked at. She felt it, the burning heat of the gaze somewhere from the right corner, intensifying with every passing minute. She felt the blaze on her right cheek, the itchiness along her spine. She felt her ears turning red, her legs stiffening. She wanted to fidget, wanted to shake off the stare, wanted to hide under the pew or simply walk away. She couldn't.

She held her breath, frozen.

'I didn't think you would turn round.' Edward brought it up months later, as he tucked his finger into the single dimple on her right cheek, the sight of it filled with the church sunshine vivid in his head.

So she did.

She waited until Old Mrs Dudley struck her fingers on the equally old organ, until the music and the hymn-singing rumbled and hovered and vibrated within the high marbled walls. She swung her neck and peered over the many heads buried in the open hymnbooks—

Blue, his eyes. An ocean undulating in the solemn white of the church hall.

It was that look – her boldness – that had encouraged him.

He was thirty-seven, Edward Hunt, newly arrived on the island, newly appointed assistant secretary at the Colonial Office. It wasn't difficult to locate the only Chinese foster child among the small circle of the expatriate community. The following week, in the name of his children, he invited all teachers and their families to a garden party in his ample mansion in Scotland Road.

The invitation arrived in a delicately designed white envelope; inside, a matching card embossed with roses at the corners, smiling out at her. *To Mr Tom Marshall and family.* She knew instantly what was to come, counting down the days.

Set up on the lawn against the blazing sun, the giant parasol trapped within it the stifling heat, the smells of tobacco and roast beef, the sweat and cologne and perfume, the cries of children in the peak of their excitement, the adults talking among themselves – all pressing onto her. *Where is he?* She stood on tiptoe, trying to catch her breath, trying to catch a sight of those blue eyes.

He wasn't there. The Marshalls were engaged in a conversation with her class teacher, yet again. *About me.* She slipped out of the crowd, walked across the green pasture and climbed the stairs into the house.

A hand reached out for her from behind the door, scooping her into the concealed corner, into a body, warm, sturdy, towering over and enveloping her. She closed her eyes, felt the heat radiating throughout her channels, did not flinch, did not make a noise. She'd been expecting it. His embrace, his wet lips on hers, his caress. The waves of tremor under her skin.

Outside, the party blared in the blazing sun, its din becoming distant, fading away.

*

It could have been anyone.

She got out of bed, rolled a cigarette from the tin box of tobacco Edward left on the dressing table, lit it with a match and curled up in the wooden rocker in a corner.

It'd been exhausting, the many roles she played. Like a chameleon, she draped on immaculately tailored skins for the right occasions to perfect her performance, switching seamlessly between a model student, a good team player in the sport field, a patient friend to ignorant school girls, and a demure, well-behaved foster daughter. Rules after rules. What to do and what not to. Even with Miss Lambie, however many cigarettes they had shared, she would not relax, always careful to let the older girl shine, herself tuned down in the guise of immaturity. All those, and the secret, the adulterous affair in the household, had left her tense and taut. Every night, restless and agitated, she stood in silence in front of the mirror and stared hard at it, the perpetual smile she wore during the day, and frantically rubbed and pulled at it, trying to smooth the skin out. Yet still, there were the tireless curves at the corners of the mouth, there was the single dimple on the right cheek, there was the polite, amiable young girl. *What have I become?* Beyond all those, she saw with acute clarity the beast of frustration waiting to burst out.

Edward relieved her. He unleashed the beast inside her.

He was surprised at her response, the intensity of it, as though she'd been expecting it, had been hungry for it. Hungry she always was in those precious meetings they managed; the animal inside her burrowed its way out, and she yielded her youthful body against his, as if trying to squeeze every remainder of energy out of him, of herself. She did not care to suppress her sighs and moans, did not succumb to Edward's occasional worried glances, her lustful enjoyment let out in full against the abundant silence. There was nothing else to pretend between two naked bodies, in those beastly primitive acts. She felt liberated; her real self stood up in triumph.

'What kind of creature are you?' He was amazed, deeply obsessed with her. He would, after their lovemaking, lie close to her, his face on the curve of her neck, and stroke her hair, loosened, cascading on her spindly back. He would watch the smooth contour of her body rise and fall as she heaved, recovering.

He would puzzle at how, when they met on occasions during the day, she was again the shy and polite teenager, a face of youthful innocence. Never seemed awkward, embarrassed.

'How many faces do you have?' once he asked, fingers fiddling her cheeks, still plump with girlish chubbiness.

'One. For you.' Her index finger landed on the sharp tip of his nose. His pupils widened with touched passion, and he took her finger in his mouth, tasting the softness of her skin, before landing his body on hers. Afterwards, as she lay face down, heart still pounding, body sticky with sweat and secretion, she squinted at the man lying next to her and realized she'd never loved him.

*

She had been a failed actor in front of her uncle.

She puffed another mouthful and stared at the smoke swirling before her. In the dissipating blue there was a face: contorted, a tinge of sadness in the eyes.

Uncle Mingzhi's.

The man she'd escaped from, unable to face him five years ago, and now, still.

She thought of his rambling, the restless fingers that knuckled the table, the stooped figure wrapped in the yellow of the hurricane lamplight, almost fading in it. 'I'm leaving' were the words she decided not to tell him.

Their meeting only confirmed the fact she had already known: she would never be able to face him.

*

After the garden party, she met Edward's wife a few times at the church. She would approach the older woman while Edward, standing to one side, watched on, alert. She would exchange smiles and pleasantries with her – pale-faced and innocent – and a sense of triumph mingling with sympathy would linger inside her. But not guilt; it never was.

Three years. Another puff, and the world before her was a smoky blur, like her life, this affair with Edward.

Outside, a cat let out an angry grunt, another followed, louder, overwhelmed, and the two mingled in shrilling shrieks as the fight began. She did not budge, did not shoo them away as she always did. She sat.

The room, hidden in an alley among abandoned warehouses, was rented by Edward. 'Safe from the eyes and ears,' he'd said. For three years they met regularly, she with excuses of spending time with her school friends much to the delight of her guardians – another sign of normality – and for him, with his position at work, there were plenty of reasons at hand to pluck from: meetings, entertaining delegations, urgent matters needing immediate attention, or something of these sorts. Plagued with a perpetual migraine, his wife, a quiet woman two years his junior, was interested neither in his work nor in the social engagements an official's spouse was sometimes expected to attend. She was glad to be left alone to tame the invisible drill behind her temples, their two children enough to add to her torment, the duty as a wife in the bedroom neglected.

Jiaxi tucked her dressing gown tighter around her, decided she would remain there, dawn only a few hours away. With the Marshalls now gone, only she and Miss Lambie occupied the big house, so she cared less.

Edward would never stay over, however intense their coupling, however passionate he could be, and she had never asked him to, the unspoken fact laid bare between them: his family was a responsibility he would never let go. It was justified, she thought, that she did not tell Edward of her plan, one that had been patiently executed for five years. She did not tell him when Father Harold, with her straight A results at hand, agreed to utilize his resources and later secured for her a precious place at London's Bedford College for Women. On her request, and with Father Harold's promise, everything was done in secrecy.

She would put the piece of gold to good use, she'd decided five years ago.

Jiaxi lit another cigarette and snuggled up in the chair like a cat. The night would not be long.

3

The Meeting

He let the rickshaw take him through the unfamiliar streets of George Town. Light spilt out from windows open to darkness, splashing yellow patches onto the night screen: warm, soothing. He noticed none of them. *Jiaxi.* He sighed as he realized he knew nothing of her still, of how she'd been living her life and what her plans would be, if she had any. Neither had he had the courage to broach it, the suggestion that had been in his head since the meeting was arranged – *Come with me, Jiaxi. Let's go home* – silenced in his throat.

A jerk, and the rickshaw stopped in front of a mansion. The meeting had begun. Invitation – under Uncle Lau's name – tendered at the door, careful answers made in response to a barrage of questions, and Mingzhi was allowed in. The room was full. Men in Western suits filled the chairs around the long rosewood table in the middle, in double or triple layers and in every possible space, their hair combed down, short and neat. He sneaked in, unprepared for the sight, feeling as though his plait, his new gown had suddenly swollen up, conspicuous; he stooped further as he found himself a vacant stool in a corner.

'. . . For twenty years we've been fighting' – standing at the far end of the table, the speaker, Dr Sun Yat Sen, glanced around the room – 'and defeat after defeat we've encountered. The failures only strengthened our determination, because we're doing this to save our people, to save our country.'

Mingzhi fixed his eyes on the great man, sailed purposefully from the land he had left behind. It was the medical practitioner turned revolutionist's first trip to the island, with a mission of setting up a foundation in the region, to gather support and sympathy from overseas Chinese.

'I believe some of you here would feel it more deeply, my fellow countrymen. It is because of the Qing, it was their cowardice, their incompetence, their brutality, that you're here in exile. For centuries we Han Chinese have been enslaved by the Manchurians, discriminated against, tortured, killed.' The room fell into a silent pause, the air heavy with sadness and indignation. They had certainly felt it, some of the attendees, the victims of the Qing's evil deeds, forced out of their country which they were forbidden to leave. And so, click, click, click, the door closed and locked behind them. Outside, they wandered, country-less, the key to their home inaccessible because there wasn't one. Like the spirits of those who have suffered untimely deaths, trapped in the underworld, drifting, sauntering. They looked down at the bodies that once housed them, lying still and stiff, so close and familiar, yet they were unable to re-enter them, nor were they able to be reincarnated, to live again, rightfully, as humans.

Like me.

In his corner Mingzhi shrank further. Perhaps it was the heat that rose and simmered in the enclosed room, his eyes were moist and blurred, and in a trance, he saw her, Jiaxi, between the bodies now kept straight and still below bowed heads, laden with emotion. He caught a glimpse of her white dress, the silky lace, the gleam of her hairpins. Walking away now, a flash of white disappearing into a doorway – but which one? Doors kept slamming and shutting, and there was only one wide open, bright, inviting, heading westwards. *No!* She didn't hear him, she didn't care to stop and listen, she didn't care to turn back. She didn't care if the rest of the doors were closed behind her. *No!*

A thunderous roar burst in his ears, a powerful voice from the front; he woke as the crowd began to stir.

'The same monster, ironically, would turn into a tiny meek lamb in front of the foreign powers.' No more Jiaxi, no more white dress. Only him. 'Such cowardice, such shameful Opium Wars, such humiliating fall of the Forbidden City. Treaty after treaty. Our money handed out, our lands signed over: Hong Kong and Burma for the British, Russia has taken the north-eastern region, the Japanese Taiwan and Liaodong. And more: French, Portuguese, German, Austrian, Dutch, American.

'They've made the Qing their slave, and we, the people, only find our lives more miserable, more intolerable.'

Focused fully now, he straightened his back, head tilted towards the only man who stood, the only sound in the room.

'It is our duty to save our country, to stop the humiliation, to liberate China from the foreign powers. To achieve this, we must first reform the nation.'

Dr Sun further explained how the doctrines he'd been championing, the Three Principles of the People –

Nationalism, Democracy and Welfare for the People – would work. The people are the most important entity in a country, he said. 'To summarize, it would be a government by the people, for the people. The rise of nationalism would free the people from imperialist domination, and together the people would rule in a government elected by the people in a democratic system like those in the West. A government by the people would then take good care of the livelihood of the grassroots in terms of food, clothing, housing and transportation.'

Mingzhi was intrigued. *Can the people really have the ability to rule themselves? How does that work?* Two thousand years now since the first Emperor, Shih Huangdi, unified the land, and there had always been a Divine ruler. A king, an emperor, the son of the dragon. His words were the orders of the Heavenly King. Mingzhi listened as the leader of resistance condemned the Qing Court for neglecting the people. The new government he envisaged, he stressed, should be one that put the people's lives, their wellbeing, in the uppermost priority.

'It's time for us to bring down the corrupt monarchy!' Dr Sun ended his speech.

'How about the Emperor? Aren't we supposed to restore him once Empress Dowager has been ousted?' From the table an elderly man with silver hair raised the questions.

Those seated at the table, he noticed, appeared elegant in their silk suits; the gold chains of their watches hung shining and important on their chests. They were among the richest in this land, their words weightier than those of the others in the room. He'd heard some of the names from Uncle Lau. Some of them were the *peranakan*, persons born and bred in this earth, who had spent time here long enough to receive education, to amass wealth and respect. Being the biggest and most far-reaching grain trader in the region, Uncle Lau would have been among them if he had come. He would have pointed out to the younger man the faces associated with those names.

Outside the encirclement of the table, sitting on the stools as he did, Mingzhi conjectured, were newer migrants. Clean and tidy though they were, their clothes appeared dull, creased and discoloured in parts, their chain-watches, if they wore one, lacklustre. Scholars turned teachers with meagre incomes who had earned their places with their elitist background, or poor peasants or roadside hawkers turned labourers turned traders, the old habit of thriftiness persisting despite their upgraded status and newfound prosperity. Once a scholar then a mandarin and now a business man, he was neither; a crossover. Not this, not that; not here, not there. He always was.

Reactions came from all over the room. 'The evil woman was the source of all calamities,' another at the front row echoed the elderly man, insisting that dethroning Empress Dowager would be enough to restore order. 'What country would it be without an Emperor? How could we abandon the son of the dragon? How could we desecrate him?'

Another followed immediately: 'It was Emperor Guangxu who supported the reformation in 1898, remember? He supported Liang Qichao and Kang Youwei. Yes, it only lasted a hundred days; yes, he's been ousted.

But he did try. And he wouldn't have been put under house arrest if he was without conscience!'

A few others agreed, proposing a constitutional monarchy instead, the Emperor's previous support for reformation not to be forgotten.

'I've had enough of the Qing Court!' A voice, deep and poignant, rose from among the less prominent crowd in a corner. 'They tore my family apart, destroyed my life into pieces.'

On his feet now, the man rolled up his sleeves, revealing the criss-crossed scars of old welts on his arms: flesh parted and squeezed out in lines of dark red, like earthworms, wriggling on dry barks that had ceased to plump up in spite of the prosperous later years. The room rustled in suppressed sighs: hands on the mouth, heads down, then silence. He'd been a market trader; a few bolts of textile a day were just enough to feed the family, who had never complained. Catastrophe befell him when, after failing to satisfy the town's organized gang, he had suddenly found himself in jail; he realized much too late that the local officials were collaborators of the criminals. Six years later he stepped out of the prison only to be told his wife had died – with their unborn child – of illness, his mother of suicide, too old to fend for herself.

The man, his throat constricted, sat back down; he stared into his wrung fingers and spoke no more. But not the crowd. More stories of a similar sort were brought out, their own or others'. High and low voices in anger, indignation and sadness bounced and hummed within the four walls of a room sealed for secrecy. Mingzhi peered at the man with welted scars and saw the tears at the corners of his eyes. He thought of the evacuees on the ship he boarded five years ago, their tales all so alike, familiar. 'Don't you know how to make money for yourself? All mandarins do!' his former superior, the district governor, had told Mingzhi when he was newly appointed a mandarin. The officials' underground activities had been unspoken facts.

Dr Sun seized the opportunity.

'We want a China for all Chinese. Not Han or Qing, but everyone in our motherland regardless of his ethnic background. Democracy is the only way forward. Only a constitutional government run by the people will serve the people and serve them well. The country belongs to the people, and it should thus be governed by the people, for the people.

'And you – are the people!'

The elderly man at the table, a supporter of an imperial court, stood up abruptly and left the room in a huff. Immediately there was a fluttering of clothes, more getting on their feet, bolting off. But there were more staying put, simmering in a room swollen with patriotic heat. Feet were stamped, allegiance pledged to the nation, blood and sweat and money promised to the leader of revolution. Around him, there were eyes red with excitement, with hope, necks strained with determination, voices hoarse with passionate shouts of 'Down with the Qing!' 'We want democracy!'

Mingzhi's long-lost patriotism sprung up alive and alert, charging towards him, boiling inside him. He found himself on his feet, shouting along, already at the top of his voice, fists thrusting, spittle frothing. An overpowering shoo from the front hushed down the clamour and a committee was quickly formed, important positions filled by the prominent figures at the table.

A donation box was being passed around; cash and bank advices flopped into it in succession. He wrote a note endorsing a sum so big his hands shook.

*

The boat he booked was to set sail to Malacca the next morning. He lodged in a cheap hotel frequented by travelling salesmen, another recommendation from the trader he had acquainted. A sweltering night in a fast-growing town on a small tropical island, a narrow whitewashed room with a small window opened out to the wall and windows of another building. No trees, no wind.

The planks of wood creaked under his feet, and it came into his head: the stilted shelter by the river. The Fisherman's Hut. The night breeze in the swaying coco-nut palms, the noises of insects, of chickens and ducks. Jiaxi sweeping the front clearing with palm fronds. Meilian feeding the fowls. Their faces intersected, then merged, flaring up in a fire so fierce, so red that he closed his eyes. When he opened them again, they were gone. No Meilian, no Jiaxi. Only him in an unfamiliar hotel room in an unfamiliar place in a land still alien to him.

The night he spent at first dismissing 'friendly' calls at the door, girls in gaudy samfus and thick powder offering cheap companionship. Whiffs of crude perfume lingered long after they left, titillating his nostrils. When he finally stopped sneezing and settled on the hard mattress, Tiansheng's face rose from the ceiling, loomed

176

large in the darkness. He thought of his friend's wordless stare when told of Mingzhi's trip northwards. His body turned clammy in a sudden cold spell. *How am I going to tell him about the donation? What will he think of it?*

4

Tiansheng

The procedures were simple:

> Step One: Pull hard at the rope and send the basketful of merchandise up, levelling it with the second-floor storage.
> Step Two: Secure the knot.
> Step Three: Climb up the stairs.
> Step Four: Haul the load onto the platform.
> Step Five: Unleash the basket and keep it in place among the existing stock.

Tiansheng sat at the top of the wooden stairs, panting and fidgeting in his shirt, sticky with sweat. He pulled it off, wiped his body with it, cursing the heat in a quick mutter that sounded more like a grunt. All the new stock was now stored and settled, but not the procedures; they rolled up in his head, flashing in bright light, one after another. Even in his sleep, even in his dream, they would come to him. Once he'd woken to find himself pulling his bed sheet as if hauling the pulley.

There were more of his work schedules: opening the shop first thing in the morning, sorting out goods to be despatched, taking them down, packing and loading them onto the carts that would send the merchandise away, attending to collectors throughout afternoon and evening, storing the stock, closing the shop. Each task had its own steps to follow. For five years he'd been repeating the acts, day and night, up and down, in and out, as merchandise came and went, the day passed and a new one edged in. He'd been managing well, with or without assistance.

Today, he had been doing it single-handedly and an exhaustion he had never experienced assaulted him.

The load had come in late. The casual worker he engaged had left for the evening. He would have called out for Mingzhi if he were there, two streets away at the Baba Lodge. *What's it about, the trip to Penang?* He had overheard vaguely, during Uncle Lau's visit, of a revolution, of the fighting against the Qing. Not much did he get out of it, for another deal was waiting, and he had to rush out, to work on it, to bring home money. *What revolution?* A slight pain rose from the small of his back, not threatening yet titillating. *Never before.* He straightened his torso, his hand reached out, rubbing.

Business was brisk, he knew, but the competition was still strong; that he knew also. There was Baba Lim gearing up for a comeback, there were small collectors racing to becoming wholesalers, there were the underground transactions requiring his constant attention. There shouldn't be a moment of slackness; an oversight would put them back to zero. He had been alert and in control.

In control he was, and beginning to become aware of it. Because of Mingzhi's reticence, preferring to retreat to the background, to visit the forest instead of the shop, he had to step forward, standing at the front.

For the first time in his life Tiansheng made decisions:

from as small as prices for a *kati* of rattan or camphor, to as big as taking over the Baba Lodge. He had forged ahead with the secret deals Mingzhi would not get involved in, pushing past the man who had always been the decision maker. No, no longer an opera apprentice, no longer a dock worker, no longer someone's assistant. The past had frothed away in the days when the ship he boarded droned forward. Bubbling off. The ocean was the divide; a swift cut, and here he was, Taukeh Tiansheng, one of the town's fast-growing entrepreneurs.

For the first time he was being looked up to; his words carried weight.

For the first time, his head held high, he gave instructions to workers, collectors of rattan and camphor, spelling out rules and restrictions, specifying requirements: what kind of rattan to collect and what not to.

For the first time he was listened to. A person, standing tall, complete and full, only here in this land. There would be no looking back; association with the place where he'd been a nobody was the last thing he wanted.

His friend's trip to the north had been troubling him.

Had he been informed earlier, he could have made arrangements for a business scouting in the north – checking out possible business partners, getting contacts and connections – an expansion he thought was right for the time, having drawn the conclusion from queries brought back by travelling salesmen. But the travel arrangement was made known to him only hours before the departure. *It was intended!* He was certain.

The air was laden with the smells of the jungle, the soil and mud and leaves, especially strong at the end of the day when the shop was loaded with forest produce.

He reached over for the bottle of wine kept on the shelf next to the stairs and took a mouthful, felt it burn his throat, his stomach, and he closed his eyes, relaxed. He had another gulp, then replaced the cap, tightened it. Two swigs, only two swigs, his reward after a day's work, another procedure ingrained in him.

A vague tune wafted through from outside the shop. Across the road a busking musician sat on the pavement playing his flute, long, trembling notes of sadness threading through the crowd noise.

The music.

Tiansheng choked on his wine and coughed ferociously, almost out of breath. Eyes bleary now, he saw a slow, gurgling river by a bamboo grove, two seated figures, small and lean, and in between them, a crouching dog. He heard the incessant talks between them, him and Mingzhi in their teens, on their first encounter in Plum Blossom Village.

'Little Sparrow? How strange your name sounds.'

'The manager chose it for me. Good for the stage, he said. If I were to choose my own name, it would be Tiansheng.'

'Tiansheng? Without a surname? Why? How about the name given at birth?'

'*Tiansheng*, from the sky, from nowhere. Just right for someone like me, without a home to return to.'

'We are friends now. My home would be yours too. I'll see to that.'

He saw his younger self shake his head, and Mingzhi, becoming anxious, grip his shoulder: 'Trust me! I mean it,' eyes bright and wide with sincerity.

The tune stopped abruptly in a tumult: the sound of

a man shouting abuse, complaining about the music. He did not look up, did not stir. Soon there were the heavy, dragging footsteps of the elderly busker, fading away. The roomful of roots and wood, the smells of forest soil and green that had come with it, pounced on him once again, even stronger.

It had been a gradual process, the void of words between him and Mingzhi, unnoticeable. Perhaps it was the workload to begin with, perhaps it was something else, and as days went by, once it was established, the guessing game came to take its place. He'd been trying to comprehend the occasional strange gaze his friend darted at him, the quiet moments Mingzhi spent contemplating the accounts, the whitewashed walls, the blank pages on the desk, as if conversing with them. Anything, just not him. And now, his trip to Penang. *Revolution? I hope not! No, never for me.*

For certain, Mingzhi would pay a visit to Jiaxi; about that, he would not worry, would be relieved. But why bother? He knew of letters being returned, news of her being withheld. Privately told to him, tales from the travelling salesmen Mingzhi entrusted with the letters described a young girl, aloof and indifferent, offering few words of courtesy, almost unfeeling. He wasn't surprised: her suspicious glance thrown at his back had not escaped him. Jiaxi had never liked him; he was fine with that, but her uncle she should at least show respect to. How ungrateful.

There was a sudden crackling over the roof; a swarm of sparrows noisily rushed past. His thoughts halted, but not the unsettling feelings, growing even heavier inside him. He needed to do something, something else that was not work. He got to his feet and put on his shirt, his once delicate fingers clumsy with the cotton buttons. 'Useless!' Cursing, he gave up, leaving the last two un-buttoned, and went down the stairs. Reaching for the loose, individually numbered planks at both corners of the shop entrance, he secured them onto the door frame. Click, click. Two large-sized padlocks over the latches, not one to be missed; the procedures swam in his sub-conscious.

*

'Dinner now?' Amah Feng greeted him as he entered the Baba Lodge, eager to wrap up the day. Her own dinner at home with her family had been delayed by her master returning later than usual this evening.

Tiansheng scowled at her slightly higher tone, at the maid's anxiety and displeasure. He waved her off. He would be going out, he said, the food was hers to take home. Amah Feng grunted, 'Yes,' and quickly walked away, didn't seem to be pleased either. *Could have told me earlier, could have saved me all the cooking, be home sooner* – he stared at the back of her head, at the long, black plait, swaying against the shapeless white samfu like a wriggling scorpion as she swayed away, reading her mind. Braised pork and roast chicken, dishes prepared at his order this morning, would now grace the table usu-ally dulled with pickled cabbage and free *kangkong* from the paddy fields. *What else does she wish for?* He shook his head, pulled off his shirt again, heading to the bathroom.

The west-facing bathroom was a steaming cauldron, bulging with the afternoon's heat. The first pail-full scorched him. The sunshine, falling through the wide, square-wired window, had been full-faced on the water for half the day; its hotness outlived the rays, which had faded an hour ago. He stuck his hand into the giant vat and stirred the water, felt the relative coolness at the bottom half. He dropped the pail and climbed into the earthen urn, telling himself he would remind Amah Feng to change the lot. He imagined the middle-aged woman grumbling under her breath, her mouth twisted this way and that, disgruntled. Even in his presence.

She'd never behaved so in front of Mingzhi, he'd noticed. Always polite, always quick to attend to her other master's orders that came rare and simple. Of course, his friend would never climb into the water tank, would never make a mess of it, of everything else.

A deep breath and he immersed himself completely in the water. One, two, three, four, five, six . . . At one hundred and twenty he re-emerged, his mouth wide open, gasping for air. *Two minutes*. He would go for three next time.

His neck rested on the edge of the vat, he closed his eyes, his body kept still, and he felt the slight current he'd stirred up, the soothing sensation of the water. All he needed was so little, a moment of relaxation after a day's hard work. On a bad day like this, he would need more, some comfort, and knew where to get it from.

He took a deep breath, took another dive. This time his limbs turned soft, almost weightless, cocooned in the water as if in a woman's embrace. Peony's arms, boneless, cuddling him. The backs of her hands on his chest. Her fingers stroking his thighs. He felt between his legs the gradual hardening. The new girl he had grown fond of, young and almost innocent, was unexpectedly attentive during his last visit, unusually passionate though inexperienced still, despite the intensive training from Madam Lim. The generous tips he had rendered to the Madam the trip before had done the trick. *My last visit!* He lost hold of his breath and water gushed in. Too slow in raising his head, he choked, stumbling to get on his feet.

Standing, he kept coughing, kept exhaling to clear his lungs. It made sense now, as he remembered Amah Feng, first puzzled, then sidling away awkwardly, when he met her during his last visit to Madam Lim's Chamber, a few doors away from the maid's home. It was another evening on which dinner was untouched, packed for Amah's children. She must have speculated on his move tonight, thinking of him preferring to dine in a brothel, served by whores. It made sense now, the tinge of scorn on her face, avoiding direct eye contact with him as though he were contagious.

The sound of the main door thumped shut. *Amah Feng.* He imagined the maid rushing home to eat a hurried dinner (the tastes of braised pork and roast chicken escape her), then ushering her family and possibly her neighbours as well to gather behind the window, waiting for him to pass by, to confirm her speculation.

'Look, Master Tiansheng! On his way to Madam Lim's Chamber!' He imagined men and women and children peering out from behind the curtain, hands on their mouths, sniggering at him. *Damn it!* He climbed out of the water in a swift movement. His earlier enjoyment of the bath fast evaporated like his dripping footprints on the cemented floor, the dark wetness disappearing in minutes as he strode out of the bathroom. He would change his plan tonight, he decided. Embarrassment wasn't on his mind, only anger. It would be a humiliation, becoming the object of street gossip from the mouth of his own servant.

*

At Wongs' Eatery, he occupied a table specially laid out by the middle-aged owner, in a corner hidden behind a pillar, the usual seat he would have when his other business deals were to take place there over a meal. Tonight he was alone, and pleased with the arrangement still. It was a strategic location, dark and secluded, and he could take in the full view of the small diner, even the kitchen, without being noticed.

Business was brisk, tables filled, the din of the diners trapped under the low attap roof mingling with the heat, the smells of food, the smoke of the wood fire from the open kitchen close to his view, the odours his to carry home. Instinctively he patted his new change of shirt, whisking off the invisible dirt he abhorred.

He took a sip of his tea and choked at the overwhelmingly strong taste, the crudeness. He thought of the braised pork and roast chicken Amah Feng and her family were having.

'Is everything all right?' Old Wong's over-smiling face emerged from behind the pillar. 'Some wine for you?' Ignoring Tiansheng's head-shaking, Old Wong turned and gestured at his daughter, helping in the kitchen: 'Ah Mooi, get my special wine for my special guest!'

Tiansheng shook his head again, a sigh. *Shouldn't have come here.* In minutes, he knew, the poor girl would obediently bring him the wine, her shy head almost hidden in her chest, her hands shaking as she filled his cup, as she, too, well knew of her father's intention, the young man an ideal suitor. 'Not to be missed, not to be missed,' Old Wong had been exhorting her. For your own sake, he had said, a better life the girl's ultimate reward.

He waited until she'd finished before rapping at the table, a silent thank-you. He could have played a trick, could have said something and then watched the girl jump like a startled lamb, her face – already blushed – redder, the wine spilt. Even just a stare, gluing on her. He did neither, fixing his gaze instead at the clear liquid in front of him, not in the mood for a game tonight.

'Taukeh Tan, this way. Taukeh Chong has been waiting for you!'

Old Wong ushered his guest to a table not far from Tiansheng's. He shrank further behind the pillar, not in the mood either for a chat with Grocer Tan and Farmer Chong, once his neighbour at the Fisherman's Hut.

'Are you sure about it?' Grocer Tan's voice was pitched high in excitement.

'Shh—'

Tiansheng pricked up his ears.

'This is between us.' Farmer Chong lowered his voice. 'I only share this opportunity with you. You don't want to just hold on to the small grocery for the rest of your life, do you?'

His chair moved closer to the pillar, just six feet away from his targets, Tiansheng eavesdropped on Farmer Chong's plan to purchase the land next to his farm and turn it into a plantation.

'I know someone who knows someone. Malay land or

not, the paperwork can be sorted. Good piece of land that is, hilly and all that, just the right sort.'

Rubber they were talking about, he was certain; the world around him had been crazy about it. Uncle Lau had recently had his lot by the edge of the jungle cleared, the seedlings ready to be planted. Time to diversify his business, he'd said. Even Ah Lim, the goldsmith next to his shop, was now quietly rushing for the new treasure, having thirty acres at hand to begin with. Another neighbour, another story of the same sort. He took a sip of tea, leaving the wine untouched, and sat back. Yet Farmer Chong was no longer whispering; his excited voice found Tiansheng on the other side of the pillar.

'Ten years I've been there and have seen no one working on the lot. What a waste. After all, who cares? People are fleeing the village – can't get much fish nowadays, can they? You should see the river – a ditch is more like it – all cluttered up with mud and sand and all that.

'I told you before and I'm telling you again: don't be put out by the paperwork, because I'm not. Anything is possible here. Only the capital I'm worried about. If I had all the money, Ah Tan, I wouldn't have sat down with you here. Think of the rubber. Think of how well they're doing in Negeri and all that. We have to move fast before someone else gets it.'

A detailed plan was broached, the exact location of the plot of land, the names of the persons who would liaise for them, the reward they asked for.

Tiansheng pulled his chair further away from the pillar, agitated as he'd been when the same subject was raised by Uncle Lau months ago. A risk worth taking, the older man had kindly advised, and Martin's howl had rung abruptly in Tiansheng's ears: *Rubber, I said rubber!*, clear and loud. 'No!' He'd risen suddenly only to find Uncle Lau sat across the table, jaw dropping, petrified.

He pushed away his tea and took a mouthful of wine. To venture into rubber was to admit his fault, to recognize Martin's foresight. A defeat. Rubber or not, they had a business that was their pride, still strong, still growing. He gulped down another cupful and hissed under his breath: 'To hell with rubber!'

A business expansion was all they – he and Mingzhi – should work on, pushing beyond Britain. America perhaps, the Golden Land. He would talk to his friend upon his return from Penang; he would need Mingzhi to draft letters. His own elementary English for a quick note of 'Rattan: 100 pounds, camphor: 50 pounds' couldn't make up a proposal impressive enough to arouse interest, to strike a deal. He would need Mingzhi also to talk to Anan, to get more rattan out of the indigenous clan. The old man trusted no one but Mingzhi. Once in the early days Tiansheng had gone to the forest alone for their weekly collection, Mingzhi being busy, learning from Uncle Lau the export procedures, the delivery orders and invoices, the customs regulations. At the path near the indigenous dwelling, Anan, a full basket on his back, pushed past him, muttering: 'For Taukeh Chai only, for Taukeh Chai only.' Back at the Rats' Nest they shared at Grocer Tan's, empty-handed, he thought he saw a tinge of a smile on Mingzhi's face.

'Oh, Anan,' his friend said, attributing the Orang Asli's behaviour to loyalty.

'Stupidity and stubbornness are more like it,' Tiansheng grumbled; that he and Mingzhi were friends and partners was not unknown to Anan. Mingzhi did not reply, turned around, hiding his frown.

He had let Mingzhi take charge of the collections since. Always, on Mingzhi's return from the forest, there were tales, not much about the transactions but about Engi, Anan's son, who was seven years old then. Engi's new front tooth was visible under his gum; Engi caught a thrush today and made it sing for me; Engi made me a mini blowpipe and we shot rambutans with it; I taught Engi numerical tables, oh, you should hear him rattling them off in Mandarin, as accurate as any Chinese boy could be . . . Engi this, Engi that, during those days when the secret business hadn't begun, when they still talked, lying a foot apart on the floor at night, the rats scuttling across the corners.

That the boy could become a replacement for Jiaxi, he couldn't comprehend. A skinny rat, always covered in mud. Perhaps he reminded Mingzhi of the son he'd never had, a stillborn at birth, he'd heard, and his wife's life taken away with it. *But does he have to spend so much time with Engi?* Get a wife – that was all he should do.

They would talk.

He poured himself another cupful and emptied it.

A light thud. A plate of steaming fried noodles landed in front of him. Ah Mooi, even shier this time, bolted without the usual 'Enjoy your meal'. He smiled in amusement, shaking his head: *As though she was already my bride!*

Go-betweens had been frequenting the Baba Lodge lately, proposals of suitable girls laid out for his and Mingzhi's consideration. Daughters of businessmen, teachers, shop owners, persons with certain status, position- or money-wise; their dates of birth readily presented on request for matching, for a detailed consultation with a fortune-teller. He wasn't unmoved. Having someone to go home to, to seek comfort from, to start a family with, was a sure temptation. But the business had been tying him up tight all over like the rattan he dealt with, and he was unable to squeeze out any room for a proper consideration. Mingzhi, always at home, had been the one to face them; would pass on to him, when there was time, information about prospective matches. His friend had asked for none for himself, he knew, his wife's demise still a grief inerasable.

Grief. He glanced up. In the kitchen, between the cauldrons and woks, Ah Mooi's spindly body moved about in front of the flaring stove. She was adding pieces of chopped wood to the fire while her mother cooked, brandishing a slice in her hand, her slight figure an elongated shadow on the wall behind her, moving constantly. Adding oil, vegetables or meat or prawns, salt and pepper, water and sauces into the wok. Stir-frying, occasionally wiping sweat off her forehead, deformed feet struggling to stand on tiptoe. All so familiar. Black-and-white images of the past spurted out in the clattering fire, bright and vivid against the red flames. Another time, another woman; the place a kitchen shed at the back of the house. And he'd been the wood chopper, loads handed out to someone who would prepare a meal for him with them, who would sew for him shirts and socks, darn them when needed.

Meilian.

She would have been mine. If only time had permitted. It hadn't.

Somewhere inside him hurt. He looked away, dry-eyed. It was then he saw him, standing tall at the door, his head ducked slightly under the beam as he crossed the threshold.

Martin.

5

Martin

There was a rap at his table. Martin squinted up from his wine and wondered at the sudden dimness in the diner. *Where have the hurricane lamps gone?* In the weak glow of the lone light by the door, Old Wong, his smile stiff like a pasted-on layer of clay, gestured 'closed', his palms clasped with a loud 'pop' and then left folded upright in front of his chest like Buddha.

'So early?' Martin grunted, in near-perfect Mandarin, annoyed yet again at the owner for refusing still to speak the language with him. Old Wong pointed at the tables around him – all were empty, plates and bowls and the residue of food cleared away, chairs rearranged, the floor swept – then at the mother and daughter standing by the darkened kitchen, leaning against each other, exhausted, waiting to go home. He clasped his hands again, moving them back and forth repeatedly: 'please'.

Martin groped for his purse, dropped a few coins on the table, took a last gulp of the wine and got to his feet.

*

At the gate of the bungalow he stopped and lit his pipe. He took a few puffs leaning against the gatepost, peering out at the gloomy structure before him. The single-storey Victorian building crouched like a hibernating white lion against the even darker silhouettes of constantly rustling palms. The lights were out, not a trace of activities visible or possible, he was certain – and relieved. He dragged himself forward.

He pushed open the door and sidled into it.

'Where have you been?' Montgomery's voice rang through the darkness like a piece of cold metal, scratching across Martin's skin, covered in goose bumps now. He stayed close to the door, blinked a few times, and gradually made out the seated figure on the rocking chair.

'That's none of your business.'

'We're doing business together, and when you walked away while you were supposed to be working, that's my business. It was your job to supervise the weeding today!'

'Well, I did. I told them what to do.'

'And you expect those coolies to work their hearts out for you while you enjoy yourself somewhere else? You weren't there the whole bloody afternoon!'

Montgomery stood up in a swift movement, the chair swinging behind him, its curved wooden blades chafing against the tiled floor, making loud galloping sounds like a horse – gallop, gallop, gallop – echoing in the ample room. Martin, standing in the darkness, listened, wished he could just bolt away like a real horse. He closed his eyes. Gallop, gallop, gallop. A real horse he was, cruising on the prairie, borderless, limitless, the world under his hooves. But there were other noises, the crackling shot of a gun at his back, Montgomery's rattling:

'The whole place is going to be a jungle. We'll get nothing out of the trees. They won't grow with all the ferns and weed around. There won't be any milk to collect if we don't get this sorted out. Do you expect me to do everything all by myself? I've had enough up to my neck. We have a deal, remember? You are the plantation manager and you get into the plantation manager's shoes. Get the workers to do their job. Clear the weed, add fertilizer, make sure the drainage works properly.

'Another two years, I say, only another two years and we can start tapping the trees. Oh, for Christ's sake, Martin. You wanted it. You asked for it. Now just stick to it, will you?'

I can't, he muttered in his heart.

In the faint moonlight filtering through the wide window, he saw Montgomery approaching, his shadow a shuffling patch of blurriness on the wall. Martin retreated; his back banged against the door and he wrenched it open and walked out, Montgomery's angry bellow locked behind him.

Outside, the palm trees planted as sunshades lined up before him, their fronds spread out like giant fans, throwing even bigger black shadows on the ground. Long arms reached out for him from above and below, and he stood inside their encroachment, enclosed and sealed in it. Like a prisoner. He held his head, his thumbs kneading his temples.

This morning he woke before daybreak to birdsong outside the window, and occasionally the cries of monkeys, the howls of stray dogs, scratching the darkness in eerie high pitch: the usual sounds of dawn. But there was something else, vaguely coming through from a farther distance, over the fields and the layers of hills. Lying very still he heard the mysterious noise gradually getting louder, gathering shape as it approached, clattering across the still-sleeping outskirt.

The first train on the newly laid railway.

The engine of his childhood rumbled into his head. Again he was the trainspotter, peering from the rise, and then blundering down the slope, chasing after the fire dragon that would not stop for him. His footsteps getting slower and slower, he watched the snaky compartments wriggle further and further away, while he, small and helpless, stood panting, breathless. He watched on as they disappeared altogether, leaving a trail of white smoke in the sky, fast dissipating. Before long, there was nothing left.

Not a trace. Only him, a lone figure on the still warm track.

He sat up abruptly, his body dampened in a sudden spell of cold sweat. How ironic. He had waited so long, had fought with all his might to get out from the small house and the small town in which he'd felt suffocated years ago, only to be trapped in another. Willingly.

He buried his head under his pillow, clasping his ears tightly.

Afterwards in the plantation, a baton-for-support in his hand, eyes looking out for snakes and boars, he walked between rows of young trees, between the workers cutting overgrown weeds around the trees, their bodies rising and falling as they repeatedly wielded their machetes. Sharp metal brushed against soft grass, swish-swish-swish, swish-swish-swish.

He watched the moving figures around him, up and down, up and down – wordless, as they were told to be, and robotic. His pace quickened, his hand kept whisking off the wanton attacks of the mosquitoes. He chanted in his heart – *One two three four five six seven eight nine ten, one two three four five six seven eight nine ten* – counting his time away. One row passed, another ahead, and another. The bloodsuckers, wilder and ravenous after the downpour the night before, buzzed not only into his ears, but his head. *One two three four five six seven eight nine ten.* 'The morning will be over soon,' he mumbled. *One two three four five six seven eight nine ten.* Then the afternoon. *One two three four five six seven eight nine ten.* Ouch! He slapped his right cheek, and a dot of black lay flat in a pool of red on his palm. More were launching their attacks, on every inch of his skin where his long sleeves and trousers were unable to reach: his hands, his face, his neck, his ears.

How long do I have to do this – coming here every day, feeding the bloodsuckers? Months? Years? he grumbled. *One two three four five six seven eight nine ten, one two three four five six seven eight nine ten.* He was trotting now, the stick hanging loose in his hand, no longer watchful against reptiles or beasts.

One two three four five six seven eight nine ten, one two three four five six seven eight nine ten. Getting faster and faster. *One two three four five six seven eight nine ten, one two three four five six seven eight nine ten, one two three four five six seven eight nine ten.* Every step he moved, every corner he turned, there were the gruelling insects converging on him, there were the silent trees lurking like vertical bars in prison cells, there were the similarly uncommunicative workers immersed in the monotonous movement.

No! He dropped his baton and ran down the hill,

oblivious to the glances of surprise from his robotic troops.

*

Five years now he'd been stuck in this place, five years in the plantation and the bungalow and this bloody peninsula. The first couple of years he was exhilarated, tagging along with Montgomery like a shadow, his friend's palm oil plantation a live classroom, and he'd learned fast, picking up every practical tip, applying them later to the land dedicated to rubber. Getting the land cleared, ordering seedlings, potting them in the nursery, transplanting them.

He watched the trees grow, an inch, two, five, a foot, and felt his heart kicking. He stood in the wideness – the trees around him, acre after acre of his sweat and blood laid before him – and wept. Unlike the business he'd run for others, for the first time he foresaw the fruits that would be his, solid and tangible, and he saw them blossom in his hands, inch by inch; for the first time also he stamped on the soil that was (partially) his, firm under his feet.

A year passed, and another. And at the end of the third year, he was deflated, only his body dragging on. Days spent in the estate on endless rounds of inspections: pets, disease, irrigation, weeding. Works needed to be done, required execution: recruiting workers, supervising the tasks. A baton in hand, he raised his voice against the gobbledygook he could never understand from the first batch of the South Indian coolies they employed.

Never let them climb over your head! – Montgomery's foremost commandment stamped on his mind, Martin, as obedient as he could be, launched his instructions: 'Keep going; what are you looking at?' 'Lunch time!' 'Back to work, no talking!' 'Too slow; faster!'

He would trudge up and down the hills, tread the river – on foot (*Never ride in the plantation; never let the horse destroy the young trees!*) – parting long grass and wild bushes, negotiating rocks and stones as he went, watchful eyes combing for beasts and reptiles he still feared.

He covered miles on end; a hundred acres of land, once a pride, was suddenly a burden too much for his untrained legs. Sweat and heat brewed and simmered inside the layer of khaki wrapped up against the mosquitoes that swarmed around him buzzing 'boring, boring, boring' in his ears; a walking oven he became, roasting not only his own flesh, but his initial enthusiasm. Charred, cracked, crumpled.

Come evening, back in the bungalow, voice hoarse, body wrecked, the mind turned blank. Hungry for a place where Montgomery's orders and instructions were not the only sound, he would abandon dinner and nest instead in his wide, silent room, a bottle of whisky in hand. Only the bitterness, only the warmth that channelled into his sinews would arouse his senses, would remind him of his existence, before the total numbness took over.

Until he opened his eyes again, and another day was waiting.

And another.

*

The long, dragging hoot of a distant owl tore across the wood. He jumped, startled, suddenly aware of the humming of insects that was becoming louder, in greater density, and the thickening dampness that would turn into dew on the tips of the leaves in only a few hours. The night, deep and black, had been taken over by the unknowns, animals and others, lurking in the darkness.

He stood small among the palms, his six-foot figure shrunken against the giant fronds. The day's events wrapped into a heavy bundle of exhaustion, thumping down on him. Bed. He needed to sit down, to sprawl on a soft mattress.

He took another glance at the white lion behind him, alive now with a single eye that glowed in the yellow hue spilling from one of the windows. Montgomery's room. He thought of the man lurking behind the shutters, his watchful eyes. He decided he would not go back in tonight.

Where will I go?

Certainly not Mingzhi and Tiansheng's Baba Lodge. He hadn't seen them for years.

The first year after the fire he met Mingzhi occasionally – behind Tiansheng's back – usually in a small coffee shop in a quieter side of the town, where they were certain their other friend would not visit. A pot of tea still, the same *pu'er*, but the taste, somehow, had felt different, oddly weak. Was it the water or the leaves? Or could it simply be him? He had never found out the answer, had never discussed it with his friend, whom he believed had shared the same thought. He had thought of making a joke of it – 'Hey, let's order a pail of well spring from Plum Blossom, via special delivery!' – but the words turned into a lump and jarred at his throat. His friend, growing even quieter, had noticed none of this, his gaze disappearing into an unfathomable distance Martin couldn't reach.

Mingzhi would no longer look into his eyes.

'Anan has weaved more baskets for us. They are good at it, he and his wife. Rattan cut into thin slices, tied up properly. Light and strong.'

Martin had not been offered one and never asked for one.

'Can you sell them? What else does he make?'

'Only for our use. To store the fruits, you see. Never thought of selling them. Not a bad idea, though. Yes, he can make them in different sizes and shapes. Would be marketable. How's the land? Ready for the seeds?'

For an hour their conversation would drag on in fits and starts: Martin dwelling on works at the plantation, the clearing of the land, seeking the right seedlings, things he'd learned from Montgomery; Mingzhi on the shop, the jungle, Anan and Engi, carefully avoiding mention of Tiansheng. The trivial of their present was laid out huge and important, the past being swept into a deep, hidden corner. Untouchable. It had been a game, painful and vain, skirting around the unspoken, forbidden topics.

'Exporting, getting the canes out of the country, seems the right thing to do,' Mingzhi said once, relating Uncle Lau's suggestion.

'Absolutely. Remember the vase?' Martin blurted out. He regretted it instantly.

Mingzhi lapsed into a long silence. Of course his friend would remember. That day they sat in a corner of a quiet teahouse by the lake in Pindong. Martin, after salvaging a delicate vase from a blunder at the market-place, came up with the idea of exporting pottery products, a vital contribution to achieving Mingzhi's tax target. Endless cups of tea they emptied, countless jokes Martin spurted out, rounds of laughter rang in the spring air.

How long ago had that been? Two years, or three? It strangely felt much longer. Martin glanced at his friend, a still figure cocooned in thought. The vase of the past sat huge like a suddenly sprung-up mountain between them; on top of it the elegantly dressed court lady leapt up from the painted face of the porcelain, waving her sleeves, turning round on tiptoes. A swirl, a flap of sleeve, and they were further apart. Martin stared at his friend, the downcast eyes below his unusually fine brows for a man, his thin lips. A shadow rose and overlapped on the solemn face. Meilian. His heart ached. He understood, all of a sudden, his friend's reticence, his averted gaze: Mingzhi saw the same in him. He saw his sister in Martin. Seeing Martin would always remind him of his dear, beloved sister.

They stopped seeing each other.

*

Light off, shutters flapped closed. The white lion had given up on him, retreating to the darkness. Still, it was there, still watching, he knew. He glimpsed the bench under the palms, tempted, but decided not to sit on it. Instead he staggered forward, stumbling in the pitch blackness.

Somewhere in the far distance a lone torch flickered through the darkness. He stared at it, long and transfixed. When he looked away, the world before him was filtered in red. *The fire!* He blundered ahead like he had five years ago, the swaying light his target, blundering through the time tunnel into that fateful night, towards the source of brightness at the other end, towards the flames, the smoke, the cries. Towards a calamity that could not be reversed. Towards broken, irreparable friendships. *I shouldn't have left her! I shouldn't have!* Towards a face now appearing large before him, smiling, smiling.

Meilian!

Loud shriek against the dead silence.

Still running, another shout, and he stumbled over an exposed root and fell.

The night wrapped around him.

6

The Morning After

Light shifted. Mist thickened and then dissipated. Lucky foxes, with the unlucky fowls' feathers stuck at the corners of their mouths, slunk back into the bushes, waiting for another night, another expedition, another abundant meal. Frogs and toads choked back their croaking, retreating into the safe world of hidden nooks and crannies.

The first smoke swirled up from an early kitchen, a lonely white thread against the partially dark sky, which changed by the second in layered hues and light. Night had lapsed into dawn, the day as unpredictable as the fast-shifting cloud.

Mingzhi stood at the bow, a hand on the wooden rail, looking out at the misty dawn as the boat chugged out of the harbour, gliding in the gentle cradle of the Straits of Malacca, southwards to where he'd come from. He would be back soon, to the Baba Lodge and Tiansheng. He turned his body around at the thought, to face other passengers on board. The boat wasn't full. Men in shabby clothes sat in measured distance from one another, dozing, finding the threads to continue dreams that had been truncated by an early rise, thin blankets wrapped over them. Families huddled together, the young ones lay on the warm thighs of the adults, who engaged in occasional small talk in suppressed whispers.

Other passengers, in suits or gowns like him, stayed in the hold, a privilege their tickets had bought them. Mingzhi, despite the captain's advice, gave up the seat he'd paid for, preferring instead to remain where he was, with a view of the openness.

The boat scissored forward, cutting through the calm water now glinting silvery orange. He could see Tiansheng walking down the stairs and out of the Baba Lodge. He could see the door being opened and closed again, the brightness that came in a flash and went. He could see himself, first traipsing in the empty house, his footsteps, however lightly he trod, echoing loud against the four walls; then sitting in the office, clicking his abacus. Day turned into night, into day, into night. Abruptly he swivelled, turning his back against his destination.

He landed his gaze on a young family encircled near the entrance to the hold, the father adjusting the drape on his wife, whose shoulder was a soft pillow to a teenage girl: mother and daughter leaning against each other. He looked on, shifted to another time, to a veranda on a house-on-stilts, where the pair's hair glowed, not in the morning rays but the evening glare. He wanted to walk to them, to wake them, to talk to them. Just a step, as though with just a step he would cross the threshold of time, to the Fisherman's Hut, to his family.

But he couldn't.

Anger rose inside him. He remembered his promise on the night of the tragedy. *I'll make the land mine. I must!* Green veins shouted out loud on the backs of his hands that were gripping tightly to the wooden rail.

———

This is it. Jiaxi flicked the ash off the last of her cigarette. She shifted and then sat up, the red imprint of the rattan clearly visible on the pale skin of her arms, her thighs, her calves and her back after a long night in the chair. She rocked lightly. Gauze curtains swayed in the morning breeze, wild in a room too bare to feel the comfort of home. She stopped the motion, got up and changed into her white dress.

The door closed behind her.

She did not tell Edward, or anyone else, that she was leaving.

Tomorrow.

To England.

Tiansheng woke to the approaching shout of '*Bao*—oh, *bao*—oh, *bao*—oh,' *dumplings, dumplings,* and the clattering of a pull cart on the partially gravelled street. The calls of the hardworking mobile hawkers were his natural alarm clock.

His eyes still closed, he fumbled for his trousers by the bedside. The first of his many routines of the day had begun. He rose: heavy torso supported by strong elbows, prising him off his bed. In his head words rolled up one after another, the major daily procedures that were his life:

Breakfast.

Shop.

Home.

And many more minor tasks in between, rolling on.

Under the hibiscus growth, Martin opened his eyes to a world of dreamy red – the sky, the leaves, the branches –

filtered through gauze-thin petals. A blossom, with its long, drooping stalk of pistil and stamens, was smiling down at him. A drop of dew rolled from a leaf and fell on his forehead, the coolness a sudden, heavy knock.

His mind cracked open—

I don't have to cage myself in here!

He had only to give it up, the rubber plantation and everything else, and he would; he decided. He looked up again: the hills afar, clear and bright in the morning sun, extending themselves beyond the horizon over to a space that was wider, more colourful, waiting for him to explore.

PART THREE

An Orang Asli in Town

1

No Stage for 'Engi Kills A Boar'

AUGUST 1905

Taukeh Chai came to the forest a week after his return from Penang. Perching on the wild rambutan tree I spotted the approaching patch of white as his pale shirt appeared and disappeared among the green foliage. *What has he got for me this time? Biscuits or meat dumplings?* I liked biscuits, though it was the chicken chunks in rich gravy wrapped in soft dough that brought out a mouthful of saliva in me. But dumplings could wait; my stories couldn't. Just the day before, I had killed my first ever wild pig, all by myself.

*

I'd been looking out for the sounder for some time, after spotting their tracks one day out hunting with Father. And yesterday, there was a mess of footprints near the river, indicating a hurried descent along the slope to the water and then further downstream. Father ignored me. He said the signs showed the boars were trotting uphill, not otherwise, which was perfectly reasonable – last night's downpour would have chased them to higher ground.

You see, you couldn't argue with Father; he was the best hunter of the tribe. As he was absorbed in parting the long grass in his ascent, I quietly sneaked away.

I traced the marks along the river, ignoring the mud, squeezing between grass and reeds taller than me. Turning a bend, the track now trailed into the woods, heading up.

They were in there.

I felt with my hand the blowpipe on my back, hesitated. It was too far to go back to Father now. I entered the woods.

The trail was cut off. I stood looking. Trees, old and young, with their huge and spindly trunks and lush leaves filled my view. No boars.

I panicked. I couldn't go home empty-handed. What would Father say of me? I thought of his crumpled face, the eyes that would turn into slits in his laughter. Father! 'Use your senses: smell, smell, smell.' His words rang in my head.

I doubled over, my body parallel with the ground like a beast's, and I combed the forest floor. The dung. Fresh and acrid, lumps of black droppings strewn sporadically on the ground that was muddy after yesterday's downpour. I inhaled deeply as though they were the fragrance of precious camphor. I was thrilled. I would not miss them.

More trees and grass. Chafed barks. Then came the sounds of grunting. I jumped and climbed the nearest tree at the first instance. There they were, about twenty of them, in the tuber growth, burrowing in the soil for the roots. I reached out for my blowpipe. My target? The biggest among them, of course.

The dart went astray, landed inches away from the boar. It was somehow alerted and startled. A loud wail, and the sounder squealed and started fleeing, running into one another in a panic.

No! In my haste I launched my second shot into the medley. More squeals, sharp and piercing among the rumbling of hooves. The earth shook and the tree with it. I closed my eyes, holding on to the trunk with all my might.

When silence resumed, I opened my eyes to a boar lying, real and still, on the ground.

*

Perfect timing!

I jumped down from the tree and rushed forward, eager to tell Taukeh Chai of my heroic adventure. Telling the story to other children last night at the bonfire was different from narrating it to the Chinaman. Yes, most of the boys were fascinated, but Sipang and Ulang were jealous of me. They had shooed me away, saying that I was lying. They put out the fire and rushed the others home, even before I reached the climax, the shooting part. Such spoilsports.

But Taukeh Chai was different. He'd always marvelled at my tales from the forest, always listened with such keenness and patience to my descriptions of the tedious processes of honey-collecting or pheasant-trapping. He would put his hand gently on my head as his eyes shone, and say: 'How clever you are, Engi. What a waste if you don't go to school.'

Over the years he'd been teaching me Mandarin, practising with me on his visits, heaping on praise after praise for my deft mastery of the language. 'But school will give you more.' He said school was a place where children gathered to learn from someone who knew almost everything in the world. *Is there someone like that, someone who knows more than Father does? Does he know my world? My jungle?* Taukeh Chai would not answer, would instead urge me for more stories, to which I would eagerly oblige. But he didn't that day. He wasn't listening. There were no biscuits or dumplings either.

'Where's Anan? Where's your father?' Cutting me off, he strode instead to the hut where Father was preparing his blowpipe for his next outing.

I stuck my head in.

'Go and play outside!' Father waved me off.

I went to the clearing around the rambutan tree, the platform of Father's evening storytelling session, and practised the Engi Kills A Boar scene to perfection for Taukeh Chai's appreciation later. A dart-less blowpipe in hand, I emerged from the back of the tree and blew from the bottom of my stomach. 'And down the beast!' I leapt and cheered, my childish, innocent voice bouncing around the woods, resounding in the vast emptiness. I hadn't the slightest idea that inside the hut, my fate had been sealed. My life would change from then on.

At lunch, Mother, surprisingly, did not tease Taukeh Chai as she usually did, about getting an Orang Asli wife. 'Diligent and obedient, who else would serve you better than our women?' she would say, and Father would nod in agreement. Instead she was quiet, fiddling with the rice on the banana leaf, while Father kept puffing his pipe, not a word.

Rehearsing in my head the movements to be enacted in front of my honourable audience, I scooped the food into my mouth as quickly as I could, impatient to jump on the stage, to deliver the performance of my life.

'Son, it's time to go.'

Father, sitting on the floor across from me, stared at me as he exhaled a mouthful from his pipe. *Go? Where?* My questions were stuffed in my mouth, cluttered with rice and curry, cooked with the wild boar I had hunted.

Father glanced at Taukeh Chai, who looked at me, nodding. Mother, with my baby sister in her bosom, started to wail: 'No, he is going nowhere. He stays with me. My Engi stays with me!'

'Oh, stop it, woman.' Father did not budge: the promise of sending me to school, to be a learned man like the *taukeh*, had steeled his heart. Mother abandoned her food and ran to the back of the hut. *What's happening?* A panicky feeling rose in me and I ran after Mother, who instantly pulled me to her bosom and began to wail, which only made me cry and cling tightly to her. Everything happened so quickly. In seconds Father appeared and prised me off Mother. 'No! Let me go!' Fear rose like night spirits that would invade our dreams (*If you don't behave*, Father had always warned us boys). I flung my limbs in vain struggle as Father dragged me away. In the midst, I turned back and found Mother collapsed on the ground, her face soaked in tears. '*Emok*, I want *Emok*!' I screamed, yet I was moving further from her. I could hear my scream tearing through the woods; I could hear the fluttering of the wings as birds scurried off; but my mind was blank, and my heart sank to an empty, bottomless abyss.

My much practised boar-hunting scene had never found the limelight I'd been anticipating.

*

We arrived at the edge of the jungle where Father and I had seen Taukeh Chai off five years ago, but this time as Father stopped he pushed me to the Chinaman.

'Behave yourself, Engi. Listen to whatever Taukeh Chai has to say to you; do whatever he asks you to do,' Father said. 'And promise me: you will never cry. You hear me?'

Father is giving me away! He doesn't want me any more! My fear escalated; my legs turned limp. In a blink Father was no longer in sight. I knew he was there, hiding in the clumps of foliage like we once did, watching us.

'No, Father! I'll behave; don't leave me here!' I shouted into the bushes but Father would not come out, and I was led away, my hand held tightly in Taukeh Chai's. The trees kept receding, becoming smaller. Soon, everything disappeared altogether.

It's a dream; it must be a dream, I repeated in my head as we walked on. Then, a sudden wave of noises came to my senses. I looked around. So many people! Most of them were Chinamen like Taukeh Chai, passing us by. Horse and ox carts rumbled past, and big houses! – tall, solid, colourful, unlike our shabby huts. I clung tightly to Taukeh Chai's sleeve and hid behind his back, aware of myself, dark and small and skinny, an ugly dwarf in a world so strange, so frightening.

It's a dream; it must be. I tried to convince myself that when I woke up, everything would be gone and I would open my eyes to my little hut, to the needles of light poking through the attap, to Mother's smile, to the familiar smell of Father's tobacco.

But which was dream and which was reality? All day I sleepwalked between the boundaries of the two, led along by Taukeh Chai, here and there, in and out. Door after door. He spoke to me as we went, names of people and buildings and hundreds of other things, noises that seemed to be the muffled buzz of a bumblebee wrapping around me.

That night, in the back room of the Baba Lodge, when I finally fell asleep in the bed as soft as a feather, the forest came to me. They were soundless, my dreams: the animals, the birds, the river. A yellow gibbon stared aloofly down at me from a treetop; it bared its teeth but I heard not the threatening hissing, only stillness. My whistling at the *burra-burra* was muted, too; the bird glanced sideways at me, its head askew, the slight, gentle movement of its throat betraying its rendition of a silent tune not for me to admire. Awake and alert, I sat up with a jerk, covered in cold sweat. No, they didn't come to claim me, but to deny me. I was an outcast.

In the real world, real sounds weaved their way through the floor, the many rooms and long corridors, to me.

'You could've discussed with me!' The suppressed anger of a man I would later know as Taukeh Tiansheng knocked the last bit of my dream from me. 'Yes, discuss . . . we should've . . . everything, all along. That's what we need to do and haven't been doing!'

'Engi is a smart boy.' Soft and feeble, Taukeh Chai's voice was almost inaudible. 'He will only be of help.'

'So let him be useful then. Let him earn his keep.'

'He's only a child—'

'Didn't you say he is capable of catching a boar by himself? The shop can't be more dangerous than the jungle, can't be more tricky than a boar, can it?' Taukeh Tiansheng's outburst shocked the house. Leaning against the headboard, I felt the wall vibrating. I closed my eyes and thought of Mother's sweet songs of river and hills that had accompanied me into dreamlands, night after night. I thought of the angry man I would share my life with from now on. I shuddered and leapt off the bed.

'Mind you, I was barely six when I . . . when I joined the troupe.' A loud bang of a door, and the authoritative tone continued from behind the wooden plank: 'No free meals in this house, that's all I have to say!'

After a long silence, Taukeh Chai came to find me shrinking in the farthest corner of the darkened room, my tearful eyes wide and fearful, staring up at him.

Everything would be fine, he said as he carried me back to the bed and tucked in the cotton blanket too warm for my comfort. He was different. He wasn't the Taukeh Chai I'd known in the forest. The Taukeh Chai I'd known in the forest was always talking and smiling, laughing even, with Father and I. But he did not now, not since we were in town. Even in the dimness I could see his knotted brow: dark shadows where the lines cut deep.

The stranger in front of me sighed. 'You'll learn from me, I promise, better than going to school.'

How many promises had he made, and would he go on making, to me and to Father? And how many had he kept? Those were sums I have never been able to work out. But one thing was certain: there was never a school for me.

*

The next morning I was ushered to the shop by the man I was to call Taukeh Tiansheng. It was a compromise – morning at Chai & Tian Company, afternoon at Taukeh Chai's study – which neither of the bosses was happy with, especially Taukeh Tiansheng. His face constantly rigid with resentment, he showered on me his reprimands, which came quick and unpredictable in harsh words, for a slip of an overloaded basket too heavy for my skinny arms (*Stupid! Wasted all the rice that went down your stomach!*), a stumble on the stairs (*Where have your eyes gone?*) or a knot too loosely tied (*How many times do I have to teach you?*). My pace was forever too fast or too slow, my speech incomprehensible, my legs too short. No, nothing was ever right.

That first afternoon, instead of going back to the Baba Lodge, Taukeh Chai took me to a teahouse a long way from the shop. In a corner partitioned from the sunlight and the crowd, I saw the first white man in my life. Unshaven and haggard with dark-ringed eyes, the man whom I'd later know to be Martin Gray towered over me like a ghost. Taukeh Chai gently released my hand and settled me next to him on a bench across from the white ghost. I sat glued to my guardian, my eyes fixed on the figure before us. Taukeh Chai ordered a chicken dumpling for me, a really big one, while they talked in a language alien to me, occasionally slipping in a few Mandarin words and sentences that sneaked into my ears between ravenous bites.

219

'I have to get out of here. This is your chance. I told you before and I'm telling you again: you'll make big money with rubber. Trust me,' said the white man.

'I can't possibly do it. You know how Tiansheng is. You know rubber was never his cup of tea. He won't agree,' my guardian muttered.

'You'll never get another chance like this. It's a good price. You have only to keep it from him. Think about it: are you going to stick with him for the rest of your life? Don't you want to do something on your own? Something legal?'

As I listened, I memorized by heart phrases such as 'a far-below-market price', 'contract' and 'agreement'.

When my second dumpling arrived, the two men shook hands.

'Deal.'

'Deal.'

*

Chai Mingzhi made his moves swiftly and quietly, with a determination and energy that I thought reminiscent of the years when he worked his way to becoming a mandarin: a legendary tale retold by men from his village, who had now landed in this same space and were, surprisingly, kept at a distance by my guardian.

During my teenage years, I would dig out from these former peasants of Plum Blossom Village snatches of stories about a man called Chai Mingzhi. His childhood, his learning with an old scholar, his passion for knowledge, the days and nights of bitter study – passing three levels of exams – to secure a mandarin post, his opium-addict father and half-brother, his deceased wife and unborn child. Bits and pieces buckled together to form an image of a scholar: kind-hearted, quietly stubborn, with an abundance of knowledge in him.

At the teahouse, I would order a pot of tea and plates of dim sum as the peasants turned coolies dwelled on the mansion Chai had grown up in, cursing and spitting when mentioning the blood-sucking landlord who was the young man's grandfather, their hate target.

Memories spilled out like water, rising up to bury the deep hole that was homesickness. Flocking together, recounting the past was their way of dealing with the present. And no, unlike them, Chai kept only to himself, staying away from his past, the place, the people; their stories were never recounted.

He embraced the present in a most pragmatic way.

The day after his meeting with Martin Gray, Chai knocked on the door of Montgomery's bungalow, a pile of paperwork ready in his hand. He'd taken me with him, of course. Shocked, furious and speechless, the Scot watched Chai lay out the documents: the legal certification of his share of the rubber plantation bought from Martin Gray; an additional statement from Martin Gray, who had then moved out of the bungalow, confirming the transfer of his share of the plantation to Chai; and a proposal detailing ways of running the joint venture.

Over a glass of Scotch, Montgomery mulled over Chai's suggestion that he, the Chinese boss, stay behind the curtain, and an experienced manager be recruited instead to oversee the daily operations; the wage, of course, would be paid from Chai's share.

Over another glass, the white man became rather impressed by the immaculate draft: the meticulously worked out details, the perfectly phrased sentences – no errors, without ambiguity – as eloquent as the writer's spoken English.

Over the third, Montgomery swallowed the bitter-sweetness as he swallowed back the initial humiliation of being forced to co-run his business with a Chinese man.

He signed the document.

'Deal.'

'Deal.'

A large, pale, hairy hand wrapped over a skinny yellow one; shaking, shaking.

2

The Lone Traveller and the
Kathakali Dancer

At the harbour a few days later, Chai saw off Martin Gray.

For the former peasants of Plum Blossom Village, and the former townsfolk of Pindong and Lixing where Chai the young mandarin had run the courts, the encounter of the two men was yet another fascinating recitation. Some said the foreign devil, with a magic box, had charmed his Chinese friend. His soul captured in it, it was said, Chai had been a slave to the Englishman: first lured into getting the finest craftsmen to produce the finest porcelain, sending them in bulk to a faraway land from where the foreign devil had come (*A robbery of our precious treasure in broad daylight!* one of the storytellers exclaimed); later taken as human shield as Martin fled the Boxers, forcing Chai to leave his country.

Others were less sympathetic, describing Chai as a traitor, too eager to abandon his roots, even keener to adopt the Englishman's language and culture which, to them, were barbaric. 'Tish!' A mouthful of thick phlegm of disgust landed with such precision into the spittoon under the table in the teahouse: a floating patch of scornful green against the otherwise clear water.

Under the louring sky that afternoon at the pier, both men were quiet. Barbarian or imperialist, traitor or slave, they were locked in a silence laden with pre-downpour heat and humidity, the smells suffocating.

'It'll only be a stopping point, this first sail to Singapore.' Martin shrugged, a bitter smile. 'Don't ask me where I'll be next. I don't have an answer to it. Australia? Africa? Or America? We'll see.'

'Write to me. Tell me how you get on, wherever you'll be.' My guardian took a deep breath, almost murmuring, as if he'd rather not say it: 'You know . . . you can always come back here.'

Martin Gray let out a light snort and shook his head, as though he'd heard something absurd. And not a word.

From behind my guardian I stared up at the Englishman, now clean-shaven: his eyes, blue as a clear morning sky, somehow felt grey, downcast. I thought of the stray dog that came to our quarter for scraps of food, slinking away when stones were thrown at it, its tail down, hidden between its legs.

I stepped out of Taukeh Chai's shadow, my head tilted up to face Martin Gray.

I was no longer afraid of the foreign man, be he devil or ghost.

*

For years to come, infrequent letters would arrive for my guardian's attention. Strange stamps, faded and illegible postmarks on envelopes in varied shapes, sizes and colours. Singapore, Bangkok, Jakarta, Kuching, Bombay, Delhi, Calcutta, Cape Town. A long list of them, places known or unknown; names that tried my tongue, knotted at attempting their pronunciations. To list them all proved impossible.

The letters were kept in a sandalwood box, in the bottom drawer under his desk. I came across it when I was once asked to look for a bill, misplaced, he said, either in the first or the second drawers. Having mis-heard, I pulled out the third and the last one to find a box so delicate that instinctively my hand landed on it.

'Don't touch it!' His face, cold like steel, only aroused my curiosity.

One afternoon, my guardian made a rare trip out to visit Uncle Lau at his sick bed. Alone in the office, with-out a second thought I drew the box out of its hiding place. There they were, a stack of mystery, arranged in reverse chronological order, about four or five per annum to begin with, becoming increasingly infrequent with the passing of time, later falling sharply to two that year, my fourth year in town.

I started with the last on the pile, dated three months after Martin Gray's departure, and worked upwards. The first was postmarked in Singapore, detailing his reunion with an English official called Bob Greenhorn.

'This is only a stop-by,' he scribbled in his wayward, carefree handwriting, all the words ending with a long tail that flicked high to the right. 'I've drafted out plans for other places, farther, more interesting.'

So he did. I read from his following letters the adven-tures of a man in foreign villages, towns, cities which, surprisingly, sounded familiar.

I recalled stories my guardian had told me at bedtime in the early days upon my arrival in town, stories of a lonely traveller who roamed the world in search of happi-ness. My guardian's voice would turn dry at the mention of his protagonist, assuming a sadness I presumed to be an intended effect. I heard tales of the young man crossing the desert with Arabian traders with their long line of camels, his near escape from a bush fire in California. In India, he dipped in the Ganges to wash away his misfortune, preparing to welcome a new beginning.

How many beginnings had he had? Every new adventure seemed to me to be a rebirth. Wouldn't he be tired of endless wandering?

'Has he ever found it, happiness?' My innocent voice had rung emptily in the dimness, only to meet with prolonged, more stifling emptiness.

Another time, as I was working side by side with him in the office, a letter of a similar kind received just the day before peeked out from under a stack of purchase orders, as they were shuffled about to make room. He was unaware of it, his head buried deep in the figures, his hand on the abacus.

From the open envelope, a thin piece of paper fell out, creased and soft, as if it would simply dissolve into water. I imagined the repeated act of folding and unfolding in the paraffin lamplight during the previous night. Did he attempt to keep in step with his friend in the streets of Monte Carlo, or Puerto Rico, or Islamabad? Draped in a robe, haggling with hawkers, eating roast meat on skewers? But the landscapes were obscure, the people alien!

And I imagined him, after replacing the letter, taking it out again, savouring again each word, chewing at each sentence, as if by doing so, the man that he missed and his life would come tumbling out from his mouth in a loud burp.

I imagined his tears dripping on the fragile sheet, dark wet patches seeping through, fast spreading.

*

Did he ever weep for Tiansheng? With the discovery of the letters from Martin Gray, I traced back my memory, finding clues and threads to identify other characters in the stories rendered in that low, gentle voice.

Aided by snatches of information from the former peasants of Plum Blossom Village, I continued to pick up images of a caring sister and a quietly stubborn niece. Of a fire, a death, and the separation between uncle and niece afterwards. But it was the teenage opera singer, that effeminate and powerless soul, the only friend to the adolescent Chai, that had me puzzled. My guardian's voice would turn even softer at the mention of the less fortunate youth, describing with admiration his special talent.

'With only a bamboo leaf' – his eyes gleamed in the half-dark – 'he let out music like a breeze swooping through a stifling night, a current running swiftly under the stream, a beam of light shining through from the end of a black cavern.'

Am I mistaken? I thought of the pair of callus-infested hands, the masculine torso, the hard, authoritarian tone of a man I called Taukeh Tiansheng, and was unable to work out an association between him and the young opera singer.

I thought of the dimness in my guardian's eyes as the story progressed, as the estranged opera singer killed a man who was the half-brother of his best friend. As that Best Friend – none other but Taukeh Chai himself,

I deduced, who had been the mandarin of the town where the incident had taken place – later saved him from a death sentence. As he squeezed himself into the colourful world of the Imperial City, into the trading enterprise. As he drifted to the tropics with that Best Friend.

The opera singer's story ended in their new world. My guardian's eyes went dimmer; there were no tears in them. (No, he'd never wept for Tiansheng, I concluded.)

Before long, the tale of the opera singer was reincarnated in the form of a Kathakali dancer the same way Martin Gray was portrayed under the veil of a 'lone traveller'.

Reality was disguised in the name of fiction. Cluttered lumps of secrets released from a near-bursting stomach with fictionalized characters, places, events; pain and suffering stored away.

Story time after dark.

It began the second night after my arrival in the Baba Lodge. Taukeh Chai came to my room after the lights were put out. A paraffin lamp in his hand, gentle steps on tiled floor. Acute like an animal's, my ears pricked up for the careful movement that would be indistinct to someone exhausted after a hard day's work, someone like Taukeh Tiansheng. Down the stairs he went, through the living room, the corridor, approaching the unlocked door.

Once inside, light, again, played its trick. The faint glow barely reached us, only cast blurred shadows on the whitewashed walls: the four bedposts, my guardian's lean figure by the bedside. Vague silhouettes shuffled in the gloom like trees in the woods, with me enclosed in them. In a trance, I was back in our dwelling, to the wild rambutan tree outside the hut, to Father's evening show time. In the half-dark he loosened up, relaxed. He was again the Taukeh Chai I'd known before, again talking, a trace of smile on his face.

'Engi, you're a smart boy.' Sitting at my bedside he said softly, 'I'm glad you're here.'

I stared at him.

He said again: 'I'm glad you're here.'

His eyes shone, watery. It was the tears that had Father's trust drown in him that morning at the edge of the forest five years back.

Many years later, as I was traipsing in the newly completed Minang Villa, a last inspection before the big move from the Baba Lodge, these words would come back to me: 'I'm glad you're here.' I remembered his tears in the darkened room as he'd said them, his vulnerable voice which I'd mistaken for gentleness, and realized with a sudden jerk that it was him who needed me. He needed me to be his fence. He was a feeble vine struggling to break away from a thick crump of bramble, to cling on to something, just something, as it headed up for the sun.

*

From his study, from his lavish collection, Taukeh Chai pulled out books, not stories about the faraway land he'd come from – these I learned during my daily two-hour reading session – but tales of his adopted world. As his recitation progressed, though, the connection between the people of this land and his homeland became apparent. The early inhabitants of the peninsula, he said, were one of the peoples of my kind. I learned that the

Negritos, as they were called, were the first inhabitants on this land, populated in the north. They had been here at least two thousand years, and possibly as far back as fifteen thousand years!

'That said' – my guardian put down his book – 'the rest of the population of this land came later from other regions, neighbouring or afar. Thailand, for instance, moving southwards.'

He blinked. 'And can you believe this, Engi?' A rare tinge of excitement in his voice; his face brightened. 'Another thread traces back to where I come from.' He ran his finger on the mattress, drawing out a source route originating from southern China to Taiwan, to the Philippines, to Northern Borneo. From there, the line forked: one went eastwards to Sulawesi – central Java – eastern Indonesia; the other south-westwards, to southern Borneo – western half of Java – Sumatra – and finally, the Malay Peninsula. And they became the Malays.

How subtle the relation between the two, his land and mine! I marvelled, even before the stories of Princess Hang Li Po and her retinue – which occurred later, binding stronger connections – came to my knowledge.

I imagined the migrations, over thousands of years, on horseback or cart or simply barefoot, on boat or dinghy, from one place to another. I imagined shelters erected and then abandoned, packed and moved on.

Was it the water or the soil? Was it the people that had made them leave, yanking out the rudimentary roots partially buried in the earth? Did the children cry as they parted with their friends? The women with their kitchens and fowls they had to leave behind? I imagined a forsaken chicken darting its surprised eyes this way and that, as it wandered in an empty hut, its occasional clatter as lonely as its shadow.

'Do you know, Engi, it was language that unravelled the migration patterns. Language doesn't lie.' He shifted between Malay and Mandarin, slipping in occasional English phrases.

'When people move, Engi, they take with them their way of naming the tools they use, the food they eat, the animals they raise.' My guardian told me that by studying the contents of the languages spoken by the people living in this and neighbouring regions, anthropologists identified the source of influence, worked out the migration patterns and tracked down the origins of the people. 'Their *external* origins,' he stressed. 'External, because their ancestral roots were from outside the peninsula.'

Sitting there, leaning against the bedpost, my mouth cracked open – my first smile since leaving home. Father was right.

That night in my dream, Father spoke in a tongue so strange I couldn't comprehend. Frantically I opened my mouth and a string of gobbledygook poured out like overflowing sewage, running between us. A river of unintelligible words: Father on one side, me on the other. Standing on the shores we peered helplessly across at each other as the water kept gushing, the land continued to part. And we drifted further apart, shrinking into two black dots, fast disappearing.

*

In Taukeh Chai's study, I began to fill in details absent from Father's stories. For instance, by 'the first of the white men' Father had meant 'the Portuguese', who sailed in with their tall ships and angry bombs in 1511, while 'the second lot of them' referred to 'the Dutch' who, in 1641, cast out the former.

However detailed the books were, something was inherently missing: the bloody red mess of chewed betel nuts and *sireh* leaves against the grey earth; the acrid smell of raw tobacco; Father's loud, comical voice and exaggerated hand gestures. I burrowed deep into the books only to find my longing for Father's vivid tales, his lively descriptions, had become more eager, desperate. No one was able to bring to life the way Father did – despite the fact that he had never witnessed them – the ferocious roars of the bombs that would shake the jungle: the trees would shudder and shrug off their leaves, the forest floor vibrate, birds dropping down from the sky, animals ˙lame with fear, fish lying dead with the white of their stomachs upturned, gleaming silver in the river. So powerful were the bombs, the Malays had to drop their kris and kowtow to the invaders. The Dutch were quick to build a fort up the hill and a port by the sea. More ships, more people came, bringing with them silk from China, tea from India, carpets from the Middle East, pepper and camphor and ivory from our land. From here they travelled again, the silk and tea and carpets and spices, in opposite directions. An entrepôt, so I learned.

Still, our ancestors kept quiet and hid further inside the woods, not wanting to bump into the white men and their Malay companions who explored the forest for camphor and rattan and other produce.

For nearly two hundred years the Dutch made money out of our land, before the British arrived in bigger ships, with more powerful bombs, more uniformed men with their fire guns. Battered and crumpled, the Dutch, following a treaty signed in 1827, fled like bees being smoked out of their nests.

I remembered how Father had raised his voice with a big grin on his face as he used his favourite description of the exodus he imagined, his spit splattering, his forehead glowing in the red flames of the fire. I would think of our bees'-nest hunting expeditions on moonless nights, Father and I. At first Father was the tree-climber and the torch-holder, while I, a wooden bucket in hand, waited impatiently underneath for the delicious honey-filled nests, before our roles reversed. On my first active mission I had my legs clasped tightly around the *tualang* tree and watched the tiny insects squeeze out of their home under my smoky flame: hundreds of black shadows hovered above my head, their deafening hum a collective helplessness. Was that how they'd fled? The white men? We were not the ones who drove them out. We never were, not to any outside men. We would only grin and bear. We took them all in.

But them?

They fought hard against one another, each wanting the others out of this land, which, funnily enough, wasn't even theirs in the first place.

*

From history my guardian shifted gradually to the more recent past. There was also a change of tone, a quiet sadness, even if events related were merry: a celebration, a reunion, a business success, or something of that kind. Upon my discovery of the letters from Martin Gray, upon realizing the possible true happenings and real people hidden underneath the narrative, I was amazed and impressed by his ability to transport his character to an entirely different time and space, a determination to eliminate traces of his past. Tiansheng the opera singer became an Indian Kathakali dancer; Martin the English trader was simply a traveller who had ventured to most parts of Asia, save China; the sister figure moved southwards from Thailand with her daughter. These characters, though, were connected to an unnamed third person.

'. . . The teenage dancer had a way of making a flute from a bamboo leaf. Music flew out like a breeze as he played with it, and he passed his skills on to *him* . . .'

'. . . From his bag the lone traveller picked up a scroll of painting. He pointed out to *him* the pond of lotus in watercolour and said: "The chance of the lotus being in the water it lives in, the chance of them being together was so impermanent, like you and me.". . .'

'. . . Over the years, the young girl returned all the letters from her only relative. She would not forgive *him*. She blamed *him* for her mother's death . . .'

Like an old man's rambling, stories flowed like a stream of emotion, slow, smooth, murmuring. Without a starting point, without an end.

*

In the tales told by Taukeh Chai, there was always a house, standing tall and important by the river. Tall, because it was built on stilts; important, because all his protagonists were, somehow, connected to it. They would eventually be drawn to it, making it their final destination. The Kathakali dancer, the woman from Thailand who was miraculously resurrected from death, her estranged daughter. Even the lonely traveller. All gravitated to the house owned by the anonymous *him*.

'And *he* named it the Minang Villa.'

The building had been his plan from the start: acquiring the rubber estates, hoarding wealth, all geared towards that purpose. It was his secret, his revenge, his gesture to the arsonist who destroyed his first home on this land, who killed his sister.

It was his means of redemption.

*

In real life, the Kathakali dancer's alter ego, Tiansheng, would only learn about the Minang Villa years later.

It was 1918, ten years after the break-up of Chai & Tian Company, which had led to the departure of Tiansheng. Passing by a grocery shop in Jalan Sultan by the Klang River in Kuala Lumpur, a salesman who had travelled from Malacca saw the boss who was busy supervising the unloading of a cartload of rice, and recognized him instantly, once a familiar face in the southern port town.

Of course he'd known of the dispute between Tiansheng and Chai Mingzhi, of the former's leaving Malacca not long after the break-up of Chai & Tian Company. The petty salesman would not miss the chance to stir up flames from a heap of dying embers. Over cups of tea, he described to the prematurely greying Tiansheng a structure erected by the Malacca River.

'Like a palace, shining gold in the sun, with edges of the roofs pointing out and up towards the sky' – the cunning man carefully observed his listener for his reactions – 'you can see it from miles away, shooting up from within the seemingly borderless RUBBER TREES.' The last two words he emphasized. 'Only God knows how much he'd hoarded with all that rubber!'

Back in Malacca, the salesman chose a busy Sunday morning and settled himself in a teahouse filled with weekend *pasar*-goers in Market Street, coolies – the lucky ones – who came out from the mines and plantations to frolic away their only day off in a week.

'He was quiet, but his face wasn't.' He peered over his cup as he sipped his tea, taking in the expectant eyes on him. 'It went red and taut. Green veins danced on his brows and neck. I could smell fire. Then, suddenly, he turned his head away, not looking at me, just gazing out at the river, not looking at anything else. "The house, of course; the house," he mumbled. He was no longer angry. He was – somewhere else.'

I sat with the storyteller long after the crowd had dispersed: impatient to pass on their newly acquired gossip.

What did I wish to find out about the man I had been eager to shrug off, whose eventual departure I had played a part in? Was I hoping to hear of his downfall or otherwise? Could I be simply curious on behalf of my guardian, thinking that he might want to know? That he might have been wondering about his old friend's whereabouts, how he'd been doing? Would I relate to him news of a man stooped under the weight of fierce competition in his line of business? Of how he'd haggle with customers for every single cent? Of his fingernails, cracked and encrusted with the flour and fowls' feed he'd been constantly carrying? I wasn't sure.

'Only forty-three, he looked at least ten years older. Dark like a *kling*, with deep lines all over his face.' The salesman finished the last of the dumplings I'd ordered for him, sat back and let out a light burp. And told no more.

I was twenty-five. I had seen Taukeh Chai's rubber estate expand with a speed reminiscent of the gushing rivers after a monsoon downpour, the boundaries redrawn over and over again. I had helped him manage the first rubber processing factory in the region. I had partially supervised the construction of the Minang Villa, and most importantly, I had taken part in securing the land where it was erected. I was elated by my achievements, thrilled at my capability, even prouder after my guardian's appreciative nods, and wanted eagerly to please him further, to prove to him my worth.

That day, after the garrulous salesman left for his afternoon nap, I sat alone in the quietened teahouse, overwhelmed by an abrupt and immense tiredness. By a sudden longing to return to where I'd come from.

I longed for Father's voice; I longed for the forest noise, the *burra-burra* and gibbons; I longed for the tranquillity.

3

Under One Roof,
Two Separate Paths

'The house' Taukeh Tiansheng referred to, I later realized, was the Fisherman's Hut, a house-on-stilts by the river abandoned by some fishermen. It was made into a home with sweat and blood – his and Mingzhi's, especially – that had bound them together as they settled on their new land. The Baba Lodge, on the contrary, was one that had separated them.

It began a week after my arrival at the Baba Lodge in 1905.

During their monthly discussion of business accounts, my guardian finally revealed to his partner his donation to the revolutionists at the meeting in Penang. According to Amah Feng, who happened to enter the office with a new brew of hot *pu'er*, Taukeh Tiansheng went wide-eyed, his fists clenched; so monstrous-looking was he that Amah Feng laid down the tray without serving the tea. He was surprisingly quiet, though. In my ground-floor room that evening, I heard footsteps scurrying down the stairs, a loud bang of the main door. Then dead silence.

In my guardian's story that night, the Indian Kathakali dancer's parents who had abandoned him as a child came to claim him.

'"We've climbed nine mountains and crossed ninety-nine rivers. We've travelled nine hundred and ninety-nine days," the long-lost father said. "Now you'll come with us. Home is calling for your return. It's always there for you." He held out his hands, expecting his son to kiss them, as he would kiss the threshold of their house on his return. But the dancer turned his back on them.

'"It was you who had disowned me," he said as he walked away.'

The same way Taukeh Tiansheng had walked out on my guardian.

*

There was no turning back for the Kathakali dancer's alter ego, Tiansheng. Planning carefully, he quietly launched a plot soon after the argument.

It was easy. You see, during those days the Chinese ran their business based on trust. Agreements could be made verbally, deals sealed without contracts. The thousands-of-years-old saying 'A promise is as heavy and lasting as gold' had always been faithfully adhered to. And based on this, the two bosses of Chai & Tian Company had since the early days agreed upon a set routine for their daily operations, defining their duties and responsibilities:

— Tiansheng would buy rattan and other forest
  produce from small collectors at rates agreed on
  negotiation. (It was managed by both of them at the
  start of the business when Chai, too, worked a whole
  day in the shop.)
— Tiansheng would record all the purchases in a book.

— Chai would come to the shop by noon and work out the total, on which basis he issued delivery notes, prepared by carefully allocating available stocks to orders received.

— Tiansheng would pack and dispatch the merchandise according to the delivery notes.

— Chai would then transfer all the comings and goings in his book by the end of the day, and check them against the money received.

— As for earnings from underground dealings, there was another account, with no other details but figures matching the cash handed to Chai by Tiansheng. The money and the book were kept in a locked coffer, the key in Chai's hand. (It was from this hoard the money was taken for donation.)

Overnight, the rules were rewritten. By Tiansheng alone.

In the morning, he strung together a few sheets, made a palm-sized notebook and hid it in his chest pocket. Against his and Chai's earlier commitment to protect small collectors, he began to press them for the lowest possible prices for the forest produce he bought, ignoring the collectors' pleas. On his notepad, he wrote down the exact money shelled out for the purchases, and in the big book, figures higher then the actual payout.

The same he did with the 'protection money': larger amounts were conveniently recorded. At the end of the day, he worked out the discrepancies and pocketed the excess.

It was even easier for his underground earnings. Cash from smuggling tobacco and gold fell gradually over time. He was safe, he knew. Chai had never talked about this source of income, and never would.

A month passed; another. Three. Five.

It was a sweltering evening. Returning home early, Tiansheng took a shower, changed into clean clothes and went off again, his new daily routine. He no longer sat at the dinner table with me and Chai.

I remember the dishes that night: a bowl of spicy pork-belly soup, braised pork and sea cucumber in thick sauce, a plate of stir-fried tofu and leek. I stuck my tongue out after the peppery soup, and was immediately soothed by the plain bean curd; with the taste buds back in action, the pot of mixed braised meat became tastier, the gravy rich in my mouth, and I could savour every one of the five spices, and the dark and light soy sauces.

'Life is about balance, Engi, like our bodies,' my guardian said; 'the *yin* and the *yang* have to be on a par.' He pointed his chopsticks first at the soup and the braised pot: 'Heat property' – then moved to the tofu – 'is balanced up with cool elements.' I nodded emptily, busied myself with chewing the succulent pork in my mouth.

In another corner of the house, Amah Feng, picking up the last round of dirty laundry from outside the bathroom, found the bound sheets on the floor. She handed them to Chai, the only person she knew in the house who dealt with 'literature'.

His face.

I saw his face turning to red, then to green and grey, his body rigid, the pages held open over his bowl of rice. Even I knew something had gone very wrong. My chopsticks still in one hand, my rice bowl in the other with my lips clasped at the edge of it, I hung on there, unsure if I should put them down or keep on eating. We sat that way for what felt like ages.

He shook his head and closed the book.

He called for Amah Feng, who was ready to leave, a bundle of the day's last laundry in her hands.

'Put those back' – he pointed at the bundle before handing her the book – 'and this.'

Amah Feng scratched her head. 'I'm washing them at home . . .'

'I said put them back to where they were!' Amah Feng, taken aback at her master's first ever outburst, bit her quivering lips like a child waiting to be punished. My guardian's voice softened. 'You'll do it tomorrow. Now, put them back and go home.'

He continued with his dinner as though nothing had happened. He picked up a big piece of my favourite sea cucumber and dropped it in my bowl: 'Eat, Engi. It's good for you,' his voice tired as an old man's. I looked up. He had aged. In that split second I saw the sudden exhaustion swooping down on him. I saw the sadness in his gaze, like the cries of a lone gibbon from a deep, mysterious end of the forest.

'I'm glad you're here, Engi. I'm so glad,' he muttered, his face partially hidden behind the bowl. As he mechanically shoved rice into his mouth, a drop of water squeezed out from the corner of his right eye.

*

There was sadness, too, in the bedtime story told by my guardian that night:

'. . . Years later, with *his* help, the Kathakali dancer escaped from the troupe and they returned to the village where they'd met. The dancer no longer danced but cooked and washed and cleaned the house, while *he* taught and brought food home. At night they went to sit by the river and played music on their leaf-flutes.

'Days passed, months. The Kathakali dancer was getting bored, beginning to miss his colourful costumes, bright lights and make-up, the applause and endless happiness and sadness of the stories and his roles. The young dancer stared at his fingernails, cracked and blackened, and thought, "No, this isn't right; I deserve better," and left.

'The room was empty when *he* returned from work, with only a torn leaf on the table, not even a flute.'

243

4

The Secret Messenger

Life went on as usual: Tiansheng at the shop with his routine, Chai at home, and me moving between the two. Seemingly.

Under this normality, I began to assume a not-to-be-spoken-of duty. I became my guardian's messenger. Every day between lunch and the two-hour study, Taukeh Chai handed me an envelope. 'Take the shortcut through the rubber estate. Don't spend too much time on the road.' Montgomery's bungalow was a mile away from the Baba Lodge. I had been there twice with Chai, had known well the path through the plantations, avoiding the main road. 'Slow down, Engi,' more than once he'd said during those trips, panting, as my forest-grown legs marched ahead, the damp soil a familiar comfort.

He'd known it from the start. There was no better candidate for the job he'd planned. He'd chosen me.

From March 1905 to April 1908, I trudged between the rows of fast-maturing trees, between Taukeh Chai at one end and Montgomery at the other, their secrets exchanged through my hands: the first harvest, the sales, the profits that came like roaring waves of the South China Sea, each rising higher, more forceful than the one before. Unstoppable. I saw, oozing out from under the skilfully peeled bark, the liquid purer than the canned condensed milk Montgomery used to make tea with, and learned from my guardian a new word: 'latex'.

Come February, I watched the leaves turn yellow then brown; I watched the wind force them off the boughs; I watched them fall and be strewn on the dried soil, whirling up, circling in the suffocating gusts devoid of humidity, sucking the trees dry. Three months of empty clay cups on the trunks, three months of reluctant holidays for the workers.

In May, I watched green leaves shooting out, white milk still dripping from fresh cuts in the afternoon heat, and shouted aloud my newly learned list: 'Tyres for carts, bicycles and cars, balls, soles for shoes . . .' But what was a bicycle? And a car? How could a steel structure move by itself? My guardian, knowledgeable as he was, had never been a good artist. His sketchy illustrations only further roused my curiosity.

At night, they invaded my dreams, the wheels and the mechanical forms, cold to the touch. I shrivelled, slunk and hid in the dark corner of a cave. The ground shook under my feet, and from above earth and dust came loose, showering on me. Outside, giant machines rolled over the forest floor, trees and brambles flattened under gigantic wheels; where they had been, there were indentations of black rubber – melted in the sweltering heat – over crushed birds and animals dotted along the trampled ground.

From the plantations I picked up mature rubber seeds, brownish black and dry, the size of a cuckoo egg. I drilled holes in them and tied them to the edges of a matchbox. 'A car.' With a six-inch stick I carefully pieced together two seeds, one on each end. 'A bicycle.' I stared at my inventions, feeling even more fearful than I was in my dreams. *What has got into me?* I could have filled my catapult with the seeds, could have shot down pheasants with them and made a barbeque the way I once used to, deep in the forest.

I didn't.

In the streets of Malacca, the first bicycle sprung up in a swirl of dust like the magic carpet in Taukeh Chai's story and rattled on the earthy gravel. Behind it, children tailed in bare feet, cheering, screaming: 'Iron horse! Iron horse!' Cling! Cling! Cling! The white man in his white suit snaked ahead, leaving another gust of yellow cloaking over the little shirtless bodies in its wake.

Two, five and more iron horses subsequently emerged in the streets and alleys. When Grocer Tan and Tiansheng began to use the two-wheeled vehicle for delivery, I wobbled on mine on the uneven path of the rubber estate, a letter in my chest pocket: hands grasping tightly at the rubber-coated metal bars, body vibrating to the hard crashing of rubber tyres against fallen boughs, puddles and mounds.

The magic of rubber. I felt it and learned practically of its usage, no longer just names and phrases, no longer the stinking liquid flowing from the tree.

The magic of Taukeh Chai. As I cycled on I became aware of the hidden power of my guardian's secret treasure.

Days lapsed into strenuous pedalling, months rolled by with the turning of the wheels. Years. As I cycled on, sheets noting galloping figures continued to travel to my guardian, the amounts doubling, tripling, safely kept in the Hong Kong and Shanghai Bank, in an account Montgomery had helped to open. Occasionally there were heavy bundles wrapped in wax paper. 'Never ever open them!' Montgomery made me tie them across my body under my shirt, to be retrieved only by my guardian; their contents, their eventual hiding place were never revealed to me.

As I cycled on, unknown to me, as to anyone else, my guardian had become one of the wealthiest men in town.

And my other duty commenced.

After dinner.

A bundle strapped to my shoulder; in my ears my guardian's repeated warning, similar to Montgomery's as he handed the similar cotton-wrapped packets to me: 'Don't you dare to tell anyone. It's a secret; our secret.'

A quick pedal to the dark alley behind Market Street, counting down the row of back doors, stopping at No. 8.

Three knocks between long pauses, followed by two quick raps.

A squeak of the door being dragged open.

The handing over of the bundle.

There were never explanations, and no questions were expected.

As I grew up, long after my night missions were over, memories and dreams of them overlapped, their boundaries blurred. I cycled aimlessly in blackness, veering into an inviting door. Inside, a corridor so long it seemed to be endless. My cycling was endless. Darkness, too. Endless also was the sharp, penetrating squeak, smothering the familiar hoots of an owl.

Before everything stopped. The images, the sounds. The fear.

*

Two incidents marked the beginning of 1908: a failed uprising at the estuary of the Yunnan River against Qing rule, and following that, the official break-up of Chai & Tian Company. Bearing equal weight, the two generated equal amounts of after-work and after-meal topics, entertaining the townsfolk for years to come.

Yet no one had speculated about the connection between the two.

Even until today, if you walk into a teahouse or an open-air tea stall, you will find eager storytellers from a table of elderly townsfolk – former coolies and shop owners with sagging flesh and loose muscles – reminiscing about the past, their only pastime. Cheeks shrunken, mouths shrivelled, lips sunk into where teeth once were, they would shake their heads as they grieve for the deaths of the heroes sacrificed in their mission.

'It was a big blow,' the elderly men would say as they relate the defeat. 'Those young bloods, some barely twenty. And think of their families, think of the people who'd put their trust in them.' And their cataract-infested eyes would be lost in an unseeable distance.

It was said the revolutionists, who'd planned an uprising, had been promised a shipment of firearms by the Japanese, their keenest sympathizers. Months passed. While they were craning their necks at the estuary of the Yunnan River, somewhere in the East Sea, the notorious pirates of the *Black Eagle* climbed onto the ship and raised their flag high on the mast, declaring it theirs.

Only the cargoes they wanted; the crew on board was killed or drowned in the wild waters.

The storytellers, eyes wide, faces red, described the scene of dispirited seamen standing in a row on deck before the roaring waves into which they fell after a barrage of gunshots. Flop! Flop! Flop! They raised their arms in the movements the falling sailors would make, as though they had been there witnessing the crime.

That the Japanese, with all the ammunition in their hold, had succumbed to the sea robbers like chickens tied on a chopping board was a question too hard for the peasant-born minds. A mystery. For the rebels, there was only one explanation: 'It must have been the Qing! They'd conspired with the *Black Eagle*, had given them the weapons they needed!' They gritted their teeth, their anger bursting like flames.

'Why on earth would some pirate target that particular shipment? Someone must have been behind them, must have wanted to see the young men dead.' Farmer Chong, one of the most indignant commentators, shook his head, yet unable to shake off his disbelief, firm as Mount Tahan. The fact that piracy was common during those days, that arms trafficking was the most profitable underground business, wouldn't change his view.

However, it was the demoralizing effect of the loss that mattered the most. Disappointed by yet another defeat, some patriotic businessmen dropped their support for the revolutionists.

That Grocer Tan, the most enthusiastic of all, was one of them, brought the patriotic spirit down to the bottom of the dark abyss. None had questioned the source of it when Grocer Tan, a petty grocery shopkeeper, continuously channelled money to the anti-Qing movement; but when he stopped, fingers started pointing at him. Besides the common remarks of 'ungrateful', 'cold-hearted' and 'turning his back on his roots', accusations of illicit activities (*How did he come up with all that money in the first place?*) were raised. As to how a grocer who ran his shop single-handedly from morning till night, with only the help of his wife, would find time to administer an underground business – the question was somehow tactfully avoided.

To a fifteen-year-old, there were only noises, loud, persistent, incomprehensible. And amid those noises, my special evening duty came to an abrupt end.

Ten years later, on that Sunday afternoon after my twenty-five-year-old self's encounter with the travelling salesman, I walked aimlessly out of the teahouse along Market Street, plodding on, into the narrow streets and alleys. I felt not the searing sun on my head and shoulders, nor its sharp penetration through my thin soles each time my feet landed on the earthy ground. I walked. Between rows of shops, front doors, back doors. Then I found myself stopping in the middle of a back lane.

A door stared bluntly at me.

Intuitively, I raised my hand, my fist a frozen surprise in the air.

'Three knocks between long pauses, followed by two quick raps.' The instruction given by my guardian years ago crept up from my memory, ringing clear in my ears.

I looked at the wooden plank in front of me, feeling familiar yet strange. The same door I had been knocking in the dark for nearly three years as a child somehow seemed different in broad daylight.

The glaring sun was a magnifier. I could see every seam, every crack, every red peel of paint on the fraying board. Too bright; my eyes hurt and I glanced down. I saw the scraps of rice and flour and animal feed strewn on the ground, the white and dark brown against yellow (soil) and red (threshold), and imagined the gunny sacks being carried into the storeroom, the contents squeezing through the seams, spilling, trailing along.

The trademark of a rear exit of a grocery.

Tan's.

I saw the bundles I handed into the waiting hands behind the door.

Bang. Heavy door thumped closed before my face.

Bang. The abrupt termination of my monthly night mission in the early months of 1908.

I dropped my hand.

Everything became apparent.

It was my guardian who had contributed to the revolutionists. In Grocer Tan's name. It was he, also, who had given up on his homeland after the failed uprising.

I searched my memory and my notebook for the early days of 1908, estimating the dates when the news from the north reached us, back-checking against signs of abnormality at the Baba Lodge. And my journal recorded my guardian's rare absence at dinner one evening.

That night, however, he had come as usual to my room and delivered a story about the unnamed third person's sorrow, after the Kathakali dancer's departure:

'*He* stood alone in the empty house. Even with *his* eyes closed he could hear the music, *he* could see the shadows shifting around *him*. The shadows of the dancer who couldn't stop dancing. *He* saw the tilting of *his* friend's head, his hands, his fingers; the kicking of his legs, the lifting of his feet, the twitching of his toes. So graceful, so delicate. So familiar. A tilt, *his* heart ached; a kick, *his* heart ached; a lift, *his* heart ached; a twitch, *his* heart ached. *He* held *his* breath, and everything froze. *His* aching turned into anger. All *his* hopes, *his* love, vanished into thin air.

'*This is it. He* opened *his* eyes, whisked the broken leaf from the table and tore it into pieces. *He* walked out, the way the dancer had walked out from his long-lost parents and later, from *him*; the door thumped shut behind *him*. Inside, the debris of wilted brown dotted the yellow ground.

'*He* would never return, never look back. *He* decided.'

My guardian's lips had clasped tight and he'd speak no more.

I should've known: everything had stopped from there on. Stories, the bundles at night, the squeaking back door in the darkness. The failure of the uprising a disappointment so great that it had led him to surrender his hope.

*

How habits rule us.

Only when it stopped did I become aware of my yearning for it, the storytelling. I yearned for the footsteps, light as a cat's, skimming the stairs, gliding through the corridor. The turn of the doorknob. The love and hatred of the characters in his tales; their adventures, fortunes and miseries.

His voice.

The shadows of bedposts on the walls like shuffling trees in the forest.

Alone in the back room, I lay awake and restless, silence weighing down on me from all sides, heavy as dawn mist in the dense woods. Suffocating, I got out of bed.

I sneaked into blackness. I was the night rider, roaming in streets deep in sleep. Wind in my ears, inside my thin shirt and sleeves, puffy with breeze slinking in and out like a child in a game of hide-and-seek. I heard not the daytime taunts of '*sakai*' but night noises from stray cats and dogs, out from the darkness, liberated as I was. The streets were mine; the town was mine. *Yes, it could be mine.* As I pedalled on the idea came to me: I would keep a record of events of the place I'd been planted in, the evidence of my existence. I would one day tell stories of my own, the way Father and Taukeh Chai did.

5

A Hunter in Town

My night-time adventure continued, without bundles, without missions. Only me and my teenage anxiety.

After dark. Lights out, noises ceased, an iron horse waiting by the inside of the back exit, as impatient as I was to burst into the open.

I marvelled at my agility, the ability to keep every movement almost soundless. Not even a click at the door, not a bump of the tyres on the threshold, of the handle-bars against the narrow panels.

It was my hunter's instinct; it re-emerged when needed.

I smiled, quietly elated. Perhaps they had never left me, had simply been in hibernation, my forest-trained body and senses.

Forest-trained legs stomped on the pedals as if they were fallen boughs strewn on the jungle floor; forest-trained eyes combed the urban streets as if searching for my next boars; forest-trained ears pricked up for movements of scavengers, humans or animals, of activities so dark even the moon was ashamed to unveil them.

I saw them all.

Behind the back walls of the town's riches, stooping skeletal figures shuffled from bin to bin, shooing away stray cats and dogs as they rummaged for scraps of food, their movement slow as battered animals'. I knew them, coolies who had become invalids, or had been used to their limit and aged prematurely in exhaustion, or had smoked (the opium) or gambled away their meagre income. Alone, penniless.

The luckier (such a word of irony) among them were the sick, the elderly and the disabled, who might find refuge at their respective clan houses – Hokkien, Teochew, Hakka, Hainanese or Cantonese – might even be granted their dream trip home.

But for many, going home was a promise never to be realized.

In shelters made of cargo planks and rusty tin pieces in secluded corners, or in abandoned huts or warehouses, the more unfortunate ones, the regretful gamblers and opium addicts, shrank and shivered in tropical winds and rain, their days counting down, each more unbearable than the last.

A life as fetid as the buckets of manure disposed of at night.

Around midnight, men with cotton wrapped below their eyes strode into back alleys, to the outdoor lavatories scattered along the lane. Out in minutes, they hunched under the two laden buckets hanging down from a bamboo pole on their shoulders.

On my first encounter with one of them in the narrow alley, I veered in time to escape a clash, my bicycle and I collapsing to one side as the man with his load scurried past, eyes fixed afar, not a glance at me. I choked at the odour, cloaking over the town like the fetid rafflesia, the giant blossom in the jungle. I retched at the sight, the spilling of the dark brown content, the wriggling maggots, threads of white against the mess. The stains.

Even in the darkness I saw them, on the masked man's trousers, his legs, his bare feet; dripping onto the ground as he marched ahead as quickly as he could, the buckets swaying at the ends of the pole, all the way to the river.

For these men, life was as filthy as the manure they carried. Night after night, bucketful after bucketful of human waste sank into the waters, washed away. And there would be tomorrow, the same routes, the same buckets, which couldn't be cleaned with a quick rinse in the shallows. Solid filth could be swept downstream by the current, yet the humiliations they bore on their shoulders couldn't. Their lives, too. Stranded mid-air, the lands they once ploughed, once stamped on, that once provided them with food and warmth, were thousands of miles away.

Such irony, that the filth they loathed, that they discarded by night, was the source that fed them by day.

I worked out their routine, learned to avoid their paths.

And there were more to be avoided.

In 1908, my journal recorded a series of petty crimes committed under my hunter's eyes. Light and quick as a mouse though the burglars were, my forest-trained eyes captured their every move: a swift crawl up the windowsill, prying open the shutters, leaping in, and then out in minutes, a bulgy gunny sack slung across their shoulders. On my pages I jotted down the dates, the locations (the street names and house numbers, or any outstanding signs of the targeted residents), descriptions of the thieves – their clothes, their sizes and shapes – to the best detail I could manage.

But something was missing. Because of the dimness,

because of the distance, the intruders' faces were too oblique to scrutinize, and getting closer was a risk I would not take. I was frustrated. I would not know their identities, a column yet to be filled in my otherwise perfect account. A flaw.

Still, I knew more than anyone else.

The day after a break-in, stories and speculation would hover around the town like whirlwinds, zooming in and out of teahouses, grocers, bakeries, the market-place, and find their way into Chai & Tian Company where I would be stacking stock. As the winds swirled and passed through the many garrulous mouths, they twisted and turned, and colours were added to the best imaginings possible of the thieves and their spoils, how they had leapt onto the walls, walked on the roofs and drugged their victims before robbing them like the villains did in the martial arts stories, popular among the Chinese.

How laughable!

I, the true witness, giggled inside while I pricked up my ears for more creative tales of a similar sort. At fifteen, after three years in the outside world, I'd learned to keep my mouth shut and my head low.

To complete this absurdity, there was even talk of the eventual emergence of a righteous hero, as usually happens in the picture books of sword-play classics, to yank out the baddies and safeguard the town! And everybody would live happily ever after. Such fantasies, unexpectedly, enriched my otherwise dull life; a sprinkle of catkins on a pond of dead water, now rippling, ring chasing after ring.

One of those mornings after, from the second-floor

storage area where I was working, I heard the comments from our petty suppliers, loud, excited, unsympathetic:

Collector A: 'Eh, it was Taukeh Gan's this time, a pair of Ming vases and nothing else.'

Collector B: 'Who'd know about the vases if not an insider? A servant or some sort?'

Collector C: 'Hush! Watch your tongue. Last week, at Taukeh Lim's, a dozen ivory cups were gone; not a trace. An insider again? I doubt it.'

Collector A: 'As I say, only someone with a magic power has the insight, and is able to move so freely at night.'

Collector C: 'Eh, didn't Old Lee say he spotted a dark shape?'

Collector B: 'You mean *"You Guizi"*, the "Black Spirit"?'

Collector A: 'Sssh—'

The air froze in a panicked silence. That was rare. I put down the load in my hands, stuck out my neck and glanced down at the men by the foot of the stairs, only to find their faces paler than rice paper. Fear seemed to have risen in the form of a sleek and slim shadow, swish, swish, zig-zagging in the room, over their heads, swift as lightning.

The 'Black Spirit'.

The local legend describes someone who summons evil power from the unknown world for his evil motives. Dressed in black and doused in oil, he would seemingly melt into darkness, his movement so quick he appears invisible to the naked eye. He would roam freely in the small hours, breaking into homes for valuables or women, who would fall into deep sleep under his spell, oblivious to abuse. The next morning they would wake to find their loss and shame, and a pool of excrement – a token of the burglar's triumphant visit, a humiliation – left prominently in the house.

No, that wasn't a 'Black Spirit', I was certain. I'd seen him more than once, that particular thief, only sneaking into the mansions of the town's wealthiest; dressed in black though he was, yet far from 'oily', and his movement visible through my naked eyes. A man bearing that evil title, I thought, would do better than that.

There had been three cases of a similar kind on my list in recent weeks: the first was the mansion of the new rubber tycoon, Taukeh Liu; the second, Goldsmith Lim's shop house; the third victim was Taukeh Lok, the owner of a textile wholesaler. Taukeh Lok! The Baba Lodge, with Chai & Tian Company now on the list of the town's top ten richest, would have been *more eligible* than the textile trader to be robbed. I thought of my guardian's newly acquired Ming painting, scrolling down prominently on the wall in the study; a celestial figure on a lotus-filled pond, fine, delicate, intriguing. I thought of the calligraphic displays, works of Master Wang Xizi. What had blinded the robber's eyes?

Despite the speculation, none of the cases had been solved. Chinese matters were never the priority of the colonial police. 'With a pile of gold in their coffers,' I imagined them sneering, 'one or two stones gone missing won't hurt.'

I could have followed him, I could have reported my findings to the police. They would reward me, would even make me a hero; with that, perhaps no one would call me '*sakai*' ever again, might even befriend me.

FRIENDSHIP was a seduction greater than the honey Father gathered, which I missed dearly. But was it a risk worth taking – exposing my little secret, sacrificing my night-time pleasure? I was locked in a self-induced dilemma, oblivious to the passing of time, standing on the top of the stairs as if in a trance.

A sharp pain burned my head before the second slap fell on my temple. Taukeh Tiansheng, standing tall, stared at me with such fury: I was the boar lamed by a shot from the blowpipe, waiting to be slaughtered. The last blow landed on my face and I stumbled onto the baskets of sandalwood behind me, their sharp edges jutting hard at my protruding ribcage. Was it the pain or did I imagine it? The world around me seemed to have sealed in a vacuum; a sudden quietness. I struggled to get to my feet; before my eyes, Taukeh Tiansheng's angry mouth was a gigantic hole, opening and closing, opening and closing in quick succession; his voice came to me through layers of water, a faraway, distorted sound wave, fading off.

That would be how I perceived sounds for days to come. When words returned to me, they entered only through my right ear. The left was silent.

I was fifteen, bursting with abundance of youthful energy. And angst.

*

Night again.

I glided down the slope, slicing through the air waves. Even the breeze would not soothe the heat inside my stomach, a volcano boiling with anger, frustration and hatred, near erupting. I was imperfect, half-deaf. I had not told anyone, not Taukeh Chai, and certainly not the man who had caused my injury. *Never reveal your fear in front of the beasts.* Father's words rang clear in my head; words I couldn't understand then were now interpreted as: 'Never expose your weakness in front of your enemy.' Overnight, after the fall, I was no longer a child.

I pounded the pedals so hard my feet hurt. I felt the rubber tyres crushing the gravel, occasional stones and branches, and my legs moved faster. Forward was the only target. Go, go, go! My body became lighter, my heart, too.

Speed, my newly discovered game of wind-chasing, of a man and his machine fighting against the power of nature, against all contradictory forces; only the stronger, the one who persevered prevailed. As I cycled on, houses and signposts rolled swiftly past like the kinescope Taukeh Chai had shown me in his study, blurring away in dimness. I was stronger, I knew. The winner. The amount of kinetic energy (another newly acquired term) I generated had far overwhelmed those forces. *Father must be pleased.*

Father.

My eyes warmed with wetness. I thought of the training Father had given me as a child.

A black shape shot out onto the street. I veered, in a curve smooth as a new moon. It was a cat, fast disappearing into an alley, not fast enough to escape my eyes. A glance, just a glance and I could tell. *Focus; always be alert. How can I abandon your teachings, Father? How can I abandon the hunter inside me?*

In the darkness shadows loomed: big or small, animals or people, foes or friends. *I am not afraid, Father. I know*

now. I know that, despite the location, despite being away from you, I can still be a hunter, an urban one; I can still put your training to full use. I will look out for my prey in a man-made forest.

The night manure men had long gone. I turned into a back lane, propped my bicycle against the wall and prepared to release myself. There was a sound. Across the gravel, a black figure was sneaking out from an open window. My heart throbbed. It was him, the presumed 'Black Spirit'. *Temple Street, No. 3 or 4.*

He did not see me; it was my hunter's instinct that I'd hidden myself in the shadow of an extended tin roof, my dark clothes and skin melting into it. *About five foot ten; skinny; brown shirt, black trousers; no mask.* Who? Who exactly was he? As I stared at the receding silhouette, my stomach rumbled with curiosity and the feeling of incompleteness – there would always be blank spaces in my record.

No! I crept in the darkness like a fox, eyes fixed at my target, and I camouflaged myself in the shadows of trees and buildings, moved as he moved, stopped as he would.

I followed him: southwards along Market Street, sidling into the alley behind the Red House, the Colonial Office, reappearing on Riverside Road. Another turn, out on the main street by the seafront. Before some scattered warehouses, he stopped, had a look around. My heart throbbed; I slid into the thin shade of a palm. I held my breath, a cold sweat running over me. *He won't see me, he won't see me, he won't see me,* I chanted in silence, my face, my body squeezed tight against the tree, merging with it into one.

Keep still, very still, Father's voice rang loud in my

head. I froze, with it the world around me. A minute, two. There came a squelch of a door, and another, then quietness. He was inside. I slipped to the ground, legs soft as water, mouth gasping for air.

I looked up. A faint light flickered from the window of one of the depots, obscured from the outside, as it was piled high with a waste tin roof and plank wood. *Unnamed warehouse, number five from the left on the main street.* My entry was complete.

The moon was disappearing. Because of the stalking, because of the walking, it was getting very late now, later than my usual outing. I could have retrieved my bike and gone home, fallen asleep soundly with a sweet smile on my face, and decided tomorrow if I would hand in my book to the police; instead I fixed my eyes on the source of brightness, eerie in the blackness devoid of other human beings. Through the slightly open window I saw shuffling figures – two, or three? *What are they doing?* I stepped forward.

Noises began to waft my way as I was approaching. A man's voice.

'. . . Marvellous! Look at this . . .'

Vague though the voice came through, it sounded familiar. I squeezed into the gap between the building and the waste materials. Startled rats squealed and disappeared into the foot of the wall, where a board had come loose. I peeped through a crevice on the neatly nailed planks, against which my good ear pressed closely.

A glance, and my mind turned blank.

It was Taukeh Tiansheng. A porcelain bowl held high above his nose, he searched its bottom for the inscription.

'"Jing Tailan pottery", an original no doubt, can be dated back to the Tang Dynasty.'

Because both of the men were standing less than two feet from me, partitioned only by the thin wall, because of the peephole effect, Tiansheng's rare, big smile magnified before me, like the sudden blossoming of a chrysanthemum. A stranger he'd become, not the irascible man I'd known from the shop.

'Well done, Ah Fook. This will fetch us a fortune. Ha, they'll be fighting their guts out over it, those foreign devils!' He patted the shoulder of a skinny man in a black shirt, the thief, who was standing behind him.

Ah Fook? I strained my eyes, could make out the features now, a teenage worker of Farmer Chong's, much praised for his diligence.

'How about this?' A third man, plump and moustached, emerged like a ghost from the darker far end of the store, where the lamplight barely reached. He held up a small wooden container as he headed towards Tiansheng, indicating the hay-padded interior.

The box was snatched. Tiansheng felt the inside thoroughly with his hand.

'Add more, at least another inch of padding. No more mistakes this time. Remember how you broke the Ming vase? People only wanted them in a pair. Those *gweilos* are not fools. They know what they're looking for. Cut the money to more than half. What a waste.' He handed it to the man, who walked his way to the back of the room, almost disappearing into the dimness.

'We'll take a break this week.' Tiansheng turned to Ah Fook. He felt for his waist pouch, shelled out some coins. 'Take this, for a great job.'

Ah Fook counted the money, looked lost. He scratched his head, hesitated: 'But . . . I need more. It's my mother . . . Two months now, and she doesn't seem to get better. She needs more medicine. My old man's letter didn't sound good.' His mutters were almost intelligible; I pasted my good ear so hard to the wall that it hurt.

'Don't worry, you'll get the rest next week. I promise. I have a bigger deal to close tomorrow; a really big one. Furthermore, there's been too much talking, you know, those people in town. "Black Spirit", ha!' He punched the youngster lightly on his arm, and teenage elation instantly overwhelmed sadness, lighting up Ah Fook's otherwise worried face.

'Your father would be proud of you.'

Immediately Ah Fook's head bowed low, his smile ceased. I looked away, my stomach sore. I felt his shame. Father would've beaten me to death if I'd ever become a thief.

There was sudden brightness. I was glued to the peephole. The back of the warehouse was now clearly visible in a flood of yellow. It seemed that the moustached man had, after fumbling to no avail for a few moments for more hay or other filling materials, lit a candle. It swayed in his grasp, as his other hand clumsily clung on to the small box, which was nearly falling.

'Be careful!' Tiansheng roared.

The container and the candle fell onto the ground. Sparks of fire spattered. The moustached man froze on his feet. A shadow darted passed him, and another, and quick successions of footsteps stomped on the rudimentary flame, which died down in minutes under Ah Fook and Tiansheng's joint effort. Tiansheng, his feet still stamping on the embers, shouted at the third man.

The angry man I'd known had returned. But what? What did he say? Too far. Only snatches of noise, meaningless, unintelligible. *Useless.* I pinched my left ear, twisting the tiny piece of flesh between my fingers, felt the pain. No sound.

I kept watching, trying to speculate from the actions and gestures. At centre stage of the pantomime, Tiansheng grabbed the moustached man by his collar and pointed to the pile of dark shapes behind him, scolding him perhaps. He then whisked the man to one side, stepped forward and pulled off a big piece of canopy cloaking over the lot; the hem of the gunny-like material that trailed on the floor seemed to have burned. Smoke rose again, a choking smell. I covered my nose and my mouth with a hand, the urge to cough pressed down, stuck at my throat; a silent burp.

In the dimness I made out, under the cover, boxes the size of standard fruit crates for shipping, dozens of them, neatly stacked up in five or six rows. With a quick sweep with his foot, Tiansheng cleared away the ash and proceeded to move one of the cargoes in the front row, closest to where the fire had been. It didn't budge. He grunted (I imagined the foul words he'd thrown on me in the shop). The other two men came forward, and the three of them, hunched under the weight, moved it presumably to a safer corner, and they continued to transfer the rest. Thump, thump, thump. The ground under me vibrated as each box touched down. Gold pieces? I scratched my head, counted: twenty-four, or more, perhaps. Could he then be richer than Taukeh

266

Chai? I gasped in silence. A chill breeze of the small hours brushed past, and I shrivelled: *If Taukeh Tiansheng discovered me spying on him . . .*

I shrank into the pile of junk and looked no more. I stayed motionless. My bike. How I wished I could jump on it, wheeling out of my quandary, but my iron horse was streets away, and no, not a noise should I be making, definitely not walking across the gravel. A cold sweat washed over me as I thought of my earlier journey trudging over it. How lucky (or stupid) I'd been, but doing it again I would be a fool.

I was trapped.

Time crawled like a snail. Amid the quietness, the occasional howling of a stray dog came through vague and distant, its slow drawl comforting. I was back in the forest, in the little hut, sprawling on the bamboo floor, cool and soothing, as I slipped into the deepest nook of my dreamland, adorned with the familiar calls of animals, of woodpeckers and owls. With Father watching closely over me.

A click of a padlock, and two, and I woke.

I watched them disappear at the turn of the corner, and climbed slowly out from my hiding place, legs heavy with pins and needles.

What would Father do if he were here? I looked at the warehouse, now immersed in the night dark as ink. I thought of my bicycle, of my feather-soft bed and pillow. I shook my head, shaking myself out of drowsiness. No, I'm the urban hunter; let him, my tormentor, be my first prey.

I tried the padlocks, twisted this way and that, but they wouldn't budge. *How unwise, Engi.* Father would have laughed at me if he were here, I knew. *The rat hole! There must be one somewhere.* I dipped once again into the mound of waste materials, found an iron bar and pried open the loose piece of plank with it. Lying down, I squeezed my skinny body sideways into the depot.

*

I pedalled as if fleeing for my life, looking at nothing, avoiding nothing. One round, two, more. Faster, faster, faster. My head spun with every spin of the wheels, yet the Baba Lodge seemed to be miles away. My bicycle kept wobbling and bouncing on the uneven gravel, as my hands and body trembled, shaken by what I'd just seen.

Before daybreak that morning in April 1908, before the town woke to its second biggest drama of the year, before Tiansheng – one of the two leading characters of the Break-up of Chai and Tian Show – rose from his river of dreams streaming with gold pieces he would never have, I arrived in the anonymous warehouse by the seafront's main street for a second time. With Taukeh Chai. I'd woken him. Perhaps it was my tone, pressing, quivering with fear, so that at the mention of Tiansheng my guardian jumped off his bed and rushed out. What did he have in mind? His friend having an accident? I sighed. *My kind and forgiving guardian.* Tailing behind, I swallowed back the initial urge to reveal the content of my find.

The cargoes were arranged in two separate piles. We started with the first. Under the paraffin lamp I'd pre-pared, I watched Chai read, inscribed in red paint on the crates, characters resembling those of Chinese, but which were not. I watched him, eyes still puffy from a truncated sleep, as astonished as I was when I first saw them. Japanese, he said, a language he was yet to learn; nevertheless, he recognized kanji, the form borrowed from Chinese letters. Although the scripts seemed to be exactly the same as the originals and might even bear similar meanings, he explained, the pronunciations were quite often different.

Painted on the covers of the boxes was the name of a factory. '"Made in Japan" and . . .' – he hesitated – '. . . some manufacturer's name.' That gave nothing away of the cargoes.

I watched him remove the cover of the first one, the one I'd earlier prised loose.

Thud! The plank fell on the ground.

Guns. Dozens of them. Sharp blades of bayonets glowed yellow in the lamplight, pale as my guardian's face, as I'd been on my first encounter.

He snatched from the floor the iron bar I had left and hurried to the second crate. His hands shook, green veins snaking on the back of them, as he worked on the lid.

More guns.

And the third, fourth, fifth and more.

Bullets, explosives, cartridges, machine guns.

A total of thirty-two crates of them, enough for the revolutionists to paralyse the Qing troops at the estuary of the Yunnan River.

It was the shipment said to have been plundered by the *Black Eagle*.

We moved to the second lot, about twenty of them, all without inscriptions. Even before opening them, as he approached the pile, my guardian frowned. He sneezed, having detected the acrid smell. 'No, not this . . .' he gasped. I knocked off the cover of the first crate, and the stench grew stronger, wafting through the room. Taukeh Chai stepped back, a hand on his nose, trying to contain a bout of sneezes assailing him. He shook his head, his hand a dismissing wave. 'No, I don't have to look at them. I know what they are.'

I stared at the blocks of coagulated black mud neatly stacked in the crate. I, too, knew what they were.

During my night excursions, I came across huts or rooms lighted till late, either tucked in secluded corners or dark alleys, or sandwiched between taller, bigger buildings, with only an insignificant entrance in sight, and a lone bulb to lead the way. I saw people go in and out: stooped, skeletal figures; some breathlessly humming snatches of out-of-tune opera, truncated in places, some wobbling all their way out. I knew them. They were the Chinese labourers. Their mouths stank with the same stench as the black cake in the crates.

The opium.

During those days, opium dens grew in number like parasites; the Chinese labourers' own numbers, and dependency on the dens, grew at a proportionate scale. One draw, they said, and gone were the backache, the cracking bones, the frozen shoulders; gone were the frustrations of long hours under scorching sun in the plantations, at the dock, on the construction sites; gone also were the homesickness, the caring wife on the other land, parents and grandparents to whom filial duties were yet to be fulfilled.

Once, on an errand for Taukeh Tiansheng, I bumped into a forest collector who had just sold his collection at Chai & Tian Company earlier that day. I'd weighed his load before Taukeh Tiansheng paid him based on the figure I reported. This was the routine my superior established, the laborious tasks now conveniently laid on my shoulders. I would steady the scale with my left hand, holding it as high up as I could, letting the basketful of rattan dangle down on one end, and on the other, adjusting the brass weight along the pole with my left hand for a perfect balance, then read out the measurement.

Six collectors came in at about the same time that morning, each with a heavy load. 'Faster!' Taukeh Tiansheng clicked the abacus in his hand aimlessly, impatient. The swift clinking of the pieces rumbled in my head, my heart raced; beads of sweat rolled down from my forehead, my eyes blurred. 'Twenty-eight *jin*,' I shouted. As I glanced up, I saw a flicker in the collector's gaze. I looked down at the scale, at where I was still holding the string of the weight: twenty-five.

I panicked. To correct my mistake meant another possible bout of scolding and slapping from my superior. I kept quiet. The collector took the money from Taukeh Tiansheng, winked at me and smiled his way out of the shop.

Later in the street in broad daylight, that very same collector dragged me into a narrow entrance between two shops, into a dim, smoke-shrouded room.

'I'm giving you a treat. You deserve it.' He made me sit on the edge of a long wooden platform, among those figures reclining on it, long pipes in their hands, looking at no one, talking to no one.

'You'll love it.' The forest collector handed a pipe to me. 'And you can always come back for more, on my account.' He winked at me. 'You know what I mean, don't you?'

I stared at the ceramic bowl at the end of it, at the black, bubbling froth; the vapour wafted right in my face. And the smell. I choked; a bout of ferocious coughing. Tears and nasal mucus squeezed their way out, splattered. The collector's laughter rang loud in my ear. I pushed aside the pipe and ran out of the den to the bright, brilliant sunshine.

And never had I set foot in there again.

Thud! I dropped the lid onto the crate of the hated contents. Closed. *No, I will not set my eyes on them ever again*. The sight, the fresh odour of the opium blocks had rekindled the old, hibernating humiliation I had been striving to shrug off. *No, they will not land in the opium dens, they will not feed Tiansheng's pocket.* I did not know yet my guardian's plan for the arms, but as he turned to walk away, I envisaged a cremation for the other lot of our find. I saw the blocks of dark filth melting in the blazing flames; fierce, forceful red tongues, licking away the last of the poisonous substance.

6

Two Boars Down with a Single Shot

Dawn hadn't fully broken when we arrived back in the Baba Lodge. My guardian ran up the stairs and burst into Tiansheng's room.

'Leave now.' Tired like an old man, he wafted emptily in the still-dim corridor. 'Send me your address and I'll arrange for your share to be delivered to you.'

I climbed stealthily up the stairs, bent over the first few steps on the top like a hunter would, against Chai's order to stay in my room. No, I would not miss the climax of the Break-up of Chai and Tian Show. I would be the sole witness of this historical moment, the best entry for my journal.

I could see Chai standing outside the open door of Tiansheng's room. There was the rustling of cloth or sheets, a grunt, a question perhaps, indistinct.

'How could you? How could you do this?' My guardian's even more tired voice was tinged with irritation. 'I don't mind you cheating on me, but those – firearms and the opium . . . The opium! You know I hated it the most, and you know why.' He rested his hand on the door frame, as if resting his entire body weight on it.

'If you must know – we could have starved to death

at the start, without that thing you hated most.' From his room, Taukeh Tiansheng raised his voice. 'Rattan? Huh! Do you really think we made enough to live then?'

'You could have told me. We could have worked something out. Something else. Anything. Just not that.'

'What else could we have done? You knew it as well as I did. You wouldn't work at the dock, nor the plantation. And could I imagine you, Mandarin Chai, carrying bricks on the construction sites? I only tried to make things easier for us.'

'But opium! I . . . I would rather starve to death.'

'Fine!' Another rustling of clothes. I imagined Taukeh Tiansheng pulling on his shirt. 'I'm sick of it – you and your so-called nobility!' Taukeh Tiansheng rushed out of the room and headed towards the stairs. I rose and retreated. Too late. I stood face-to-face with him, who brushed past me with a grudging stare. 'And your *sakai* spy!'

Taukeh Chai turned and saw me standing. A glimpse of – surprise? – in his eyes.

'I don't owe you anything. Not any more. I've done enough for you.' Taukeh Tiansheng threw his last words as he headed to the main entrance.

The door slammed closed. Thump. A string of vibration in the quietness.

*

I propped the ladder on the shopfront and started climbing, the morning sun full on my face: a brilliant red behind my eyeballs. I felt the burning sensation on my skin, tingling. I didn't mind. I tilted my head upwards, taking it all in. Two more steps, another. I reached out for the signboard, a hammer in my hand, and I prised loose the first nail. The second, the third and fourth. Done.

CHAI & TIAN COMPANY fell to the ground, breaking into pieces. How fragile.

A crowd gathered, the loud thud a prelude to the Speculation of the Break-up of Chai and Tian Show.

Amid the buzzing 'What happened?' and 'What's going on?' I felt in my pocket for the key to the shop, now mine to man. 'You've learned enough, Engi,' my guardian had said earlier that morning, the key readily handed out; not another word.

My enemy was gone. At the click of the padlock, as the heavy bundle of metal dropped in my hand, I smiled. Without having to look at a mirror, I knew my eyes had squeezed into slits. Like Father's once did.

Father, you would have been proud of me. Two boars down with one single shot! I was a real hunter, in or outside the forest. Not only had I taken revenge on the man who hurt your dear son, but also put an end to the so-called 'Black Spirit's' night activities. How could I have done this without the skills I acquired from you? If I were in the jungle, there would be a bonfire at night. I would perform my heroic, unprecedented Two Boars Down with One Single Shot act to an eager, slack-mouthed audience, the way I did after hunting down my first wild pig.

I imagined Father's toothless laugh, the two dashes where his eyes were. I quietly sidled into the shop and replaced the door plank. I sat myself down at the foot of the stairs, the commotion outside an accolade to my achievement.

I sat. Time lapsed. The noises gradually assuaged, the passers-by having resumed their day. Gossip could wait; their lives, the many stomachs to be fed at home, could not. I was relieved, but not for too long. Very soon the small collectors would come with their harvests. I knew I should open the shop, but instead I sat still. I needed time. Everything had happened so quickly. I needed to think the whole thing over. I held my head with both hands.

Light from the outside filtered through the seams between the planks, intruding, as it sliced open the inside dimness. Thin, faint lines fell on the walls, the floor, my seated figure. What a display: a burst of even, parallel and illuminating beams filled with iridescent, dancing particles! I held out my hand, saw the patch of orange on my flesh where it caught the light, felt the warmth on my skin.

It was real.

It was for me to decide when to open the shop and when to close it, how much to pay the collectors, when and where and how and whom to send the merchandise to.

Mine, the shop was.

I stood up in a quick movement and headed straight to the door. My clients and suppliers were waiting.

*

'Don't you ever venture out at night again.' My guardian's voice appeared as firm as his face. A heavy chain tightly secured my iron horse to the latch, only to be released when daylight came.

That night I sprawled on my bed, fingers flicking the

remaining pages of my journal. Blank. *How do I fill them up – now that Tiansheng is gone, away with the drama of which he has been a major part?* And with the secret outing now forbidden, even the smallest matters of cats and dogs would not find their place in my book.

In the faint glow of candlelight, I stared up at the ceiling. In a corner, there was a black dot, moving in the air, floating. I blinked, then again, and looked up once more: eyes narrowed, focused. It was a spider, gliding on its web, fluttering in the breeze from the open window. Perhaps it was aiming at its target, closing in on it, a target so tiny that it escaped my naked eyes in the poor lighting. Perhaps it was merely striving to survive the wind, possibly tearing apart its woven home, thought to be safe in a secluded corner of an enclosed space.

I curled up abruptly, hands over my knees. Nothing was safe for ever. And what was for ever? I once thought my life with Father and Mother, us in the forest was.

Nothing.

I thought of Taukeh Chai, his now seemingly *safe* existence. How long would it last before everything came crumbling down?

I knew how to put my notebook to good use. I had a clear target: Taukeh Chai. I would record his prime, the same way I would his downfall, his end.

PART FOUR

The Minang Villa

1

The Grand House by the River

MAY 1938

Mingzhi opens his eyes one morning to a gleam of sunlight creeping through a crack on the attap roof, and remembers the sparrow he scared away in the Fisherman's Hut. His House Number One. He stares up, squinting, and thinks he sees it again, the same tiny brown sparrow, fluttering in the haze, squeeze itself out through the torn attap into the same clear blue sky and land on the same piece of white cloud. He imagines it building a nest for its family in the giant boulder-like cloud as he'd once imagined.

A little bird settling in its mobile home, rootless and rooted.

Everywhere and anywhere is its nesting place.

Mingzhi blinks, and the bird is gone. He is back in his Minang Villa, his House Number Four. Or Five, or Six? He has lost count of them. But does it matter now? He shakes his head.

Today is the day.

He has to get ready. He grasps the sides of the brass bed-frame, gives a laborious pull and is up, sitting, breathing heavily. He takes his time. His feet prowl about on the floor, finding not his sandals but the sudden touch of coolness from the linoleum. A shudder, a sneeze, and he is fully awake now, eyes raised to the giant scroll on the wall opposite his bed and the only character on it:

家

Black ink against white paper, in clear, powerful brush-strokes.

'The dot and the cover-like constructions underneath make up the roof of a building.' A gentle, soothing voice wafts through time and space into his ears: vague, distant. *Uncle Liwei*. Mingzhi's heart clenches. He slips back into the courtyard of his childhood days, into that spring morning when his uncle told him '豕' meant 'pig', and the cover-like strokes above it meant 'roof'. Uncle Liwei said because every household reared pigs under its roof, the combination of these separate parts made the character 'house', or 'home'. His uncle carved the strokes on the sandy gravel. The thin bamboo stick sketched the outline of a curve-edged tiled roof, and underneath it, the shape of a pig with a tiny rounded head, four skinny legs and a springy tail.

'*Jia*,' Mingzhi read after his uncle.

He was six, and was thrilled by the discovery, the way the character was formed. *But if the house is filled with pigs, where do the people – where do Mother, Father, Grandpa, Sisters, Uncle Liwei and I go? Where do we sleep and eat and play?* He thought of asking his uncle. But when Uncle Liwei took out the book of *Sanzi Jing*, the 'Three-Character Classic', and started reading, asking Mingzhi to repeat after him, the boy quickly forgot his questions.

That was then, when his uncle was still his uncle, when 'house' meant the mansion. The Chai Mansion.

Mingzhi grew up without being able to grasp the true

meaning of 'home'. Even when Father, Grandpa, Sisters were still alive; when he was still there and hadn't left Mother and Uncle Liwei behind.

Even when he thought he finally had a family of his own.

*

The Minang Villa is hidden away in the lush of palm trees at the edge of the rubber plantation. Stilted, attap-roofed, sharp edges pointing to the sky. A brown agate hibernates within a mesh of green, kept cool all year round by the luxuriant fan-shaped leaves.

The house was constructed based on the traditional Minangkabau architecture, popular in the southern part of the peninsula, especially in Negeri Sembilan, where the Minangkabau culture, which originated in Indonesia, has been widely adopted. One will easily spot a Minang-kabau house among other local dwellings, and will never mistake it for something else. Buildings of this type stand prominently among the usual kampong houses-on-stilts, boldly displaying the buffalo-horn-like roof edges, point-ing high and sharp into the sky.

The front clearing is a multipurpose meeting place. In those days when parties were held at night, oil lamps were lit on the bamboo poles around the house. Long tables filled with pots of fish, chicken and lamb curries, fried rice and biryani rice, jars of red syrup drinks and Chinese tea. Men and women danced to loud music under the suddenly reddened sky, while pigs grunted and chickens clattered in their pens.

On afternoons when wages were counted, Indian labourers stood impatiently outside the residence, while their toddy waited patiently in the toddy hut. And, while their wives sat on the straw mats at home thinking of a hundred ways to escape the inescapable beating, their rubber-tapper husbands thought of a hundred new ways to beat them. Their noises droned in the ample compound.

It was in the front clearing of the Minang Villa also that a court order was delivered to Mingzhi, by a newly promoted police lieutenant. A Malay. Lieutenant Kassim would not let Burhan the driver, or his wife, Khadijah the house servant, pass the letter on to their master. He would not enter the house either, insisting on getting Mingzhi outside, meeting him under the sun.

'Who knows what people would say? Chinese *taukeh belanja kopi-O*? Too big the treat; bigger even the risk.' The new officer smoothed his moustache as he cleared his throat, his voice raised as if he was giving a public lecture: 'I am a people's servant and I work for *my* people.'

He turned to Burhan and Khadijah: 'If I were you two, I would've gone by now. Back to where you came from. *Balik* kampong. Back to the village. Be with people of our kind. Grow some paddy, catch some fish. Anything. Anything but serving a Chinese *taukeh*.'

Gazes of puzzlement were exchanged; not knowing what to anticipate, the husband and wife, after calling out for their *taukeh*, nudging each other, slowly retreated into the shadows of the villa. They watched their master, a walking stick in his hand, questions under his raised eyebrows, emerge from the house, tok-tok-tok, descend the stairs and approach the visitor. They watched Lieutenant Kassim wave the paper before the Chinese *taukeh*.

'Three months. You have three months to pack and go. What is not yours will never be yours.'

The timid Malay couple saw the smirk on Lieutenant Kassim's face, and on their master's, flashes of green and pale white. It was a windless, stifling afternoon, but they saw the letter wavering – no, it was their master's hand that was holding it, shaking like the threads on Khadijah's spinning machine. They saw surprise, anger and queries in their master's widened eyes between tightly knitted brows.

'Like you Chinese always say, "A sheet can never wrap up a fire." Phew, the secret has burned its way out, Taukeh Chai. We're taking it back, this land; it's ours. OURS, Taukeh Chai.'

They saw that their master's thin, withered lips were quivering, and nothing came out of them.

'Three months, remember. Bundle up and leave. Clean and clear. Don't make my men *help* you. I don't think they'd like to do that.' Lieutenant Kassim dusted his shiny boots before walking away.

'You're lucky, Taukeh Chai; no rent has ever been charged for – how many years? Fifteen? Twenty? We've been kind. We've always been kind to you lot. Too kind, indeed.' The officer's voice lingered long after he'd left.

Burhan and Khadijah watched their master stand alone on the yellow earth, frozen in the direction of the departing visitor, the sheet still in his raised hand. They heard the lieutenant's voice still ringing loud in the wide clearing, punctured only, towards the end, by a single burp from a hen that had been woken from its nap between the stilts under the house.

Ka. A single burp, and they saw Taukeh Chai's hand

drop to his shin, the letter scrunched up in his balled fist. They saw green veins dance on the back of his hand, wrinkled and turned scrawny by age.

They saw him toss the paper on the ground, turn and walk towards the villa. Tok-tok-tok. One tok for one step. They saw him disappear through the door, which closed behind him.

The couple did not see then what would happen two months later, right there at the clearing. They did not foresee a crowd, with torches in their grip, file into the compound of the Minang Villa, in hundreds if not a thousand. Their fellow Malays, residents of the town and neighbouring villages. Young and old, men and women, the latter with infants in their arms and toddlers by their sides. Voices raised, abuse shouted, the fire in their hands held, high up towards the night sky.

'*Pergi! Pergi! Pergi!*' They would chant. *Go! Go! Go!* Accompanied by the wailing of the young children, an outburst triggered by the ear-piercing noise, the heat, the squeezing against one another.

Burhan and Khadijah would, once again, hide in the safe shadows of the stilts under the house. They would shudder and huddle together, as they watched the mob form a human ladder, reach out for the board above the door of the Minang Villa and throw it into the bush.

They would stay put as their master lost his balance and fell to the ground.

They would hug each other tighter and shrink further into the darkness.

But for now, Khadijah glanced at the slanting after-noon sun and the patch of dark cloud that was coming their way and murmured, almost unintelligibly, as she moved towards the back entrance to the house where the kitchen was: 'Lamb *rendang* for dinner tonight. Low fire for at least one hour. No time to be wasted.'

Burhan, his eyes on his wife's full, swaying bottom tightly wrapped under her sarong, scratched his head and returned to the car. Parked inside the garage next to the main building, the Mercedes had its bonnet raised high like an imploring glare, as if urging for the service work interrupted by the visitor to be resumed.

*

That was three months ago.

Today, the clearing is quiet.

In fact, it has been quiet for some time.

A lone hen, the only surviving daughter of the one that witnessed the lieutenant's visit three months ago and the riot two months after, strolls languidly, and launches occasional attacks on the soil at the edge of the gravel around the house. Dirt-red earthworms twist out of their broken homes, offering their fresh and fat bodies to the lean fowl. Against a bamboo pole from which fierce flames once illuminated the party-goers, a stalk of spindly hibiscus leans. Its surviving leaves hang sparsely, turning yellow; the only two blossoms cling pitiably to the boughs: the petals shrivelled, a faded red.

Beyond the house, beyond the palms, acre after acre of rubber trees stand in straight, evenly spaced rows, extending to the horizon. Like obedient schoolchildren at their desks in the exam hall, waiting to be told what to do. Sunlight hovers above the layers of leaves that grow in luxuriant abundance, and underneath, mosquitoes drone in the cool, humid air of their paradise. Grass snakes cruise between the overgrown weeds. Families of monkeys trot around surreptitiously, combing the edge of the plantation for bananas and rambutans.

Inside the house, Mingzhi is sitting. Alone.

The light has faded away. Mingzhi smells dampness in the air, and outside the palm leaves rustle. Tokoh the giant hen has long gone to hide in her shelter between the stilts under the house. Mingzhi hears her occasional surprised blurts of ka-ka-ka from below. She has smelled the torrential rain that is on its way.

The latex! Mingzhi gets up, thinking of the beads of rain drumming on the brimming cups of milky sap. Diluted white fluid spills onto the brown earth, seeping fast into the soil. *I have to give them a hand! Too many trees and time is too short.* Bare-footed, he hurries across the room, raises the curtain at the door to a sudden brightness—

He stops and lets go of his grip.

The thin piece of cotton slaps down, casting a dark shape over his face. The workers have stopped coming after the riot, he remembers. Mingzhi stands motionless for a moment before turning round.

Engi will be here soon, he murmurs and nods, walking slowly towards his bed. *I really have to get ready.*

He lowers his body and peers into the dimness under his bed; his hand ventures deep inside for his sandals.

There is something, he feels it, caught in the crevice between the floor planks where the lacquered mat doesn't reach. Some papers. A book, perhaps. He yanks it out and the dust rushes to his nostrils. A loud sneeze, and Mingzhi drops his find on the floor. A man in an ancient

Malay royal costume stares out at Mingzhi from the tawny, tattered cover of the illustrated book. His hand rests on the kris on one side of his waist, partially inserted into the gold-patterned *songket* tied around his body. The title reads:

PARAMESWARA

It is a name he's come across so many times, in books and snatches of stories circulating among the townsfolk, Chinese or Indians or Malays. He's even related the tales to – who? Ali? But the child had known them all from the book. He pauses, shakes his head and pauses again. Yet still, memory fails him, and he concentrates on the title instead. It's a name, he now remembers, closely tied to the history of the land in which he now lives, of a particular town called Malacca. Of the wars, the exile, the confrontations, the connections with the faraway lands where he came from. Of the glory and the declines. Some say he was a hero; others dismiss him as an oppor-tunist, a murderer, a betrayer.

Still, he is remembered.

That's his story, their stories. How about mine? How about my story in this land?

Mingzhi picks up the book, wipes the dust off the cover and turns the page—

The annals of the ancient realm blunder out from the faded sheets, fleeting past scene by scene like the silent movies shown in the town's only theatre. With light and motion and captions, added to and intersected with more images that Mingzhi conjures up from his memory. Images of his own encounters in this place he calls home.

He flops on his bed, the open pages in his hand, an imaginative book of his life in his head.

In his sixties, sitting by his bed in his Minang Villa, Chai Mingzhi, tired and alone, slips into the far and present past: *theirs* and his, old and new. Sweat and blood, tears and anger, joy and laughter, love and betrayal.

They intersect and overlap.

2

Tokoh the Lone Hen

It rains. Sporadic silver bullets puncture the loose yellow soil, dashing out dark surprised patches across the front clearing, embellished with green and brown (new and old) fallen leaves. Before long, it turns into a deluge and erases its own creation.

It drums on the roof like a machine gun over Mingzhi's head, like hundreds of soldiers trotting, rushing towards him, to haul him out of the house.

Mingzhi curls up in his bed like a shrimp.

The rumbling buries every other sound. It swallows up Tokoh's incessant rattling of shock so that Mingzhi, in his room, wrapped in his blanket, can't hear her. In her comfortable nest of coconut husks under the house, the giant hen's curious eyes dart here and there, pleading for the rain to go away perhaps or, more likely, looking for Ali.

The hen was Ali's pet. Every three months Burhan, Ali's father, would buy two dozen chicks from the market to replace those he'd consumed or sold to the Chinese housewives, whom he often visits door-to-door during fruit seasons with basketfuls of rambutan, *manggis, langsat* or durian on his bicycle. Instead of rearing kampong chicken that run wild in the country like most Malays do, Burhan, with his surprisingly acute business mind – against the stereotypes – caged his meat-fowls in the handmade den behind his house, feeding them with generous servings of crushed corn and leftover rice from the Minang Villa.

His son Ali has never been interested in them.

The seven-year-old is a keen reader and listener of folklore. Three months ago, he spotted an unusual red mark on the chick's beak that resembles Tokoh the Heroic Cock – who rescues an entire flock of chickens from the hunter eagle – in a picture book he'd just read. The boy picked it up from his father's new supply and declared its name Tokoh. A hero. Four weeks later, as it grew, he discovered it was, in fact, a *heroine*. That didn't alter the bird's privileged status. While her counterparts were contained in the den behind the house Ali shared with his parents, Tokoh enjoyed the freedom of cruising in the open the way Ali enjoyed his freedom in the Minang Villa. With Mingzhi's permission.

Occasionally the hen wandered to the back of the house and peered through the wire cage at her pals. Perhaps they were jealous of her privilege, perhaps her bluntness was mistaken for arrogance, Tokoh's quest for old friendship was always met with fierce clatters and forceful pecks from the flock of her same breed, and she bolted, innocent surprise on her face. Head held up, eyes wide, neck turning here and there. *Why? Why? Why?* Yet Tokoh, all by herself, still strolled over, was still chased away. When Ali related this to Mingzhi, the Chinese *taukeh* said, 'You can't trust your friends. No, not anyone.'

By then, Mingzhi was all by himself in the Minang Villa, with only Burhan the driver and his family for company.

He didn't tell Ali it was wrong to segregate the chickens in the first place, a lesson he'd learned following that tragic fire, when Martin decided against sharing a roof with him and Tiansheng, and moved into Montgomery's bungalow instead. That marked the beginning of the end of their friendship.

*

Life has never been the same after Ali and his family left, even for Tokoh the hen. With most of the chickens now sold or slaughtered and her master away, Tokoh, alone, looks startled in her lonely nest.

They lived in an annex behind the Minang Villa: Burhan, Ali and his mother Khadijah the cook, cleaner and washing lady. Burhan drove Mingzhi in his Mercedes and ran errands for him. For ten years the young family had been living there, working for Taukeh Chai, their Chinese boss, until a week ago, when Mingzhi was discharged from the hospital where he'd been receiving treatment for a stroke.

Every evening after dinner boss and driver sat on a bench under the old *saga* tree in front of the house. A few pieces of *kemanyan* burning in a clay bowl, a cup of sweet milk tea (for Burhan), a pot of *pu'er* (for Mingzhi), and they would chat, of the rubber estate, the Indian workers, the prices from Mingzhi; and from Burhan, his harvest of fruits, the chickens, news from his village. Ali.

Mingzhi, already fluent in Malay then, intentionally slipped English phrases into his stories to his attentive audience. 'Rubber *sudah* dropped two cents.' 'Samy *pukul* his wife again. *Teruklah*.' The kampong boy listened and learned by heart.

Burhan was only eighteen when he came to the Minang Villa. Mingzhi had inherited the young man from Montgomery when he bought the Scot's share of the plantations and his bungalow. 'I've had enough of Malaya.' Montgomery, overcome by a sudden longing for home, had decided to return to Scotland with the money squeezed from the colony.

The bungalow Mingzhi turned into accommodation for his estate managers. As for Burhan, the Chinese boss generously offered him a gardener's position, to tend the two-acre orchard next to the house.

Burhan was reluctant at first. Working for an English colonist was one thing; working for an immigrant Chinese *taukeh*, another. Mingzhi assured him of a secure job in a secluded orchard (*You don't have to answer or to see anyone*). Thinking of his fiancée in the village and both parents' urge for a wedding, the young man gave in.

Two things happened two years later that propelled Burhan to an unexpected promotion. The first was Mingzhi's decision to turn the orchard land into a workers' quarter; as more rubber trees were maturing, more workers were employed from south India. And the second was Driver Wong, who had come to Malaya as a five-year-old, responded to the patriotic call from the Motherland and returned to China to join the Communist Party, to fight for the nation's pride. Burhan, efficient and a quick learner, seemed to be the obvious successor. Mingzhi paid for his driving lessons; he didn't say no.

Mingzhi watched Burhan grow from a shy young man to a confident, mature person. He was surprised when Burhan, who had only primary education and spent most of his time in his village, uttered his first 'Where going, Taukeh?' and answered: 'No problem, Taukeh.' Mingzhi watched him bring from his village his new bride, to whom the *taukeh* gave a job. When Khadijah had a difficult labour he let Burhan drive his Mercedes back to his village for the traditional midwife.

He watched Ali, as an infant, lie on his mat, then start crawling, then walk his first steps into his childhood.

Ali – honey-skinned, bright-eyed, round-faced – clambered up the stairs and walked through the back door into the Minang Villa, into Mingzhi's world. Light, tiny footprints stamped across all corners like postmarks. Delivered. The proofs of his existence, of memories inerasable, which, years later, would rise from where they were imprinted. From the lacquered mat in the sitting room (where the boy did his first *joget*). From the rosewood dining chair (to reach for the table). From the foam couch (a comfortable place for an afternoon nap). From the stools in the kitchen in front of the cabinet (to reach for the sugar jar).

From a book stuck between the floor planks, titled *Parameswara*.

Tiny, light feet landed heavy prints on Mingzhi's memory.

*

Drip, drip, drip. Rainwater slips through the crack on the attap, dropping on the linoleum. Lying there, his ear pressed on his bed, he hears the rain-noises amplify. Drip, drip, drip. Crisp and clear on the waxed surface, strong and ponderous on Mingzhi's heart. *How could something so small make such a huge impact?* he wonders.

Drip, drip, drip. DRIP, DRIP, DRIP. **DRIP. DRIP. DRIP.**

A bucket, I need a bucket! He pops his head up from his cover.

'Khadijah! Khadijah!'

Silence. His voice, breathless and hoarse, disappears into the rumbling downpour.

Of course, they've left. Mingzhi uncurls himself and flings off his blanket.

Everyone's left save me.

He walks out of the room, carefully avoiding the wet patches, avoiding the drips. He enters the spacious living room furnished with one of the first leather sofa sets (an olive-green three-piece suite) in town, past the long, gloomy hallway, now bereft of sunlight. Past the drawing room with the never-been-played giant piano (moved from the bungalow with much effort) inherited from Montgomery, which Khadijah had to polish once a week. Past his study with four wall-shelves full of waiting-to-be-read books peering out from the wide-open door—

Something rustles under Mingzhi's feet. He looks down.

A paper, some colourful drawing. Blown off from the wall where it was pasted, out of the room, and caught under his slippers.

He picks it up.

RUMAH SAYA

My House. The incipient writing of a child crawls across its top and underneath, a big house-on-stilts with familiar, recognizable sharp edges of the roof. Black for the outlines, brown for the roof, red for the wall, yellow for the ground. Next to it, a smaller building stands side by side, almost merged, with the former.

The Minang Villa.

Mingzhi turns the sheet over. In the same handwriting, printed: 'ALI, Darjah 1A'. *Ali, Class 1A*.

For little boy Ali, his house included the Minang Villa, including Mingzhi.

The painting is one of the child's early works. When Ali started school, an unspoken routine was established. After lunch, the boy would walk through the back door with his books. First the homework at the long oak desk in the study: light HB pencil scribbling 'ABC' on double-lined exercise book; little head being scratched over simple additions and subtractions, multiplications and divisions; colour pens sketching a bright red sun (with sparkling rays of light around it) against the green mountains and paddy fields underneath. And chickens! Their yellow bodies and three-forked claws dotted across the grassland.

Then the story time in the kitchen. Two cups of warm milky Milo, a plateful of Marie biscuits on the table and they would plunge into the time machine, entering the realms of the ancient and the wild. Ali had a full collection of illustrated *The Annals of Hang Tuah*, *Hang Jebat* and other warriors of the past. The legendary heroes of Malacca – their love-hate relationships, loyalties and treacheries – fascinated the child, but it was the tales from the forest that grabbed him the most. Sang Kancil the witty mouse deer, Tenggiling the hatch hog who defeats Sang Gajah the giant elephant, and the lazy earthworm who becomes blind. Stories Mingzhi gathered from his numerous trips to the jungle in the early days, for rattan and camphor. Stories from Anan, his Orang Asli friend.

Ali's preference was Sang Kancil. Remembering every word by heart, he would act out his favourite scene, all by himself.

'Ooi, Sang Belang, the one and only mighty gong is there on the bough. Can't you see it? It plays the most beautiful music in the world!' Ali would squeal, effeminate voice raised high, pretending to be the witty mouse deer, tricking Sang Belang the tiger into hitting the beehive.

'*Aiyo! Aiyo!*' Now the role would change; the boy was the bee-stung tiger, holding his head, blundering around in the kitchen, before the drama ended with Ali clambering up onto the stool for the jar of sweets on the cabinet: his synonym for the delicious honey his hero Sang Kancil was after.

Mingzhi let him, indulging the boy.

But he's gone, Ali.

Everything stopped even before the child was gone.

Mingzhi takes the drawing to the study, pastes it on the wall above the desk and lands himself on the chair.

As the price of rubber began to falter a few years back, there were nights when he sat in his study, trying in vain to fiddle magic out of his old abacus. Click, click, click. The faithful wooden beads rang out the facts he wished were otherwise. Over the years the figures slumped like an air-filled rubber ball, descending all the way from the top of the mountain to the foot. Click, click, click. Lonely, crisp sounds hitting hard in the quietness, in his heart. He would push everything away and stare up at the sketch, at the building, and think of the boy who takes him in without wonder. And feel warm.

Whatever happens, he thought then, *I will still have it, the Minang Villa, will still be with Ali and family. My family.*

He smiles bitterly. Perhaps the fire, years ago in the Fisherman's Hut, was a premonition. Perhaps he should've succumbed to fate: he will never own a house, not anywhere in this land that doesn't want to own him.

Outside, the wind has grown wild, howling, shrieking. Trees are hurled this way and that; palm fronds twist and whirl. Wind at the front and back doors, at the windows. Wind inside the house, gushing down the long hallway. Door curtains roll and bulge and slap. The house swells.

Rain forces in through seams and cracks and chinks, through the gaps between the wooden shutters onto Mingzhi, sitting by the window.

The sudden sprinkles on his bare arm trickle a vague memory. He brushes down the wetness with his hand and sits thinking.

A bucket, I need a bucket. He gets up, and a sudden dizziness assaults him, a tearing pain grabs at his chest.

I give him the bucket.

The door was unlocked when I arrived, two days after the messenger found me in the forest. The rain had stopped; the sky a polished, unadulterated bright blue. In the clearing, puddles glared white in the fierce after-rain sun, like shards of mirrors on the gravel, sharp and blinding. A lone hen sauntered, busying itself with earthworms shot out of the soil loosened by raindrops. Not a glance at me.

I found him on the floor of the study, his right leg twisted under the chair; he had tripped on its foot. I felt his breath and the faint throbbing of his pulse before calling the hospital.

As I helped him up and carried him to the living room, the man Father told me to call Taukeh Chai, the man whom I remembered standing tall and spindly at the edge of the forest one morning thirty-eight years ago, seemed to have suddenly shrunken in my arms, small and light. He muttered, 'Bucket, I need a bucket,' pointing at the corridor leading to the kitchen.

I did not tell him it was no longer raining.

3

Ghost from the Past

Here I am, in the Minang Villa. Sturdy stilts built under my supervision, still intact, still strong; distinguished structure designed with my approval – before the final nod from the real master – the edges of the roofs reminiscent of buffalo horns still sharp, still pointing towards the sky; walls woven with nipa on my order, the colours faded.

And the floor creaks under my feet.

Walking on it, my heart cringes with each step I land. I wouldn't have let that happen if I had always been here. It had been my pride, the project of constructing the Minang Villa.

I remember the instructions from my master twenty-eight years ago.

'A Malay house. A distinctive yet authentic Malay house.'

It was one of those brooding afternoons, after a morning of prolonged downpour, a pattern that had been repeated over the past few days. The no-rubber-tapping day. The workers and the factory had been idle. No rubber sheets, no sales, no income.

Not wanting to be locked under the same roof with my master, I frolicked my time away in my favourite teahouse in Market Street, where willing storytellers gathered, eager to share tales and gossips. Over the past days, I'd been indulging them with pots of strong *o-long* and plates of hot dumplings; while they fed on them, I fed on the episodes of my master's pre-Malaya life. That day, a town called Pindong, his first venture out of Plum Blossom Village, was the topic.

'A busy town that was. Been there once myself. So many things to see. Hm . . . beautiful women . . .'

'Busy it certainly was. I almost got lost in it. Think of him, a feeble bookworm, in those streets . . .'

'That you don't have to worry about. With a grand-father like that, with the money they had . . . Getting lost? No way!'

'Aye, a room and a servant. That's a different world.'

'He called the place Little Hut of Leaping Fishes, that small room he had.'

'Eh, he was after money and fame all the same. Even an illiterate knows what it means once a fish has leapt over a dragon gate.'

'Aye, status and prosperity come tumbling in.'

'But he was no illiterate. He was a scholar. Perhaps he'd other meanings.' Words poured out of my mouth before I realized it, only to face the disapproving stares.

And they talked to me no more.

I sipped my tea and thought of the long afternoon, now certainly more unbearable. It was then that the new house boy from the Baba Lodge came to me.

'The *taukeh* wants to see you.'

Back in the house, I found my guardian poring over a book in the study, his head buried deep in the open pages.

'Here.' He did not look up, but I heard in his voice a rare tinge of enthusiasm. His finger directed me to a sketch, a building-on-stilts with the edges of the roof pointing up like the horns of buffaloes.

Minangkabau Architecture: Rumah Gadang

The 'Big House'? I stared at my guardian, the glint of excitement apparent in his gaze.

'The Minangkabau people,' he said, 'came from Sumatra, an island in the west of Indonesia. Can you believe it, Engi, the Minangkabau culture adopts a matrilineal tradition? Thinking of all the feudal male-dominant communities around it.' My guardian, who'd become increasingly reticent in recent days, doused me with his babbling about the people and their culture.

Because of this unique culture, he said, women were placed in the centre of society. 'And Engi, you'll be interested to see how this concept has been absorbed into the architectural design. A Minangkabau house is designed for the priority and convenience of women rather than men. It reflects women's status in society.'

He looked straight into my eyes. 'You'll find out more.'

Me? Why?

He closed the book and handed it to me.

'I want this house.'

*

In the house he wanted, in the central-hall-for-living-room, my former guardian seems to have fallen asleep on the recliner, his brows knotted.

I traipse in silence, inspecting the house as if for the first time. The house I helped to build, lived in for fifteen years.

The architecture of a rumah gadang *reflects a woman's life cycle, from the entrance to the rooms and then the kitchen.* Words from Taukeh Chai's book crept into my head. With that in mind, I had the architect draft his plan abiding by the traditional model, putting into focus the main three areas: the central hall, the rooms and a special area called *anjung*, reserved for honourable guests, and the kitchen with a large space in front of it where visitors would be received.

A spell of sunlight breaks through the rain cloud, a sudden brightness inside the house. *I want the best of the daylight* – another instruction from my guardian.

Of course I know and could dwell on them, every minute detail of the structure. Those days and nights I spent researching and discussing with a team of the top architects in the peninsula had been excruciating. The project had drained me, leaving me limp with exhaustion in bed at night, begrudging Taukeh Chai for the decision to build a house distinct from those of the Chinese in town. A double-storey mansion would have been easier: square structure, brick walls, tiled floors, solid and secure. It would also have saved him from adding another topic to the townsfolk's basket of gossip, already packed with his stories.

'Why would he live in a Malay house, and worse still, one that prioritizes women's status and power? A woman's house!' they'd laughed. 'Has the shrewd *taukeh*, for once, been blinded, lost his common sense?' The questions and ridicule had been directed at me time and again, only to find a casual shrug of the shoulders for answer.

Why?

I walk out of the hall into the long corridor, past the rooms on both sides, and head towards the end of the house. Steering away from the kitchen, I descend the *anjung* at the farthest end. It had never been used, the *anjung*, the most important and revered room, a forbidden corner. Its secret had been sealed by a heavy padlock, its key held only by my guardian. Even Amah Feng was prohibited from entering this part of the house. It was the only room whose furnishing and decoration were not for me to take charge of.

I'd seen my guardian quietly sidle into it, night after night. I'd noticed, escaping from under the door, the faint yellow of a candle, and imagined the darkness inside, wondering. Always, when he finally re-emerged, hours later, the sadness on his face was a pond of bitter water, enveloping him in a world impenetrable to anyone else.

I stare at the door. My heart thumps. It's empty where the padlock had been.

I stand there, a thin piece of wood away from a mystery I have longed to uncover. I feel my hands clammy with sweat.

I push it open.

A woman stares out at me from an enormous portrait on an altar, the only furniture in the wide room, her eyes bright and clear.

Instantly I know who she is.

I should have known. Of course it's a woman's house. This place, the Minang Villa, is for his sister, Meilian.

Is she now looking down at him? Did she witness the attack on the house – her house – and her brother?

Silence was the only answer. Back in the living room I gaze at the figure now curled up in the recliner like a child, wheezing, short, faint, intermittent, like the last puffs of a steam machine as it grinds, heavier and heavier, the smoke lighter and lighter.

I sit there, watching. Is it the ending? – of the story about a man and his land, and the house he determined to build on that piece of land.

Of the man who dominated my life, who took me out of the forest and, without any warning, 'returned' me to where I'd come from.

4

A Question of Snake or Egg or Rhinoceros

It was 1925, twenty years after I left the jungle. I was supervising the workers in the plantation when a horse cart hurried towards us and jerked to a halt. I was surprised to see Taukeh Chai, a rare visitor to the site, rushing out of it, looking worried.

'Hurry, your father is dying,' he said, urging me to get on the cart with him. *Father? Dying?* My mind turned blank. Was it Taukeh Chai who pushed me into the cart? The next minute I was already in it, heading back to the forest.

It was dim inside the hut, the door closed against the afternoon blaze at Father's request. Let my soul be trapped indoors, he had said. Sweat grew like beads of pearl in the humid air; they rolled down my brow and landed lightly on my lashes. I blinked, and they broke into salty splashes, filtered through my lashes into my sockets. My vision blurred.

Was that him, Father, the man who lay sideways on the mat facing the wall, shrivelled and shrunken like a dried leaf? Shame was an invisible troll's slap, landed loud and heavy on my face.

When had I last seen him? Two years ago? Three? Or

more? Even before that, my trips had been short, infrequent. And when I was there, my mind wasn't, crowded with work and trivia from the rubber estates. There were always new hands to be trained, labourers' living quarters to be prepared and maintained. There was the mandatory daily inspection of workers for slackness and mistakes. A slip of attention and the consequences would be drastic: a slow worker brought in less latex, which coagulated fast as the heat increased; and a bad cut not only hurt the tree but halted the flow of the milk. There was the wage-cash to be ready for the workers, in correct and adequate amounts, every Saturday afternoon. There were fights among them to be mediated after their end-of-week-if-not-end-of-day-toddy. One after another, always demanding, never ending.

A cup of tea, a quick meal with extremely white, imported rice (our self-grown rice was yellow and coarse) and cans of (again, imported) baked beans and sardines in tomato sauce, and I was gone, my heart filled with pride for being able to bring my family the luxuries they would otherwise not have.

'Tell me, who else do you know among us has tasted these?' Mother would say when she set down the red, gravy-rich dishes in coconut shells. A wide smile was Father's response, his eyes drowning in it.

How I had been blinded. It wasn't his smile that had sketched out his slits; it was his wrinkles, more, deeper, squeezing against one another, overlapping. Like the dried-up bark of a hundreds-of-years-old *neram* tree on the riverside; his eyes were simply smothered by the loose, leathery, drooping lids. In my mind's eye I saw only the hunter I'd known as a child, always strong, always agile.

How naive I had been, refusing to acknowledge my changed fate, changed life, changed self. Memories of Father and of the forest had frozen on the day I left, aged twelve.

Father survived just another day.

At Father's deathbed, my guardian pressed into my hands a cotton bundle, light and small. 'Your time with me has come to an end, Engi.' He held my inquisitive gaze. 'I've kept my promise. I'm returning you to your world.'

My world? Where exactly is my world? Furious, I glared at my guardian, who looked away.

I opened the package. A cotton-like material unravelled itself in my hands. Brown, stained with age, pungent with dampness, torn in places. It was the loincloth I'd worn twenty years ago. *My last loincloth.* I felt the carefully woven bark with my fingers, so soft it almost melted to the touch. I imagined how, over the years, it had fermented in the humidity of the tropics. I imagined how bacteria had threaded and chewed through it the way they gnawed at my childhood, my innocence. Melting away.

When he spoke again, my guardian's voice was dry.

It was an agreement between him and Father, he explained, that I be taken to be educated, to learn skills, and later, upon Father's death, to take Father's place in the family. (*Family? Mother died five years ago and I wasn't informed, and both of my sisters were married, having families of their own.*) A school for the children of the forest was Father's condition, he said. 'And you, Engi, are to be the teacher.'

So matter-of-fact; so – impassive. Did he have tears in his eyes, for parting with someone who had lived and worked with him for twenty years? I recalled those story-telling nights, moments when tales of the lonely traveller and the Kathakali dancer were told, how I had speculated whether he had wept for either or both of them. I recalled the morning Tiansheng was asked to leave the Baba Lodge. I couldn't remember seeing his eyes, couldn't remember seeing him weep.

*

After the funeral, Taukeh Chai gathered a few young men from the quarter. His instructions were simple: a structure made of bamboo, to be built next to Father's shelter – now mine. Poles were conveniently cut from the growth by the river, joints secured with strings made from palms. A sack of rice each was his only promise to his helpers. I looked at the suddenly lit-up faces of my tribesmen, and my heart ached at two immediate realizations: first, I would never again be as content as them (this hurt the most); second, my guardian had become a real *taukeh*, a shrewd, calculating businessman.

I recalled tales of Taukeh Chai's childhood, narrated to me by former peasants from his village. Heavenly God dictates our fates and no one can alter it, rich or powerful, they had said. Words rolled intermittently in sticky circles in their mouths, stuffed with dumplings I paid for at the teahouse. Nodding in pretended seriousness, they had told of how, against his grandfather's wish for him to become a scholar and a mandarin, my guardian had on his first lunar birthday chosen a ledger over calligraphic brushes, scissors, copper coins, books, five grains, shovel and mandarin costumes, among others, a varied selection of items, prepared for the pick-a-career ceremony.

At the teahouse I'd heard cynicism in stories squeezed out from underneath the bulging cheeks. He'd tried to turn himself into someone he wasn't meant to be, one sniggered. A scholar? Of course, they had all the money to cage him in a mansion of books. A mandarin? That was a reward for the game played by the rich and the powerful, and the false, convenient relationships forged between them.

With a resourceful and determined grandfather and an imperial scholar for a father-in-law, they had pointed out, Taukeh Chai's reward had come early and easy. 'That was merely a child's toy, a treat or a trick or a test, from the Heavenly God,' a toothless old man had murmured, having finally dislodged with his tongue the dampened dough sticking on his palate, his wrinkled face crumpled with presumed wisdom. 'The Almighty knows the right time to put you back on the right track, the one He has planned for you. Your true destiny.'

As though he were the Almighty Himself.

If that was my guardian's destiny, what was it for a forest child, after wandering in an outside world, the initial strangeness gradually turned into familiarity, being returned to where he had come from?

A teacher in a jungle?

The awkwardness of it was equal to that of the case of a forest child in an outsiders' world.

Not here, not there.

Not this, not that.

I watched the elderly man devour the last bite of his dumpling. A lump the size of a rubber seed visibly moved downwards along his throat; skin that was loose and saggy suddenly pulled tight where the food-lump was. I remembered, as a child, once out fishing with Father by the river, seeing a snake swallow a crocodile egg the size of a baby boar that bulged like a boulder under the slick skin, as though it would explode any minute. 'Why doesn't it crack open?' I asked. 'How could the egg remain intact inside the reptile's stomach?' Father said the big feast would be consumed and disappear in a few days. He said everything would melt away inside the beast. 'The difference comes in how long it takes, and however long it takes, everything will turn into water inside its system. It's only a matter of time, son.' An experienced hunter's experienced talk, confident, matter-of-fact, leaving no room for doubts.

'It can take in anything, anything that comes in its path, even a giant rhinoceros; that'll keep his belly full for months,' Father whispered in my ear. 'Imagine a rhino-shaped snake! Guess from where would it start to devour its big meal? The head, the tail, or the legs? I'd say the tail.' He stared ahead at the riverbank in the near distance, a hand rubbing my short, curly hair, smiling, as if the rhino-shaped snake was right before us. I didn't smile; I didn't see the rhinoceros or the snake that had possessed it. My eyes were glued to the scene in front of me: the egg being pushed along the soft, unsettling cylinder. 'If the egg is inside the snake's body, can we still call it an egg?' I asked. Father scratched his scalp, on his face a rare awkward expression. He patted my head and led me into the bush away from the river and the snakes: the real one, adorned with an egg shape in its body; and an imaginary one, rhino-shaped. The question, along with the answer he could not find, were left in the gurgling water, washed downstream.

*

The elderly man in the teahouse had never seen the snakes, of course, egg-shaped or rhino-shaped. The world of the tropics was one he shunned, the true fact that he was in it conveniently ignored. His stories instead dug deep into a land so alien yet vaguely familiar to me; familiar, because time and again sparkle and shadows of it were cajoled up from memories of the bedtime tales of my teenage years. My guardian's nightly murmurs.

What did they, those storytellers, expect, pouring out from their hearts snatches of the people and their lives that were now so distant from them? I'd seen in their eyes love, hate, longing. Sadness. Yes, sadness. Even when they were smiling, the tilt of the corners of the mouth only revealed a past impossible to revisit in person. Even when there was an occasional glint of happiness, it appeared rare and brief; it was that rareness, that briefness, that made it feel even sadder.

I'd always been amazed at their ability to preserve the past, in volume and clarity. Like a vat of timely un-earthed, century-old wine, because it had been sealed air-tight, had been buried underground, not a drop evaporated, not a sip adulterated. So perfectly had it been brewed, that with just a sniff the taster would accurately reveal its every ingredient, every stage of the brewing, the temperature, the source of the water used.

As though they had witnessed the entire process, not one detail was missed.

I had believed so until I, too, became a storyteller.

*

Storytelling began at the school on the first day. Four rattan-woven walls, a bare floor, eight gawking, snotty students sitting crossed-legged on the mats. Before them, a stranger that was their unprepared teacher, with half a day to be filled without any books at hand, and an accent suffused with years of speaking the Chinese tongue.

Father's jungle tales came to the rescue. Spirits and animals, gods and ghosts, a rhino-shaped snake (which made them giggle, baring toothless gums), the witty mouse deer. The good and the bad, the predators and their victims, all stumbling out of my head through my mouth as though they had always been there, always ready, only waiting to be summoned, to leap out of their hiding place. To reclaim their lives.

How easily I had imitated Father: his tone, the way he would raise his voice for attention, the way he would hush down for suspense, his sudden shouts that made us jump. How easily missing details were filled up, lost episodes recreated much to my amazement. Words flowed like water, running down the stream, colours added by the green and yellow, brown and red from the twigs and leaves collected along the journey; body twisted and turned, shaped and reshaped by boulders and bends. Enriched, beautified.

Gaps closed, stories completed.

Wasn't that how they had told their stories, my guardian and the peasants from the faraway land? Imagination was the trick; I should have known.

The past was a century-old porcelain vase, displayed prominently on a tall cabinet, too high to be reached. Because it was unreachable, because it was too sacred to be profaned, one could only crane his neck, tilt his head and stare up at it; his eyes filled with admiration, his mind swollen with longing. Day in, day out, the details painted on it were magnified in the memory: the delicate patterns became more elaborate, hues that were faint as watercolour somehow intensified, lines deepened and ran in places where they shouldn't be.

The blank spaces of truncated memories were stuffed with inventions, glorious, colourful, abundant.

In my newly built school, my hidden power of imagination flooded in. It was a game of join-the-dots. Sentences were made, linking up the vague clues dug out from memory, of 'a mouse deer called Sang Kancil', 'a tiger called Sang Belang', 'a beehive', and 'the mouse deer got the beehive he coveted'.

'Sang Kancil shuddered at the sudden appearance of Sang Belang, who bared his teeth at him. "I'm keeping watch of this gong for the King of the Forest," Sang Kancil, trying to stay calm, told the tiger, pointing at the beehive on the tree branch. "It's the King's precious instrument. Only the great and the mighty would be able to make sounds from it."

'"A gong?" Sang Belang was intrigued. "I have good ears and I love music. I'm sure I will beat out of it the loudest and the most beautiful music. I'll shake the jungle to life. Let me try, please," he begged.

'Sang Kancil sniggered inside, but he appeared sombre, hesitating: "The King would not be happy—"

'"He won't know if you don't tell. Just once, please!" Sang Belang pressed on.'

The dialogue rolled on, quick, without a pause. The lies of the little Sang Kancil I dwelled on with such detail I'd never thought I would be capable of. I looked at the children before me, the sudden brightness in their eyes, widening with the power play between the strong and the weak, the twists and turns in my reconstructed animal kingdom. Then, in a blink, I saw myself sitting in the teahouse. I saw that I pricked my ears the way the children did, to tales similarly alien to me. Those childish faces became mine: eager, transfixed, not a doubt.

How vulnerable I had always been, confusing creation for truth, being manipulated!

Father, you'd foreseen this, hadn't you, as a storyteller yourself? You had foreseen the inevitable blight that would be bestowed on us, with the outside world closing in on us, the outside men striving to rob or coax the forest from us. *No.* I stared at the innocent faces before me. *They will not be manipulated, Father, I'll see to that. They'll be as witty as Sang Kancil under my care. They'll protect our homes, our lands for generations to come.*

I continued, voice raised, tones clear, actions animated.

'Sang Kancil hid behind a bush and watched the tiger beat the beehive with his bare hands. Once, twice. Not a sound, certainly not the loud gong he expected, but a wave of rumbling buzz. Bees, thousands of them, swarmed out of the hive, found their obvious target, Sang Belang, and launched their attacks!

'"Ouch, ouch! Help!" Sang Belang first tried to flap

away the bees, but they were all over him. His body burned with pain, as if there were thousands of pins and needles sticking in it. He let out a howl so loud it shook the jungle floor, before fleeing for his life.'

The children burst out laughing, relaxed now, elated at the scene of a defeated tiger.

There was a snigger too, from outside the shelter.

'What a storyteller he is, just like his father.'

Suppressed whispers and exclaims of approval rose and ebbed from the outside of the shelter, from a sea of bobbing heads. The elderly and toddlers too young to be at school, and the women, babies tied across their bosoms, had been gathering, as curious as the young ones inside. 'School' was a term too new, too alien to their forest-born-and-grown ears.

When the newness turned stale, when curiosity subsided, when they decided 'school' was nothing more than a place to formally impart our oral tradition, and when I added the moral implications of the tales (*Always respect the elders like we respect the gods and spirits, never be as greedy as the hippopotamus-eating snake and always act only according to our might, and learn to use our brains as the mouse deer do*, to name a few), by mid-morning, the crowd gradually dispersed. Noises ceased, shuffling figures receded.

I let out a sigh, relieved. Only me and the children. My students. The future of my tribe.

*

I heard them, the people of my tribe, calling me 'the town-man' behind my back. A stranger who spoke with a strange tongue.

317

I began to find slabs of meat at my doorstep in the evenings, fresh, generous cuts of boar or deer or monkey, and once, tiger. Tokens from the hunters. *A gift from the Unknown.* I smiled to myself, for, so fast, so surreptitiously they did it without me noticing, that it felt like a treat from some forest spirit.

Sometimes, awake at dawn, I lay on my mat and imagined the men, barefooted, marching in single file the way we would when we trod the narrow jungle trails. I imagined them, in their loincloths, their blowpipes on their naked backs, machetes tied to their waists, heading towards the heart of the wild.

They never knocked on my door, never stopped, never extended invitations to their expedition, just observed me from a distance. On occasions when I emerged in time to greet them, they would nod and grin, curious gazes thrown at me, trudging on. Backward glances.

One afternoon, I heard light footsteps outside my shelter, soft crunches on leaves and boughs. Approaching, close, away. *How I wish I could come with them – yes, I'll join them!* I rose abruptly, seized Father's blowpipe and the basket of darts in a corner and rushed out of the shelter.

All was quiet.

Where are they? I strained my eyes, looking in all directions, trying to peer through the still-dim wood, dense with mist like layer upon layer of veils, weighed down with dampness. There were only dark shapes of trees, barely visible within five feet. No shuffling figures, no sounds of human activity. Not a trace of the hunting team.

No! I wanted to call out for them. *Never ever, in any event, make loud noises in the jungle.* Father's voice came in time, a flash of lightning in my head. The shout that was ready to come up was suppressed in my throat. No, I would not offend the spirits of the wood.

I swirled around, looked once more, and again, and saw no one. Disappointment grew and spread inside me, a load of tangled wire, weighty, sinking fast. I glanced at my shelter, a gloomy black patch sitting small and ugly. I thought of the bare four walls and floor, another day of unbearable idleness in it.

No, not today! I will catch up with them, I decided. The blowpipe and the basket swung onto my back, I headed towards where I thought the footsteps had disappeared.

Father, here I come again! I'll bring home an even bigger boar, I promise. You'll be proud of me like you used to be.

I trudged on. Before long, paths narrowed into trails. Soaking now, my cotton trousers were glued to my body like a thin film of skin, increasingly uncomfortable with every move. At every step, I pulled at the hems, only to find them fast sticking back, heavy on my thighs.

There was still no sign of them.

Half an hour passed, perhaps a full hour. The trails vanished, the trees and foliage thick and dense and gloomy around me, a cocoon of dark green, and I was caged in it. I groped at my waist. *My machete!* Frantically, I felt around me once more – it wasn't there, the uppermost important survival tool in the jungle! *How could I have made this mistake?* I sighed. Too late to turn back now. I gritted my teeth and started using my hands to push aside anything that came in the path. This way, I squeezed slowly through drooping rattan tendrils, vines and ferns, between long grasses, thickets of undergrowth, young trees and branches.

Ouch!

A sharp pain. I stared at my left palm, a bloody mess where it was cut. I tore at the hem of my trousers and wrapped the strip of cotton around my palm. *I must find them, I will find them!* I picked up a couple of fallen boughs from the ground and wielded them, one over my head, the other around my body, as a shield from the irritating tendrils and grass and branches.

But I was too slow! At the foot of a slope now, my stomach was rumbling, empty since this morning; my throat dry, cracking with thirst. Food and water! Another mistake. I looked around: no durian, no rambutan, no other edible fruits! Frustrated, I thrust at a clump of foliage with a stick. Taking another look around, I gasped. There was still nothing but tree after tree after tree. No food, no water; no way out!

What would Father do if he were here? I squatted down, my head in my hands, thinking hard. For certain, he would not turn back.

Be focused, I told myself, *and break your way through to the trail they've cleared.* I paused and pricked my ears, listening to the calls of the wild, figuring out where the river and the mountain might be, speculating where the men might have headed to – for a boar or a couple of monkeys? I decided to ascend, to locate my target from a higher ground. I rose, retrieved the sticks and resumed working strenuously, grabbing at the roots at times, climbing up the slope.

Occasional streaks of sunlight sieved through the layers of leaves, sprinkles of brightness, flashing. It was noon. I felt the grinding inside my stomach, intensified. *I will not give up, I will not give up, I will not give up,* I chanted quietly, paused again, concentrated.

There was a sound, faint yet crisp. Splashing water! Of course, it was the waterfall Father frequently took me to as a child. The source identified, I bent and squeezed below a fallen trunk—

Cut branches, pulled foliage, trampled soil: a clear trail. They'd been!

My heart throbbed. I pushed aside the drooping vines, pressing myself forward, the tumbling of water becoming louder in my ears. I moved faster, almost running—

I was on the edge of the waterfall.

I saw myself stepping on it, the slippery moss-green boulder, driven forth by the unstoppable momentum.

I heard my scream, a sharp tear across the tranquillity, the forest woken.

I saw the frothing cascade before my eyes, white, beautiful.

I saw the pool below, a crystal-clear green.

Halfway in the air, I somehow glanced up and saw faces, surprised, peering down at me from the top of the cascade.

A loud splash, and then blackness.

*

The school was closed for a month. I wobbled restlessly around the hut, waiting impatiently for my left leg, broken at the shank, to heal.

The long, brooding rainy season added to my misery. One afternoon, sitting by the door, watching sheets of water roll down from the attap roof, my craving for meat dumplings rose suddenly and grew like the puddles in the front yard. The succulent, juicy minced pork; the warm, soft dough! I held tight to my crutches, pushed myself up and started moving around the room, opening and closing drawers, rearranging things that did not need to be rearranged.

And then I saw it, a bundle, hidden in the deepest corner of my wooden chest. My journals! I took it out, unpacked and counted: seventeen. One for each year since my third year in town, documenting my everyday mundanities, occasional excitement, work and leisure, a record of my urban dealings.

I read through them. People and their faces emerged and rumbled in my head in a surge of waves. Close or distant, they threaded together in a mess of love and hatred, tears and laughter, anger and sadness. Loose or tight, the lines intertwined, knotted; a complicated web of relationships and emotions.

I began to conjure up stories from the notes. Like Father once did, I set aside after-dinner hours, a cup of tea at hand, a distinctive world constructed between occasional sips. The only difference being that I used written words, on stacks of paper that came with the monthly supplies for the school, on my order, courtesy of Taukeh Chai.

On good days, I sat on the bench under the old rambutan tree outside my shelter, with sheets on a hard board across my knees. An English fountain pen in my hand, I felt the light breeze in my hair and glanced up occasionally at the setting sun, flickering with red and orange like the fervent passion of young lovers. If it rained, I moved my literary platform indoors; a candle

322

lighted next to me, the evening was prolonged until the last drop of wax waned.

Father would have been proud of the talent I inherited from him, would have thrilled at my stories. But these were no tales of forest and its being, of spirits and men's dealing with them. It was my life outside of all those related to the forest – or I'd thought so, until I read through them one day, the stories and the journals.

I found between the pages a shadow, huge and prominent. I saw it extending its limbs over me like the tentacles of an octopus, sticking on, twining round, though not squeezing. I saw that it existed in every inch of my existence.

And I realized it was his life I'd been documenting, and the stories I created were snatches of adventure and mystery, ups and downs, love and hatred, of a man who had changed my fate.

He, Chai Mingzhi, my boss, my guardian of twenty years.

How he had dominated my life.

The intended lead was reduced to a cameo, appearing only for the sake of a more important role, the all-over-the-place protagonist; even in scenes without him, his influence lurked, invisible yet powerful, gripping. Without him, everyone else, everything else was meaningless, and nothing would have happened.

*

School resumed.

In the classroom I looked at my students, always glancing up at me, always smiling, eager and trustful. Now that their initial nerves and uncertainty had evaporated, their

323

youthful faces opened up like a blank sheet of paper they had not a chance to see. Soon they would be filled up, those empty pages, with knowledge of the outside world too complicated for their innocent minds: middle men, loggers, developers, and ardent, persuasive religious officers who offer food and materials to lure them into a faith that is not theirs. The greed, the slyness of these outsiders. A sudden pain gripped at my heart.

I strolled around the room. Twenty years of life in the outside world broke into separate episodes, by time, by events. Characters capered in my head: Chai Mingzhi, Tiansheng, Martin Gray, Farmer Chong, Grocer Tan, the storytellers and listeners in the teahouses. Faces rose, magnified with sadness, anger, anxiety, vague traces of smiles, overlapping one another.

I had only to dwell on them, on the nature of the men of the outside world apparent in those snatches.

I strolled on. I saw the child hiding under a tree between bird's-nest ferns with his father, his eyes on the first outside man he had ever met. I saw him asking: 'Why doesn't he just leave and go home?' And I saw, five years later, the child that was my twelve-year-old self, leaving the forest. I cleared my throat, the first episode ready to be let out, and there would be more to follow.

And yesterday, I began a new episode: The Journey Towards Acquiring the Minang Villa.

5

The Journey Towards Acquiring
the Minang Villa

APRIL 1908

From five shops away he could see Grocer Tan, sitting as if riding a horse on the long wooden bench where they once played chess, fumbling in a sack of onions between his open legs, pulling loose skins off them. It was late afternoon; for half an hour he'd been in that position, with the right side of his body – in only rolled-up trousers – laid bare to the increasingly hot sun. Grocer Tan raised his head and wiped sweat off his brows with the back of his hand. At that split second, he saw him approaching, Chai Mingzhi, walking on the shopfront pavement along the row of buildings. He saw the black-and-white flash of the immaculately tailored gown in the bright sunlight. Grocer Tan cast his gaze down on his onions.

Too late.

Mingzhi, eyes fixed on his target, had caught the signs of not being welcomed. For a moment he slowed his pace, hesitated. He thought of the purpose of this trip – *I must talk to him!* He strode forward.

Grocer Tan did not glance up when his visitor greeted him. He did not invite him to sit down, nor was tea offered. 'Hm,' was his reply. *Hm,* a snort of the nose.

Mingzhi, his feet crunching on the tissue-thin brown peels on the ground, brushed off those on the bench, smoothed the hem of his gown and sat himself down, the sun on his back. He tilted his head sideways to Grocer Tan, squinting over the sack between them.

'See who's here. Has the wind blown the wrong way round?' Grocer Tan, still not looking up, did not stop with his chore, working even faster. Crisp outer layers of onions torn between stout fingers, drifting, falling into heaps on the floor around his legs. 'What can I do for you, Taukeh Chai?' His 'Taukeh Chai' sounded unnecessarily loud and shrill.

Mingzhi held his breath. *Call me Mingzhi, like you used to,* he screamed inside. On the outside, there was silence amid the crispy noise of onion skins. He turned to stare down at his hands, the palms flat on his knees.

'You've always been very helpful, Ah Tan.'

'Too helpful indeed – stupid enough to have gotten myself into carrying the blame for you: ungrateful, traitor. You name it.'

'I didn't know it would turn out that way. I couldn't let him know. Tiansheng would not have agreed with me.'

'That was what you said. I trusted you then.' Grocer Tan hurled a rotten onion into a bucket-for-a-bin by his leg. Mingzhi watched it hit the tin base, bounce, hit the side of the bin, before falling back down. A crisp 'thud' came at each contact with the surfaces. He stared at the mash crumpled in the bucket, the lump of brown-ish black against silvery white. Then Grocer Tan's voice wafted through: 'I'm not sure now,' as if coming from the bottom of a brimming pond, vibrating, obscure.

Through the deep water the distant voice kept rising and eddying:

'You cheated on him. All those things you did behind his back . . . behind ours. The rubber estate and who knows what else . . .

'. . . He'd been working so hard at the shop . . .

'. . . And you conspired with the *gweilo* . . . How could you . . .

'. . . How naive I'd been . . . to have let you use me . . . channelling the money for you time after time . . .

'. . . Who knows where exactly those notes came from . . .

'. . . Had they known, those revolutionists, they wouldn't have taken your money . . .

'. . . I thought, eh, he didn't forget his country . . . How selfless he was, giving out his earnings . . .

'. . . And suddenly you realized how stupid you'd been, throwing away your treasure, and stopped supporting them . . .

'. . . Of course they thought it was me . . . Traitor, heartless . . . that's what they called me . . .'

Inside the shop, Grocer Tan's wife was sweeping the floor, the business being quiet at this hour of the day. *Did he tell her all this? That I used him, cheated on him, on Tiansheng, on the townsfolk? And she to her friends and everyone else?* Mingzhi imagined the skinny middle-aged woman, standing between sacks of rice and flour, red and green beans, barley and chicken feed, whispering to her customers, housewives of various ages. He saw them nodding and shaking their heads, their mouths twitching with disgust, as they hissed into one another's ears.

'. . . Perhaps you and Tiansheng did it together . . . Opium and firearms? . . . Dirty money all the same . . .'

He saw the women, at home, proclaiming loudly at the dinner table to their husbands of a liar they had mistakenly trusted as a serene, honest man.

'. . . Clever you . . . made me the scapegoat . . .'

He saw the surprise and excitement on the men's faces in the paraffin lamplight. *A dog that doesn't bark kills*: he heard the rounding-up comment.

'. . . How long has this been going on? Three years, five, or more? All the time it takes for *your* rubber trees to grow? . . .'

No, it was my money, my rubber money. Nothing to do with Tiansheng, nothing to do with opium or firearms. Mingzhi stared at Grocer Tan's mouth, his magnified lips opening and closing, opening and closing, like those of a thirsty goldfish.

'. . . And you dumped him when you started getting the milk . . .'

It wasn't me; it was him! It was Tiansheng who cheated on me!

'. . . You and that *gweilo* with your estates . . . two thirds of the lands in this surrounding area are now yours . . . All these years you've been making money quietly . . . Lucky you . . . started early and earned pockets full . . . Unlike me . . . still another year before the first harvest – oh, no!'

Grocer Tan stood up abruptly. 'This is it. The land, isn't it? I'd been asking myself, why have you come, what else could I do for you, now that you've got everything in your hands?' As he pulled his right leg over from the other side of the bench, the sack of onions was knocked over. Little light-brownish balls spilled onto the ground.

'Not my land, Taukeh Chai Mingzhi. We've been working so hard on that estate, Farmer Chong and I. It's our future. It's for my family, my sons.' Grocer Tan strode into the shop.

'You may get everything else in the world, but not my land. Never!' His last words leapt off the waters, swooped into Mingzhi's ears, no longer bobbing. He was back to the reality he dreaded.

Sitting still, Mingzhi watched the onions roll into the drain half a yard away from the bench. Little balls stuck in the frothy, stagnant waste accumulated from the row of shops, floating, pale against the dark mess.

*

The sun was setting when he arrived. The river soaked in red and orange, colours of the clouds above, and at a glance, it was unclear which was the origin and which the reflection. The two merged into one, and the skyline blurred. He stood on the riverbank, where once water gurgled, now shamefully retreated after years of heavy silting, and after the conscious decision to ignore the silting. The river and the port were being left to their death by the colonists; their love, their passion for Malacca had long travelled hundreds of miles southwards to a small island at the end of the peninsula, where bigger steamers could dock in deeper, safer water. Singapore, the island was called, from where he, like Parameswara, his predecessor of five hundred years before, had fled.

And now, it was the villagers who had fled the place

329

they and their ancestors had been living in for five hundred years or more. Their boats stranded, abandoned in the muddy shallows, the fishermen and their fish-selling wives moved north-eastwards to the coast for fish that could still be netted in abundance, in wider and wilder waters; or ventured further inland to farm a few acres of paddy or durian. A more treacherous life at sea for the former and a relatively peaceful one for the latter, only whipped up their memory of the one they had been forced to leave behind. The unchanged fact was the meagre income they still earned.

Since the fish in the river had dwindled and the villagers left, the kampong disappeared, along with it the stamp of 'Reserved' on the land. Stilted houses turned into rubber trees laden with milk, liquid money ready to spill out in a constant flow like water pumped up from an underground reservoir. Not theirs. Not a single tree was.

From between the trees, a long stick awkwardly shot out. He fixed his eyes on it and immediately recognized it to be the flag pole once erected at the front of the mosque. How had they, Grocer Tan and Farmer Chong, done it, getting the land transferred to their names? He wondered. *Engi. Engi will be able to find out for me,* he was certain. There was nothing in this town that would escape the boy's eyes and ears.

From where he stood, gusts of evening breeze sent forth noises from a bend yards away, hidden in a luxuriant growth of reeds. Loud voices of men between splashes of water: one or two obscene comments on women and their bodies, and what they could do with these women and their bodies, followed by peals of dissolute laughter, amplifying in the quiet air. It was the plantation workers, he knew, taking a bath after a long day's work.

It was they who had occupied the compound where once the Fisherman's Hut had been.

Because of its proximity to the river and to Farmer Chong's own farm, for convenience, Farmer Chong and Grocer Tan built the workers' quarter on the ground flattened by the fire. A row of five wooden houses, with four walls and tin roofs, crude and basic. Slack laundry lines pulled across the coconut trees in front of the dwellings. In the clearing, a few chickens sauntered, pecking languidly at the gravel for earthworms and seeds, feeding themselves well in order to feed the workers.

He found the *bayan* tree on which he had once put up the SUNGAI BERTAM board. Where was the man with his whiskery white beard? Did he see all this coming with his ancient wisdom?

The fire hidden inside him flared once more. As the flames began to burst out, he shook them off. In his mind's eye, a house, big and tall, came into shape.

The land will be mine, he mumbled, *it will be mine.* He turned and left, huge strides firm and quick.

Behind the houses, rows of young rubber trees thrived, waiting for their first dribble of milk in a year or two.

*

'News has travelled fast, Taukeh Chai.' Farmer Chong waved him off at the entrance to his farmland before Mingzhi uttered a word. 'Not a chance, I say. Not a chance.' A click, and the fence-gate latched against the lean figure.

'It's a shame that Tiansheng isn't there. He was the one who did all the work and all the talking for you, in those days. He'd come round in the evening, share a pot of tea with me and the workers. You'd never come. Too dirty, too lowly my place was for a scholar? I'd let him take home a bunch of pak choi now and then. Your sister craved it, he said. How caring. It was just a little thing I could do, so why wouldn't I? He offered a hand at the farm now and again and wouldn't take my money. Of course I'd teach him. Of course I'd show him how to grow the greens, how to rear chickens and ducks and pigs. My workers willingly helped him mend the house. They went with him to the jungle to look for you, if you didn't know already? It was for Tiansheng that they offered their help. Not you.' Farmer Chong's rambling from the other side of the gate bobbed in his head as he walked home. The path, the river, the sky were a blur, the ground underneath floating.

He felt himself drifting.

*

Everything was floating in the Baba Lodge, too, in a yellow pool of paraffin lamplight. His office, the desk, the abacus he had been fiddling with.

Click, click, click. The wooden beads of the abacus crashed against one another, loud and piercing in the wide room. Click, click, click. The beats bounced and rebounded against the walls, the ceiling and the floor. Click, click, click. The furrows on his forehead cut even deeper with each rebound. He'd worked out his worth, all he could offer for the land, far exceeding its value.

They have only to take it! He brushed away the abacus, the beads spinning on their fulcrums, a swirl of red.

They spun in his head, quick, so quick that only whiteness prevailed, dazzling, blinding, and nothing else. No land, no house, no Meilian or Jiaxi.

No! He grabbed the abacus and felt the vibration of the beads under his fingers, weak, tingling, yet alive. The way he'd always been, always fighting, always having hope. Yes, he would fight on, he decided.

Anything, I would do anything, no matter what it takes.

He reached for the pair of scissors on the desk, pulled from his back the plait he'd kept since the age of ten, held it high up in the air. Crack! One quick move, and a thousands-of-years-old weight of morality detached itself from its host, falling heavily to the floor.

Not a sound was heard.

*

A transfer at the colonial office, followed by the arrival of a new official, unexpectedly smoothed things out for Mingzhi.

*

Sunday, and it was busy in the Club. Since mid-morning, planters, traders, miners and government officials had been flocking in. In a sea of blond and red and brown heads, a few drops of black bobbed, the carefully oiled and combed-back dark hair of the richest among the local businessmen, in immaculate Western suits. Their average five-foot-five build somehow looked even shorter, weighed down by their gratitude for the permission to be granted Club membership, as they tilted up their heads, a perpetual flattering smile on their faces. Always staring up, always smiling, while the tall figures of the foreigners towered over them.

Tall or short, colonists or colonized, under the red tiled roof of the Club, as they dined and exchanged pleasantries, an unspoken common purpose hovered over the marbled floor, and swirled around as the ceiling fans stirred the air across the room. It swelled with the excitement of waiting, the afternoon breeze generated by the whirling brass blades. Amid the eating and drinking, speculations scurried in sibilant whispers:

'Young man under forty with zero experience. From a senior tax officer escalated to the top post of this territory! What has he done in Singapore that impressed the governor so much, I wonder?'

'He certainly knows the game. Arrived just yesterday and doesn't waste time in making his first appearance here—'

'Well, he isn't here yet.'

'That's what we've been told.'

'Let's see. Let's see.'

Words rose and ebbed like tides in the wide room, sweeping into Mingzhi's ears. His hair combed back sleek and neat, his gold watch hanging from the chest pocket of his new suit, this guest member of the Club had been occupying a small table in a quiet corner between two pots of tall palms – an inconspicuous spot strategic enough to capture all actions in the room. Sitting there, watching, listening. Not a word passed through his ears unnoticed, not a guest that came through the door escaped his eyes.

He'd been putting together information gathered by Engi:

Point One: Through some channel, Farmer Chong and Grocer Tan had reversed the status of the land by the river where the Fisherman's Hut had been, legalized the purchasing of the land otherwise exclusively reserved for the Malays, and turned it into a rubber plantation.

Point Two: It was under the old administration, the old secretary, that the above took place.

Point Three: A new official was taking over the office.

Point Four: The new man would show his face in the Club today.

Mingzhi sipped his tea. *Bob Greenhorn. From Singapore.* The name sounded familiar. Where the man had come from made a convenient association to a past episode on the small island, his first experience of Nanyang. He hoped he was right.

There was a clamour at the entrance. A tall figure strode in, a man in his thirties. Blond, moustached, a scar on his left cheek.

Mingzhi's heart throbbed.

It was him.

The crowd drifted to the newcomer like bees after honey. Bees they were, humming out flattering words, and names and titles too important, too long to be remembered: *Congratulations and welcome to Malacca. I'm Tim Heinemann, Director of Heinemann Plantations. Graham Mitchell, Executive Director of Mitchell Shipping Company. Pleased to meet you. Charles Wayne, Head Engineer of Cannongate Mines. How do you do?*

He was shown to his table, tea and cakes offered. More hand-shaking, even more talking and smiling. Before long, occasional bouts of laughter began to burst from the centre of the crowd. Loud, careless, familiar.

The same laughter. Mingzhi was relieved, convinced the man had not changed.

He waited. One hour, two. He sat. On the far end of the high ceiling, a gecko appeared from a crack on the wooden border, its brown body a smear on the white paint. It moved languidly forward and then rested on the decorative panel and peered down at the hoo-ha below. *What does it make of this unrehearsed yet smoothly acted-out play of competing-for-favour, dominated by a line-up of second- or third-rate actors? A comedy, a farce, a satire?* He imagined the gecko's eyes, cold and indifferent. Like his.

Two hours passed. Tea drunk, cake eaten, people met, the most important guest of honour stretched his arms and held up his head.

'Have I missed anyone?' Bob Greenhorn glanced past the faces surrounding him, to and around the quieter ends of the hall. His gaze fell on a Chinese man in a corner. Mingzhi stood up. His chair pushed back, he emerged from the shadows of the palms and headed towards his target, steady steps on solid marble.

He held out his hand.

'I am Chai Mingzhi, a friend of Martin Gray.'

The widest smile of the afternoon cracked on the face of a mutual acquaintance: brows raised, eyes brightened. 'Ha, I've heard so much about you from the man himself!'

A big, hairy hand rose and wrapped over the awaiting palm. Two hands squeezing against one another, blond over yellow. Shaking, shaking. A friendship was established.

6

Engi: What I Didn't Tell the Children

'So this Bob Greenhorn got the land for him?' Siaan, the oldest of the class, stared up at me. Others voiced their views, too.

'That's very kind of him.'

'So lucky, that Chinese *taukeh*.'

'But that's too easy!'

'Yes, too easy!' the children said in unison.

How quickly they've learned to be doubtful, I sighed, beginning to be worried. *Have I corrupted them with my tales of the outside world?*

Of course I did not describe to them the full picture. Who would want to harm such innocent souls with stories so cruel, people with their plans and actions so insidious? I did not tell them my part in that episode. That, I keep to myself.

It had taken another year before my guardian finally got hold of the land. With my help.

*

It rained heavily one evening, months after I took over the shop following Tiansheng's departure in 1908. Two collectors came in when I slotted in the first door-plank, closing for the day. They had walked a long way in the rain, and were eager to get rid of their harvests in exchange for food and drink. I took them in: weighing the load, making payment, stacking up the stock, a chat with them about the forest and the people they met there (no, none fitted the descriptions of Father), and an hour passed.

The Baba Lodge was quiet but lighted when I returned. I peeled off my sweat-sodden shirt and went straight into the dining room. Taukeh Chai wasn't there. I removed the food cover on the table. Underneath, the dishes and two bowls of rice were untouched.

A sound of coughing came from behind my back. I turned around.

A stranger! I almost shouted, but a second look made me gape – it was Taukeh Chai. His plait was gone, and he wore his hair and his clothes like those white men's. He appeared lighter, paler; an apparition drifting into the room.

'You're late,' the yellow-white man in front of me said. 'You shouldn't be, and you certainly shouldn't do it again from now on.' He pulled a chair and sat down at the dining table. 'Because there are other things I want you to do for me.'

*

I got my bicycle back.

Night riding resumed, with a mission: find out how Farmer Chong and Grocer Tan got hold of the land now planted with rubber.

More detailed instructions followed. My focus was, of course, the back lanes. But this time, I had a clear target: the colonial staff residences. On occasions, I had also to keep an eye on the front entrances, to study the official comings and goings.

Hush, hush. Hush, hush. Not a word.

To accommodate the governing white men of the Red House, bungalow units had been built in the quiet corners of the Bandar Hilir area, behind the high school, within walking distance of their office. It was quiet. I crept gingerly into the neighbourhood, my iron horse propped up near the entrance of the back alley, hidden in the bush.

Camouflaged in a dark corner in my black shirt and trousers, I munched my dumpling-for-dinner, specially made by Amah Feng on Taukeh Chai's order. The boy is too busy with the shop, he'd said. Amah, still adjusting to her master's new look, did not notice the sudden widening of my pupils, the shock of hearing my guardian's first bare lie in front of me. *Father, you never told me changes in a man's appearance mark the changes in his heart, too.* I pinched my thigh; the sharp pain made me wince. That wasn't a bedtime story; this was real. I stared up at him, and he looked away. 'Be careful,' he muttered as he left the kitchen.

Two days, three, and a week passed.

From the front entrances, I began to establish the pattern of Life-as-a-Colonial-Official: nine to five at the Red House, the Club after work, coming home drunk at night. In between, in scenes I did not witness myself, there were poker, drinks, women.

In the back alley, I watched lonely wives sneak out to meet their equally lonely lovers, both parties quaking with illegal passion absent from their respective legal partners. I watched lucky poor servants (lucky to have landed a job with white men) in their sparkling clean, starched uniforms handing out bulging bags of something to waiting hands, sometimes of a child, sometimes of a woman, usually shabbily dressed. For a more honest maid, that something would be the residue of a big feast; for a less trustworthy one, foods intentionally put aside for a special treat, clothes and silver carefully picked from less prominent piles, to exchange for a few dollars in the black market.

At the rear exit also, I watched men from the underworld slip bulky envelopes into slightly gapped doors. On occasions like this, I would retreat further into my hiding place, the risk of being discovered too high. Tales of the rivalry between the two major Chinese clans, the open confrontations and secret executions, had been circulating in all nooks and crannies. Life was cheap in the foreign world. In the name of 'clan honour', they were constantly competing for territories, protection money, business opportunities – legitimate or otherwise.

On my return to Baba Lodge, I reported my observations to my guardian, who would spring forward from his studies at the creak of the back door. I described to him every detail of the night, but none was the news he'd been expecting. He would stroll back into his study, his footsteps dragging, laden with disappointment.

The moon rose and retired. Ripened to fullness, then waned; an invisible hole in the dark sky. And the cycle rolled on. Like the pattern that was my life: out in the early evening, waiting like a hunter, back by midnight. Reports, falling flat in bed, opening the shop in the morning.

Days moved like my bicycle wheels: their turnings, dependent on my feet, became slack over time.

It was leading nowhere. My guardian's anxiety had become mine, seeping into my dreams. Darkness. Deep, long darkness. The howling of a lone dog. Alleys with no ends, like a maze. I wandered in them, disoriented, panicked, rushing from one lane to another, the animal's shrill cry drilling into my ears. Still, there was no way out. The buildings began to narrow on me from both sides, hemming me in. Suffocating, I pressed myself against the walls, hands and head and shoulders squeezing. *Let me out! Let me out!*

I sat up abruptly, heaving, my body, my bedclothes clammy with sweat, the linen crumpled after a night of tossing and turning.

'What have you done, Engi, boy?' Amah Feng grumbled when she entered my room at daybreak. 'You sleep like a monkey would. All this mess.' Eyes ringed dark, I crawled out of bed every morning at a shake of my shoulders by Amah's strong hands. A pull at the sheet and she sent me rolling down the bed, impatient to get it remade. 'Go, get yourself ready before the master does!' A shout, a push on my back, and I was out of the room.

At the kitchen, I drained the tea Amah Feng prepared – black enough to drive me out of the door – grabbed a couple of dumplings, and munched all the way to the shop.

Outside, Ah Fook was waiting, pacing up and down in front of the linked shops, a sack on his back. He must have spent his only day off yesterday from Farmer Chong's plantation combing the forest. Fruits, aromatic wood, camphor, gutta, dammar, traps of pheasants or fruit bats. Anything he could find. A few extra dollars would buy more herbal remedies direly needed by his ailing mother in the village.

It was aloe wood this time. The routine of weighing and storing. From my ridiculously large pocket specially sewn by Amah Feng on Taukeh Chai's order, I shelled out the money for purchasing stock, counted and handed it to Ah Fook.

'Four *kati*, here's what you get.'

'You said five. Five *kati*. I heard you clearly,' Ah Fook insisted. 'Weigh it again if you like.'

He knew I couldn't. He'd earlier watched me empty his load into a big rattan basket, adding onto the existing stock. *Not again!* I sighed. It had been three or four times, or more, in just one week? The same mistake had been repeated. I should have recorded the figure in the book immediately after weighing, announced it out loud as I wrote, getting the sellers to witness. Black ink on the white sheets. No room for arguments or false claims.

Too late now. Reluctantly, I gave Ah Fook the balance claimed. I waved for him to leave, without another look at him.

I slumped down on the stairs, remained seated long after Ah Fook was gone. It was a quiet morning; in fact, the shop had been quiet in the past weeks. Visits from the regular suppliers were becoming more irregular with each passing day. When they did come, they were offering inferior produce: the shapes awkward, small; the scents felt dull. Without a doubt they were rejects from a shop newly opened by Baba Lim, who was staging a return. And orders, too, had turned scarce.

The air smelled damp. I stared out through the wide-open door to a darkening sky, laden with heavy clouds. In the street and on the pavement, dust and leaves and scraps of paper capered in gusts of wind, whirling, rushing into the shops.

I gazed down at the floor, at the rubbish just blown in, black and brown dots and patches against the grey cement, all over the place. My place. My pride. *And such filth!* Anger rose within me. I got on my feet, whisked the broom leaning next to the stairs and brushed the floor with such strength that my arms hurt. Swoop! Swoop! Swoop! Dust and dirt swirled up like a cyclonic shield, covering me, assailing my nostrils, my ears, my mouth. My eyes!

'Damn!' I hurled away the broom and rubbed them with both hands, the pain aggravated.

'Damn!' Tears squeezed out. I fumbled to the stairs and sat myself down again on the steps.

Thunder roared, the sounds of a crackling sky torn apart by blinding lightning. I peered out with my bleary eyes to beads of rain, first sparsely puncturing the earth, later turning into sheets, rattling on the roof, cascading from the eaves. The street was a blur – or was it my sight? The world seemed to be fading before me. Or was it I who was disintegrating, dissolving, crumbling into the yellow soil? Hundreds of drums rumbled inside my stomach.

I got up and paced the room, my steps as unsettled as my mind. At the flash of lighting I stopped abruptly; a sudden realization came to me: *He doesn't care!* My guardian, he cared less about the business. My heart sank. The shop wasn't a reward for my hard work, but a transitional placement, a cover-up for what was to come.

He didn't need the business, a drop in the sea of wealth he'd hoarded.

It would eventually be closed, would no longer be mine.

I felt the chill running through my spine.

But what was coming? What exactly would his plan be? What was awaiting me? I held my head, heavy as a boulder, bursting with thoughts, thousands of them, and none would untangle to form a perfect thread. I glanced up at my familiar space, the carefully arranged shelves and baskets, the giant brass hook – which I polished with Amah's groundnut oil every other day – hanging down from the scale: glinting, reflecting the sudden flash of lightning. No! I kicked the baskets on the floor, swept the shelves with my hands and trampled the mess on the ground. *Who cares? Certainly not him!* I flung the scale with such force it bounced back; another push, and another. My only good ear buzzed with the clinking and clanking. The world swirled around me.

I did not go home for dinner that night.

*

I felt the heavy blows of the raindrops on my body as I left the shop. I felt them on my head, on every inch of me. I felt my flesh sink where it was hit and imagined the bruises it induced, imagined the black and blue and red patterns on my dark skin, imagined Amah Feng's curses as I asked for ointment from her – *How many times have I told you not to get into a fight?* – even though I had never got into one.

The rain rumbled on and Amah Feng's voice ceased, together with the imagined bruises and ointment, my mind emptying. I walked on. The town was almost vacant. One street ended, another began. My eyes blurred. My legs kept moving. I felt the rain rumbling inside my stomach, a churning, sickening mess, bursting.

'Ah—!' I let out a shriek and broke into a run. The rain and the wind sliced my ears and face like thousands of piercing knives. I ran, rushing past corners, entering the dark alley, the usual route I would take every evening. It was then, as I brushed through a bush in a back alley, I realized I could no longer feel it, the rain, the wind and the scratches of the branches.

There was only numbness, and the constriction at my throat as I heaved, gasping for air.

Even the groaning of my empty stomach was drowned out by the roaring deluge.

I squatted under a clump of hibiscus, my shirt and trousers soaking wet, clinging tight to my skin. Rain slashed down in fierce gusts of wind from all directions, bout after bout. If I had gone home, my guardian would have insisted that I put on a cape and a hat. *Town-rain isn't the same as that in the forest; it will make you sick,* he would have said. But I didn't go home, didn't even want to wonder if he had been waiting for me, if he had had his dinner. Boughs and stalks of flowers and leaves swished against my naked face, neck and shoulders, and then fell lame, before another charge of wind came in full force, another attack: ferocious, merciless. I felt nothing.

I was trapped in the rain the way I was in this world. Trapped under the watchful eyes of my guardian, in his many secret plans of which I'd never had an inkling. Caged. Couldn't move. Stuck.

But why here? Why under this very hibiscus growth? I stared up. Traces of light seeped through the seams of the closed windows in the back lane: scattered, faint, shielded by sheets of water. I fixed my gaze on them, the houses that lurked in the dark, and remembered now the reason I was there, the task I had been assigned to. Vaguely, I became aware of the importance of my night mission, that my future would somehow depend on it.

I realized in that instant that in order to break free, I would have to prove my worth.

I was not to fail my mission.

My senses returned, my hunter's eyes gleamed, my mind focused. I adjusted my posture – head lowered, body down, shoulders hunched, hair raised – my back curved like a beast on high alert, watching out closely for its prey.

Today is the day, my hunter's instinct told me.

I stayed still. One hour, two, three. The patience of a hundred-year-old forest dweller.

It was a black silhouette to begin with, small at first as it turned into the back lane. Gradually, I picked out the figure of a man, unusually big and plump. I blinked, concentrated, looked again. Now I made up the outline of a pointed straw hat and a knee-length straw cape, a perfect disguise, if not protection from the rain, in a late-night outing, a stealthy one.

I shrank further into the hibiscus clump: body level with the ground, eyes on my target. I felt the thumping of footsteps, firm but not heavy, fast approaching despite the downpour. *A tall and stout man; a hard labourer, someone who is capable of long hours working in the fields or on construction sites; young and agile.* Certainly not Farmer Chong or Grocer Tan. My initial excitement deflated. Who could that be, then? I listed in my head the men in town who might fit the description. Young Ming? Mad Cow Liong? Big Liu? That led nowhere, as almost half the townsfolk fell into that category. I fixed my gaze on the dark shape, getting closer.

Lightning struck in the far distance, a sudden flash on a youthful face.

Ah Fook. Farmer Chong's worker, and the presumed 'Black Spirit' who was once Tiansheng's accomplice in his illicit activities.

I breathed out, long, relieved, though still watching. That explained it. Who else was in more dire need of money than the young man, now that Tiansheng was gone?

In the faint light sneaking through the window seams, I saw Ah Fook knock on a back door, the assistant secretary's. I saw him take out a packet. I saw a hand held out from the gapped door, where the brightness of a paraffin lamp flooded out. I saw the packet being transferred from a yellowish brown hand to a pale white, almost translucent one.

At that split second I thought of another time, another back lane, the little parcels I delivered to another man inside another door, on Taukeh Chai's order—

He did it on someone else's orders, of course! Immediately, Farmer Chong, Ah Fook's rightful employer, stood out from the background.

Was it a monthly payment, or bi-monthly, for the land title? I would find out soon. I had to act fast. I stared at my target, my heart throbbing with excitement.

The door closed; Ah Fook stood alone in the dark shadow. *Now!* I leapt out from the bush, rushed towards him and with a quick move, punched him in the face and locked his arms behind his back before he could react. He groaned, in too much pain even to struggle.

'Ssh.' I pressed him down. 'You don't want anyone to know why you're here, do you?'

'You, crazy *sakai*!' My trademark accented Mandarin did not escape him. 'What do you want? Let go of me!'

'Let's make a deal. Do what I say and you'll get the money you need. Otherwise . . .' I scratched my head, thinking hard. 'Otherwise, the whole town will know you've been cheating on me. Think it over, Ah Fook. No one would buy anything from you then; not Baba Lim or anyone else. Think of your mother; think of the medicine she needs.'

In the dark, I couldn't see his face; but Ah Fook's head drooped like a beaten dog with its tail between its legs, not another word.

I'd had my prey in my hands. *The land will be yours soon, Taukeh Chai.*

7

Mingzhi: What I Couldn't
Tell Engi

JUNE 1910

It's mine. Standing on a mound of river sand, Mingzhi peered ahead: *All this.* Still a distance away, yet he could already see the structure, the sharp edges of the would-be roof that rose high, pointing at the sky, the wooden pillars erected from the concrete foundation, the two stretches of horizontal beams, one on the top, the other a few feet from the ground, that would respectively form the ceiling above and the floor below.

It was real. Everything was in place, everything was on schedule.

He could also see Engi, dark and small among the labourers, yet standing out, confident and in control. The young man was giving instructions to workers, as the first delivery of nipa arrived, to move the palm leaves into a shelter twenty feet away from the building site, where women would begin weaving for the walls. Under another thatched roof supported by four lone bamboo poles, carpentry work was underway. Stairs, tables and chairs, cabinets, bed and bed poles.

Nothing was overlooked.

He watched Engi threading like a dwarf through men

and women at least one foot taller than him, agile and at ease. He saw how they listened to Engi, their shoulders dropped, their heads and eyes lowered.

The young man. Mingzhi sighed, surprised at how quickly, how naturally he now called his charge *the young man* instead of *the boy.*

He was seventeen, Engi, his build still that of a boy, his face too. An eternal tinge of naivety absent from the faces of the townsfolk lingered on, only punctured by occasional traces of seriousness, the locked brows and pursed lips. Those symbols of maturity, Mingzhi noticed, were new additions. Perhaps they were not new but, as to when it started, he scratched his head, couldn't settle on an answer. Could it be a month ago, when the groundwork of the Minang Villa had commenced? Or perhaps a year prior to the construction, when one afternoon he, Engi, had left the shop closed and rushed back to the Baba Lodge.

It was a quiet afternoon. Mingzhi, in his study, heard Engi's hurried footsteps approaching. As he burst in, face red with excitement, he flashed a few sheets of paper before his guardian.

'The agreement between the assistant secretary and Farmer Chong and Grocer Tan, their secret deal, and the forged transfer of the land title,' said Engi. 'I asked Ah Fook to go over all the past events, told him to search for the documents. Farmer Chong trusts him like his own son. When the boss goes out for chess and mah-jong and business talks with Grocer Tan in the evening, and the boss's wife is busy with the children and all that, he has plenty of time to roam the house.

'Lucky for us he can read. Lucky for us the papers are not just in English but Chinese, too,' Engi had babbled on. 'August the twenty-sixth, nineteen and six – that was the date the land title was transferred, with a stamp from the office and a clumsy signature. An imitation is more like it – must be the work of that white assistant secretary.'

Mingzhi snatched the documents from Engi. Black and white. Chinese and English. Square characters and crab-walking alphabets. All stating the same terms: the job to be done, the money involved, the payment methods, and finished with three signatures – one in English (by the assistant secretary himself), the others Chinese (by Farmer Chong and Grocer Tan) – equally big, equally clear, equally prominent. The names magnified in his eyes, and he saw nothing else, certainly not Engi, who stood to one side, waiting to be praised.

That night at Bob Greenhorn's, Mingzhi choked on his first glass of Scotch as he watched his host read the document. He saw that the new secretary's face changed from surprise to anger, before turning to excitement.

'It's time for housekeeping,' Bob said. *How convenient.* He'd been eager to stamp his foot on the new ground, to prove first to his superiors in the head office his worth, then, to his new charge, his capability. To impose and install his authority, to smother the grievance, the doubts over his age and experience. He grabbed the letter like a piece of precious Chinese silk, waving it as if it were a magic wand. Within days, the assistant secretary was sacked, the administration reshuffled, important positions conveniently filled with the head's confidants. The new official's position was now safe and firm in the southern Malaya town.

'Now, what can I do for you, my friend?' When Bob Greenhorn's words finally came, Mingzhi did not hesitate. His reward was quick and satisfactory: new documents, under his name, installed; old ones destroyed. Everything became rightful, lawful, unquestionable.

It's real. Mingzhi held before his eyes the land title he'd been yearning for, wavering in his trembling fingers. The signatures, the seals, the wording. His name. Because it was in his hand, because he did not know what else to do, he drained the glass of Scotch handed to him by Bob Greenhorn. He did not choke this time, savouring every mouthful of it.

It wouldn't have happened without Engi. It had not been easy, and Engi had been hiding it from him, deploying Ah Fook discreetly, only revealing everything in the final moment. Mingzhi remembered now the gleam of elation in the boy's eyes, the yearning to be praised, and the sudden disappearance of his shyness.

Perhaps more had disappeared from Engi then; perhaps it was then he had crossed over the threshold that separated CHILDHOOD from ADULTHOOD. That the boy under his charge would use an older man's attempt at fraudulence as a weapon, and top it up with a monetary reward to press Ah Fook into spying for him, he now reflected, was unthinkable.

The boy who had once been afraid to sleep alone at night, the boy to whom he had been telling bedtime stories, had now slipped into power-play, just like any townsfolk in business would.

What have I done? Mingzhi wiped his face down with a hand; his eyes remained closed long after, the bright sunlight a web of red at the back of his pupils. The low murmuring of the river seemed to amplify in his ears, the trotting of hundreds of thousands of troops. *WhathaveI-done, whathaveI done, whathaveIdone.* His head buzzed.

In a blink, he saw the whiskery old man standing by the ancient SUNGAI BERTAM board he'd picked up from the shallow. He saw the path between the long grasses. He knew where it led.

Of course he knew where the path led. Mingzhi took a deep breath. He opened his eyes and stared ahead.

The roof, the beams, the pillars. Real and solid. He remembered that night, years ago, when everything was dark, when smoke rose from the blackened remnants once called the Fisherman's Hut.

He bowed; a long sigh of relief. *It's ours again, Meil-ian. The place is ours, and no one is going to take it away from us ever again. No one.* He muttered, felt the warm wetness gathering in his eyes, wiped them with the back of his hand.

As he straightened, Mingzhi shook his head, blinked, and looked again at the building site. He saw that, underneath the freshly sanded wooden structure, there were Engi's busy steps, back and forth, in and out of the spaces which would be the rooms, which would make up the Minang Villa, where the Fisherman's Hut had been. He shuddered, overwhelmed by a sudden realization: that boy had put his prints on it before he did. A cold spell swept over his spine.

He stepped forward, heading to the framework of the

house that was his. He would tell Engi to spend more time instead on the rubber processing factory, newly constructed, newly in operation, needing more attention. He would tell Engi he would take charge of the work here from now on. A hand on his forehead shielding the blazing sun, eyes on his target, Mingzhi proceeded, feeling the heat under his soles, the eagerness of his strides, quick and big and steady.

The eagerness to claim the place he owned.

Which would then be reclaimed: the land that houses the Minang Villa and the rubber estate surrounding the mansion.

Twenty-eight years later.

8

Pergi! Pergi! Pergi!

TWENTY-EIGHT YEARS LATER

Two months after Lieutenant Kassim's visit with the court order, Mingzhi, inside the Minang Villa, smoothed out the letter from the officer salvaged by Burhan. The driver had somehow felt vaguely that it might be important, and had on that strange afternoon rushed out of the garage and got hold of it when the first raindrops drummed on the tin roof. He had quietly left it on his master's desk.

Mingzhi sipped his after-dinner tea, noted that Khadijah had finally become adept at brewing the perfect *pu'er*. He let the bitter-sweetness fill his mouth, linger on his tongue; a flush of warmth. *How long have they been living with me? Seven years? Eight?* He glanced at the drawing on the wall. *Rumah Saya. My House.* Three big and one small skeletal figures, standing side by side next to a house-on-stilts. Ali's handwriting slanted leftwards, quivering like chicken claws. Mingzhi smiled, wondered if the child had, instead, *Keluarga Saya* on his mind. *My Family.* Smiling again, he shook his head, trying to shake off the boy's big, toothless grin, to eliminate also his own fantasy.

He returned to the letter.

. . . Recent investigation concluded that you have been

illegally occupying a Malay reserved land with the plot number noted above . . .

. . . You are henceforth required to vacant the abovementioned property by the date noted below . . .

Running his fingers over the wall calendar, he traced and circled with his new fountain pen the date he'd been ordered to abandon his property, worked out the time left for him to – take action? Consult a solicitor? Tomorrow, he decided, he would have a chat with Lawyer Lam. Returned from England five years ago – with a degree sponsored by his very own Chai's Foundation – and now much praised for his acuteness, the young man was one of a handful of the first local barristers. *Local!* How easily the word had come to his mind! Mingzhi shook his head again. He could have used 'non-white', 'non-British', or 'non-Westerner', the way he had in the early days. He didn't.

It's mine, the land. I've been working on it for more than twenty years. Over the years, he had felt every drop of his blood and sweat dripping on it, that piece of land, as the latex dripped into the clay bowls tied around the rubber trees. He saw the milk overflow, smearing the earth with rich abundance of white. He saw his coffers filling up also, overflowing. He let it drip into his clan house, into schools, Chinese or Malay or Indian, into a foundation he set up for bright students from poor families, Chinese or Malays or Indians.

Haven't they seen that? Those so-called true *locals? Haven't they seen I am part of them? Don't they know that they need me?* He whisked the letter from the desk, scrunched it once again and hurled it into the bin. It was then he heard the noise, the low droning of a crowd, indistinct, becoming louder as it gradually approached.

'Burhan! Khadijah!'

The house itself was silent. He raised his voice.

'Burhan! Khadijah!'

Nothing came in reply.

He walked out of the room to a vacant corridor, to the noise that had seeped through seams and crevices and windows, ghostlike, circling within the four walls, amplifying against the quietness, encircling him. He shuddered, hurried through the emptiness towards the source of the clamour.

He pushed the main door open.

A wave of heat and light and din rushed to his face.

'Pergi! Pergi! Pergi!' Go! Go! Go!

Figures loomed. Angry glares and shouts launched at him; fierce flames of torches lurched. He blinked, a hand gripping tight to the railing around the narrow platform on the top of the stairs, another on his forehead, shielding, the sudden brightness blinding.

'Pergi! Pergi! Pergi!' Go! Go! Go!

Young and old, mostly men.

How many of them? Dozens? Hundreds? A thousand? He wasn't able to count, wasn't able to get a clear picture; saw only silhouettes now, many, overlapping one another, changing places, floating forwards and backwards, light as night spirits.

'Pergi! Pergi! Pergi!' Go! Go! Go!

Loud, clear, rumbling, like thunderstorms before a swift, unexpected downpour. His ears buzzed. *Where's Burhan? Where's Khadijah? Ali must be scared. Did they tell the boy to hide in his room?*

357

'Go back to where you came from!'

Shadows shuffled, quick, coming his way, climbing up the stairs. Too quick! A shove, and he fell onto the platform. A tearing pain ripped through his shoulder. Intuitively, he buried his head in his elbows and knees, anticipating the blows and kicks that never came. Curious, he stole a glance from between his hands.

The men moved fast, two or three of them, stacking up on one another's shoulders, reaching up.

The board!

His heart sank.

A thunderous cheer rose from the crowd. It was in their hands now, his CHAI FAMILY.

'No!' He got on his feet, rushed to the young man holding his ancestral pride. 'Give that back to me!' But the other men on the platform immediately stepped out, blocking him. He nudged and kicked frantically, achieved nothing, but lost his balance, stumbled and fell off the veranda.

A body flew in the air, light as a thin sheet.

A loud thump.

And Mingzhi was face down on the ground below the platform. *I have to get it back! I have to get it back!* He struggled to get up, but immediately fell back down.

Another thump, and something fell into the clump of long grass several feet away from him. He raised his head slightly and glanced up from under his lids.

Fire. Dancing before his eyes. Like snakes. Split tongues of orange and blue fondling CHAI, licking away FAMILY, winding over them.

His eyes widened. It was eerily beautiful, the flames, illuminating, bright against the darkness. *How strange.*

Like the lights and lanterns on the stage, on the opening night of the opera performance on his grandfather's sixtieth birthday. Even the noises – *how familiar* – the sounds of gongs and drums, trumpets and clappers, erhu and *sanxian*, swimming in like tides, rising and ebbing to the climax and anticlimax, close to his ears. In between them, there were faces, fading in and out as light and sounds faded in and out. Mother. Uncle Liwei. Meilian. Jiaxi. Martin. Tiansheng. Big, clear, staring down at him, gazes of deep sadness.

A sudden tightness gripped at his chest.

'Engi, where's Engi?' he muttered, as the sounds subsided, lights dimmed, the world before him a swirl of red.

*

'Engi, where's Engi?'

The name seemed to have always been lurking there, in some part of his mind, and it would spring up by itself: in the deep of the night, on hearing a bird chirping, at the fluttering of leaves. Any time, anywhere. When being struck by a stroke, or like now, when regaining consciousness in the hospital.

'Engi, where are you?' he murmured as he stirred, gradually regaining his senses: the acrid smell of a hospital, the blur of white.

'It's me, Boss.' Who? He strained his eyes, focused. A face swayed before him. Burhan's. Filled with shame and regret.

*

A week of intensive care, and Mingzhi was allowed back to Minang Villa.

359

Despite protesting strongly, Burhan eventually succumbed to the Chinese *taukeh*'s request for him to leave. 'Go home now. Go back to your kampong. I don't want to cause you and your family trouble,' he said, pushing a bulky red-money-envelope into Burhan's hand; it was pushed back.

'You've given me enough, Boss; and it's not right what they did to you,' Burhan said as he held the older man's hand for the last time.

In his recliner Mingzhi watched them walk out of the door. Only Burhan and Khadijah, for the couple had sent Ali to Burhan's parents in the kampong after the mob attack. He listened to their footsteps, taking the young man to his final errand for his former employer: get a messenger, send him for Engi.

He heard the gate being closed and latched. When it opened again, it would be Engi who would walk into the house.

Engi, my son.

So long it had been; so much had happened; so much to tell.

And *the boy* would come, he knew.

Epilogue: Engi

Come back I did, only too late.

In the Minang Villa, everything has halted before the ambulance arrives. The pulse, the final puffs of breath. The last of the raindrops from the eaves. Even the lone hen now tucked in her safe nest under the house has ceased ka-ka-ing, as though she knows her grand master will no longer respond to her.

I pull up a stool and sit by the recliner, the way Taukeh Chai sat by my bedside, years ago, with an abundance of stories to nudge away my fear of being in an alien world. I stare at the man once my storyteller: his lifeless eyes open blankly to the ceiling, his withered face distorted with deep creases. It isn't pain or worry; it's fear, indignation. The reluctance to let go.

I smooth down his eyelids with a wipe of my hands, carry his body and lay it on the mat on the floor. With much effort, I prise open his fists, tightly balled, as though he'd been getting ready for a fight, and straighten his limbs. I pull a batik cover from the sofa and drape it over the body.

*

I stand alone in the long hospital corridor. Men and women in white hurry past, swift steps on crisp cement; past endless doors on both sides of the passageway, one of them opened to a body that once was my guardian. I do not know what to think. I do not want to think. I want to go home.

I wait.

Fixing my gaze on the square of light that slants on the greyish floor through the wide window, I watch the brightness expanding itself across the ground, inch by inch, until at last, Lawyer Lam taps me on the shoulder. I press the death certificate into his hand. He will take over from there, and I will return to my students.

It's being passed back.

'He named you his adoptive son.' The solicitor pulls out a stack of papers from his heavy suitcase and reads the last line from Taukeh Chai's will, my name clear and jarring. It's been added only the week before, he says. *A week after the attack.* 'With this, you will be able to administer his funeral, legally, indisputable.'

What? I clasp my bad ear with a hand and prick up the good one, tilting it towards Lawyer Lam. He repeats, shouting into it.

A surge of heat rushes to my neck, and up. My temples throb, bursting.

I am unaware when the lawyer presses into my hand some paper, and stuffs into my pocket a thick sheaf of notes, his voice the buzzing of a caged bee: '. . . Money put aside for the ceremony is plenty . . . Spend as you wish . . . He wanted you to do it . . . Only you . . . You don't have to assume the mourner's role, though . . .' fading away, as his plump figure swaggers off along the wide passage, before disappearing at the turn of the corner.

I lower my head, eyes fixed on the grey cement under me, lips quivering. From the floor, the hospital smells rise with the rising afternoon temperature, acrid and suffocating. I pant, gasping for air, and choke, my throat sore as if it has been torn open.

I lean against the whitewashed wall, the copy of the will in my hand. I stare at it. ENGI. ADOPTIVE SON. Black and big. His seal, the same I've seen during my years living and working with him, a striking red. I stare hard at it until my eyes hurt, flashing green; until the sheets shake in my tremulous hands. *It's real.* I decide, in that instant, I will carry his family banner, I will bear the title of the son he never had. I will do what he wished.

*

I ponder over the last of my stories about the man now lying cold and still inside the coffin in front of me.

Midnight now. The clan-house-for-funeral-home is quiet, the air hot, heavy, stifling, pressing against me from all sides. The Taoist monks have long gone, with them the ear-piercing clapper and wooden fish. Gone too is the night-long chanting, monotonous, incomprehensible, unsettling (*How would a solemn soul like his settle in those noises?*). Gone also are the town's rich and famous, the *taukehs* and *tuans* and sirs, after two respect-paying nods: one at the body lying flat and cold in the coffin, the other, so mild that it could barely be called a nod, at the immediate family – I, Engi, on all fours, the only representative, nodded back.

Why is he here, that sakai? *Did he come back for his money?* I could almost hear them as they strolled out, to the Club perhaps, where more stories will be conjured up, laden with imagination, distorted by jealousy, about a man called Chai Mingzhi, a man whom they had hardly known, despite the amount of beer and wine they had shared at the Club and the many parties and dinners held for and by big bosses and officials.

Because only I know he would have preferred tea. *Pu'er*. Hot but not scalding. He would have preferred to stay at home, sitting for long hours in his study, alone, in the company of his books, letters from afar, memories of the distant past, sweet or bitter, pleasant or sad, plunging deep into them.

Only I know.

I smile, then cringe with a sudden realization – it is the memories of him that have plunged deep into my mind! I shake my head, unable to shake off the image of a lone figure, a silhouette in the darkness, a cup in his hand; in another, a stack of papers, his face buried in them. But I can see him, the sharp cuts on his brows, his sad eyes, clear, teary, peering at me. I shake my head with a greater force, yet the pictures persist. Still kneeling, I straighten my back, and immediately the sickening smell of decomposing flesh wafts to my nostrils. I shudder and choke, coughing ferociously. I lower my body once again, taking care to rearrange the white linen strap draped over my shoulder. I also smooth out my white gown, the attire for a son in mourning I'm yet to get used to.

Light flickers blue and yellow on the long sticks of white candles, casting a mess of dancing shadows on the fragile walls of the miniature Minang Villa, a replica displayed prominently next to the coffin. Paper for walls, bamboo for pillars and stilts. His sanctuary in the underworld, a point of reunion for his family. He'd spent his life dreaming of it, building it, loving it, only to be cast out after his death.

I glance up at the altar. My former guardian peers out from the giant portrait, his sad eyes staring back at me. I avert my gaze.

Everything will be over tomorrow.

I reach out for a stack of silver paper from a pile next to the coffin, pull the tissue-thin string off it, spread the sheets out like a fan between my palms, loosening them, and throw them into the burner. A stack for a million dollars; a rich man would be even richer in his afterlife. How absurd. What would he spend them on in the underworld if he'd never consumed much on real materials above ground, never entered the town's brothel, never kept a mistress? Could he buy a passage to the past, so that he could correct his fate? I imagine him knocking on the door of Yama, the King of Hell (*Yes, he will be in hell*), the money readily held out: 'A trip to Plum Blossom Village, 1875 (to start his life all over again), or 1900 (to go back in time to before the fire, before Meilian's death), please.'

The chuckle itch heaves and rises up to my throat, tickling every inch of my nerves, and it bursts—

'Ha! Ha! Ha!'

I hear my own voice in the quiet hall, bouncing and echoing, bouncing and echoing. *Stop it!* I hold my cheeks with both hands, pressing hard, but the laughter keeps sneaking out, filling up the emptiness – 'Ha! Ha! Ha!' – bouncing and echoing, bouncing and echoing.

I feel my stomach hollowing out, all the clouds and heaviness rumbling out with every continuous bout of laughter. I feel it becoming lighter, my inside, which has been bloated all these years.

I flop down on all fours; my hands land on the hem of the long strap of crude linen draped over my shoulder, slanted across my body, trailing on the floor. My head drooped, I stare at the brown linen, part of the attire for a Chinese son-in-mourning. I stare at myself, the arms that escape from the sleeve of the mourner's gown, the dark brown of my skin against the pure white cotton. An Orang Asli in a Chinese mourner's costume. How awkward, how eccentric. Like a tapir. Resembles nothing, belongs to nothing.

He has a body like a boar's, but half black, half white; nose like an elephant's, though shorter; eyes like a hippopotamus; legs like a tiger's; tail like a cow's. Yet he's none of those . . .

Father's voice drifts in my ears, his rendition of the story of a young tapir who is lost in the jungle.

The sun sets. Night closes in. Hungry and scared, the tapir goes to knock on the door of the boars. 'Go away! You're not my son,' the Mother Boar roars. He finds his way to the elephants, and again, being chased away . . .

I see the helpless tapir wander from the boars to the elephants, to the hippopotamus, the tigers, the cows.

And none would take him in.

I feel the warm wetness squeezing out of my eyes, rolling down.

picador.com

blog
videos
interviews
extracts